The Squid and the Spaceman

The Squid and the Spaceman

by

Randy Ross

Epsilon Books

Copyright © 2024 by Randy Ross

All rights reserved.

ISBN-13 (paperback): 978-1-945671-35-7

ISBN-13 (ebook): 978-1-945671-34-0

Published by Epsilon Books

Printed in the United States of America

First Edition

DISCLAIMER: This is a work of fiction. Any resemblance of characters in this work to real individuals, living or deceased, is purely coincidental.

In loving memory of my father, Gavin Thomas Ross

"I am the cat who walks by himself, and all places are alike to me."

—Rudyard Kipling

"Being alone never felt right. Sometimes it felt good, but it never felt right."

—Charles Bukowski

"Ambivalence is a wonderful tune to dance to. It has a rhythm all its own."

—Erica Jong

I

THE ASCENT

Reorganizing my medicine cabinet is an exercise I always find calming.

So far this morning, I've grouped all sprays, solids, and creams by orifice on the top two shelves.

The bottom shelf has things I haven't used in a while but may need any day, namely the insomnia collection: pills, gummies, extracts, earplugs, nose plugs, masks, and mouth guards.

Because I haven't had overnight company in a while, meaning I'm overdue, I hid the good stuff (Vicodin and Percocet) in the cabinet under the sink.

The doorbell rings. I glance at my watch. Joey's late. I head to the living room to buzz him in and immediately have to take a piss.

When I come out, Joey is sitting cross-legged on my couch, holding my script, red pen in hand.

Joey is a theater instructor at Boston's Emerson College and my acting coach. He's also my first cousin, and someone I've looked up to since I was little, even though we're only six months apart.

"Hey," I say.

"Hey," he says. "Sorry. The kid had a meltdown. You ready to go?"

Eight years ago, I got laid off from my job as an editor for a computer magazine. Joey said, "Swing for the fences," so I took a trip around the world and wrote a novel that was actually published. This past year, I decided try my luck as a professional storyteller.

Both Joey and I know it's a long shot.

I take my place in the middle of the room, facing him, trying to imagine an audience of more than one.

He gestures with the pen. "Burns, you're on. Remember: Slow it down and no foot shuffling."

"OK, got it."

I exhale.

"Bangkok. Bang ... Cock. The name alone sounds skeevy and from the moment I ... *ahh* ... I ... *ahh* ..."

"Stop." Joey throws a hand up. "What's going on? Last week you had this nailed."

"I did. You told me to rehearse an hour a day, write it out long-hand, perform it at double speed, then half speed. I did all that. I do everything you tell me to do."

"Is this about Harriet getting married?" he asks.

I say nothing.

"OK, whatever. Concentrate on the work," he says. "You need to get this piece down. Bulletproof. Try it with your eyes shut."

I deliver a few lines, eyes shut.

"Better," he says. "Now try it standing on one leg, eyes open."

I deliver a few more on one leg, eyes open.

Joey chews the end of the pen.

I pause. "Is that my pen you're chomping on?"

"I'll buy you a box. Now focus. We've got a deadline."

He hands me a pair of headphones. "Put these on and take it from the top, no stopping. If you botch a line, keep going."

I put on the headphones and hear machine-gun fire, whistling artillery, and, in the distance, some guy screaming.

Joey scribbles as I say my lines, while I imagine his intestines spilling out.

Ten minutes later, I take a bow.

Joey studies the script covered in red ink. Finally, he looks up, takes the pen out of his mouth, and says to me, "I think you're ready."

A week later, I am the featured performer at The Harvard Square Storytelling Hour. The event has been running for fifty years, long before the *Moth Radio Hour* was a pupa. Spalding Gray once performed here, and Boston-area celebs like Mike Birbiglia and Eric Bogosian still pop in to test new material. I'm only here because Joey called in a favor. He was supposed to come but bailed at the last minute. Something about family night with the wife and kid.

A half-hour before show time, I grab a beach chair in the great room of the Co-Living Commons, a communal house previously known as The Commons House, until it rebranded to be in line with the rest of Massachusetts, where everything is now "co," "bi," or "poly." A few feet away, a woman wearing a flannel muumuu and Tevas with wool socks adjusts a mic stand on the small stage. When she bends to add a log to the fireplace, her buffalo-plaid rump assaults my sight line. But, instead of engaging in snarky internal commentary, I remind myself that it's 2015 and, yes, I skimmed the memo about inclusivity and the new non-standard notions of beauty. I also remind myself she's probably the MC.

I finger the three Ricola honey drops in my pocket that I plan to dissolve in my mouth at three-minute intervals before I go on. Three is my lucky number; it's also the number of Red Sox championships since 2000 and the atomic number for lithium, which might have saved my last relationship.

But I don't have time to dwell on the savagery of middle-aged women because the room is now packed with thirty or so people seated on various couches, bean bags, weight benches, and tatami mats facing the stage. In the adjacent kitchen, pots clang and a disposal grinds, while a few more people wait in line for the open mic signup. Eventually, the MC lumbers into the spotlight, waits for the noise to subside, and announces the event's two rules: One, every story must be memorized, and two, it must be true.

She attempts to warm up the crowd with a story about a Brad Pitt look-alike ten years her junior who couldn't keep his hands off her. Considering what I've seen of her, she's already broken rule number two.

When the first performer takes the stage, a woman who calls herself Herman, I pop a Ricola. By the time I've finished the third one, a half-dozen storytellers have gone, and I can't remember anything about them.

The MC retakes the mic and squints as she reads my bio from a scrap of loose-leaf paper. "Tonight's featured performer is Randall Burns. Randall is a writer, performer, and web consultant. His fiction and humor have appeared in the *Vermont Quarterly*, the *Hockomock Swamp Rat*, *The Bagslam Review*, *Pancreas*, *Bean Flicker Magazine*, *Spooge Review*, *Itch*, and the *Boston Herald*. His short story, "Smells Like Fish," was a finalist for the 2013 Brown-Eye Adult Fiction Contest. In 2014, his novel *Skid Marks on the Ceiling* was published by Sweet Diesel Press. His one-man show *The Chronic Single's Handbook* has been featured at fringe theater festivals in Paris, Maine and Berlin, New Hampshire. Tonight, he is going to tell a story called, "One Day in Thailand." Please give a mindful, heart-centered welcome to Randall."

No matter how many times I perform, my body responds the same way when I'm announced: leg numbness, intestinal contractions, debilitating fatigue, waves of burning pain, dizziness, fever, hopelessness, paranoia, and suicidal thoughts. But eventually, I find my way on to the stage.

I wrestle the mic from the stand and immediately notice a bearded guy in the front row who seems particularly interested in the zipper of my khakis. Is it just the pants? Or is it the whole package — cap-toed oxfords and white dress shirt —

while everyone else is sporting flannel, fleece, or camo, ready for panhandling or varmint hunting? There is one exception: a lone Asian woman in the back row wearing a black bowler, fitted suit, and crimson lipstick. She smiles as she sees me looking her way.

I look away to refocus.

"Bangkok. Bang ... Cock."

A chuckle from the crowd.

"The name alone sounds skeevy and from the moment I get off the plane, I'm on high alert. I'd read about the deep-fried scorpions, tuk-tuk scammers, and locals who play volleyball with their feet."

As I clip along, my mind wanders to what I had for dinner, my new skis, my old car, Harriet.

"The airport bus drops me downtown, where the sooty, humid air stings like a lung full of red ants."

Eventually, I hit cruising speed, switch to autopilot, and survey the room: the MC nodding in approval, a guy scrolling his phone, a couple smiling meekly, and one guy staring at me, lips tightened. Is he challenging me? I direct my next lines his way and stare him down.

"I approach a guy with a mossy blond beard growing down his sternum. He's wearing a wide-brimmed hat with the chinstrap pulled snug against his jowls."

My challenger looks into his lap, and laughs awkwardly. We know who's in control here. Joey would be pleased.

The Asian woman catches my eye. She's listening, eyes wide. I send a few lines her way.

"The guy tightens his chinstrap and says, 'I was an MP back in Saigon. One of the last guys out ... last guys out. This whole area is built on a swamp. I'm going to retire here ... retire here.'"

She responds by peeling off one sleeve of her jacket, and then the other to reveal a shimmering black blouse and a slice of collarbone. Her gaze never wavers.

I hear myself stutter. A skip. A lapse. A 404 Not Found error. The blue screen of death. I look at the ceiling, the ground, the muumuu, anywhere but the Asian woman for the next line.

The disposal starts again, and the MC stomps toward the kitchen. I repeat one of the stuttered phrases under my breath, hoping it will catch and restart the feed. Joey always says that performing is about getting on stage, trusting that your lines will come, and letting the audience know who's boss. What a load of crap.

I blow into the mic, *puh-puh*, and repeat the phrase again, this time out loud. A few more words surface, a sentence, not sure where it belongs but I go with it.

"He smiles and tightens his chinstrap again: 'From here, Soi Cowboy is just a few subway stops ... subway stops.' Then he exhales into his hands and sniffs his breath."

OK, I've skipped a whole section of my piece, but this has happened before and the audience never seems to notice. Besides, the punch line is up ahead. I deliver it, pause, and let it land.

"In less than two minutes, this guy has confirmed my worst fears about Southeast Asia. This place can do things to you. Permanent mind-warping things. I put on my hat, tighten my chin-strap and walk away ... walk away."

Titters. The Asian woman is laughing out loud. The crowd joins in.

Back in my beach chair, I am pleased, relieved, spent, craving a beer, a cigarette, and a nice, long shit.

After the MC's closing remarks, the guy who stared at my fly heads my way. The Asian woman, wearing her jacket, follows.

"I liked your piece," the man says. But before I can say, "Want-to-buy-my-book?" he adds, "I've been to Thailand."

I know this type. He's not interested in what I have to sell or say. He just wants to relive *his* trip to Bangkok. Sure enough, he prattles on about Soi Cowboy, Pat Pong, and the city's other red-light districts, unconcerned that an Asian woman is standing next to him. As he's raving about an all-night backrub at a spa named Tugs, two amber fingers appear behind his head in a "V" shape. The Asian woman winks at me. I wink back.

The guy finally mentions something about going for a drink with a few other people.

I point to the woman and say, "I'll go if you go."

We end up next door at Paddy O'Wong's, an East-West fusion of reclaimed pine and polished steel, stained glass and Kanji, golf umbrellas and drink umbrellas, part Celtic bar and part pu-pu platter, another institution that's co, bi, and confused.

I grab a seat by the woman still wearing her bowler but get stuck on the other side with Señor Tugs, who introduces himself as Hank, which could be an alias. The MC is there, too, along with a few others from the event.

A waiter pulls up to the table and addresses the Asian woman: "I'm Kim. I'll be your server tonight."

"I'm Jackie," she says, and then gestures toward me. "And this is Randall."

Kim ignores me and continues: "Tonight's special is a vegan haggis stuffed with kimchee and seaweed."

"Give me a Beefeater on the rocks with a twist," Jackie says.

"Budweiser," I say.

"Is that it?" he asks me.

I look at Jackie. She shrugs.

He shakes his head and continues around the table. Several people order the haggis; others opt for the fair-trade lychee bread, the wellness bubble tea, and the probiotic Irish coffee. Jackie touches my arm, and a jolt of oxytocin practically knocks me off my seat. Like I said, it's been a while. Like months.

"So," she says, "What was a nice guy like you doing in Bang ... Cock?"

I smile and feed her my standard answer. "Oh, that. Eight years ago, I traveled around the world and had a rotten time. Except for Bangkok, Vietnam, and Cambodia."

She smiles, looks me up and down, and says nothing.

I feel a little exposed, embarrassed, and aroused.

When the drinks arrive, Jackie runs the lemon twist around the rim of her glass. She's wearing a thumb ring and a slim gold bracelet. "You know these garnishes are a magnet for E. coli and other nastiness," she says. "The gin kills some. But just in case ..."

From her jacket, she pulls out a pocket-sized bottle of Purell. She shoots a clear gob into her palms, rubs her hands together, and then rubs them all over mine.

"Who knows what you caught over there," she says.

As she scrubs, I notice the fine lines around her mouth, a hint of eye socket, slightly sunken cheeks, probably about my age. After fifty, it's either a slim body with a gaunt face or a plump body with a plump face. My friend Abe, who like most married guys, thinks he's a relationship expert, claims I always go for scrawny women in need of a cheeseburger or an IV drip. He's right. I'll take slim and gaunt every time.

"And what's a well-dressed girl like you doing at a shaggy storytelling event?" I ask Jackie.

"It's the anniversary of my stepfather's death, his yahrzeit. He used to read his poetry in the Village. In his honor, I wanted to attend some kind of literary event."

"You're Jewish?" I ask.

"My stepfather was Jewish and my mother is Chinese. Jewish men seem to have a thing for Asian women."

"I'm Jewish," I say as evenly as possible.

She looks at me over the rim of her glass as she sips.

"You don't say." She pauses for a moment. "So, your one-man show is *The Chronic Single's Handbook*? That must bring the women running."

"It's just a show," I say, "and I'm done apologizing for it."

She raises her nearly empty glass. "I'll second that."

The waiter comes by and Jackie orders another round for us. "This one's on me," she says.

The drinks arrive, but before we can toast, a younger guy to her left says something and she turns to him. I lean into her and detect citrus and tobacco. She leans back as if in response. She's probably five-four and no more than a hundred pounds. Under the bowler, she has neck-length black hair with blonde streaks. In an exposed ear, a black stud that could be a spade or a bat.

Hank, noticing an opportunity, is off again telling me about go-go girls in Cuba, bar girls in the Philippines, and hostess bars in Saigon. When Jackie finally turns back, I leave him mid-sentence rhapsodizing about a bar girl who could juggle ping-pong balls without using her hands.

"So ..." I say to Jackie, tapping her now-empty gin glass with my half-full beer bottle.

"So, welly-well," she says. "A nice Jewish boy goes to Bangkok and ...?"

"And ... he visits lots of temples." I sit up in my chair.

"I bet." She sits up in her chair. "Happy endings are a given, but the real men go for the hot lady-boy action. Did you know a lot of women watch gay porn? The more cocks the better."

"You don't say." I sit back and cross my legs to regroup. Her mouth is slightly open. I catch another whiff of citrus shampoo and tobacco.

"Something tells me you're not like a lot of women," I say.

"Well, I'm old enough to remember the Jackson 5, but you can still bounce a dime off my stomach. So, yeah, I'm probably not like a lot of women."

She leans forward and pinches my stomach, testing for firmness. "Not bad," she says.

No boundaries and no filter. My kind of girl.

The waiter drops off the check. People throw down money and stand to leave. Jackie considers her empty glass.

"Walk me to my car?" she asks.

On Mass. Ave., we walk along a row of parked cars.

"Guess which is mine?" she asks.

I gesture to a Range Rover.

"Too small," she says.

I point to a Mini Cooper.

"Ha ha," she says.

I point to a white BMW, then a red Mercedes.

"Too girly, too kraut," she says. "I only buy American."

She draws a key fob from her coat pocket and pinches it, rousting a black Hummer spanning two parking spots. The interior lights flood half the street along with Jackie's face, which is tilted away from me, exposing the sleek underside of her jaw, a length of amber neck, the top of her collarbones.

"OK, not what I was expecting," I say.

"Oh, really? You were expecting something?" She flexes her eyebrows. "Where's yours?"

I decide not to tell her "mine" is a bicycle locked to a parking meter near Paddy O'Wong's' entrance. "How about I let you guess next time?"

She smiles, takes my hand, folds it over a business card, and then whispers in my ear, "You're on, Mr. Smooth Operator."

I sense some sarcasm.

Back in my apartment, I call Joey to report on the show but get voicemail. I fire up *Pornhose.com* and peruse tonight's recommendations: "Boston Cream Pie," "Peleton Housewife Finger and Squirt," and "Hot Stepsister I, II, and III."

I'm too wound up to watch and call Abe, who lives around

the corner in Boston's Back Bay. It's before ten, so even though he's married, he's probably still awake.

He answers after four rings: "Burns, what's up? I'm busy here."

Through the phone, I hear the chime for *Pornhose* in the background.

"Hey, Abe, shut that crap off. You've got a wife to service. And this is important. I met someone at the storytelling gig tonight. Which, by the way, went very well."

Before he can respond, I hear door knocks on his end and a woman's voice — Amy, his wife.

"Abe, why was the door closed?" I hear her say.

"I got Burns on the line. He just met someone. Locker-room talk."

They continue back and forth, something about their ten-year-old daughter. I click on a video called "Plumber Chick Cleans the Pipes" and turn the volume up so Abe can hear it. So Amy can hear it. His voice gets louder. Amy's voice gets louder. Then silence.

"I'm back," Abe says. "Amy's got a tarantula up her ass. Anyway, tell me about the new lady."

"She's age-appropriate. Jewish. Well, sort of. From Long Island and drives a big, black Hummer."

"What kind of Jewish chick drives a Hummer?" Abe asks.

"An Asian one with a Jewish stepfather."

"Let me guess. She has the bony Karen Carpenter body you like."

"And no kids or pets. She wears makeup, dresses like an adult, likes foreign movies, drinks gin. She's over fifty and still parties. She's an outlier, a Renaissance woman. These don't come on the market very often."

"Burns, finally, someone who recognizes your genius. Especially since you haven't had a date in like three years."

"Abe, it's only been three months."

"Has she seen your car?"

"No."

"Good. What about your bicycle? Do you still cover the seat with a trash bag?"

"I'm hoping she'll think I'm a struggling artist and want to hang out with the band. Her stepfather wrote poetry."

"She's cute and single? Got to be something wrong with her."

"Like I said, she's from Long Island. And sells real estate. And has a condo in Brookline. She said she's trading in the Hummer for a new Camaro. She wears jewelry and watches lots of TV: The Entertainment channel and *Sex in the City* reruns. She's got JAP written all over her. Pun intended."

"So what? Amy has a Ph.D. and watches that crap. What else you got?"

"She's been married three times. She says she likes being married and would do it again."

"I knew it. Need I remind you that you've never been married and can't stand to be around anyone longer than four hours."

"I know," I say. "This is never going to work."

There is another silence while Abe and I ponder *Pornhose* on our computers.

"But," I add, "She likes to ski, has a gun permit, and voted for Reagan."

"Great. You'll be perfect together — two low-information voters. Maybe she'll listen to your rants about how middle-aged white guys are victims. What did she think about your Bangkok story?"

"She laughed. I mean she really laughed. But who drinks gin these days?"

"Right. That's a red flag, too."

I hear Amy again in the background. I check email, half-hoping to see a note from Jackie. Instead, there's an ad for Asian brides. *Pornhose* must be listening to my phone calls.

"I'm back," Abe says.

"And get this," I say. "She talked about sex constantly. Women who do that are usually desperate or prudes." An ad for lube appears on my screen. I click on it. "I have to stop getting so excited about these things, Abe. They never work out."

"Amy says all her friends talk a lot of sex trash. Anything else?"

"Middle-aged sex is always a crapshoot. What if she's a saggy disaster under those nice clothes? What if we have sex and my dick gets finicky? Maybe I should get a regular job and rent twenty-year-olds like Lenny does. How do you do it, Abe?"

"Burns, at our age sex is a chore. You just do it."

I decline an ad for Viagra. Too scary. With my luck, I'll be the guy who gets a three-day zeppelin and ends up in the ER, where a sleep-deprived resident has to puncture it with a railroad spike.

"Are you still in front of your computer?" Abe asks.

"Yeah."

An icon flashes on *Pornhose*: One of my Facebook friends, a guy from Boston with a wife and kid, is on the site.

"Abe, looks like *Pornhose* just added a new feature that recommends videos my friends are watching."

"What will they think of next? Check out 'MILF Rub and Tug.' Some of those women look fine."

We skim a few videos together. According to *Pornhose*, Abe has given this clip two thumbs up.

"I don't know, Abe, there's something I really like about this one."

The phone slips out of my hand onto the floor. I pick it up.

"Burns, calm down. This chick has a lot of 'yeah, buts,' so just do what I tell you. Email her in two days, a short note:

'Enjoyed talking to you the other night, let's go for drinks.' Choose an adult place near the T so you don't have to pick her up in your car. Dating is like performing; your job is just to show up. If she likes you, it won't matter what you say or do. Amy was just saying the other day that after ten years without a date, you're overdue."

After hanging up with Abe, I check the Celtics news, my web traffic, and *Match.com*. There's a message from "Edgy and Artsy," a poet from Cambridge.

Randall: Checked your website, impressed you got a novel published. Watched videos of "The Chronic Single's Handbook." You are hysterical! Unfortunately, you seem to know a little too much about being single. Good luck with your search!

Her note triggers a visit to the Dark Place.

Who am I kidding? Fifty-six and never married. I'm pathetic. Fucked up. Even Harriet is getting married — again.

My last shrink, Dr. Moody, tried to help me to accept my reality. "Marriage is no barometer of mental health," he'd say, suggesting I reread *Solitude: A Return to the Self*, a book about famous people who never married but fell in love with their work.

What work? A degree in journalism, senior editor for a computer magazine for fifteen years. Laid off and no interest in another corporate gig. Cue the solo trip around the world that mostly sucked and a novel that barely sold any copies. And now a one-man show with mediocre reviews at a couple of local theater festivals. Joey's a mensch for helping me, but we both know I'm going nowhere.

A fleeting memory of blonde highlights under a black bowler.

At least I have a date next week.

But it's always good to have backup.

On *Match*, I key in "artsy," "thin," and "aged forty to sixty."

The results:

A tall redhead with the handle, "Cares 2 Much."

Her summary: *I adopted a blind kitten, a three-legged greyhound, and an autistic child of color. Family-oriented, daughter is my best friend, love my new grandchild. Cuddly, glass half full, always smiling. Three is my lucky number. Let's be silly together!*

She sounds pathetic and we share the same lucky number. I drop her a note.

"Drop Dead" sounds edgy and has a small tush.

Her summary: *My daughter made me get on this site. Not sure what I'm doing here. If you are a liar, cheater, or would sleep with your girlfriend's cousin from NJ, don't message me!*

I message her.

I skip "God Comes First," even though she looks great in a bikini and has recently quit hard alcohol.

"Ivy Leaguer" is cute but probably out of my league.

"Needs Luv" is wearing a short dress and very high heels.

Her favorite things: Wagyu beef, yacht shopping, polo ponies, and generous men.

I log off *Match*.

This is pointless. Life is pointless. I've got nothing: no hair, no fancy job or hedge funds; no criminal record, creepy tattoos, or other bad-boy cred.

If God were handing out report cards, I'd get all C's:

Material Success: C+

- Had a decent job, have some savings, middle class.

- Current career as writer/performer promises slim-to-moderate success at best.

- But, considering eighty percent of the world goes to bed hungry, I'm doing OK.

Plays Well with Others: C-

- Love Life: Fifty-six, never married, longest relationship: two years.
- Family: First cousin, Joey, married with kids, which means he can't be counted on when I get old. Evil stepsister, mostly estranged. No other close living relatives.
- Friends: Considering I dislike most human beings, I have a fair number of friends.

Health: C

- Mental/spiritual: Believe in God when I need luck.
- Physical health: Mother died of cancer. Her cousin committed suicide. Whereabouts of biological father, unknown. Stepfather deceased. Various relatives have done time in homeless shelters, mental hospitals, and white-collar prisons.

Prognosis: D

I'm going to die alone like my Uncle Heshie, a shoulder surgeon who had it all — money, lanky women, Upper East Side address; he probably slept with Needs Luv. He never married, either. My stepsister and I were the only people who visited him in hospice. Where were all the models and nurses he dated before he got sick?

Three days later, I email Jackie and suggest an eight P.M. drink at The Beacon Hill Lounge, which is near the T and the health club where she teaches spinning two nights a week.

She texts back:

What took so long?

I arrive at 7:45 and secure two seats at the bar, side-by-side, my preferred seating configuration for a date, intimate but not too intimate. It provides an opportunity to dip in and out of her personal space, avoids unnecessary eye contact, and offers plenty of built-in conversation fodder: in this case, a Celtics preseason game on the tube, a dip-shit twenty-something bartender, and a mirrored wall for people-watching.

The bartender trudges over, blue hair held in place with a cloth hairband à la Rosie the Riveter, silver lightning bolts protruding from wet nostrils, and a black, untucked T-shirt featuring images of dead rats. His ink: "Team Satan" on the left forearm and "Mary Was a Whore" on the right. How do these kids get through HR?

"What can I get you, sir?" he mutters.

I'm dressed in navy chinos and a button-down dress shirt — tucked in — a little equestrian above my left pec, a spray of brown and grey chest hair at my open neck. I'm guessing that calling me "sir" was not a sign of respect.

"I'm waiting for a friend," I say. "A glass of water would be much appreciated."

He turns away to his cell phone. My water can wait.

I turn to my little spiral-bound pocket notebook and review the game plan for the evening:

- Be a good listener, and if she's monologing, let her run.

- Keep her guessing: Be aloof one minute and solicitous the next.

- Get that first kiss out of the way early, during the date rather than at the end, when there's a higher degree of difficulty.

- Try to have fun.

At 8:15, Jackie texts to say she's running late.

At 8:25, I'm not having fun and order a Budweiser.

At 8:35, the bartender looks up from his phone. Thunderbolts twitch, dead rats flinch. I watch Jackie's entrance in the mirror.

She's wearing a black sweatshirt, hoodie up. She looks frisky, like a baby seal. Snug jeans, narrow snaky hips, and red Converses without laces. Scarlet lipstick. The sweatshirt has an image of dead bats with the words "Teach Kids to Worship Satan."

As she makes her way to the bar, men check her out, women check her out, the bartender checks her out. I want to marry her.

I swivel and stand to pull out a bar stool for her.

"An old-school gentleman," she says. "A girl could get used to this."

She kisses me on the cheek and compliments my outfit before reaching into my personal space to pet my chest hair. "I like fur on a guy."

"Thanks," I say. "Nice threads."

"Ha," she says, settling onto her stool. "I just like messing with the millennials."

She notices my half empty beer. "Sorry I'm late. My class ran over."

"No problem," I say, "The Celtics are getting schmeared. I needed a drink."

Jackie places her phone face up on the bar.

"How was your class?" I ask.

"Sold out. First ten drinks are on me. Let's get you a real one."

I roust the bartender from *Tinder* or whatever he's swiping and order two Beefeaters on the rocks with twists.

Jackie checks her phone and puts it back on the bar.

I glance down at her shoes: "Did the warden take the laces so you don't hurt yourself?"

"So I don't hurt anyone else." She gives my chest hair a little tug. "I'm a stand-your-ground kind of girl. Second Amendment all the way, baby."

She mentions husband number three, something about a silver spoon and a prenup. The marriage only lasted two years, about the length of my last relationship.

"I got reamed in the settlement," she says. "But got to keep my guns. My ex had a boat and always worried about getting robbed at sea. Now, I live on the mean streets of Brookline. Some dirtball breaks into my place, he's going to get a taste of the old ultraviolence, *pow-pow-pow*, right in the nut bag."

Something stirs in my chinos. I collect my drink and my thoughts.

"To the old ultraviolence," I say, tapping her glass. "I saw just the place for you outside Phnom Penh: Bazooka Joe's Shooting Range. You can shoot chickens with a machine gun or cows with a rocket launcher."

"You'll have to take me for Valentine's Day."

Jackie checks her phone again.

And again.

I start to feel myself drift, shifting from participant to observer. My last girlfriend, Ricki, used to complain that sometimes I'd disappear right in front of her. "Hey, Walter Mitty," she'd say, knocking on my forehead. "Anyone home?" Sometimes Ricki was a real dick. Like Harriet.

I sip my gin. "You expecting an important call?" I ask Jackie.

"Sorry. Got a deal pending. Just want to make sure the buyer doesn't flip out on me. She's done it before."

"Jewish?" I ask.

"Worse. Chinese."

She checks herself in the mirror behind the bar, applies lip gloss, and adjusts her hoodie. Fine skin, small pores. Tear-drop eyes.

I feel a light tug on my chest hair. "Hey," she says, "You're too far away. I need a big strong man to protect me."

I move my seat closer and kiss her on the cheek. In the mirror, I picture Maury Povich and Connie Chung, Mark Zuckerberg and Priscilla Chan.

Jackie smiles and uses a finger to rearrange the ice in her drink.

"You're not one of those Jewish guys with a weird Asian fetish, are you?"

"Me? No. Of course not."

"That's too bad."

I kiss her cheek again.

"Ever been married?" she asks, looking at me out of the corner of her eye.

I tell the truth: "Not exactly but got close a couple of times."

I go on, not sure if I'm still telling truth: "I'm trying to stay open to whatever comes along."

Then I work in my usual talking points:

- I own a two-bedroom condo in Boston.

- Used to have a good job.

- Socked away money so I could quit and try my luck as a writer and performer.

- The gist: I'm on a budget, commute around Boston by bike, and own a crappy car by choice, for my art.

She parries with what I assume are her talking points:

- Works out five days a week and likes a guy who is fit.

- She's ABC, American Born Chinese "with an emphasis on American."

- Looking for a relationship, not a hookup: "I don't date men, I marry them."

The last comment generates a cold stripe of sweat down my back. I glance at the clock above the bar: We've been here an hour and a half, the right amount of time for a first date.

I excuse myself to go the bathroom, where I stare into the mirror and reflect. Jackie pulls her weight in conversation and asks questions. She's nice looking, likes the way I dress, and offers to buy drinks. She even made the first move. Is the Universe finally cutting me some slack?

I watch my expression shift.

Yeah, but ... A grown woman who refuses to act it. Seems girly but dresses ghetto. Talks about cocks, and then says she's not looking for a hookup. Who is really under that hoodie?

When I come out, the bartender is smiling and talking to Jackie.

I pull up and say, "How about the check?"

"She just took care of it." He waves the receipt in my direction and heads to the cash register. Little prick.

"Thanks. I'll get the next one," I say to Jackie, not sure if there's going to be a next one.

I hold the door for her as we head outside. As I'm contemplating my next move, I feel two hands on my collar. She pulls my face to hers and whispers, "I'm free next Friday."

A week later, and the day after another testy rehearsal with Joey, I bike over to Jackie's place. It's early November, daylight has been saved, and it's cold and dark, better for sleeping. I'm decked out in New England old-school: brown leather bomber jacket, burgundy corduroys, and Timberland boonie-stompers that have never seen the boonies.

Jackie lives in Brookline, home to pet psychologists, kosher Szechwan restaurants, and double-digit real estate appreciation. An average two-bedroom condo costs $600K. If she's had three husbands, she must own her unit and a few others.

She buzzes me in and I climb two flights. Her door is open. The Allman Brothers' "Whipping Post" is blasting from two large floor speakers. *Sex in the City* is muted on a large-screen TV. There's an iPad and a laptop, both switched on and scattered on the couch. Entertainment multitasking, the sign of a lonely person.

I hear the jingling of glassware coming from the kitchen. "Be right out," she says.

The room is sparsely decorated, though she said she's been here for five years. The paint scheme is Boston Rental: off-white walls with glossy white trim. The upholstered furniture is beige, neutral, and unlikely to offend. Where's the European walnut, New Zealand wool, top-grain hides, and brushed nickel she must have collected from her marriages? Is this place being staged for sale?

The most distinct pieces in the room are three hat racks in the corner. Floor-standing jobbies, a hat on every spindle: bowler; Stetson; pork pie; beret; O.J. Simpson black watch cap; Red Sox, Patriots, and Bruins lids; a furry mad bomber; coonskin; pith; and some girlie-looking toppers with flowers and feathers. One hat has a button that says, "My Heart Is an Idiot."

Jackie emerges with a serving tray holding two shot glasses, a flask, and a bottle of Jack Daniel's, the hazing choice of frat guys everywhere.

"Cigars, cigarettes, Tiparillos?" Jackie asks, parading by me. She places the tray on a wood-inspired coffee table that probably required some assembly. We sit on the couch. She pours two shots and gives me one.

I tap her shot glass and say, "*Ganbei.*"

"A clever boy, who can even toast in Chinese," she says, as if narrating the scene for a third party, possibly her good friend Carrie Bradshaw.

We do our shots.

"Yummy," she says.

"Hardly," I say.

A queasy silence ensues.

I look around the room. "Nice pad," I say. "Where do you keep your guns?"

"In the bar, next to the bourbon." She laughs. I laugh.

She's wearing her black bowler, a black turtleneck with hint of breast, olive fatigues with a hint of tush, and black paratrooper boots. Her makeup is delicate, light on the eyes and lips. Paramilitary yet girlie.

"I found a quirky French film at the theater around the corner," I say.

"After my day, I need a laugh. How about *A Clockwork Orange*? It's playing there, too."

She shifts her black bowler to my head and considers me for a few beats. Her eyes grow large, soft, and wet. I want to hold her, rescue her, own her.

She smiles approvingly. "Want to catch a buzz before we go?" From behind her ear, she produces a nicely-rolled doobie.

I haven't smoked in months.

"Sure," I say.

We each take a few hits, and then she slips the stub into a pack of Newports, the cigarette of ghetto ass-kickers everywhere. She picks up the flask from the tray, fills it with Jack Daniel's, and stashes it in a thigh pocket of her fatigues before grabbing another bowler for herself. I watch as she slips into a zippery motorcycle jacket and think: You are the coolest woman in the world.

A warm feeling washes over me. This could work.

On the walk to the theater, she talks about her day. A little of this and a little of that. I listen for a few minutes and start to drift.

Once in a while a fabulous woman locks on to me for reasons I never understand. Last year, I swore if it ever happened again, I was going stick it out, no matter how bored or crowded I got. If the relationship was going to end, she'd have to end it.

Why am I scrolling ahead like this? I just met this girl.

This weed must be good.

As we turn the corner, I realize Jackie is still talking about her week.

I'm not a fan of women who yak.

Yeah, but what's a little yakking, when it means no more online dating? I imagine the things we'll see and do: skiing in Vermont, double dating with friends who thought I'd be single the rest of my life. No more praying for a girlfriend to St. Jude, the patron saint of lost causes and hopeless cases — more great advice from Abe.

Maybe it worked.

If someone asks about my show, I'll be able to say, "*The Chronic Single's Handbook* is about a middle-aged goose-egg who can't get a hot woman." Then I'll point to Jackie and say, "In other words, it's not about me if that's what you were thinking."

I glance sidelong at Jackie, her jangling leather motorcycle jacket, her smooth athletic walk. Just being next to her feels good. A knot loosens deep inside my chest.

In the theater parking lot, I catch a guy checking her out. She doesn't seem to notice because she's looking at me, smiling. I smile back. She pulls out the left-over joint and lights it. We finish it off, and then share a cigarette. Everything feels natural, as if we've been doing this for centuries.

I'm thinking of kissing her, when she peels back her jacket and thrusts out her chest. "How would I look with D-cups?"

I'm guessing Jackie has B-cups now, which work for me as I prefer small and tight over big and sloppy. And implants can have unforeseen consequences: Ten years ago, Ricki got a boob job and promptly dumped me.

Jackie's eyebrows are raised. She's waiting for a response. This is a test.

I lean over, kiss her cheek, and whisper, "You're perfect just the way you are."

"Lying dog," she says, laughing.

The theater is half full. We grab two seats by the aisle and take turns swigging from her flask, as we watch the previews.

Jackie's arm is resting on the shared armrest. I rest mine close to hers, elbows touching. Hers stays put.

The movie finally begins, and I contemplate lassoing my arm around her but nix that idea because my arm always falls asleep. Instead, I edge my knee against hers, which stays put. Dating hasn't changed much since high school.

She leans slightly forward, transfixed by what's on the screen. Maybe it's a bad angle or the lighting, but her face seems older, more drawn. Then the lighting changes and she's young and beautiful again. I close my eyes and then blink them open again. Still hot. I repeat. Now, not so hot. I make a mental note to get my eyes checked.

Without taking her eyes off the screen, Jackie shakes my forearm with both hands. Alex and his thugs are beating up a drunk. Jackie is grinning. I lean over and whisper in her ear, "You're a real sicko."

"That's what they all say," she says.

When Alex and his boys break into a house, stuff a tennis ball in the husband's mouth, and ravage the wife, I cover Jackie's eyes with my hand and whisper, "A nice girl from Brookline shouldn't be exposed to this kind of thing."

She moves my hand to her mouth, kisses it, and tosses it back in my lap.

Behind us, someone says, "*Shhh.*"

"Sorry," Jackie says, a little too loud.

On screen, Alex picks up some lolly-licking chickies to bring home.

"Time for a little of the old in-out," Jackie says.

I put my hand on her thigh and spider crawl to her crotch.

"You horny dog," she says, squeezing my hand and leaving it there.

Someone behind us says, "Please be quiet."

Jackie caresses my hand where it rests on her thigh, which feels warm and promising.

I lean over to kiss her neck, but she is leaning again toward the screen where Alex and friends are breaking into the house of an old lady. I lean back. Alex grabs a sculpture shaped like a giant cock and yells at the lady, "You filthy old *soomka*!"

Jackie and I stifle laughs. I lean toward her again, and she turns to look into my eyes. I pause. We're both suspended, waiting, anticipating, when I'm walloped with a head rush, then a body rush, then a spinning Bonzai pipeline of J.D., THC, testosterone, and oxytocin. The next thing I know, I'm kissing her cheek, her chin, her lips, and she's kissing me back, full on.

A flashlight shines in my face, then Jackie's, and then back to mine. A zit-faced usher.

"Would you two please act your age, or I'm going to have to ask you to leave," he says.

On screen, Alex is bashing the old lady over the head with the giant cock.

Jackie doubles over, hooting and snorting.

"Yes sir," I say to the usher, putting my hand over Jackie's mouth to quiet her. I feel her tongue sliming my palm. When the usher slinks off, I wipe it on her thigh.

"You're an animal," I say, leaning in for another helping of her neck. She squeals and tilts her head giving me full access.

"Will you guys shut the fuck up!" someone yells from behind us.

Jackie busts out laughing again. I grab her hand and drag her out of the theater.

In the hallway, I press my body against hers and hold an

index finger to her lips. She sucks my finger into her mouth, holding my gaze. "You filthy old *soomka*," she mumbles with my finger still in her mouth. Then she spits it out and withdraws her flask. She feeds me a swig, and then takes one herself.

Jackie grabs my hand. "Come on, Daddy. I don't want to miss the part where Alex licks the dom's boots."

The words "Daddy" and "dom" linger, as I follow her back into the movie.

After the movie, we walk back to her place, my arm around her snaky hips. At the corner, she changes sides, saying, "The man should always be on the street side to protect the girl."

Traditional on the outside and kinky *soomka* on the inside?

At her door, I start to follow, but she stops and turns to face me.

"That was fun," she says, putting one hand flat on my chest. "I'd invite you in, but I have to get up early tomorrow."

And then her lips are on mine, engulfing them, viper style. Her tongue shoots between my lips, boring into my mouth. There's nothing soft, sexy, or delicate about it. I withdraw and try to restart the process. I press my mouth gently to her lips but here comes the tongue again, ham-handed and ruthless.

We separate. "That was nice," she says.

"Yeah," I say, feeling slightly violated. "I'll call you."

The next day, I go with my friend Lenny to the Minuteman, a health club on Boston's waterfront, where I met him and Abe in the late nineties, back when I was employed and had money. Since getting laid off in 2007, and taking various left turns, my new career hasn't generated enough to pay the buck-fifty a month for the Minuteman.

Today, Lenny is treating. "Abe said Jackie stuffed you at the door the other night," Lenny says. "Chicks can sense desperation. A little massage will take the edge off."

Lenny knows about dry spells and desperation. He went

through a three-year drought when his mother got sick, and he was the devoted son. When she finally died in 2009, he found himself alone and rich. He now refers to himself as a "not-so-poor orphan." His friends call his six-million-dollar Boston penthouse, "The House of Rumpus."

A few years back, he hosted a guys-only "Viking Party." The engraved invite said, "A bachelor party with no guy sacrificed on the altar."

For that event, Lenny had his oriental rugs covered with plastic sheeting on which fifteen wooden eating bowls were spaced a few feet apart. No silverware. No napkins. We were all instructed to strip to our boxers and dig in. A team of waitresses in short-short kimonos served us IPA, New York strip steak, heirloom potatoes, shitake gravy, Bananas Foster, twenty-year-old port, and thirty-year-old scotch. After the meal, the waitresses cleaned us up, and several masseuses from the Minuteman appeared. We each took turns in one of Lenny's three bedrooms where the masseuses rubbed and, if we wanted, tugged.

Over time, Lenny adopted a steady diet of strippers, hookers, champagne rooms, and mother-daughter tag-teams. For six weeks, he toured the Phnom Penh sex bars I visited on my trip and many more I didn't. Upon his return, he embraced the teachings of Charlie Sheen and his guiding principle became: "If it flies, floats, or fucks, you're better off renting." Lenny's lucky number has eight figures, which apparently protects him from guilt and consequences.

Recently, he decided to mix it up and now has an unpaid, age-appropriate companion named Deborah who appears once a month. His solution for the crapshoot of middle-aged sex: "Variety." But just in case, he keeps a mint bowl of Viagra on his Italian marble coffee table.

I haven't paid for sex since my trip. Not only am I on a budget, but I worry that my recent dating drought and inability to land a relationship in the last ten years could somehow be karmic punishment. But today I should be safe because technically I'm not paying — Lenny is.

We head to the spa where we change into bathrobes, and then take seats in the waiting room. None of the all-female staff is wearing nose rings, tattoos, hipster clothing, or playing with their cell phones. They're wearing navy blazers over white camisoles and address Lenny as "Mr. Rosenfeld."

Lenny gives me the club scuttlebutt. "Remember that masseuse we called 'Trixie?' They fired her. Just when the girls get good, they shit-can them. It's usually because someone's wife catches on. That's why Abe couldn't come today. I got you a session with my new favorite, Shay-Shay. You'll like her. She's thin as a wand. I ordered you the Kowloon Special. If you want a beer, ask for a 'cold tea'. That's still the same."

"*Same-same*?" I ask, using Lenny's favorite Bangkok slang, which means "similar enough to cause problems."

"*Boom-boom*," he says.

When my name is called, I follow Shay-Shay, who is wearing a lab coat, hair bun, and thick black-framed glasses, into a treatment room. She looks like Buddy Holly's phlebotomist.

"Something to drink?" she asks.

"Cold tea, please," I say.

"Please remove your clothes, wrap your waist with a towel, and I will return shortly."

She reappears with a plastic cup filled with beer. A sign on the wall says, "No alcohol allowed in the spa." The sign is slightly askew.

I swill half my beer, then lie chest down, nose and mouth in a face-sized donut cushion at the head of the table. Shay-Shay works my calves, my hamstrings, and reaches under my towel to work my glutes. She spreads my cheeks and grazes my stuff.

I'm aroused and embarrassed, but mostly I'm aroused.

"Please turn over," she says.

I roll over onto my back and shift the towel over my unit. The towel resembles a small pitched tent. Her face reveals nothing.

In my experience, if a masseuse is going to tug you off, she'll wait till you're on your back, as I am now, and start working up your shins, knees, thighs, and then ask if you want her to continue. If you say 'yes', she'll either negotiate a price or leave it to you to leave a big tip. Lenny said that fifty dollars is the recommended amount. "If you want her cell number to set up a house call, leave a hundred," he said.

After Trixie got fired, Lenny had her come to his apartment once a week. He eventually bumped her to two-fifty a visit. Then she moved in for six months and got a monthly allowance of $3K. After six months, Lenny got her a cushy front-desk job with his Back Bay dentist and moved on to another masseuse.

I feel the tips of Shay-Shay's fingers pause at the edge of my pitched towel. She returns to my thighs and lower legs. I feel myself twitching beneath my little tent.

"More tea?" she asks, unimpressed.

"That would be nice. Thank you."

She takes my empty cup and leaves.

As the tent deflates, I think about Jackie. I think about that good night kiss — what a bummer. I think about risking karmic wrath for a hand job. I've gone months without sex so what's another week? Does tipping qualify as paying?

Shay-Shay returns with another beer. Fifteen minutes later, she cleans me up and smiles professionally when I tip her a hundred dollars.

Saturday night, a week later, I meet Jackie at Toon Village, a restaurant in Boston's Chinatown. She's wearing her snug jeans, black hoodie, a black O.J. Simpson burglar's cap, and black leather trench coat. She looks like she's dressed for a home invasion.

The hostess seats us in a booth. The restaurant is mostly filled with Asian couples and families. Jackie points out ones she identifies as Chinese.

"They always look so oblivious, lost, like they're in this country for the first time. I bet most have been here thirty years and still can't speak English. See how they all look the same? No style, straight black hair, glasses, MIT wannabees. That's why I got contacts, changed my hair color to blonde and then red. When that got old, I went to hats." She looks around contemptuously. "God, they're so cheap: Look at the one over there checking every item on the bill."

"Anyway," she turns back to me, "remember I can't stay out too late. I've got three showings tomorrow."

She's checking her phone again, when a waitress hands me a menu in English and gives Jackie one in Chinese.

I order a scorpion bowl to start, and then challenge Jackie to see who can eat the spiciest food.

"You're on, white boy."

When the waitress returns with the scorpion bowl, Jackie orders for both of us in Chinese.

As we're sipping our drink through three-foot straws and playing footsie under the table, Jackie glances over my shoulder towards the front door.

"Here we go. Another Asian cliché," she says. "Fifty-year-old white guy and pretty, young Chinese girl dressed like a hooker."

I look over my shoulder and see that it's none other than Lenny with Shay-Shay, whose exposed midriff sports a belly-button ring.

The hostess seats them in a booth at a far corner, where they sit side-by-side facing me, examining their menus.

"You're too far away," I say to Jackie, swinging around to the seat next to her, our backs now to Lenny and his date. I give her thigh a playful pinch and she wriggles closer.

I consider the karma. I imagine Lenny and Shay-Shay stopping by to chat. I imagine Shay-Shay thanking me for my generous tip last week.

"I have to run to the bathroom," I say to Jackie.

From a stall, I text Lenny:

In Toon Village with Jackie. You can't miss her. The one across the room in the black hoodie. Meet me in bathroom. STAT!

Lenny greets me at the sink, as I'm washing my hands for the third time.

"What's happening, my man," he says, massaging my shoulders. "Got a good look at Jackie. You're right. She's pretty hot — for an old lady."

"Ha ha. Look Lenny, she can't meet Shay-Shay. You have to get her out of here."

"No can do. We already ordered and her uncle owns the joint. It'll be fine. Shay-Shay's a pro. Now, go close the deal."

When I get back to the table, Jackie is putting her phone away. "You were in there for a while. Poopies?" she asks, in a little girl voice.

"A gentleman is always discreet," I say sitting down next to her. "Anyway, you know the guy who walked in with the Chinese girl? I ran into him in the bathroom, and I know him. Lenny. He's actually a friend of mine. Small world, right? He goes to the Minuteman where I used to belong. He's not a bad guy. His mother died a couple of years ago." I hear myself babbling but can't stop.

Jackie leans forward to take a hit off her straw. "Who's the girl?"

"Someone from the club."

"Really?" Jackie twists around to take another look. "I heard the Minuteman is pretty expensive. Is she a member?"

I mumble through my straw. "She works in the spa. I think he said her name is Shay-Shay."

Jackie turns back. "Interesting. Does Mr. Bang ... Cock know what Shay-Shay means in Chinese?"

I shrug.

"It means, 'thank you'. She must do a lot of favors for people."

I detect some sarcasm.

"Shay-Shay must be very friendly," Jackie persists. "Why don't we go say hi?"

Just then, one might even say, auspiciously, our appetizer appears: dried red pepper husks, brown sauce, spongy round ovals with a soft little bone inside that reminds me of a toenail.

"Duck tongues?" I ask.

"Impressive. I guess you did pick up a few things in Southeast Asia."

I scissor a morsel with my chopsticks and offer it to her. She looks me in the eye, as she clamps her lips over it. Then it's my turn, and then hers again. And so it goes until the entrée arrives: pale gray meat strips, fried onion-ring-looking things, Chinese cabbage, light brown sauce, and more red pepper husks.

The meat tastes like pork. The fried-ring things have the consistency of a loofah sponge. A fishy loofah sponge. A spicy, fishy loofah sponge.

"Those are fish maws," Jackie says. "You know, swimming bladders. They have collagen for young-looking skin."

She points to her smooth cheek. I kiss where she's pointing.

I pop a hot pepper husk into my mouth and feed her one.

We chew, gazing into each other's eyes. My throat begins to simmer and my nose begins to whimper. My tongue feels sunburned.

"I thought you said this meal was going to be spicy," I say, wheezing.

Jackie smirks and then looks up.

Lenny and Shay-Shay are standing there in their coats. My nose and eyes are streaming. I point to my throat to indicate that

I can't speak. Jackie introduces herself and all three exchange hellos and nice-to-meet-yous. Shay-Shay barely glances in my direction.

They leave.

Jackie says, "She seemed to recognize you."

Is this a test? How do women always know these things?

In a ragged voice I say, "She did wonders for my Achilles tendonitis a while back."

"I bet," Jackie says. "Lenny seems like an *interesting* guy."

I sit in silence.

Jackie sits in silence.

I wipe my face, my forehead, and my nose with a napkin.

Jackie checks her phone, taps a few keys, and waits for a response.

I think, this is never going to work. I'm not relationship material, and she's a pot-smoking, gun-toting, self-hating Asian who parties like a frat boy. And what is it with the goddamn phone?

The silence simmers.

I glance over at Jackie. Her face has morphed. She looks a little haggard, like she's about to cry. We both poke at our food for a while. I take a chance and put my hand on her knee.

She dabs her eyes with a napkin and puts her hand on mine.

"OK," she says, not looking at me. "Full disclosure: I hate my job, and I'm worried that I may get canned. My ex-husband is stalking me and I'm drinking too much. Then I meet a sexy, Jewish guy who looks like Bruce Willis, who is kind of quirky, makes me laugh. Honestly, my life is kind of a mess right now. Sorry."

She separates her hand from mine and dabs her eyes again with her napkin.

"Wow. Sounds like you've got a lot going on." I caress her knee, wondering if I should hug her or give her some space or if I'm about to get the old heave-ho.

"I'm a pathetic loser," she says, shoulders shaking.

"At least you've been married."

"And what do I have to show for it?"

She grabs my hand and turns toward me. "I'll make a deal with you: You don't ask about my marriages, and I won't ask why you're over fifty and still single."

I smile and hold up a pinky. She does the same. We lock pinkies and seal the deal.

She leans her head on my shoulder. "I like the fact that you've never been married or divorced. No bad habits. You're trainable and can probably clean up after yourself."

She sits up and dabs her eyes again. "My seventy-five-year-old mother goes on more dates than I do. Most guys think I'm too much."

I squeeze her knee as if to say, not for me!

We each poke at our food, which has grown cold.

Eventually, she puts down her chopsticks, cradles my face with her hands and looks into my eyes for several seconds. Then she smiles and whispers, "You have a giant booger in your nose."

"What? Fuck!" I grab her napkin and throw it over her face, cover my nose with my napkin, and race to the bathroom. From behind me, I hear her giggling.

Back in front of the mirror, I remove the offending sludge and watch a smile develop on my face. Women like this don't come around that often. Complicated? Yes. Crazy? Possibly. But not boring. I need to cut her some slack. I need to cut us both some slack. Maybe this can work.

When I return, Jackie is standing by the table, coat on, texting madly on her phone. She looks up at me, red-eyed, lips twitching. "Sorry, I can't ... I have to go." She throws down some cash and, without another word, bolts out the front door.

I watch her disappear thinking: I just had to get the fucking massage, didn't I?

I sit down. Three twenties are scattered on the table. I'm trying to sort out what just happened, how to proceed, but come up with nothing. I finish the Scorpion Bowl and text Abe:

Out with Jackie tonight at Toon Village. Ran into Lenny and Shay-Shay. Things seemed to be going great. But when I got back from the bathroom, she just took off. No 'call me' or 'I'll call you.' She just bailed.

He answers immediately:
Have faith my son. She'll be back.

I text Lenny and he answers immediately:
Shay-Shay got a bad vibe from her. You can do better.

Then Joey:
Sorry to hear that. Sounds like you really liked her in your own twisted, ambivalent way. Hang in there. See you tomorrow for our acting session.

The next day Joey comes to my place looking like a theater person: strafed bomber jacket, glasses with clear frames, and a Colonel Sanders chin strip and moustache. For acting lessons, I pay him a low-ball thirty-five dollars an hour, which is what I charge him for help with his website.

After the Harvard Square gig, Joey reviewed an audio recording I made of my performance and gave it a thumbs up despite my brain freeze. He also finally convinced me to sign up for the biggest amateur theater event in North America, the Moose Fin International Fringe Festival in Alberta, Canada, next spring.

"I did it five years ago," he said. "It's a big deal but let's just say, it's not Broadway or Edinburgh. A lot of knuckleheads go. Farmers dressed like livestock doing one-man shows. Pole-dancing grandmothers. They love the edgy stuff. Did I ever tell you about this one called 'Onion Dip'?"

"Sounds tasty," I say.

"Hardly. It opened with one guy using a turkey baster to stuff another guy's asshole with mayonnaise. Then the guy strutted around naked before taking a white crap on the stage. They scraped the mess onto a plate with crackers and dared the audience to try it. The show sold out every night and got a four out of five-star review. My show got four-and-half stars and I barely rehearsed. You're going to get five stars, full houses, awards. You're going to get noticed."

Joey takes out my script. "Read me your show pitch."

I stand and do as I'm told.

"Decent," Joey says. "Now, run the 'Domination for Dummies' scene."

I perform while Joey red-lines the script. When I finish, he starts in.

"Look Burns, you've got to be sadistic, nasty. Really sell the line: 'Your twat stinks so bad, seagulls follow you home.' Sure, some people will cringe. Maybe you'll get a few laughs. Maybe you won't. Whatever they do isn't your problem. Give the line some room to hit and then move on. Trust me on this."

We move on to the scene where my character visits a Phnom Penh body spa named "The Curious Finger."

We work for three hours straight. After being nitpicked and bossed around for most of it, I want to smack Joey.

"You look like you could use a massage," he says.

Why not? Jackie bailed last night without a word, so I've got nothing left to lose.

For twenty years, Joey has been happily married to a French woman, Monique, an entertainment lawyer with a fondness for spiky hair, sheath dresses, and ankle boots. She paid the bills, while Joey raised their daughter, Jan. Since Jan has been at boarding school, Joey has returned to work, and he and Monique have rediscovered sex together and, occasionally, apart. Once a year, Monique returns to France to see family and to sleep with an old girlfriend. Once a year, Joey gets to visit a massage parlor.

Today is one of those times. "Let's try someplace besides the Minuteman," I say, thinking: I went eight years without paying for sex and now I'm doing it twice in a month?

Joey checks *TugRater.com* and picks the Joy Luck Spa, a massage parlor with five stars. Joey puts an arm around my shoulder. "Only five-stars for us."

We enter the spa from an alley off Newbury Street. Enya is playing on the sound system. There are flowers in vases and bamboo flooring underfoot.

In a teak-paneled locker room, Joey and I change into plush bathrobes. A half-dozen other guys are there, too: Guys in suits, guys with blue collars, guys with wedding bands. No one is talking, but we all know why we're here: the chilled cucumber water.

I follow a stocky woman into a steamy, tiled room for my table shower. She says, "Welcome to the Joy Luck Spa" in a British accent. In addition to a phlebotomist outfit, she's decked out in rubber gloves, rubber boots, and a rubber smock: She's either going to wash me or gut me. I disrobe and lie on the table.

She grabs an industrial spray hose and gets busy. She washes and sprays, then wipes me down, hands me my bathrobe, and leads me to an adjacent room where a long blonde greets me. "Welcome to the Joy Luck Spa," she says in a Russian accent. I remove my robe and lie down on a massage table, face in the donut pillow. She covers my tush with a towel and determined hands start on my calves.

I drift, thinking of Jackie who still hasn't answered my texts.

As Enya wafts through the sound system, I think spiritual thoughts: With every action, we either move toward or away from what we want. Was I moving forward with Jackie or just hovering? What does it matter? I'm going to die alone. Enya sings about something called the Orinoco flow. Women never make sense.

I turn onto my back, and the masseuse ignores my pup tent.

This whole scene reminds me of a bit from my show, in which the narrator visits Tent World, an outdoor gear store. He encounters a salesman who has just backpacked around Asia and knows more about happy endings than he does about travel products. I think about Hank from the Harvard Square Storytelling Hour. I think about Joey and Lenny and what my show reveals: the profound, universal truth that guys like hand jobs from twenty-year-old women.

I'm going to be a hit in Moosefin.

I pay the Russian one twenty-five plus a fifty-dollar tip for good luck, both hers and mine.

Later, I text Jackie one last time:
Should I contact missing persons?

Three more weeks pass and I've all but given up when I get a text from Jackie:
Help me pick up a Chanukah bush. I need a big, strong man.

There's no mention of her disappearing for a month, no apology, nothing. I don't press it.

Two days later, Jackie picks me up in her new, black Camaro. When I get in, she offers soft, wet eyes. I ignore them. She's wearing a red, fur-trimmed down coat, black tights around slender thighs, each of which would fit in one hand. On her head, a wool-knit Patriots hat with a pom-pom, and on her face, loaded makeup: eyeliner, blush, scarlet lipstick. I ignore it, them, her, the whole package. I'm not falling for her bullshit again.

The Pats game is on the radio. As we idle in traffic, Jackie talks about Belichick's girlfriend's new outfit and some other nonsense. I focus on the play-by-play.

At a red light, Jackie turns to me, "I was going to cancel the holidays this year," she says. "But I'm not letting the Grinch win."

A woman making no sense. What else is new?

She offers me a cigarette. We smoke in silence.

After the Pats win, she shuts the radio and pops in a CD. When we hit the highway, she hits the gas: g-forces, tailgating, road rage, Ozzy Osbourne's "Crazy Train" on eight speakers, shaken-passenger syndrome. She swerves into the break-down lane to pass a BMW while checking her phone. I hit my limit for distracted, impaired, crazy-train driving. "Let me hold that for you." I snatch the phone out of her hand.

"Easy there, pale face," she says.

She appears angry, but I can see a smirk developing in the corners of her mouth.

"One of these days, I'll put you over my knee," I say.

The smirk widens.

She turns down the music. Her mouth and eyes do the softening thing. What a performer.

"Did you miss me?" she asks.

"I missed everything but the part where you took off for a month."

"I'm really sorry. Extenuating circumstances. Can I take you to dinner, if I promise not to behave?"

Before I can answer, she screeches across two lanes of highway traffic and comes to a stop at a roadside Christmas-tree stand. A sketchy guy comes out of a sketchy trailer. He has a few trees and a few ear hairs. He tries to sell Jackie his most anemic specimen. No doubt, he thinks she just got off the boat. I step away and chat with an old woman wearing a trench coat over a housecoat and, on her feet, terrycloth slippers striped with mud. His wife or mother.

A few minutes later, the guy is smiling. Jackie is smiling. I strap a lush, nine-foot evergreen to the Camaro's roof.

Jackie squeezes my arm. "Jewed him down," she says.

"Always a good move before Christmas." In spite of myself, we high-five.

Back in the car, we hurtle towards Kmart. The store is filled with last-minute shoppers. Aisle-rage.

We shop for a tree stand, tinsel, strings of lights, a yule log, and more Christmas tchotchkes. I'm bored and itchy but Jackie seems happy, which reminds me that sometimes just showing up can make someone happy. I start to put my arm around her, then reconsider, and retract it.

We stuff the bags of holiday crapola into her Camaro and move out.

As we idle in traffic, I light another Newport and look out the window.

Jackie reaches for my hand. "You're coming next Thursday for Christmas Eve, right?"

I'm instantly irritated, then happy, then claustrophobic, then hungry. Normally on Christmas Eve, Lenny rents a Chinese restaurant for all his Jewish friends. On Christmas day, he and I ski at Okemo in Vermont.

"Let me get back to you," I say.

We pull into a mall and I scan the restaurant options: Capital Grille, Cheesecake Factory, Morton's Steak House, Legal Seafood, Miki-Maki Sushi, Chili's.

"Let's go to Chili's," I say.

"I can afford something nicer," she says.

"I'm a simple man with simple tastes like Budweisers and wings."

She does that thing again where she appears annoyed but then smirks.

At dinner, I think about her bailing at our last meal. I think about her driving. I think about red flags and checkered flags and checkered histories, hers and mine. I think about a recent conversation with Abe.

"Burns, relationships are supposed to be boring," he said.

"I'm never bored when I'm alone," I said.

"Right. You're too busy in the Dark Place."

A family is sitting at a nearby table. The husband and wife are holding hands. Their little boy taps his feet on his chair leg, content. Jackie squeezes my hand under the table.

When the check comes, I let her pay without comment.

At her apartment, we drink eggnog spiked with bourbon and set up the tree. After the lights are strung, she sets a bunch of wrapped gifts under the tree.

"I got you a few things. Don't worry if you didn't get me anything. I sprung this on you last minute, but I've been thinking about it ever since we saw *A Clockwork Orange.*"

I read the labels on the gifts: "Randall," "The Jewish Alex," "Storyteller of the Year," "Spalding Burns." They're all for me.

A boneless chicken wing flutters in my stomach. Enya plays in my head. I feel angry, then sad and pathetic. I kiss her on the mouth.

The last time I spent Christmas with a woman was ten years ago with Ricki when we visited her family in Bangor. She prepped me on the drive up. "First, there's my mother side. I know it's politically incorrect to call them retards so let's just say they're on the spectrum. My father's side? Central casting for *The Beans of Egypt, Maine*. Welcome to crazy town."

At Christmas dinner, the men ignored me. I made one friend, a teenage niece in a tube top who rubbed my knee under the table and invited me to smoke a bone after the meal, which I politely declined.

While I was helping Ricki's mother put away the silverware, she mentioned that manic depression and borderline personality disorder ran in the family. "That's why Ricki's father divorced me. Don't blame him. One minute I worshipped him, the next I wanted him dead."

She handed me the poultry shears.

"My psychiatrist calls it splitting. I was splitting so my husband split."

She laughed and handed me a carving knife.

"I quit drinking and that's helped. I'm hoping Ricki does the same. Did she mention that breast cancer runs in the family?"

She handed me a cleaver.

"We're all so proud of Ricki. She was the first of us to go to college, even if she never graduated. Don't tell her I told you."

She handed me a turkey hatchet.

That night, Ricki and her mother had a two-hour fight. Back in Boston, Ricki and I had our first two-week fight, which led to our first two-month split. No cutlery involved.

Jackie and I sip our eggnogs in silence on her couch, knees touching, listening to Ozzy singing "Grandma Got Run Over by a Reindeer."

Crazy driving, crazy train, crazy town. Maybe this is my destiny.

On Christmas Eve, Jackie greets me at the door with a gentle kiss; no face swallowing, no tongue-attack. She's wearing an elf hat, Star of David earrings, green eye shadow, red lipstick, and a red body stocking offering a bas-relief of clavicles, B-cups, abs, and a camel's toe at thigh junction.

In the living room, our tree glows red and blue. Muted on the TV, *How the Grinch Stole Christmas*. In the air: cloves, cinnamon, turkey, tryptophan, and Ozzie singing "Please Daddy, Don't Get Drunk this Christmas."

The coffee table is set for dinner with lit candles in a pewter menorah; Budweisers in an ice bucket that says "Drink Me"; candy canes, marzipan, and fortune cookies in a bowl that says "Eat Me"; and green and red paper napkins and paper plates, dinnerware for single people who'd rather dispose than clean.

I sit and sip a beer while she brings out plates of white meat, dark meat, mashed sweet potatoes, green beans with almonds, tsimmas, and hot and sour soup with pepper husks bobbing on the surface like water moccasins. Platters teeter on the coffee table, on end tables, on top of the TV.

She takes photos of the dinner and sends them to her mother in Florida. She takes a photo of me and sends it too.

"Are you man enough?" she asks, serving me soup.

We slurp and cough, wheeze and sneeze. She wipes my nose, I wipe hers.

"I think it needs more hot peppers," I say.

By the time we finish, our eyes and noses are streaming.

We take hits off a joint, and then attack the turkey and fixings. After I clear the leftovers, I sit next to Jackie and rest my head on her shoulder, sink into her, her couch, the holiday scene.

There's a long, soft, easy silence.

Then she stirs. "Time for dessert! Have a fortune cookie." She holds out the bowl of them.

I rally, crack one open, and read: "Thanks for making this Christmas special."

She whispers in my ear: "Sorry to be such a cornball."

My body feels warm, awash in tryptophan, cuddle hormones, and cannabis. I could get used to this. Then I notice two new lines around Jackie's mouth. The lines disappear, then reappear, then disappear.

I light a cigarette, which we share back and forth, until we get halfway through when she lets me have the rest. She knows I like the ends, like the ends of a roast, well done, the most flavor.

She puts her head in my lap and looks up at me, eyes soft.

"Your nose-hairs are getting long," she says.

I tweak the B-cups.

"Hey, it's for your own good," she says. "In case you have a job interview later tonight."

I tickle the camel's toe.

She shrieks: "Help, help. I'm being assaulted by a hairy-nosed Jew."

I grab her green elf hat and use it to wipe my nose. Her face clenches. We both pause. I've crossed some line, struck below the belt without knowing it. She snatches the elf cap from me. "Don't ever mess with my hats."

She sits up. We share another cigarette in silence. I take the remaining plates into the kitchen.

"Sorry for snapping at you," she says when I return. "We're still learning each other's operating instructions. I should have sent you the cheat sheet."

We return to watching the happy, little Who families on TV.

I take a sip of beer. "Were you ever interested in having kids?" I ask after a while.

"I was more interested in having a nice, tight cunt."

A hot pepper detonates in my stomach. I cough into my beer.

I've never dated a woman who didn't want to have kids. Not in forty years of dating. Even Ricki wanted kids. And Harriet has two.

I light another cigarette for us to share.

After the Grinch, Jackie loads a remake of *The Secret Life of Walter Mitty*, starring Ben Stiller. "It's about a middle-aged Jewish guy like you who travels the world, comes home, and falls in love with a fifty-something Asian hottie," Jackie says. "It's my favorite."

I consider calling her a cornball but think better of it.

I consider saying that she probably tells that to all the Jews she dates, but think better of it.

I think about Ricki knocking on my forehead and calling me Walter Mitty and then I don't.

We watch the movie, arm and arm. A few minutes in, she falls asleep, head on my shoulder. I carry her to bed, still in her elf outfit. She whispers, "Sorry we can't have sex tonight. I'm having my period." She opens her eyes and pauses. "Kind of a relief, right?"

It is, but I don't say so.

I kiss her and tell her I'll come to bed after the movie. She smiles.

I pop an Ambien, my first sleeping pill in three months, light my fifth cigarette of the night, more than I've smoked in three years, and watch the rest of *Walter Mitty*. In one scene, Mitty has to rent a car and is offered a choice between a red one and a blue one.

red pill or blue pill
single or married
adrenaline or oxytocin
rabbit hole or velvet coffin
free fall or safety net
anxiety or lobotomy
die alone or die of boredom

Why is everything in life either-or? The Ambien pauses my thoughts. I climb into bed with Jackie and fall asleep.

In the morning, I awake to a soundtrack of *clangs, bangs, binks, plinks*, and the theme from "Pop Goes the Weasel." Jackie is laughing. Is she watching The Three Stooges? Have I mentioned that women like this don't come around very often?

The bedroom door is closed. The clock reads 9:50. I sit up remembering how she tried to wake me earlier, yelling: "Happy Jewish Humiliation Day. Merry Crotchmas!" I opened one eye and said, "Every year an elf dies after waking a sleeping Jew. Now *amscray*."

"OK," she said. "I'm giving you till ten, and then I get my shotgun."

Stacked along the bedroom wall are several white milk cartons filled with socks, panties, bras, and sweaters. An overflowing shoe bag hangs from the closet door. On the floor, a swarm of boots overwhelms a shoe rack. I get out of bed and step on a plastic dry-cleaning bag filled with folded clothes. Millennial furniture and a millennial-slob mentality?

The living room is still lit red and blue, sublime and extraterrestrial. Beneath our oversized tree, a dozen presents lay scattered like clues. A pot bubbles in the kitchen making the air warm and moist, sweet and spicy, a cinnamon mist. The dishes have been put away.

"Come sit with me," she says. "The Stooges are plumbers trying to fix the healthcare system."

No trace of last night's little beef — vanished, resolved, and settled. I can roughhouse with her but just can't mess with her hats. No problem. We all have our shit.

She hands me a half-smoked joint. "Wake and bake."

"I'm good for now." I kiss her on the mouth. She's still in her elf outfit with a fresh coat of makeup and lipstick.

We sit side-by-side watching another Stooges' episode, the one where they're all married to harpy wives. "You know," Jackie says, "If we get married, we'll need a ceiling fan because you fart in your sleep."

Married? I spread two fingers and poke her abs, "Plink."

She spreads two fingers and pokes my unit, "Bink."

"I heard on the street that you need to act your age," I say.

"Make me," she says.

During a commercial, she brings out bagels, lox, cream cheese, diced red onion, and capers. I eat, then close my eyes, and once again settle into Jackie, settle into the couch, into our domestic scene.

"Snap out of it!" she says. "Time to open presents."

My sense of well-being vaporizes. Adrenaline replaces oxytocin. I've survived twelve hours with her, slept in the same bed, but now I'm facing the final leg, the Heartbreak Hill of Christmas — exchanging presents.

Shopping for her was stressful. I didn't want to overdo it

and come across as some lovelorn, pussy boy with a sleeve of hearts. But now, looking at all the food, the decorations, and the gifts, I realize I've underdone it. I thought spending a hundred dollars was adequate, considering she ditched me for almost a month and invited me over at the last minute. But now I'm going to look like a cheapskate, which I am, but she doesn't need to know that yet.

She reaches under the tree, grabs the box I brought for her, and reads the card: "To Daddy's Little Girl, from Burns."

I watch as she opens it, remembering how much time I spent worrying about how to sign the card: "Yours," "Best," "Love," "*Lurve*?"

Inside, a handful of gifts I wrapped myself, including a pair of shoelaces imprinted with little bats and a card signed, "Your Big, Strong Man."

Also in the box: a bottle of hot sauce labeled with skull and crossbones, *A Clockwork Orange* T-shirt featuring the domination scene she liked, *A Clockwork Orange* cock paperweight, and a large bottle of Woodbridge bourbon.

"Seems someone likes it when I swing from the chandelier," Jackie says.

She hands me a succession of small gifts, starting with a plastic Oscar statue and two golden balls on a string. "Some kvetchers spend their lives wishing they had the nerve to try what you're trying," she says. "A toast to your brass balls."

We each do a bourbon shot.

I emerge from a sour mash spell and whisper into Jackie's neck. "Thanks for making this Crotchmas special."

She hands me more presents: new ski mittens, which I told her I needed, a paperweight-sized Porsche. "One day when I'm rich, I'll buy you a real one," she says. An electric nose-hair trimmer and a sleeping blindfold. "You can keep these here in case you ... " She doesn't finish the sentence.

Then she hands me a lap-sized box. The card reads, "Now

we can both mess with the millennials." The contents: the rat-motifed T-shirt the bartender wore on our first date, a pair of Converse sneakers with the laces removed, a black Polo Lauren hoodie, which must have cost two hundred dollars, and *A Clockwork Orange* T-shirt. "We can be twins," she says. Her cards are signed simply, "Jackie." I'm relieved and disappointed.

She summons me to the Christmas tree for our first selfie and doesn't seem concerned that I underspent on her gifts. She's a good actress; all women keep score.

She sends the photo to her mother, and then hands me the phone so I can see the picture. My cheek is pressed against her head, against the elf hat she's wearing. I look high and happy. She's staring into the camera, intent on getting the photo, a moment worth preserving or evidence or both.

When I told Lenny about my plans for Christmas this year, he warned: "If you spend Christmas with a chick, it means you two have either a past or a future."

I look closer at the photo and see a hint of doubt in my eyes. Her face also looks a little chubby.

"Let's do another one," she says. As we're setting it up, me sitting on the couch, her sitting on my lap, her phone buzzes. I peek over her shoulder. There's a text from someone named "Dickface." She swivels off my lap, skims the message, and starts to cry, softly at first. I sit next to her, rub her neck, kiss her shoulder, and wait. We watch the muted TV. She grabs the remote and shuts it off. "I have something to tell you."

I knew it. She's reconnected with the ex. Or she's not really having her period, she just prefers dyke to dick. Or, I whiffed on the gift giving and she's been holding it in.

Ask me if I care.

We had a few good dates, even a Christmas, and now it's time to move on. I'm almost relieved. It'll be a clean exit. No awkward, this-is-not-right-for-me phone call or overpriced, dyspeptic closure dinner. Later tonight, I'll catch Lenny and some of the massage girls over at his place and spend more money I don't have.

Jackie lights a cigarette and offers me a puff, a farewell smoke, the firing squad.

"It's my ex-husband," she says.

I stand and put on my khakis over my Christmas-themed boxers.

"He owns a lot of apartment buildings, including this one."

A cute, real estate chick choosing a developer over a struggling non-artist? What else is new? Brass balls, my ass. My heart is an idiot.

"As part of our divorce agreement, I'm supposed to have free rent, but now he's trying to renege."

I stop dressing and listen.

"He also got me the real estate job."

I start dressing again. "What did you do with my shoes?" I ask.

"They're in the bedroom. Where are you going?"

"Home. In any love triangle, the guy who hears about the other guy becomes the third wheel, the hypotenuse, the poly-*gone*, whatever the fuck it is; he's the one who gets the heave ho-ho-ho."

"Where do you get this nonsense? That guy Lenny? Please sit down."

I stop dressing and join her on the couch.

"I had to leave you at the restaurant to meet him."

I start dressing again: "I don't need the gory, puss-filled details." I lace up my shoes.

"Wait a minute. He knows I'm seeing someone. That's why he's busting my chops. I need you. I think my apartment is bugged. We've got enough food and booze for a week."

She needs me?

I run my fingers along the knuckles of her spine, her baby

back ribs. I look around the room, which is now familiar, and smell the cinnamon. Jackie did this all for me. Ricki wouldn't have done this for me. No one in my entire life ever did this for me. Not even my mother. I put my arms around Jackie for a few moments. I start to relax, to settle in again.

Did she say a week?

She shoves an iPad into my hands. "Can you Google 'how to debug an apartment?'" she asks.

I sit up, take charge, and find the necessary info.

"OK. We'll need an empty toilet paper tube, a flashlight, and your cell phone fully charged," I say. "We'll go room by room, inch by inch. This could take months." I put my hand on her shoulder. "Let's start here in the living room. Daddy's got this under control."

She dashes off and returns with a paper tube and a flashlight.

"Nice work," I say. I consult the iPad. "Step One: The woman has to take off all her clothes."

"Let me see that."

"OK, we'll skip that for now."

According to the iPad, we're supposed to look inside flowerpots, light fixtures, and other places that might harbor a hidden mic.

When she bends over to check an electrical outlet, I pull the waistband from her tights and use the toilet paper tube like a telescope to look down her ass crease. "All clear down here."

We check under couch cushions, the coffee table, and kitchen shelves for miniature cameras. We inspect jars of herbs labeled in Chinese. We walk room to room listening for clicks or buzzing that could come from motion-sensitive cameras. We turn off the lights and look for tiny red or green LEDs.

I kneel and look through the paper tube telescope at her camel's toe. "I think I found something fishy."

She flicks my ear with a thumb and forefinger, "Plink."

We check the mirror above her headboard for tiny glimmering lights that could indicate pinhole cameras.

I pretend to recite from the iPad: "Be sure to check the sex-toy drawer."

She pokes my stomach, "Clang."

It's now five P.M. and we've been at this for four hours and found nothing. She's still in her pajamas.

"Will you stay over tonight? I'm a little scared. And I'll give you a naughty Asian massage, better than anything Shay-Shay could do."

In the morning, Saturday, I leave her apartment and walk through the neighborhood, noticing nearby buildings and stores, hoping to see more of all this. Could Jackie be the woman I've been waiting for? Someone who will think about me, miss me, and pick me up after a colonoscopy? Someone who is always there for me?

Someone who is *always* there?

When will I get time to myself?

I exhale and feel like I've been holding my breath for the last forty-eight hours. It wasn't that bad, but by the end, I had to get out of there.

I do a quick calculation. Four days until Lenny's New Year's Eve party. I invited her to be my date, so I'll have time to recuperate and recharge. When I mentioned I was an introvert on the first date, she claimed to be one too; introverts recharge by being alone, so a four-day break should be fine by her, too. I take a deep breath and listen to the quiet, soothing *pttt-pttt* sound of the snow hitting the asphalt.

At home, I check my phone and find no text from her, which is a relief and a disappointment. In the quiet of my apartment, I notice the usual gnawing, grinding emptiness has been replaced with humming and purring.

Sunday
A.M. No word from Jackie. Perfect!
P.M. Ditto. *Hmmm.*

Monday
A.M. Still no word. Gnawing thoughts: What if she goes back to her husband? Think about her once an hour, then once every fifteen minutes.
Early P.M. Text from Jackie:
Looking forward to New Year's. My bed smells like eau de Burns. Yum!

I wait two hours, then text:
Me, too.

Immediately, my phone rings. See it's her and don't answer.
Late P.M. Text from Jackie:
Hope you had a great day. Called earlier just to say hi.

My insides roil. I'm happy. Then annoyed. Then happy and annoyed.

Tuesday
Late A.M. Call her back. Her voice is perky, which irritates me: "Did you get my call?" she asks.
"Sorry, I was working."
She talks about *her* work, her working out, more about her work, then about nothing in particular. I hang on until I'm ready to scream. "Gotta run," I finally say.
P.M. Text from Jackie:
Where are you? I'm in your neighborhood. Thought I'd pop by.

I'm home working and should be happy but I'm not. Do I have to report in with my whereabouts at all times? Or be available whenever she wants?
Abe doesn't answer, so I consult Lenny. His advice: "Throw

the brush-back pitch: Text her tomorrow, something cryptic and sports-related:"Oh, no! Manning PEDs?"

I consult Joey: "Lenny is an asshole. You like this woman. Be nice or at least fake it. Tell me you won't do anything stupid till after New Year's."

Later that night, I text her back:

Sorry I missed you. More soon.

Wednesday

A.M. I visit a flower shop and explain my relationship status to the girl at the counter. She suggests a yellow rose, saying it's too soon for red. I buy a four-dollar dark chocolate bar and write a little card: "Thanks for making my New Year's special." Is the card too much?

Joey says it's fine.

Abe says: "You like this girl, it doesn't matter what you do, your life is ruined."

Lenny emails:

Burns,

You're clearly whipped but it's going to pay off — My crystal ball predicts some hosing in your near future. I know you're out of practice, so here are some tips once you get her in bed:

Start with a little Tongue Congress, then ease her into a Reverse Lorax, and slowly progress to a Seated Frankenheimer.

If she's not responding, mix it up with either the Greasy Weasel in Pike Position or a Dixie Horse Collar, and finally, finish her off with the old Rusty Flugelhorn.

Extra credit: If you locate her Foona Lagoona, work it clockwise with a pinky hay-maker.

The next day, she'll either brag to her friends or call the police.

Go get 'em, Tiger!

The email includes a clip of Dr. Seuss characters humping each other. I laugh. Then I think: Is he really fifty-six? Am I?

Sure enough, a few hours later, I get a text from Jackie:
Where are you?
   Home
Busy?
   Not really
Be right over

She arrives at four in sweats and sneakers with no makeup, as if she's ready for a home improvement project. She's wearing a large backpack.

She pecks me on the lips. "We need to get this over with. I have a showing at five. Where's the bedroom?"

I stop her mid-stride.

"Do you mind taking off your shoes first?" I ask.

"Oh, right, of course."

She flings her dirty, wet Chuck Taylors onto my hand-loomed wool rug, shuts off *my* stereo, and then grabs my hand and leads me down *my* hallway.

She drops her bag on the previously unscratched hardwood floor in my bedroom, and then helps herself to the adjoining bathroom. I pull back the covers, and then stand there for a few seconds looking at the rumpled sheets. When was the last time I washed my bedding? I start removing my socks, stop, and sit on the edge of the bed.

I should be happy.

She comes out still clothed.

"My turn," I say.

In the bathroom, I regard myself in the mirror and wiggle my eyebrows for effect.

Show time.

Then I'm hit with leg numbness, intestinal contractions, waves of burning pain, dizziness, debilitating fatigue ...

I open my medicine cabinet for reinforcements, locate the Ricolas, and pop one. And then another. And another.

As the familiar sweetness fills my mouth, I start to relax and realize I *am* happy. I really like this woman, and she obviously likes me. Let's do this.

When I come out, the lights have been turned off, and my blackout shades have been drawn. I turn on the bedside light.

She squints from the light. "What are you doing?"

"This is a big step. Let's get to know each other a little better," I say, sitting on the edge of the bed, still fully clothed. "What's your love language?"

"We only have forty-five minutes."

"I understand completely," I say stroking her cheek. "Anyway, when you're feeling stressed, would you like your partner to:

"A) Say, 'I know it's difficult and I admire your courage.'

"B) Take you out to ... "

She grabs my head and pulls it to her face. I kiss her lips gently, and then withdraw, looking into her eyes. I start back for another kiss and pull up.

"If you could have dinner with one famous person, who would it be?"

"Ron Jeremy. Now, will you cut the shit?"

"Don't you want to hear the love poem I wrote for you?"

"We don't have time!"

"There once was a lovely, intelligent, Asian woman from Nantucket ... "

"Don't even ...!"

She shuts the light. I feel two petite, single-minded hands grab my arms and tug. I sprawl next to her, fingers on flesh and something that feels like a starched badminton birdie.

"How disrespectful of me," I say, immediately retracting my hand from a B-cup.

I feel her sit up. "Help me get this thing off," she says. As my eyes adjust to the darkness, I see she is sitting with her back to me, holding her hair up.

I manage the clasp without a hitch, undress, and then, you know, a touch of this, a touch of that, some tweaking and twisting, a little nibbling and gnawing, followed by panty-whispering and trilling. I spell out the Hebrew alphabet with my tongue. When push finally comes to shove, I watch my alarm clock and last the national average of seven minutes.

As we are lying side by side, I hear her say, "That was nice."

"Yeah. It was nice," I say.

"OK, I gotta go."

After Jackie leaves, I head for the living room thinking, my drought is over. Maybe I'm more relieved than satisfied and that's OK.

There was just one, tiny issue: the fleshy skin tags, the size of pencil erasers, I kept encountering on her body. But I decide I'm not going to dwell on it. Them. Those bulbs the size of pencil erasers.

I call Abe, who misquotes Woody Allen and says, "Middle-aged sex is dull and miserable. But as dull, miserable experiences go, you could do worse." Joey and Lenny don't answer.

I roam the apartment cleaning up after Jackie: dirt on the carpet, a spent toothpaste tube that missed the garbage, an emptied toilet paper roll that she didn't replace. As I'm changing my sheets, all I can think about is how she said she doesn't date men, she marries them.

I throw away the card I bought her. Then the flower. Then the chocolate. An hour later, I fish them out of the trash. The card is stained with juice from the tuna I had for lunch, and the flower is beyond repair.

I rewrap the chocolate in today's *New York Times* and go out to buy a new card and flower.

Thursday: New Year's Eve Day

A.M. Call from Jackie: "Still lots of leftovers, want to come for lunch?"

Three hours later. Another call from Jackie: "Forgot to ask: What time should I come over tonight?

I call Abe: "She's driving me bonkers. She's calling and texting twice a day."

"Welcome to married life."

"Abe, I'm not married."

"You're on the slippery slope in dress shoes, pal. You're used to going days without calling people back. Not anymore."

Lenny says: "What did I tell you? Doing Christmas with her was going to be trouble. Throw her the backdoor slider: Don't answer any more calls or texts. Call back when you know she's busy."

Joey: "She's not doing anything outrageous. She obviously likes you, which is more than most women you date. If you respond promptly, she'll feel secure and won't call or text as much."

I hang up and text Jackie:
Can't make lunch. Can you be at my place by 6?

New Year's Eve

She arrives wearing her backpack and towing an expedition-size wheelie suitcase. She kisses my mouth and cheek. She smiles when she sees the flower and the chocolate bar gift-wrapped in newspaper. She helps herself to my bedroom and bathroom to shower, blow-dry, and suit up.

I use my galley kitchen for a green room. I shave over the sink and use the stainless-steel toaster for a mirror. My outfit for tonight is a yellow bowtie, ruffly tuxedo shirt, and jeans. Not skinny, below-the-navel jeans that show your ankles, but classic at-the-navel Levi's that I don't have to keep hiking up and that break slightly on my cap toes.

Jackie emerges from the bedroom. "How do I look, Daddy?"

Black bowler, vintage-store tuxedo, ballet slippers on her feet.

"You look terrific," I say.

"Introducing me to your friends is a big deal," she says. "Are you sure you're up for this?"

"Of course," I say, realizing she has a point. How am I going to introduce her? As my girlfriend? I want her to feel special, but I don't want to look like an idiot if she bolts again.

"It'll be fun," I say, kissing her on the mouth.

On the way out, with Jackie on my arm, a young couple from the second floor says, "Hi," as we pass. They never say "Hi."

The Waldorf Residences, where Lenny lives, is forty stories and overlooks the Boston Common. After the doorman buzzes us in, the elevator takes us directly to the foyer of Lenny's penthouse.

Stepping out, Jackie says, "I remember this listing from four years ago. Twenty-five-hundred square feet, three-bedrooms, twenty-foot ceilings, fifty-foot deck, a master suite on the second floor, three parking spaces for only six million dollars. Does Lenny live here alone?"

I don't answer, distracted by the smell of winter on wool and seafood on ice. I can hear the tinkling of glass, the thrumming of bass, and the synthetic laughter of a hundred lonely people. For once, I'm not one of them. I kiss Jackie on the lips, which part slightly for some tongue tag.

We hand our coats to the coat check and stroll by Lenny's art collection: a surrealistic painting of a Black couple performing sixty-nine, a Mapplethorpe-esque photo of a woman servicing another woman with a strap-on, and Lenny's most prized piece, a black-and-white print of what could be a piglet with a beard or a road-kill possum. Underneath the print, a small plaque says, "Eastern Hogged-Back Growler." Jackie stops to take it in.

"You really don't want to look at it too closely," I say, steering her into the living room, which is thick with people. Most of the men are in either full tuxes or black dress shirts and old-man jeans. Most of the women are in little black dresses or white dress shirts and old-man jeans. The notable exceptions are the young women in short-short kimonos: spa club workers, Lenny's hairdresser and her staff, and Lenny's dry cleaner and her staff, who are all circulating heaping plates of hors d'oeuvres.

"Is that Shay-Shay?" Jackie says, pointing to a slender young woman in the kitchen supervising.

"I think so," I say, steering Jackie in the opposite direction.

"Are they a thing?" Jackie asks.

"Lenny likes to hire his friends. Can I get you something?" I gesture toward the carving station, the champagne spigot, the raw bar, and the whisky bar. Jackie stands close, holding my arm stiffly.

Lenny waves to us from across the room. I hold up a finger to let him know that we'll be over in a minute.

"I need booze," Jackie says, in a low voice.

"OK, you got it."

We move to the whisky bar, where I order two ten-year-old bourbons.

Jackie scans the room. "Taupe, grey, and white palette; polished concrete floors," she says. "It's nouveau something or other. To be honest, I was expecting a lot worse. Like say, a stage and dancing pole."

I say nothing, tip the bartender, and grab our drinks.

To our right is a sunken living room with a couch the size of three trampolines. Lit swimming-pool-style steps lead down to the couch, which faces a wall with an embedded gas fireplace and a stadium-size TV. We cram into a corner of the couch to sip our drinks. Our knees touch briefly. Jackie pulls away.

"Engelbert Humperdinck would love this place." She turns and faces me. "How many of these women have you slept with?"

"None," I say, hoping this will turn out to be true.

"Oh, look, here comes your good friend, Shay-Shay, with some pot stickers." Jackie says a little too brightly. "Want something?"

"Maybe later."

The TV is playing a Guy Lombardo New Year's Eve rerun. A digital display on the wall counts down the time. Two hours left in 2015. I snake my arm around Jackie's shoulder, but she shimmies away.

"What?" I ask.

"What-what?" she asks. "You've been acting all feely and needy since we got here."

I tap my drink to Jackie's. "*Ganbei*?"

She frowns and then shoots her bourbon as I shoot mine.

She slips her arm through mine. "OK, I feel better. Give me the lowdown on who I'm going to meet."

"There's Abe, the big round guy standing next to Lenny. I've known him twenty years. He likes fast American cars, and owns a Mustang that he says will beat your Camaro."

"Fat chance," she says. I feel her body relax.

"His wife, Amy, is a pain in the ass." I don't mention that it's because she thinks I'm a bad influence on her husband, odd considering she likes Lenny. Amy is probably still miffed because of the time she set me up with her best friend, who not only turned out to be out of my weight class, but spent our date ranting about her ex-husband, and then stormed out when I offered to let her split the check.

"Interesting. Which one is Amy?" Jackie says.

"The little round one arguing with Abe. They've been married for twelve years."

"Then there's my cousin Joey who I've told you about, on the other side of Lenny. He's married to Monique. She's French, a corporate climber, and rarely talks. She's probably on the deck smoking her European cigarettes.

"Is she attractive?" says Jackie.

I'm not sure where she's going with this, but eventually I say, "Joey thinks so."

"And Rachel is an old friend. She belongs to the Minuteman, too."

"Where is she?" Jackie asks.

"I don't see her right now. Oh, and there's Deborah, Lenny's date tonight. They met on some fetish website. She's six-one, a little klutzy, and wears floor-length gowns even when no one else does. We don't know her real age. She says she writes erotica and once slept with Lou Reed. Joey nicknamed her 'Anais.' Abe refers to her as 'Lola.' She claims to have homes in Montreal and Davos, and says she 'attended university' in Singapore."

"Is that her?" Jackie says, pointing to a red-head in a long-sleeved, emerald mermaid dress.

"That's the one."

Jackie sits silently for a minute, and then stands up, hands her empty glass to a kimono girl, and applies lip gloss. "Let's do this," she says.

We head across the room to the floor-to-ceiling windows overlooking the deck and Boston Common.

Lenny is dressed in a white tuxedo, tails, and a top hat.

"Lenny, you remember Jackie?" I say.

"Of course. She and I have a lot in common. I'm also a Long Island Jew."

Jackie gestures toward the living room décor and then at his outfit: "I never would have guessed."

Lenny turns to me. "Your girl's a pip."

I wrap an arm around Jackie. Her body feels tense again.

"So, Lenny," she says, "I was admiring a photo of yours. The one of an Eastern Hogged-Back Growler. I've never heard of one."

I know what's coming and tap Jackie's hand to warn her.

"That's a picture of my cock and balls," Lenny says with something resembling pride. "When I pledged my college frat, one of the things I had to do was make a copy of my junk on the library Xerox machine. Now, all my sperm have an extra flipper and swim around in circles. Great birth control."

Lenny pauses and smiles. Jackie smiles back and slides an arm around me. I exhale.

Deborah comes up and kisses the top of Lenny's head. "Hello, Burns," she says in an accent I still can't place. "Hello, Deborah," I say.

Deborah glances at Jackie, then steps forward to hug me. Her muscular hugs always make me a little uncomfortable.

"This is Jackie," I say when we break.

"A pleasure," Deborah says, bending to embrace Jackie. In the process, knocking Jackie's bowler to the floor.

"I'm so sorry." Deborah bends to retrieve the hat, providing a view of her generous cleavage. Her throat is flush with what could be embarrassment or hormone treatments.

Jackie accepts the hat, flicks some dust off it, checks it from different angles, and places it back on her head.

Deborah waves for Shay-Shay to bring some appetizers.

Jackie squeezes my tush.

I call over to Abe and Amy who are several feet away, looking out the window at the snow and lights.

"Hey, Abe," I say, "I want you to meet Jackie."

Amy hands her plate of food to Abe and cuts in front of him. She gives me a quick hug and abruptly pats my back, as if she's already had enough of me.

"So, this is the date I've heard so much about. Hello date," Amy says, holding out a hand, "I'm Amy, and you are?"

I cut Amy off. "Oh, right, where are my manners. Amy, this is Jackie. Jackie, this is Amy, Abe's wife."

"What a cute couple," Amy says to Jackie. "You look like you've been together forever."

Abe must have told Amy about Jackie's one-month hiatus. I feel the twisting of an internal organ I didn't know I had.

"Since October," Jackie says.

"That's long-term for Burns. You get a gold star for letting him take you to *A Clockwork Orange*."

Behind her, Abe's face blanches.

"Actually, I took him," Jackie says. "He's on an artist's budget, you know. We each wore bowlers, smoked some weed, and made out like teenagers. Best date I've had in years."

I smile at Amy who yanks her plate from Abe and mumbles something about getting another oyster.

Abe mouths something I can't make out and slinks away.

Joey comes over wearing a porkpie hat, black leather blazer, and black high-top sneakers. He says hi to me, and introduces himself and Monique to Jackie. Monique, like Jackie, is wearing a vintage-store tuxedo and black ballet slippers. Something like a smile passes between the two women.

Handshakes all around.

"What did you think of Burns' performance in Cambridge?" Joey asks Jackie.

"He was great." She smiles at me, and then turns back to Joey. "Burns says you deserve all the credit."

Monique, who has barely said two words to me in the fifteen years I've known her, cuts in and says to Jackie, "Want to dance?"

Jackie turns to me and hands over her purse. "Hold this for me, Daddy?"

Joey and I watch Jackie and Monique glide onto the dance floor. "Burns, don't blow this one," he says.

Rachel, still recovering from a bad breakup two years ago, joins us. She's let her hair go grey and is wearing a slouchy beige sweater and baggy pants.

Fifteen years ago, when we were all single, Lenny, Abe, Rachel, and I started the Chronic Single's Club. We threw parties at local bars and invited anyone we knew who was single. That's where Abe met Amy and Rachel met Arturo. Abe and Amy got married, but Arturo dumped Rachel and went back to his ex-wife. Eventually, the Club imploded, but it still lives on in my one-man show. Rachel is a good friend but that's all it's ever been or will be.

"Heard you have a girlfriend," Rachel says, giving me a hug.

I smile and nod toward the dance floor. "The one in the bowler dancing with Monique."

"She looks like your type," Rachel says, watching. "She even reminds me a little of Ricki. Joey said your rehearsals have been going well. Got a relationship and a career. Congrats."

Jackie and Monique join us again, sweaty and laughing. Jackie wraps her arm through mine. I'm about to introduce Jackie to Rachel, when Jackie whispers, "Daddy, I'm hungry."

I mouth, "Talk later" to Rachel as Jackie and I excuse ourselves and cross the room to the sushi buffet. We load up a plate with shrimp, salmon, and tuna rolls, and head over to a far corner, where we take turns feeding each other with chopsticks.

"Buy you a drink?" Jackie asks.

She heads to the bar. As usual, various people, both women and men, check her out. While she's waiting in line, a guy approaches to chat her up, but she points toward me. He leaves. I get a shot of oxytocin.

She returns with a beer for me and a kiss. "You're the hottest guy here," she whispers.

"And you're the hottest chick," I say, standing up. "Be right back. Got to hit the head." I take two steps, and then turn back and kiss her again. "I'm also the *luckiest* guy here."

When I get back, Jackie is by the bar talking to Adam, one of Lenny's real estate buddies. I wave. She waves back. They're probably talking business. I decide not to crowd her or be one of those sorry guys who can't let his girlfriend talk to another guy for two minutes.

I notice Rachel standing alone nearby with a drink in her hand.

"Hey, you," I say. "How are you holding up? Abe told me the dating scene has really sucked lately."

"Abe is the biggest gossip. But yeah, just when I didn't think it could get worse, I get stood up by a software engineer who can't write a complete sentence. Another guy turned out to be married, and another had a rap sheet. They all seemed normal, you know, photos of them shirtless, holding a striped bass."

"I think you need a hug." As I wrap my arms around her, I say, "Hey, if it happened for me, it can happen for you."

I glance over at Jackie who is watching and smile.

"Burns, whatever you do, hold onto her," Rachel says, before releasing me. "You don't want to go back out there."

Abe slinks over.

"Excuse us for a second," I say to Rachel, grabbing Abe's elbow and pulling him aside.

"Abe, what the fuck is it with Amy?"

"Yeah, I know. Sorry. She's on the warpath. The other night, she started going off about the Minuteman spa again. I either had to give her something to chew on or get a lawyer. Your relationship problems always make her happy. I owe you. It won't happen again. This time I mean it."

We shake on it, and he starts talking about something else, maybe his kid or couple's therapy. I half-listen, watching Jackie, who looks relaxed. Every once in a while, she glances over and smiles. I smile back.

"Abe," I say, interrupting him, "How long can I hang out with, say, a friend like you, and ignore a date during a party like this?"

Abe says, "About five minutes. Why? Is your time up?"

Lenny's real estate buddy Adam now has his arm around

Jackie. She seems to be enjoying it, even encouraging him. He cups his hand to her ear; she shakes her head and points to me.

Lenny pulls up. "Burns, I suggest you go over and claim what's yours."

As I reach them, Jackie puts her arm through mine.

"Adam, this is my boyfriend, Randall. Randall this is Adam. He used to take my spinning classes. He's a developer."

Adam and I exchange handshakes, as if we didn't already know each other, and he immediately excuses himself.

"What took you so long? Too busy hugging other women?" Jackie says, punching me a little too hard in the chest. "If you're my daddy, you need to take care of me."

"I knew he was in real estate and thought you might want to talk shop without me around. I didn't want to crowd you."

"I was about to kick him in the balls, but we're at your friend's party. You're the only one I want hitting on me. I want you to crowd me. Stop acting like you're still single."

I think: First, you tell me I'm too needy and now you want me to crowd you? What the fuck, woman!

I grab her by the arm, pull her face inches from mine, and then jam my tongue down her throat.

For the remainder of the party, I lead her around by the hand, stand next to her, claiming her. I have to admit, it's a nice change to be at a party and have a base, an anchor, and not be free floating like a lost balloon.

As we're waiting at the coat check, I point to Jackie's blouse. "You spilled something."

When she looks down, I give her nose a gentle, upward flick. "Plink. Got you."

"Anyone ever tell you, you need to act your age?" she asks.

"Only you."

Fireworks begin over the Charles River. I lean down to kiss her.

"A writer who loves clichés," she says.

That night, she stays over for the first time.

Over the next two months, we settle into a routine where we sleep together one night during the week, and then hang out Friday night through Sunday afternoon. We talk, text, and email every day, which seems to be working, until one day Jackie says she's not happy with my response time.

"With my friends," I say, "we have a rule: messages have to be returned within twenty-four hours."

"I'm not one of your friends," she says. "We're in a relationship. I'm sucking your cock."

I can't think of a response.

When we're together, we spend hours on her couch, me in her bathrobe, her in my flannel shirts, smoking cigarettes, drinking coffee, sipping bourbon, and watching romantic comedies. There is no such thing as personal space. I reach into her pockets for car keys, she reaches into my Jockeys for the hell of it. Time vanishes, the Bermuda Triangle of relationships.

One day I overhear Jackie talking to her mother on the phone: "We do nothing and everything, talk about nothing and everything, and the hours just zip by." The phrase "nothing and everything" circles my brain. I'm not sure what it means but it sounds shallow. Is she an airhead? Am I?

Over the next few weeks, I attempt to engage her in substantive, contemplative conversations. I rummage around her past, rifle her present, and frisk her psyche. I like what I find.

Personality Inventory for Jackie Chin-Rosenthal:

Family History: At age five, her biological father was killed when his little car was crushed by a big car. Hence, her affinity for Hummers and muscle cars. At age six, her mother remarried her Jewish internist. "The cliché of all Long Island clichés." Jackie has no siblings or other close family. When I tell her that I only have an evil stepsister who I barely talk to, Jackie asks,

"Is she pretty?"

Education: "Some college, a local school." In Boston, this kind of vague response can only mean Harvard. Though Jackie doesn't present as Ivy League material, she possesses a dark sense of humor, which has been linked to high intelligence. She also seems to have an impressive knowledge of communicable diseases.

Career: Security guard at the Museum of Fine Arts, waitress at Howard Johnson's, bartender at the Scotch 'n Sirloin, inside sales for Boston Phoenix adult classifieds, inside sales at Fidelity Investments, real estate rental agent, Howard Johnson's redux, real estate salesperson, bartender at Four Seasons, real estate broker/developer. She mentioned having several "very odd jobs," but refused to elaborate.

Relationship History: She married her first husband, a musician, at age twenty and divorced him six months later after he cheated on her. Her second husband was fifteen years older and died of cancer after ten years of marriage. Her third husband is the real estate mogul currently stalking her. Follow-up questions led to her terminating the conversation one of two ways: By asking why I never got married or by spiraling to her own Dark Place, where she refers to herself as "the Asian Zsa Zsa Gabor."

Things She Misses Most from Her Youth: Baba Louie and El Kabong, Shake-A Pudding, KC and Quaaludes, The Ronald, the Go-Gos, two-for-one happy hour, three-for-one happy hour, four-for-one happy hour, bathroom cocaine parties, men in suits, both of her fathers. "The eighties were our generation's Roaring Twenties," she said, adding she doesn't miss anything about the nineties or beyond. "But maybe, Burns, you can change that."

Worldview: The one thing Jackie despises more than millennials are those Little Free Libraries popping up around Boston. "All those gross people bringing books from their filthy homes filled with unwashed kids and pets. Those books carry scary shit like Chlamydia and crabs." It's hard to argue with her logic.

Assessment from Drs. Abe Gorman and Lenny Rosenfeld: Spotty career and marriage history coupled with a preoccupation with clichés and germs, all key indicators of dysfunction and criminality. "She's an antisocial deviant like you Burns."

Clinical note: Dr. Joey Silverman wanted no part of this exercise.

Sometimes when Jackie and I are together, I shift from participant to observer and see a guy who seems normal and think maybe I can do this. Maybe I just never met the right person or wasn't ready, and after forty years of dating and therapy, things have finally aligned. Then I wonder if this is just another performance, which ends when one of us wanders backstage and sees the wires.

Periodically, we get off the couch for a meal, for the gym, for liquor shopping. Every activity is a date that we dress or undress for. And there's regular sex, two to three times a week. On Sunday, it's time for me to split, to recharge for a few days, and rehearse my show.

When I leave, I always notice the quiet of her neighborhood and how the old gnawing sensations have mostly disappeared. Having a girlfriend puts a floor on how low I can spiral and inoculates me from the Dark Place. A little monotony seems like a fair trade off. I haven't thought about Harriet in weeks.

The married couples in my building now talk to me. Because I'm in a relationship, I'm no longer the creepy, single guy who might flash their wives if I got them alone in the laundry room.

Jackie and I are becoming the standard by which relationships are measured. One night, we were sitting at the bar of the Beacon Hill Lounge, and I was watching basketball while Jackie hummed and played with her phone. Every once in a while, I'd kiss her hand, wrist, forearm, Gomez Addams style, while she stroked my head like a sex organ. Two different couples nearby gave us the thumbs up.

Then one night, after sex, Jackie said, "I think I'm in love with you." I can't remember the last time someone said that to me. I heard myself say what I was supposed to say. I immediately felt bored. Then crowded. Then I kissed her. The next day, I bought her a toothbrush to keep at my place.

These days, Jackie is drinking less, smoking less, and wants to hang out at my place more. On the other hand, I am drinking more, smoking more, and wanting to keep my place as a refuge.

I read somewhere that you only meet three people in your life you can marry. In my case, it was Dani in my thirties and Ricki in my forties. Neither worked out. Jackie could be the one. She also could be my last chance.

But I'm still concerned about our middle-aged sex life, those exposed wires backstage.

The second time Jackie and I had sex was after Lenny's New Year's Eve party. At my place, lights off, condom on. I didn't cum. Jackie didn't cum. Was that sex? The next morning, I found a small pelt, that looked like possum road-kill, a hogged-back growler, on my dresser that turned out to be her hair extensions. Jackie slept in a bandana and when she took it off in the morning, I noticed her hair was thinning. Ah, the hat trees. I felt had, then sad. I tried not to think about the fleshy, pencil-eraser moles on her body.

The third time we had sex, Jackie said we didn't need to use condoms because all of her eggs were old and rotten. Lights off as usual. After trying missionary, she got on top and appeared to cum or maybe she deserved my mini-Oscar statue. Regardless, I did my best, topped the magic seven minutes, and came.

The fourth time we had sex, she left the lights on and the pencil erasers were all I could see. She noticed me noticing and said nothing. We tried a reverse cowgirl with her on top facing away, the moles less noticeable: She appeared to cum. I came.

To be fair, Jackie never comments on my body, my varicose veins or my little stomach roll, which is just as well. I couldn't handle the scrutiny. Yeah, I can dish it out but can't take it.

The fifth time, we got stoned beforehand. What moles? What thinning hair? All I noticed were the toned arms, smooth throat, slim thighs, lovely face. Everything was great until a post-coital discussion of her love of anal, and how she had sex with her first husband every night, and how she had sex with her third husband every night, and how he liked it when she stuck things in his ass. She said sex is like chocolate: the more, the better. I found the chocolate analogy in bad taste. When I returned to my apartment alone that night, I watched porn nonstop to see how many times I could cum. Between Jackie and *Massage Parlor Mayhem*, I hit four times in twenty-four hours, something I hadn't done since my forties. But my schmeckle was sore, depleted. I failed to have a morning boner for days but luckily managed to summon one the next time I slept with Jackie.

The sixth time, she talked about her vag, her va-jay-jay, and, of course, her cunt. When she grabbed my unit, she said, "Time for a little beef chow dong." I was turned off. We argued. She complained that she was the man in this relationship and I was the girl, that she was the dom and I was the bootlicker. She said I was gay. I said she was gay. She dared me to prove it by letting her dress me up like a woman.

She was making no sense. What else was new?

One night, I let her put a wig on me and make me up with lipstick and mascara. She wore a fake beard and moustache. We went to a local bar, the public library, and Whole Foods. No one noticed because too many other guys were dressed as women. At home, Jackie called me her "lady boy." I banged the shit out of her — moles, thinning hair, and all. We both came.

Four months into the relationship, we've settled on sex three times a week, at least once every time we're together, usually in the morning, usually after coffee, occasionally after bong hits. But I still have concerns about her sexual appetites, her husbands' sexual appetites, and my ability to keep this up, keep it up. Also, I don't like the gulping, gobbling kisses and the gulping, gobbling blowjobs. I wonder if she's angry about something. But she is beautiful. My friends think she's beautiful. How can you be so in love with someone and not like having sex with them?

I consult the experts.

Abe:

"Amy and I have sex twice a month, and sometimes we forget." He talks about sex and chores and how, in a few years, Jackie will lose interest. "Quit whining. Ride it out. Pun intended."

Joey:

"How many moles does she have?" he asks.

"I counted seven, but she wouldn't hold still long enough for me to check for more."

"Jeez Burns, you made it sound like at least fifty. Love the moles, kiss the bald spot, ignore the other stuff. Focus on things you like: the arms, the face, her body in clothes. And if you're really not in the mood, be a man and say no."

Lenny:

"You could dump her and rent someone younger. But I get that you like her, and you get depressed without a girlfriend. Whatever you do, don't let her stick anything thicker than a finger in your ass. Or maybe two. By the way, I can give you some Viagra, that's what I use whenever I let Deb stay over."

One night in early March, Jackie and I meet Monique and Joey for a drink near Monique's office in Copley Square. The hostess seats us at a corner table.

Joey talks about my show and our recent rehearsals. "The Moosefin Fringe Festival is a big deal," he says. "If we do it right, the domination scene is going to shock the Canadian audiences and generate some press."

Monique covers her mouth with her palm, feigning shock, then smiles, and puts her arm around Joey.

Jackie yawns.

Joey, always the gentleman, changes the subject, and asks Jackie about the real estate market.

"Crazy busy," she says, ordering another drink.

She and Joey talk about prices in his South End neighborhood.

Monique turns to me, wanting to know more about my show. Monique never talks to me about my show. Monique never talks to me about anything. Must be the Jackie effect.

After two rounds of drinks, Monique and Joey say they have to go. They leave and Jackie heads to the bathroom. When she returns, her eyes are wet and swollen. She sits down and says nothing.

A minute passes.

I ask, "Are you all right?"

She pounces. "What the hell were you thinking? Don't you get it? You are not single anymore. You can't talk about sex like that with other people in front of me. How do you think that makes me look?"

I look at Jackie, and then around the room. Were we both at the same table, with the same people, in the same city, on the same planet?

"I'm totally humiliated," she says, dabbing at her eyes.

Is this the same woman who talks about anal and va-jay-jays and cunts and stuffing things in her ex's asshole?

"And you flirted with Monique."

"What are you talking about? Monique is Joey's wife. I wasn't flirting with her," I say. "That's the first time I've ever had a real conversation with her. I'm assuming that's because either she's got the hots for you or because she thinks I'm normal now that I have a girlfriend."

She glares at me. "And what am I supposed to do while you're at your fringe festival with all those Canadian theater sluts?"

Jackie blows her nose. "I don't trust women," she says. "Besides you, I have one friend, my ex-husband, and now he's trying to screw me in more ways than one."

I'm her only friend? Should I be happy that I'm literally her one and only? My spleen twitches several times.

Jackie sniffles. I try my best to reassure her and apologize even though I'm not sure what I'm apologizing for.

"Now I see why you've never been married," she says.

This seems a little below the belt, but I say nothing and file this away under "Jackie Operating Instructions."

By mid-March, month five as a couple, we're holding steady at three sleepovers a week and having a pretty good time, considering what we've been through: Valentine's Day, my birthday, the Patriots not making the Super Bowl, and the ensuing depression that descends because there's no more football for seven months. Jackie gets bonus points for knowing that the Red Sox and Celtics are no substitute for the Patriots.

Then one day when I'm over, Jackie comes down with the flu. I got vaccinated back in the fall but she didn't. "My mother says flu shots are bad for Asian people," Jackie said.

Instead of wishing her well and heading out the door, I stay and take care of her, something I haven't done for anyone since my mother got sick three years ago: lung cancer, dead in four months, and she wasn't a smoker.

I follow Joey and Abe's advice and sleep with Jackie in her infected bed, buy groceries, cook, and then schlep her to the doctor. Jackie asks me to come into the exam room with her but her doctor says, "Sorry, only family allowed."

Jackie says, "He's my fiancé."

I get hit with oxytocin and panic at the same time.

Back at her place, I sit vigil as she ignores the doctor's advice and instead follows the advice of her mother, who sends musty Chinese herbs and other random remedies, some of which I try. Our favorite is the salty sinus flush that we blast into each other's nostrils with a squirt bottle. It generates a searing head rush as the heated liquid shoots up one nostril, into the sinuses, and exits the other nostril, flushing out a ropey goop that swings from our noses like spinach linguine. We compete to see who can handle the highest temperature and the most salty powder. We even add Tabasco sauce.

On the fifth day, Jackie develops a sloshy cough that keeps us both up at night. We return to her doctor who prescribes codeine cough syrup, which we drink from shot glasses while watching hours of *Snagglepuss*, *The Three Stooges*, and *Jackass* movies. We manage to polish off a whole week's worth of codeine in two days. Jackie weasels another prescription from her doctor who explains that "sharing a prescription, even with a fiancé, is a crime." Jackie and I agree that not sharing is a bigger crime.

Two days later, her bedroom is filled with empty beer cans and take-out containers stuffed with cigarette butts. Her bedspread is stained with bong water and something that resembles spinach linguini.

"I'm not sure how much more my immune system can take," I say.

"I'm sorry, Daddy," she says with a little-girl cough that sounds forced. "I need a hug."

I give her a hug and a shot of codeine, clean the place, and make dinner for the seventh night in a row.

The next day, she is better and I am finally free to go. I spend the next several days in my apartment, alone, recuperating. I call Jackie every four hours as instructed.

As a thank you, she sends me a bouquet of flowers and a sinus flush kit.

A week later, we're back in her apartment on the couch, the flu episode long gone. She lies down with her head in my lap. Does she want sex? We had sex yesterday and I'm not up for it, but I don't want to spoil the easy mood.

I stretch my arms out on the back of the couch to avoid encouraging anything.

"Everything OK?" she says, looking up at me. "You seem a little jumpy."

"I ... actually, I kind of feel like going to the gym," I say.

"That's OK. Me, too," she says. "But first, I had this great idea for us."

"OK," I say.

"Let's go to Bermuda — on a cruise. That way we can be together and have sex every day."

I can think of nothing to say except, "Oh, wow."

Later, I consult my panel of experts, and they all agree there's no way I'm getting out of this one.

In early April, Jackie models a one-piece bathing suit for me. "You look great," I say. "But it's forty degrees out."

"Ha ha, silly boy. This is for our cruise."

I reach for the bourbon.

She parades in front of me wearing a new floppy sunhat and sunglasses. I light a cigarette.

"I get it," she says, coming over and sitting on my lap. "It's not really your thing, but we need to live a little. And it will be good for us." She pauses. "I told you, I'll pay for the tickets." She pauses again. "But I can count on you picking up incidentals like meals and drinks, right?"

For the record, I've never been on a cruise nor ever wanted to, nor had I any interest in seeing Bermuda, which I've heard has all the charm of Tijuana. But I'm in a new phase of life. I need to be flexible, open to possibilities. And Jackie could be my last chance for not dying alone.

The coming weeks have their challenges.

Monday
Wake at seven A.M., eyes crackly, mind cranky. An image of a cruise ship pops into my head. Fall back to sleep.

That night, shift around in my bed like a dog looking for the right spot. Never find it.

Tuesday
Wake at three A.M., stare at ceiling. Toss. Turn. Check clock. Six A.M.

Stay at Jackie's that night. Pop two Nyquil, take a bong hit, have mirthless sex. Two hours later, she wakes up, and plinks my forehead: "Wake up and go to sleep." I find some leftover cough syrup in her fridge.

Wednesday
Wake hung over, Jackie already at work. Recall journalist's credo: Three of anything is a trend. This is the third bad night in a row. My old therapist, Dr. Moody, always said to nip insomnia before it got rolling. I go to the gym, then to happy hour with Jackie. "You were grinding your teeth last night," she says.

That night, I sleep alone at my place, barely.

Thursday
More of the same.

Jackie drops off a care package her mother sent for me: Herbs and estrogen cream, which "calms the body." Jackie rubs cream into my arm "Don't worry, you won't grow a va-jay-jay." We have requisite sex, and then she leaves to sleep at her place because I've been keeping her up. I throw the herbs out the window for the squirrels and wash down my last Ambien with a beer. In the morning, I'm too groggy to remember if I stayed up all night.

Friday onward

I worry about insomnia once an hour and develop bed dread: a fear of nighttime. Abe drops off some of his Ambien and a bottle of Nyquil. Every morning feels like a morning after.

Jackie offers reassurance. "This cruise will fix everything! You are going to love it!"

In the past, my bouts of insomnia could last a year. My first bout was at age six. I didn't want to wake my mother and stepfather, so I'd get into bed with my stepsister, Harriet, who was seven years older. After a few nights, she called me a little perv and kicked me out. From then on, I'd go into the bathroom and read labels on medicine vials and household cleaners until I got tired, which could take hours. I was always tired. At thirteen, I discovered pot smoking, which helped me sleep but made me depressed, which was marginally better than not sleeping. When I started dating in my teens, I noticed that some women I could sleep through the night with and some I couldn't, which often indicated whether the relationship would last.

This is the worst bout I've had in five years.

I consult my team of medical experts.

Abe: "Get your own script for Ambien, you cheap fuck."

Lenny: "Shay-Shay is stopping by with a friend. You in?"

Joey: "Make an appointment to see Moody. Get this under control before the cruise. I want you in good shape for Moosefin."

Dr. Moody and his shrink wife live in and practice out of a large Victorian in Newton, a big-ticket Boston suburb. After my previous shrink moved to Maine in 1998, I started seeing Moody, but stopped soon after my mother died in 2012, when he seemed to be mailing it in, telling me the same thing over and over, something about sitting with things instead of reacting.

But when Moody was on, he was great. He noted that I was drawn to people and situations that made me uncomfortable, a trait he called counterphobia, which made sense. I'm terrified of germs but when I was a kid, I'd touch my poops three times for good luck. I'm also afraid of heights but bungee jumped three times, once in South Africa and twice in New Zealand. And even though I'm introverted, I'm drawn to women with crazy train, over-the-top personalities like Ricki, Jackie, and Harriet, who once sent me to kindergarten wearing lipstick, the same Harriet who also held me down when I was seven and diddled me in front her best friend. And she called *me* a perv?

Over the years, Moody helped me understand my regular visits to the Dark Place and to accept that relationships were a challenge for me because I tended to frame them as winner-take-all power struggles, although I've often wondered if this was more his issue than mine.

Today, Moody greets me in his foyer. The receptionist and espresso machine are gone. He also seems to have upgraded his wardrobe from shirts too large and ties too loud to a black, mock turtleneck and tan, fitted jeans. He's lost weight. He's lost his bald spot. He has a moustache and goatee and could pass for an Emerson College theater instructor.

"Nice to see you again, Randall," he says, in an even, professional tone.

We walk in silence down the hall to his office, which is strewn with half-filled boxes. The walls are bare: no modern art and no photos of his lumpy wife and kids. We're seated in folding chairs that could have been stolen from a Harvard Square Storytelling Hour.

"What happened to the leather couch and rolling, high-backed shrink chair?" I ask.

"Was that a dig?" he asks.

"You tell me, you're the doctor."

He says nothing and pulls out a yellow legal pad, Bic pen poised. "So, what brings you in? Your phone message said something about a girlfriend with lots of moles."

"Right. I've been dating this woman Jackie for about six months. The relationship has been great. Mostly. Except she talks about marriage all the time, and then she booked us on a one-week cruise to Bermuda. I've stopped sleeping. That's always my early warning that a relationship is a bad fit."

"Any trips to the Dark Place?"

"Not since I started dating Jackie."

"Does she have the same body type as your stepsister Harriet?"

"Yeah. Jackie is slender. So what?"

"Do you still have erotic dreams about Harriet?"

"Not since I started dating Jackie. And, for what it's worth, Harriet is getting married again."

"Are you working?"

"I just wrote a one-man show called *The Chronic Single's Handbook* that I'm performing locally. Remember my cousin Joey? He talked me into signing up for a big theater festival in Canada. It's like Sundance for live performers, where people go to get discovered. I'm trying to follow your advice about chasing dreams but not betting the 401k on the outcomes."

"So, you've got interesting things happening in your life. If this is the wrong relationship, why are you bothering with it?"

"I'm sick of being alone, and she's the best woman I've ever dated. Except for the insomnia. And the fact that I feel like I'm drowning when I'm around her too much. Also, she wants sex five or six days a week. And the moles are a turnoff. Should I send her a postcard and tell her I ran away and joined the circus or moved in with you?"

Moody looks up from his pad. "Not unless you want to share a room with my wife."

Shrinks with separate bedrooms? This seems worth a dig but I resist.

"Actually," I continue, "I love Jackie. She's quirky and fun to be around. On our second date, I wanted to take her to a foreign film to impress her. She suggested *A Clockwork Orange* instead, and then pulled out some weed and a flask of Jack Daniel's. We laughed so much we almost got tossed out of the theater. It was the best date of my life. Until the next one and the one after that. I feel normal around her. Even the people in my building treat me differently now. They let me pet their dogs and kids."

I glance out the window where a lone car is idling at a red light. When the light changes the car sputters away, its exhaust fading into a thin gray ribbon. I look back at Moody. He's squinting at me as if I'm fading, shrinking, becoming invisible.

"Randall, you're fifty-six years old. You've never been married. And you just wrote a play called *The Chronic Single's Handbook*. Marriage may not be in the cards for you."

"You've said that before. And by the way, I just turned fifty-seven."

We stare at each other in silence.

"Is it possible that you contribute to the power struggles as much as I do?" I ask.

"In therapy, all things are possible," Moody says, checking his watch.

I check my watch.

"As for the sleeping," he says. "We've tried everything from lithium to Prozac to Ambien to CPAP to meditation. I'd like to help you more, but I'm going through changes of my own. I'm getting divorced and leaving this practice. Starting next month, I will be the prescribing psychiatrist for a chain of medical marijuana clinics. I'm sorry, but I'm going to have to give you the old heave-ho."

"You're dumping me? What am I supposed to do?"

"Clearly, you've got two things going on, the relationship and the insomnia, and I'm not sure they're related but neither is fatal. Slow everything down. Take the relationship a month at a time. Go on the cruise and don't think about breaking up until you get back. Keep practicing your self-care and awareness."

He tosses around more chestnuts about hypervigilance, assertiveness, and his favorite, ambivalence.

"As we've discussed before, you need to sit with the anxiety, the discomfort, the uncertainty, the boredom, the grey and beige. See where it all goes. When you come out the other side, you'll be better able to deal with it next time it appears, and it will appear, again and again. Remember to have fun. For the record, you seem calmer, more centered, less combative. I think you're in a good space for a relationship."

Moody scribbles on his yellow pad, tears off the sheet, and hands it to me.

"Here's another sleep specialist to try. I wish you good luck in all your new endeavors," he says in a tone I don't recognize but which could be sincerity.

"And you as well," I say, standing up. "By the way, would you mind if I hit you up for some weed next month?"

The next day, I call the sleep specialist, Robert Fleagle, M.D., and reach a receptionist with a sing-songy African accent. The good doctor is booked through September 2017, eighteen months from now. I ask to see someone sooner, preferably a man and add that this is an emergency. I'm offered an appointment with a nurse practitioner, Radoslav Vetochkin.

"He's new and is taking patients with great enthusiasm," the receptionist says.

I'm transferred to Vetochkin and get the voicemail of a man with a gurgly Russian accent that I can barely understand. I am not enthusiastic and hit zero to be transferred back to the front desk. A man with a Spanish accent answers. Once again, I mention the gravity of the situation. "I'll take a man or a woman, anyone who is a native English speaker. Sorry."

"*Si, Señor*. No worries." He suggests a physician's assistant, Mindy Rothstein. First, I think assistant, as in secretary. Then I think, probably Jewish and probably a native speaker.

The next morning at eight thirty, after another endless night, I find myself in the waiting room of the Hollstone Sleep Medicine Clinic. The front desk staff is stationed behind a plexiglass barrier, which looks bulletproof. The staffers wear an assortment of headgear: bonnets, turbans, and skullcaps.

I approach a Black guy wearing a white veil. He says that sleep medicine is a specialty service and my copay is forty dollars, which is twice what I normally pay.

He rings up my credit card and says: "Please be seated, sir. We will address you when Dr. Rothstein is available. In the meantime, please complete this questionnaire."

I collapse in a seat across from a wall plaque that says: "We understand your time is valuable. If you've been waiting longer than fifteen minutes, let us know."

The other patients look like they've been waiting all night: hanging jaws, hanging eyes, half-empty cups of coffee. There are dripping children, sniffling college students, men in slippers, women in bathrobes, old guys in night shirts, dirtbags in cockroach stompers, bed-wetters, snorers, insomniacs, narcoleptics, sleep-apneacs, and sleepwalkers. I've never seen so many busted up, down and out, white people in one place. Apparently, sleep medicine, like psychotherapy and skiing, is a Caucasian indulgence.

The TV is blaring daytime talk shows, while the overhead lights are bright enough to tan pale skin. A coffee machine in the corner features free coffee–anything to keep us awake.

I take a seat and start the questionnaire, the same questionnaire I've filled out dozens of times. I list allergies (scallops), ailments (too many), family history (too much). For next of kin, I consider putting Jackie but instead put Joey.

I sit, drink coffee, and finger my wallet, which seems forty dollars lighter. I watch the clock and recount my experience with sleep clinics. Fifteen years ago, Moody sent me for an overnight sleep study. At bed time, a technician wired up my eyelids, nose, chest, legs, and any other place he could stick an electric lead. He strapped an elastic belt around my chest. I lay there while the little creep video-taped me scratching my balls all night. They eventually diagnosed me with sleep apnea and prescribed a CPAP machine, a router-size device that shot air up my nose and down my throat all night, and they wondered why I didn't sleep.

I read somewhere that doctors who can treat, do. Those who can't, open a sleep clinic. I also read that twenty-five percent of medical treatments fail. But that was fifteen years ago, the early Moody days. Maybe the science has improved.

After twenty minutes of *Live with Kelly and Michael*, I approach the bulletproof glass. A receptionist in a red fez says: "Please sir, be seated. I'll check on Dr. Mindy."

"I was told she's a nurse. Did she earn an M.D. while I've been waiting?"

The receptionist ignores me. He's probably used to this kind of behavior.

Five minutes later, Dr. Mindy appears. She has blonde hair pulled into a bun and grey, Brillo-like eyebrows. Her lab coat fans behind her into an A-frame, another overweight health professional.

In her office, we sit opposite each other. I smile. She smiles. I try not to look at her wool socks and Tevas. Dr. Mindy puts my completed questionnaire aside and asks me the same questions I just filled out.

She hands me a five-page privacy document and checks the clock on her desk. I scribble my name without reading a word and hand it back to her.

She asks about my health, sleeping habits, and social life. I describe the burning sensation behind eyes, how my body feels hot and crispy, my brain fried. She takes my temperature, my pulse, my blood pressure. "All normal. You just need to relax."

I tense up.

She hands me four pages of instructions and talks about sleep restrictions and stimulus control. She discusses compressed sleep cycles and Ambien abuse, which can lead to walking in your sleep, eating in your sleep, and driving in your sleep. She tells me I also need to record the time I get into bed and how often I wake during the night. I also need to start getting up at seven in the morning instead of sleeping until ten.

This whole discussion makes no sense, but I take notes as she talks and types. We both work as fast as we can. Our time is valuable.

If I can't fall asleep after twenty minutes, I'm to get out of bed and perform one of the following relaxing, non-stimulating activities:

- knit, dust, sift cat litter

- sharpen knives, write poetry, listen to music

- read catalogs, actuarial tables, *Eat, Pray, Love*

It sounds like I'm going to be too busy to sleep.

She stands up and hands me a prescription for Ambien.

"Make an appointment with me in two weeks, before your cruise. You're going to be fine."

I follow Mindy's instructions for the next week and notice a pattern. I average four hours of sleep per night and wake up foggy, anxious, and horny whether Jackie is with me or not.

One night, I dream I'm Leonardo Di Caprio in *The Revenant* after he spends the night sleeping in the body cavity of a disemboweled horse. In the morning, my mouth tastes musky and Jackie's underwear is stuck to the ceiling. She's in a good mood, which makes one of us.

Another morning, we have a post-coital discussion about large birds that can eviscerate you with one kick: Ostriches. Cassowaries. "There's one more," I say. "Begins with an 'E.' Egret? Eagle?" I madly search the E's in my memory. Then I search the birds again. No luck. Jackie searches on her phone: "Emu!" she says, triumphantly.

The next night, I double up on Ambien. The following day, I start forgetting the names of movies and actors. Who are those Boston guys? Matt Damon and Ben, what? Ahh, fuck! Oh, right, Affleck.

Next, I'll be microwaving my keys. I had forgotten that Ambien doesn't help you sleep, it makes you forget you were awake. Did I already say this? I feel like someone ran a magnet over my head: corrupted files, scrambled partitions, bad sectors, lost clusters. If this continues, can my memory be restored? I reduce my Ambien dose by half for two nights and smoke more weed.

I call Mindy and leave a message.

Three days later, she calls back: "How is the sleep going?"

"Bad."

I tell her I increased the Ambien. I tell her I drank and smoked weed with the Ambien to make it clear the treatment is not working, and that she needs to return my calls promptly or I will do something crazy and it will be her fault.

The strategy backfires. She says she will not refill my Ambien. I need to calm down and give the program some time. It's only been a week. Then she contradicts herself and says my sleep problems should have improved and suggests that I may have an underlying psychiatric issue. She recommends a sleep psychologist named Noreen Nussfeld.

I call Moody. He recommends a sleep psychologist, indeed, the same Noreen Nussfeld. He says he will give me a prescription for Ambien. "Remember: Insomnia is not the end of the world and won't kill you — unless you keep reading all that crap on the Internet."

The next morning, I see Nussfeld. She contradicts Mindy. "You're nocturnal. You need to go back to sleeping later in the morning. Waking at seven is like waking in the middle of the night for you. Try melatonin. And don't worry."

I fork out another forty-dollar copay and worry.

That night, I sleep alone but can't fall asleep. Though my memory is shot, my hearing is suddenly superhuman. I hear a refrigerator, a dripping sink, a leaky toilet. I check my refrigerator, sinks, and toilet. No dripping or leaking. The noise must be from my neighbor downstairs. Then my heating system kicks on. And off. There are drunks on the street. Somewhere in Boston a TV is blaring. I hear cars on the street. Boston traffic doesn't start till five A.M. Is it five? Have I been awake for the last five hours? I get out of bed but instead of sharpening my knives or opening *Eat, Pray, Love*, I go into the bathroom and read the labels of medicine vials and household cleaners.

The next morning, Jackie texts me:
Great news! I just picked up our tickets!

II

THE CRUISE

According to the glossy brochure Jackie left on my bed last week, our cruise ship, the *Dorian Whisper*, which I immediately dubbed the *Durian Whisper*, is quite the specimen. With a crew of eleven hundred, she boasts an indoor mall, a health spa, a three-hundred-seat theater, a disco, a rock-climbing wall, an ice-skating rink, a basketball court, two casinos, two pools, and ten restaurants. Endless opportunities for us to indulge our senses and wallets in around-the-clock activities, including: shopping, dance parties, duty-free shopping, talent contests, lectures about shopping, socials, super bingo, a Mr. Sexy Legs competition, a Wacky Putt-Putt tournament, and, of course, Broadway musicals. The ship is a floating game show. Our vacation is a seven-day infomercial. I'm ready for it. All of it.

The always thoughtful Abe emailed me a cruise-ship exposé by David Foster Wallace, featuring his personal account of antiseptic tourism, sterile simulated experiences, socio-economic alienation, status anxiety, brand fetishism, conspicuous pampering, porcine excesses of food, drink, and adiposity — and the unbearable sadness of the entire gyrating, gelatinous, neo-bourgeois spectacle. The article was concerning but, in the end, I concluded that Foster Wallace was just a very literate kvetch.

The always helpful Lenny pointed out that taking this trip would score huge points with Jackie, meaning she'd ease up on the marriage pressure. "But," he advised, "stay out of your cabin except for shitting, sleeping, and hosing. Close quarters are where fights happen. You know if you cram too many rats into a cage, they start eating each other's babies."

"Lenny, I didn't know that."

"For real, I saw it on *Mutual of Omaha's Wild Kingdom*. So, get time to yourself. If you're with her too much, she'll start reading your mind; old ladies are really good at that. If she starts some shit, go alpha. Chicks dig it when you tell them to fuck off."

Joey suggested a pre-cruise discussion. "Spell out your expectations," he said. "Both of you, but mostly you."

One night, after some bourbon over candlelight, Jackie and I drew up a contract specifying, among other things, how often we'd have sex, when I'd get time to myself, when I'd get time to rehearse, and our signal — the Carol Burnett earlobe tug — when one of us wanted to leave an event. Instead of signing in blood, we each taped a lock of pubic hair to the agreement, which is now in the side pocket of my suitcase and stored on our phones.

On Friday, May 6, 2016, the seventy-ninth anniversary of the Hindenburg disaster, Jackie and I line up in a hangar-sized terminal on Boston's waterfront at one P.M for a four P.M. departure. From where we stand, the thousand-foot Durian towers over the pier with its layers and layers of portholes and balconies and lifeboats spanning fifteen decks stacked 150-feet high. The capacity is 2,200 passengers, all of whom seem to be boarding at the same time. The temperature is in the fifties, so most people are wearing down vests over their radioactive cruise wear.

Jackie's idea of cruise wear is stack-heeled motorcycle boots and skinny red jeans, along with her latest, guaranteed-to-offend hoodie, which has a mug shot of Patriots tight end and convicted murderer Aaron Hernandez.

After visiting a tanning salon yesterday, her face is bronzed and creamy; she even added a Marilyn Monroe-style beauty mark this morning. I slide an arm around to cup her ass and bend to kiss the side of her head.

It takes two hours of waiting in line for our luggage to be searched and tagged, and then another hour to have our carry-ons searched. During those lost hours, I start to feel unbearably sad until Jackie points out a sign that says, "No illegal drugs." She stifles a laugh and squeezes my hand. "We're going to rip this boat a new one," she says. And for some reason I feel a little better.

After being scanned by a muscular guy with a metal wand, we face two women wearing holsters, brandishing spray bottles. "Washy-washy," they say in unison. I follow Jackie's lead and extend my palms like a preschooler as they saturate both sides of our hands.

Welcome to antiseptic tourism.

In addition to rogue waves, speedboat terrorists, and rum-soaked captains running aground, the biggest concern on a packed cruise ship is an outbreak of the flu, salmonella, Legionnaire's disease, or the ever-popular, barf-inducing norovirus. Two giveaways that an outbreak is underway are help-yourself buffets that have been replaced by manned serving stations and no salt and peppershakers on the tables.

Before our hands dry, we are confronted by a guy dressed in navy whites: white pants and a white jacket with gold buttons and gold and black epaulets. A pin on his jacket says, "Free hugs."

"Hi there," he gushes. "I'm Mango Mike your cruise director, welcome aboard the *Dorian Whisper*! Are you ready for the vacation of a lifetime?"

He takes in Jackie's hoodie and his smile dims. Without another word, he forks over a map of the ship and a list of its restaurants.

Next in line are his two chirpy assistants, Kit and Kat, also in white. They hand Jackie a goody bag with coupons for, among other things: the spa, the chocolate shop, a bucket of Bud Light, a jug of Sutter Home, a case of Pepsi, and a bag of gourmet pork rinds. Kit recites tonight's special events: A chance to meet Spa Director Dr. Elke, a garnet seminar at the jewelry store, and a tequila-tasting at the duty-free liquor store.

I think, porcine, neo-bourgeois consumerism. Then I think: Can't let Foster Wallace get in my head.

There's now only one person between us and our cabin: a man in a navy blazer with a salt and pepper, Amish-style beard. No doubt the boat's surgeon general. He studies Jackie's hoodie, says nothing, and watches us board.

Our room is on Deck 10. We skip the lines at the elevator and take the stairs, which are empty. The hallways are cramped, single-file passages with wall sconces shaped like torches. The rooms to our left face the interior of the ship and have no windows. "The cheap seats," Jackie says.

When we reach cabin 10-130, Jackie's inserts her keycard and flings open the door. "The love nest," she says, arms held wide.

The love nest is narrow, maybe twenty feet by ten, and features a bathroom the size of a closet, a dresser, a bed with a mirrored headboard that engulfs a third of the room, and, at the far end, an armless couch facing an LCD TV. The walls are paneled and wood-like. Above the dresser is a piece of abstract wall art, likely from the *Ecole de* Marriott period. Our luggage is piled in front of the bed.

Jackie throws one of her suitcases onto the bed and pulls out a plain, brown box with Chinese writing, a care package from her mother. She tears it open, grabs a canister of Clorox wipes and throws a pair of rubber gloves to where I'm standing in the doorway. "Want to come in and help?"

In the bathroom, I wipe down every light switch, faucet, and hard surface in the toilet, sink, and shower areas while Jackie brushes her hair. I move on to the couch area, attacking every handle, knob, and armrest. Jackie wipes down the minibar. I place the TV remote control in a clear plastic zip-lock I brought.

Sitting on the bed sipping a wine cooler, Jackie points to the dresser. "I think you missed a spot." I remove the decorative bedspread and matching accent pillows and throw them into the hallway.

"What the hell are you doing?" Jackie asks.

"The word on the street is these things are rarely washed and are a breeding ground for your favorite organism, E. coli."

"Always thinking of me," she says, smiling as she drops her empty wine cooler into the wastebasket.

I savor the reassuring smell of bleach and the phrase "sterile simulated experiences" wafts through my brain. Jackie flips on the room fan.

I remove the rubber gloves and flop onto the denuded bed. My arms hang over the sides. Definitely more full than queen. I'm tempted to ask Jackie, "So, where's your bed?" but I'm distracted by something impaled on the overhead light: a towel coiled, twisted, and knotted with dark, empty eyes.

Jackie aims her phone at it. "A monkey!" she says. "My mother loves towel origamis."

I get up to survey the cabin for escape routes and safe rooms but, other than the bathroom, there is only a floor-to-ceiling glass door that leads to the small balcony outside. It will have to do for now.

After Jackie shelves her clothes and hangs her jackets, I cram my stuff onto the remaining half shelf.

When I turn around, Jackie is wearing a surgical mask. She cocks a finger and says, "Hands up, pants down."

We have sex. I work around the moles and stroke her face, breathing in the smell of her vanilla moisturizer. She kisses my head. We exchange I love you's, and settle into each other.

Minutes later, we're fog-horned awake by the PA system. "Greetings all! This is Mango Mike, your cruise director with a few announcements. Please join us on deck now for our Bon Voyage party and complimentary Bud Light. At six, join Kit and Kat for a tour of the Duty-Free Mall and a Belgian chocolate tasting. Dr. Elke will be giving a lecture on low-priced, liquid facelifts on Deck 9. And don't forget our specialty restaurants: Listeria, offering the finest in gluten-free, vegan cuisine and Papilloma, our Argentinian steak house. Both are taking reservations right now."

"Listeria?" I ask.

"I think he said 'Wisteria,' " she says,

"Papilloma?" I ask.

" 'Papillon,' funny guy," she says, springing to her feet. "Let's dress up and hit the Bon Voyage party."

I put on an oxford shirt, a paisley tie, khakis, and loafers with socks. Jackie wears a black T-shirt, black leather pants, a jean jacket, and loafers without socks. I kiss her and squeeze her tush. She pushes me away. "Not now, you horny dog. We have a party to go to."

On Deck 12, we pass a pool too small for laps, three hot tubs on raised platforms, steel drummers in a salmon-colored gazebo, and gelatinous crowds in Red Sox, Celtics, and Patriots' jerseys milling between the spread legs of a two-story statue of David in a pink thong. We make our way to an uncrowded serving station, where we grab sixteen-ounce cans of Bud Light, and then move to the railing, waving to people on shore. I stand behind Jackie, my arms circling her, and press my cheek to the top of her head.

She lifts her phone, tilts her head to show off her new beauty mark, and snaps a selfie of us kissing with the pier in the background.

A middle-aged couple pulls up to the railing a few feet away. He's sporting a grey hoodie that says, "Sons of Belichick" above an image of the grim reaper wearing a Patriots helmet and, on his feet, orange Crocs with wool socks. All four pockets of his cargo shorts bulge with cans of Bud Light.

The woman's hoodie has a Patriots logo and the words:

"You are now leaving Foxboro. Sorry for the ass-whooping." On her feet, white flipflops with white bows identical to ones Jackie owns.

Him: "Goodbye, you frickin' retards."

Her: "Hey, those are my kids waving down there."

Him: "Don't have a spaz attack, Charlene."

Her: "Come on Tommy, don't get too hammered. We haven't even left the harbor."

There is an uncomfortable silence, then they bang a U-ey and leave.

I say to Jackie, "That could be us in ten years."

"You should be so lucky." She shimmies her tush against my thigh.

We head to the serving station to grab two more Bud Lights and a flyer of tonight's activities.

I open the flyer and read out loud: "Tonight's movie triple-feature: *The Poseidon Adventure*, *Outbreak*, and *The Perfect Storm*. Musical review: *Syphilitic Inbreds: A Tribute to Grand Ole Opry*. Snack specials: Twenty dollars for unlimited Shaefer, Doritos, and Ring Dings."

Jackie rips the flyer out of my hand. "Cut it out, Burns. Let's check out the gym."

I see a sign for the gym on the far end of the deck, but Jackie leads me down a nearby stairway. We pass a liquor store, a cigarette store, a jewelry store, and stop at a Purell station. I tap the foot pedal for Jackie who rubs her hands together like mating weasels. She taps the pedal for me, and then grabs my wrist to examine my watch, as if she's noticing it for the first time. It's a plastic Timex, the same thirty-dollar model I buy every ten years. The watches never die but the bands eventually break, so I figured out how to repair them with a combination of Super Glue, Bondo, and Velcro.

"Easy on the merchandise," I say, as Jackie scrutinizes my repair work from different angles.

She drags me by the wrist into the jewelry store.

The sales girl is dressed in a little white smock, something Shay-Shay might wear. She introduces herself as Chelsea and smiles as Jackie places my wrist on the glass counter above a display of Movado watches. I try on a few models, which are impressive but not for eight-hundred dollars.

Eventually, Chelsea loses interest in me and turns to Jackie. "I like your earrings. Is that cassiterite? We have some pendants that might work with them."

Chelsea launches into a discourse on precious stones, semiprecious stones, precious-semi-precious stones, two-for-ones, trunk shows, appraisals, guarantees, duty-free fifty-percent offs, tennis bracelets, rings, friendship rings, engagement rings.

I cut in: "Did I read something about an eight-hundred-dollar limit on duty free?"

Chelsea motors over my question: "Caribbean charm," "one of a kind," "tanzanite," "hemimorphite," "morganite," "melanite," "moldavite, ammolite, malachite."

Last week, Jackie and I had a jewelry discussion. Not *the* jewelry discussion but *a* jewelry discussion. "The stuff I'm wearing is all from my ex-husband. I'd rather wear something from you. Doesn't have to be expensive."

I interrupt Chelsea: "Do you have any hermaphrodite Israelite?"

She ignores me: "Citrine," "aquamarine," "and, as I mentioned, the two-for-one trunk show." "Authorized dealer," "Effy, Mikimoto, Pandora," "gold and silver charms."

Foster Wallace is in my head again — something about brand fetishism and socio-economic alienation.

"What was that?" Jackie, the mind reader, asks me. I detect an edge in her voice.

"I didn't say anything."

Over the PA system, a now-familiar voice booms.

"Good evening, ladies and gentlemen. It's Mango Mike here, with some reminders and more specials for this evening: At our Professional Portrait Studio, photos with yours truly. At Effluence, our poolside bar, Bud Light is hosting an LGBTQ happy hour. For all you high rollers, we have $2,500 Bingo tournament in the Balut Royale Casino. And there are still a few spaces left for a free cellulite assessment with Dr. Elke in the spa. Finally, don't forget to make dinner reservations at our premium restaurants: Rice 'N Spice, our sushi restaurant. Hungry now? The Munch House Buffet is open."

"Did he say 'Effluence'?" I ask.

"Try 'Affluence,'" Jackie says.

"'Ricin'?"

"Cut it out, Burns."

Mango Mike trills on, and I have the sudden urge to visit a Purell station but then think of Joey's recent advice: "Burns, you love this girl and want her to be happy. If it's not killing you, do what she wants some of the time."

I'm actually contemplating a purchase, even though I haven't bought jewelry for a woman in ten years, when Jackie tugs on *my* earlobe and turns to Chelsea. "We were just passing through. Thanks for your time."

Once we're outside the store, Jackie says, "I got the message when you started acting like a dick."

I decide the best tack is to say nothing and trot after her.

Eventually, we make it to the gym, which features a full bar and cocktail servers. On the walls, motivational sayings: "You got this," "Your workout is my warm up," and "Unless you puke, faint, or die, keep going."

Passengers in Red Sox and Celtics jerseys are sprawled on the weight benches in various increments of inebriation. A guy who is older than his hair color, waves a red frozen drink in Jackie's direction and slurs. "Exercise is my *blish*."

This group doesn't resemble the triathletes and Zumba

babes from the cruise brochure except for one woman doing crunches in a crop top, accordion abs and all.

I sense Jackie stiffening beside me.

"I'm going to check out the men's locker room," I say, kissing her cheek.

A row of lockers, a row of urinals, a row of stalls, everything looks normal except for the toilet seats, which have an automated, rotating assembly line of paper covers. If you want to double- or triple-protect your seat, additional covers hang from a wall dispenser.

Above the sink, there's an eleven-step guide to washing your hands with diagrams, decision trees, and Boolean conditions that would have confounded Alan Turing. By the door, a Purell dispenser, a tissue dispenser, and a sign: "Feel free to open the door using a paper towel." I like their style.

I exit just as Jackie is coming in to check on me.

Hand in hand, I lead her into the aerobics studio to our left, which is stocked with balls and yoga belts. I pick up a Nerf football and draw Jackie in for a huddle. "You're the quarterback," I say. "It's fourth down, fourth quarter, fifteen seconds on the clock. We're going to fake a bubble screen, then I'm going to break like it's a corner route, then cut back on a skinny post. Got it?"

"Yeah, sure, whatever you say."

I circle the room a few times, pinching Jackie butt each time, and stop at the far end of the room.

"Moss is open in the back of the end zone," I say. "Brady looks and fires. Hey, Brady, yeah you, with the cute ass, look and fire."

Jackie windmills a few times and finally hurls the ball, which knocks over a lava lamp, which smashes to the floor. She covers her mouth with both hands.

Later that evening, I'm hanging out in my retreat (the balcony), listening to the *sploshing* of the ocean and the thrumming of the engines. Jackie is sitting on the bed with her back to me reading a magazine. We've changed into our casual attire of shorts and polo shirts.

"What do you say we eat at the Coprophagia Café?" I call out.

Silence.

Finally, she says "I'm going to the *Fantasia* Café, but why don't you go ahead and eat at the *Coprophagia*, Mr. Comedian." She pauses and turns. "I just looked up that word. A little much, even for me."

Two women in holsters greet us at the Fantasia entrance. "Washy-washy," they say.

Jackie and I grab a booth.

"Salt and pepper shakers on table?" I ask Jackie.

"Check," she says.

"Unmanned help-yourself buffets?"

"Check."

"Serving staff wearing latex gloves and scratching their balls?"

"Check."

We fill our plates with Hibachi beef and return to the booth. She sits next to me. I move over to make room.

"You're too far away," she says, tapping the seat next to her.

I move an inch and then another as she keeps tapping until we are sitting thigh to thigh, skin to skin. Her legs are hot and sticky and not in a good way.

The room is filled with diners, most of whom have changed out of their sports jerseys into cargo shorts and fleece vests. Several of them resemble characters from Foster Wallace's article, including a large red-faced woman on the pasta line who looks like Jackie Gleason in drag and a wispy-haired guy sitting alone filming his food, the décor, and the water view out the window with a camcorder mounted on his shoulder like a small bazooka. I watch him, hoping someone will join him.

Jackie is gazing out the window nearest us. "Nice sunset," she says.

Strips of pink and orange settle into an immense, endless blue-grey ocean. Something inside me releases a little. I spear the juiciest slice of beef from my plate and feed it to Jackie. She takes a bite, smiles, and squeezes my thigh.

It's midnight when we get into bed. Kiss-kiss, sex-sex. Afterwards, Jackie covers her head with a spare pillow, rolls over, and goes to sleep. I pop an Ambien, slip in my night mouth guard, place my sleep blindfold on the night stand for later, and open *Eat, Pray, Love*.

The rocking of the boat is soothing, amniotic, and after twenty minutes, I feel dozy and turn the light out. But after twenty more minutes, a buzzy sensation starts in my wrists and inches up my forearms, over my shoulders, up my neck, and into my ears. Bed dread.

I hear a *yip* followed by a *yap*. Wasn't this cruise pet-free?

I start composing a complaint to Mango Mike.

The yipping is replaced by ponging and echoing à la *Voyage to the Bottom of the Sea*. Then rushing and whooshing. I imagine a mega-ton, cruise-ship septic flush spewing acres of toilet-seat-cover flotsam. I check my watch: I've been lying here for forty minutes. Sleep experts say I should get out of bed.

I look over at Jackie. Face exposed, peaceful and beautiful. I should buy her those earrings.

She stirs and covers her ears with the pillow. "I can hear you thinking," she says. "Wake up and go to sleep."

"Sorry, I'll try to keep it down."

She flutter kicks a few times under the sheets and goes back to sleep.

Now I detect a smell: sweet and sour, salty and savory, fermented and gamey. I sniff my armpits, then lift the sheets and sniff. My Asian girlfriend smells like soy sauce. I am a racist Jew.

"What the hell is wrong with you?" she asks.
"Nothing my little honeysuckle. Wake up and go to sleep."
"Cut the crap already."
She snatches the sleep blindfold.
"This thing is all wet."
She throws it on the floor and covers her head again with the pillow.

I kick the sheets off my legs. Then I'm cold and tug them back on. My body thermostat is old and unreliable. Buzzy blood starts circulating again, tingling. Then a sphincter twitches. Crawly skin, humid pits and crotch, body damp and scratchy like I'm in a giant bathing suit filled with wet sand.

I get up to take a piss but don't flush. Sitting on the toilet, I fold and refold a towel into an origami that looks like a folded towel and then, after popping another Ambien, I crawl back in bed.

The next day, we have a room service breakfast and, at noon, hit the pool area on Deck 12, the site of the Bon Voyage party. The same band is playing the same calypso music in the same salmon-colored gazebo. The chaise lounges are plum-colored and S-shaped, like cavorting dolphins. I move my chaise next to Jackie's before she can start with the tapping. She kisses my cheek.

A waiter materializes and Jackie orders a frozen daiquiri.
"I'm all set," I tell him.

The ship has only been sailing for twenty hours, but we're already off the coast of Virginia, and it's now about seventy-five degrees under a big blue sky and a few frothy clouds. I'm bedecked in a wide-brim hat, long-sleeve rash-guard shirt, SPF 50 swim tights, and windsurfing gloves — the outfit I wore on my trip to fend off the sun in Venezuela, Greece, Thailand, Vietnam, Cambodia, and Australia.

Jackie is wearing her scarlet lipstick and a scarlet one-piece that makes her tan pop. Her cover-up is an oversized T-shirt that says, "In a world where you can be anything, be a douche."

From our beach bag, she takes out her book, Zig Ziglar's *Secrets of Closing the Sale*. I take out mine, *The Artist's Way* by Julia Cameron. I also take out my little spiral-bound notebook and plot out a rehearsal schedule for the week.

"What are you always writing in there?" Jackie asks. "Dear Diary, Jackie is such a bitch; she made me have sex with her again."

I stare at Jackie over my wrap-around, polarized sunglasses. She continues.

"Zig Ziglar says, in a relationship it's not good to have secrets. He was married to the same woman almost seventy years. They met when he was seventeen and she was sixteen."

"I guess that makes him a child molester as well as the world's greatest salesman."

She lunges for the notebook and I pull it away. She lunges again. I pinch the soft smooth skin on the inside of her thigh.

"Ow! Security! Security! This strange man dressed like the mummy just tried to touch my unit."

People in nearby chaises turn in our direction.

Jackie says to me in her outdoor voice: "People are watching. You better behave yourself, Mister Roscoe Bernstein, room 12-170."

A waiter appears with her drink. Jackie orders chicken fingers with extra French fries, and winks at me as if to confirm that, per our agreement, I'm paying for incidentals, such as drinks, snacks, and extra French fries. I wink back.

The remaining chaises in the pool area fill up. The crowd resembles what Foster Wallace referred to as the "bovine herds" with middle-aged skin conditions: pustules, liver spots, varicosities, spider veins, sebaceous cysts, lipomas, and lots of belly button hair — on the men, too. The fitness models must be in the gym.

Three sentences into my book, I'm interrupted by a tap on my shoulder.

"Would Roscoe care for a chicken finger?"

"Roscoe is good right now."

"Would he care for a French fry? A rim job?"

People look in our direction. I feel myself blushing and getting hard.

I return to my book. Or try to.

A nearby kid starts screaming. Then another kid starts crying. A few rows from us, a plump, pink, freckled guy gets to his feet. He looks younger than the rest of the crowd. Nestled in his red chest hair is a Star of David. He calls the kids spoiled brats. A pink woman with short hair, in a T-shirt that reads, *"Oy Gevalt,"* tells the guy not to yell. He calls her a spoiled brat. I hide behind my book, hoping no one will connect me with these people, my people.

Moody would probably ask if I'm jealous of this guy.

Why? Because in thirty years, when he is my age, he'll probably be retired, on the board of this and that, and spending his time with grandkids, instead of chasing childish dreams of being an astronaut or a performer?

I return to the same page I've been reading for the last hour.

Jackie starts grunting. She's struggling to open a bottle of tanning oil.

"What you got there, little Missy Miss?" I ask.

"My lucky stars. A big strong man has come to my rescue."

I open the bottle and return to my book.

"Oh, Roscoe. Does the artist's way include rubbing oil on a lover's back?"

I kneel on her chaise, straddling her little tush, rubbing oil into her smooth, tawny skin. I massage it into her shoulder blades and neck, kneading her upper back. She purrs, adjusting herself against my growing erection. A smile creeps up the side of her face. She adjusts again.

This isn't so bad. The noise from the masses has settled into a soothing hum. Everyone seems to be having a good time. Even the Jewish tribe has quieted down, their kids splashing in the water. I bend forward and kiss the back of Jackie's head and whisper, "I like you. A lot." Another smile.

Looking around, I continue to rub her back and notice she's one of the few on the sundeck with color, of color, the only Asian, tawny in a pale, pink sea. Does this ever bother her? Maybe this is why she does everything she can to stick out, as if to say, "Hey, fuck you. I'm not hiding just because I'm outnumbered."

On my trip, I was in places where I was outnumbered but it never felt like an issue. Or maybe I was just invisible. Or maybe everyone had plenty of *others* to other. The Greeks hated the Turks. The Thais hated the Cambodians. The Cambodians hated the Vietnamese.

Once, at a youth hostel in New Zealand, I was drinking beer with a bunch of guys: a red-faced, overbearing Aussie, a dark-skinned Māori, and a few pink Europeans. At one point, the Aussie put his arm around the Māori and said, "Isn't that right, you black cunt?" In this context, I was pretty sure that "cunt" was meant as an endearment. Still, I wondered what would happen next. When the Māori hugged the Aussie back, I wondered if he did it because he was outnumbered or whether being called a "black cunt" wasn't such a big deal. Later, the conversation turned to the Scots, and then the Jews, and which group was cheaper. Was I offended? A little? A lot? I considered saying something even though I knew this was just a bunch of guys busting on each other. The Māori didn't make a fuss when it was his turn. In the end, I mentioned that I was Jewish and that, yeah, some of my relatives had a thing about money. And then someone mentioned that all Americans had a thing about money. Then someone went inside and bought a round of beers. And then I bought a round of beers.

My conclusion at the end of the trip: Scratch the surface and we're all a bunch of racists.

Still, I wondered if this is something that Jackie and I should discuss. I kiss the back of her head again, dismount, return to my chaise, and prop open my book. Jackie returns to her book.

How do you bring up this kind of thing? Jackie and I rarely have serious conversations, and when we do, she says I interrogate her. I put down my book. Jackie puts down her book. We look into each other's eyes. Then she rolls toward me, and reaches into my swim tights. "There's an old Chinese saying: If you tickle your boyfriend's balls on a crowded cruise ship, it brings good luck."

Back in the room, Jackie takes a shower and I rehearse using the towel monkey as my audience. Jackie exits the bathroom before I'm done and rolls her eyes. "Oh, for god's sake, can you please take that outside?" she asks, pointing to the balcony.

For happy hour, we decide to check out the Chiki Tiki on Deck 13. I've changed into a polo shirt and board shorts. Jackie is wearing a "Free Whitey" hat backwards, mirrored state-cop sunglasses, a new coat of in-your-grill scarlet lipstick, and a white wife-beater over a lacy bra. Her hair, which she's been growing out, hangs whip-like between peaked shoulder blades — Asian for bad ass, my Chinese Kate Moss.

The fluorescent, thatched tiki roof is adorned with plastic flamingos wearing green fez hats. Polynesian war clubs and ceremonial paddles hang from the walls. On the TV, a Red Sox game.

We sit on grass-skirted stools and wait for the bartender. Jackie plucks maraschino cherries and pineapple chunks from the bartender's garnish tray.

"I can't take you anywhere," I say.

She opens her mouth and points to the half-chewed remnants.

"That's not very lady like."

Her eyes widen. She chews, swallows, and leans forward to whisper, "Incoming. A mating pair of Lane Bryants, portside."

The couple lands in the two seats kitty-corner to us. They're wearing matching lime and turquoise outfits. His picturesque Aloha shirt is opened to show off a belly fuzzed with grey hairs. She's wearing a kaftan cover up.

"Oooh, Ortiz is up with two on," the woman says, eyeing the flat screen.

They slap plastic cups half-full of something red and frozen on to the bar, then remove their fanny packs, and heave them on the bar, too. The woman adds her pink, rhinestone-encrusted phone to the pile. I notice that Jackie's phone on the bar is pink and rhinestone-encrusted, too.

They introduce themselves as Frank and Janice.

Janice: "So, where you guys from?"

Me: "Back Bay."

Jackie: "Me Cambodia."

Janice: "How fun. We're from Quincy. We never met anyone from Cambodia."

Jackie: "Me Boston long time. Work massage parlor." Jackie lassoes her arms around my neck. "Kemosabe best customer." She kisses my blushing cheek.

Janice and Frank pause, glance at each other, and then stir their drinks with the world's longest straws. Jackie sticks her tongue in my ear. I flinch.

Me to Janice and Frank: "She's kidding. About everything."

Jackie removes her arms from my neck: "Me no kidding!"

Janice and Frank look around the bar, which is starting to fill up with people.

As Frank turns his head, I notice a diamond stud in his ear.

A bartender comes over to Jackie. "What can I get you Miss?"

"We'll have two Jack Daniel's on the rocks and split a Bud tall boy," Jackie says in perfect English.

Frank turns back to us: "You two are a *real* hoot."

Janice stands, snatches their gear, and then Frank. They depart without another word.

I feel a moment of embarrassment, and then whisper into Jackie's ear: "Dude, you should be doing the fringe festival, not me."

She whispers into my ear: "You're the only audience I care about."

We kiss. Our drinks arrive. Ortiz lines a single into right field.

Ten minutes later, the bartender sets out little signs around the bar: "LGTBQ happy hour, drinks half price." He switches the TV from the Sox game to reruns of the seventies' sitcom *Maude*.

"I used to love this show," Jackie says, roping her arms around my neck again, which feels hot and slick and not in a good way.

Another couple grabs the open seats near us. The guy looks about my age with appropriate-colored hair and clear-framed glasses. But it's the logo on his polo shirt that catches my attention: "Moosefin, Alberta."

Jackie whispers in my ear. "Let's hit the bricks."

I hold up a finger for her to hold that thought.

I lean over. "Excuse me," I say, "Have you ever heard of the Moosefin Fringe Festival?"

"Been many times," the guy says. "We live there."

"Really? I'm performing there next month," I say, extending a hand. "I'm Randall Burns."

"I'm Geoffrey," says the man shaking my hand, "and this is my wife, Theo."

"And this," I say, circling an arm around Jackie's shoulders, "is my girlfriend, Jackie."

"Me Cambo..."

I spin around and mouth, *Don't*.

Theo orders two Macallans, neat, which the bartender brings right away. I order another beer for Jackie and me to share.

Geoffrey is wearing seersucker shorts and Top-Siders without socks. Theo is wearing a man's seersucker jacket over a white camisole that's crowded and busy.

Geoffrey slides his seat nearer. "Where are the two of you from?"

"Boston," I say. "You're not a performer, are you?"

He smiles. "I'm an appreciator of theater and the Dean of the English Department at the University of Alberta in Moosefin. Some of my grad students have performed at the festival. But we're going to miss it this year. We'll be out of town. Have you done many fringes?"

"A couple of small ones in the U.S." I mention my published novel and describe my show. Geoffrey, Theo, and I talk on about our favorite authors and playwrights.

Jackie cuts in: "Yep. I'm dating a guy who wrote a show called *The Chronic Single's Handbook*. So, what am I? Frickin' retarded?"

Geoffrey and Theo sip their scotches, looking more bemused than offended.

"Not to change the subject but there's a great show on the cruise called *Betsy Carmichael's Bingo Palace*," Theo says. "It started on the fringe circuit and broke out. I think they're from Buffalo."

Jackie sighs.

Geoffrey says, "We're going one night this week. Want to join us?"

Jackie pretends to check her closed phone case. "I think we have plans," she says.

I keep my eyes on Geoffrey and say, "We could probably change them."

Jackie sighs again, and orders a shot of tequila.

Theo leans over to say something, but I can't hear because the bar is crowded with tanned, slender men.

Geoffrey hollers to Jackie: "Is your earlobe bothering you?"

"Oh, she's fine," I say, rubbing her knee under the bar top. She pushes my hand away.

Theo puts a hand on Geoffrey's arm and says something. Geoffrey looks at his watch and turns to me.

"We have a dinner reservation in ten minutes at Wisteria. We could try to get a table for four, if you'd like to join us."

Beside me, I hear Jackie shout, "No, I'm not married." A guy half my age is standing next to her, his arm resting on the back of her chair.

I turn back to Geoffrey and shout, "How about we take a raincheck."

They get up and gather their things. Geoffrey hands me a business card. "Very nice meeting you two. Hope to see you around."

"Nice meeting you, too," I say.

Jackie says nothing. The guy who was standing there is gone.

The minute they leave, I open my mouth to say, "What the hell?" but Jackie beats me to the punch and yanks my earlobe. "You're the syphilitic inbred," she says.

We walk in silence down the stairs and through the catacombs toward our room. As soon as we're inside, Jackie says, "I hope you'll excuse me. I have to powder my beaver." She slams the bathroom door shut.

I grab the cigarettes from her purse and go out on the balcony to smoke and, in my little notebook, jot down some advice Geoffrey offered about the Moosefin fringe festival.

Fifteen minutes later, Jackie exits the bathroom and heads toward the balcony. I leap up, slam the glass door shut, and stick out my tongue.

She yanks the towel monkey off the overhead lamp, leaps

on the bed, spreads her legs, and humps herself with the monkey. She sits on its face. It sits on her face. Then she whips it at the glass door and yells, "At least somebody loves me!"

I yank the door open and point, "Get out here, now!"

Lenny would be pleased.

She takes her time putting on her shorts and eventually saunters outside. I light her a cigarette. Her eyes are soft and wet.

"Sorry," I say.

"Oh, did you do something wrong?"

"I guess I was kind of a jerk."

I list my offenses:

- Excluding her from the conversation with the Canadians.

- Cutting off her Me Cambodia routine.

- Ignoring the earlobe signal.

- Ignoring the second earlobe signal

- Ignoring her after I was done ignoring her.

"Is that everything?"

"Close enough," she says. "No biggie." She wipes her eyes with what's left of the towel monkey. "And I'm sorry for flirting with that dude to make you jealous."

"No biggie," I say. "Do you want to order in?"

After a late dinner, we sit on the balcony, Jackie in my lap, listening to the slosh of the ocean and the hum of the boat.

At midnight, I take a shower and get into bed.

Jackie is under the sheets, flipping through a magazine. I lift her arm and sniff her pit. "Washy-washy?" I ask.

Jackie yanks her arm away. "What kind of *fakakta*, twat-sniffer name is Theo?"

I chew my lip thinking, Is this another test?

"She had the worst boob job and, by the way, how could you not see that her little Geoffrey was hitting on you?"

"What?"

"He wanted to put his poly, LGBTQ, happy hour cock in your ass so bad. And you were loving it."

"Are you completely nuts? He's a college professor. What about that twenty-year old hitting on you?"

"Well, you were ignoring me. For a change."

"C'mon Jackie, they live in Moosefin. They can get people to my show."

"I don't care! This is *our* vacation, not a promo tour for your fucking *Chronic Single's Handbook*. It's a *VACATION*. You *AND* me. Not Theo Epstein and Geoffrey Dahmer, the blow hard, fudge packer. Mr. Oh-did-I-already-mention-five-times that I have a Ph.D. from East Moosefuck University?"

Her eyes are wet again.

I consider recent advice from Abe. "In a fight, once she goes irrational, which will be most of the time, logic is useless. Just apologize and keep apologizing."

"I'm sorry for being a jerk," I say.

Perfunctory kiss. Perfunctory sex. We shut off the light. Whooshing and swirling, ponging and echoing, whirring and clicking. My mind pitches and yaws. I fall asleep.

In the morning, I awake chewing on something and realize I've bitten through my sleep mouthguard. Good thing I brought two spares. And on the plus side, I slept a few hours.

The daily newsletter of activities slides under our door. I read it out loud:

"Tonight's movies: *The Towering Inferno*, *Contagion*, *Typhoid Mary*. Plus, the original Broadway cast of the musical comedy: *One Day on the Achille Lauro*."

Jackie rips the paper from my hand. "Enough already, Jack Benny. Just don't forget you promised we'd be contestants on

The Best Couple game show on Thursday evening in the cabaret room."

We make in-room coffee and drink three cups apiece on the balcony, listening to the sound of the ship thudding through the waves. Jackie moves from her chair onto my lap. Then my back starts to feel crawly and itchy. Jackie hikes up my shirt to examine me.

"You have red marks that look like little bites. Three between your shoulder blades. Three in middle of your back, three above your ass crease."

"Groups of three?" I ask.

"Kind of."

"Bedbugs!"

"What?"

"Group of three bites — breakfast, lunch, and dinner — telltale sign of bedbugs."

"How come I don't itch?"

I check her back. No bites, smooth, tan and toned, except for a mole that I never noticed before.

"C'mon you flea-bitten Jew. I'm taking you to sick bay. All that showering? Ha!"

We race down four flights of stairs to the infirmary. Out of breath and over-caffeinated, I sign forms without reading them. We're directed to an exam room with a sink, an examination table with a fresh paper covering, an IV stand with tubing, two carts with drawers, a row of cabinets above a long counter piled with little boxes of stuff. Jackie pulls out a wooden tongue depressor. "Didn't these go out with Dippity-Do?"

I pull out a wooden tongue depressor. We don surgical masks.

"On guard," she says.

"I think the phrase is *'en garde'*."

"Stick 'em up, Canadian homo-snob-lover."

"*Allez! Allez!*"

Lunge, parry, riposte.

My reach is longer. I poke her breasts, her stomach, then her crotch. "Savoir-Fair is everywhere."

"But Klondike Kat always gets his trouser mouse," she jabs my crotch and retreats to a corner. I spin her around and hold my depressor to her back. "Bend over and spread 'em."

"I thought you'd never ask."

There's a knock on the door.

We both stand at attention.

The man with the grey Amish-style beard is standing in the doorway. The gold buttons on his blazer sparkle.

Jackie says, "Wow. Did anyone ever tell you that you look like C. Everett Koop, may he rest in peace?"

"The name is Dr. Rosen."

"A member of the tribe?" I ask.

"The tribe? I'm German but not Jewish if that's what you mean." He pauses and considers us. "I don't think those masks are necessary, do you?"

We toss them into a metal garbage pail.

"How old are you two?" asks Dr. Rosen.

Jackie and I look at each other and smile: a straight man for our romantic comedy.

"When I'm not around her, I'm fifty-seven," I say.

"He's six months older, so I've been following his example," Jackie says.

"But girls mature faster."

"Not this one."

Rosen interrupts our "Who's on First" routine and gestures for me to sit on the examination table. He checks my back.

"Looks like nonspecific dermatitis."

"Sounds like a restaurant," I say.

"It's a minor skin irritation. Just to reassure you, we'll send someone to check your room. Bed bugs leave tell-tale signs on mattresses and a distinctive odor."

I sniff Jackie and whisper. "Washy-washy?"

Rosen hands over a tube. "This should help your skin. But as noted in the forms you signed but probably didn't read, medical charges on the ship may not be covered by your health insurance. Enjoy the rest of your cruise."

As soon as Rosen leaves, Jackie says, "What a needle dick."

"He wasn't so bad," I say. "Let's go lift."

At the gym, we work out at top speed for an hour, and then stretch out on yoga mats. After a couple of beats, Jackie asks, "Ready for lunch?"

"We just ate."

"We're on a cruise ship. Get with the program."

"You go ahead. I have to go to the room. I'll meet you."

"I'll come with you."

"If you don't mind, I need a little privacy."

"Going to snap the rooster? Pinch a loaf?"

"You're gross. I like that in a girl. See you in a few."

Back in the room, I bolt the cabin door. Women are sneaky and don't respect boundaries.

When I was little, Harriet used to bathe me and spend what seemed like a lot of time cleaning my little wiener. "More, more, more!" I'd say. Other times, after I pooped, she would spend what seemed like a lot of time wiping my tush.

When I was older, my mother used to check my armpits for hair. One day she found one. The next day, she left a stack of books in my room on how babies are made. Dr. Moody says I obsess about this stuff. You think?

When I'm at Jackie's, I always take my daily dump before my nightly shower, water running as white noise. I never let Jackie go down on me if I'm not pristine. And if she has anything funky going on, I skip it. Anal sex? Obviously, not.

I thought I'd gotten over my issues with bodily functions while I was in Southeast Asia, where I had to use squat toilets and wipe my ass with my fingers.

Nope.

I bolt the bathroom door, place down a toilet seat cover, and settle in, cozy and safe, like a cat in his litter-box house.

I haven't gone in two days, which means time to bust out an anaconda. I start seated, detecting a pressure in the depths, ponging and echoing in the recesses. Five minutes later, the pressure eases, nothing to show. I stand up to adjust and feel the pressure building. I sit again. After another five minutes, still nothing. I consider reading more of *Eat, Pray, Love*.

My phone dings, a text from Jackie:
Need a hand?

I text back:
No, thanks, I'm good.

Another five minutes of sitting, standing, and bearing down. Still nothing. I worry about pushing too hard, damaging the plumbing, shearing an orifice.

Another ding from Jackie:
Did you fall in? My mother says if you sit on the toilet too long, you'll get piles.

I start to feel annoyed:
I'm fixing my hair.

The genius of squat toilets is that they provide a more natural position, unkink the intestines, put less stress on the fixtures. I haul myself up into a squatting position, hover the bowl, and start to get some action: motility, twinging in the recesses, and finally I feel a snake head peek out.

Another ding from Jackie. A photo of a butt hole with hemorrhoids. The snake head retreats.

I shut off my phone and focus, bearing down without bearing down, bathroom Zen. I picture a baby squatting behind a couch, my neighbor's dog squatting in my parking spot.

A full, deep inhalation. Hold. A slow, cleansing exhalation. Then a bolt to freedom, followed by a buzz down the alimentary canal and up the spine. Maybe this is what people like about kundalini yoga and anal sex.

I stand and survey the situation. A coiled rattler that swallowed four pregnant eggplants. Nice.

I press the toilet handle and watch the blue flush rise, lap at the rim, and fail to recede.

Another ding from Jackie:

Remember to wash your hands. Hot water, soap, and sing happy birthday three times. No poopy fingers in my va-jay-jay.

I hear a key struggling in the cabin door followed by three sharp knocks. "Burns, open up. I need to get my bag."

"Be right there." I look into the blue muck that still hasn't receded.

Two. slow cleansing exhalations.

I open the door for Jackie.

"Burns, why is your arm all blue?"

After lunch, we share a cigarette on the balcony, as the ship docks at our port-of-call in Bermuda's Royal Naval Dockyard, one of the Island's three main tourist spots.

Today's newsletter included warnings about Dockyard pickpockets, alerts for Dockyard shopping discounts, and the usual puffery, propaganda, and advertorial mush. The Dockyard was once a giant fort, and from where we're sitting, it still looks like one. There are no pink beaches or swaying palm trees. Only stone barracks, stone warehouses, stone storehouses, stone edifices, and ramparts and parapets, whatever those are. There's even a pair of stone clock towers that are part of a mall, as well as a fort within the fort that's now a dolphin petting zoo, and a former prison for the convicts who built most of this stone stuff.

Welcome to the penal colony of English Bermuda.

"Isn't it beautiful?" Jackie puts her arm around my waist. "This is my favorite place in the whole world."

I pull her close and try not to think about how much I hate sightseeing. The Greek ruins reminded me of an unfinished parking garage, and when I went to Angkor Wat, I couldn't get out of there fast enough. Ditto Stonehenge. My conclusion: If you've seen one pile of moss-covered rubble, you've seen them all.

But I'm not in Bermuda for me. I'm here for the brownie points.

Per our signed agreement, I'll shop with Jackie for three hours, and then we'll go our separate ways for three hours before meeting up again.

We follow the bovine herds down the gangway, off the boat, and onto North Arm, a walkway into the Dockyard. We pass sandwich boards, booths, tents, gazebos, pagodas, kiosks, pavilions, and small storefronts hawking hair braiding, henna tattoos, island tours, reef adventures, parasailing, ice cream, and hand-rolled Bermuda cigars. On our right is a pirate-themed floating bar; we pass it, and take a left after the Bonefish Bar & Grill.

"Where are all the hucksters, scammers, and low-lifes?" I ask.

"This isn't Bang ... Cock," Jackie says.

At 1:07, we reach the Clocktower Mall. I start the timer on my watch.

A Union Jack hanging in front droops in the heat. Inside, there are lofted ceilings and two floors of stores. I follow Jackie around, heeled at her side, embracing my role as the boyfriend, the shlepper of little bags.

In a store called Furbelows, we scour the bounty of locally made minutiae, frippery, and feculence. The Queen's Flummery boasts an exclusive selection of luxurious yet unaffordable, fashion-forward yet Olde English, exclusive yet world-renowned, Bermuda-made *chazzerai*. Jetsam Outfitters is bursting at the seams with bold, Bermudian-sourced, East Indian-inspired detritus. The Deep-Six Apothecary tempts us with their inspired collection of banana-leaf dolls, Bermuda Triangle tea towels, and hand-carved, cedar crapola.

I embrace a new philosophy on site-seeing: Unless you puke, faint, or die, keep going.

"What?" Jackie asks.

"I didn't say anything."

"Let's get a drink," she says.

In the Spirit of Bermuda pub, we savor the locally made Goslings Black Seal Rum.

Over our second shot, Jackie says, "You've been a very good boy this afternoon. I'm going to let you go twenty minutes early. But first come with me."

I follow her out the door and along a brick path that leads to a stone arch shaped like a wedding band. There are a few couples lined up in front of it. I read a sign. "Lovers who kiss under this arch will be assured a long and happy life together."

I read it twice.

"Burns, are you crying?"

When it's our turn, I hand the couple standing behind us my phone for a photo, and give Jackie a long, deep kiss.

When I get back to our room, a freshly folded monkey towel is hanging from the overhead light. I rehearse my show for an hour with the new monkey as my audience, and then grab my computer and head out.

The ship's library, tucked away in the bowels of the boat, is windowless with mahogany paneling, Paris club chairs, a lit fireplace, and jazz on the sound system. There's a bar offering high-end whiskies, cask-conditioned beer, and not a single frozen drink.

The washy-washy girls are in cocktail outfits and serving

the crowd, mostly men wearing collared shirts, Bermuda shorts, and loafers without socks. Not a Gronk jersey in sight.

Frank, the guy from Quincy with the earring and wife with the rhinestone-encrusted phone, is standing at the bar by himself. He gives me a quick nod, and then turns away. The seats are all taken except for one behind a desk with an LCD monitor. A little sign says, "The Librarian Will Return Tomorrow." I assume the seat and consider taking out my laptop, but I'm too relaxed, too relieved, too safe. No Jackie. No shopping. No pressure.

My body sinks deep into the leather chair. My head finds my folded arms on the desk.

Ten minutes? An hour later? I awake to a commotion in the hallway outside the library. Mango Mike, Rosen, and two uniformed guys are trailing a leashed beagle. A new bedbug infestation?

I walk over to Frank, still at the bar. He looks at me, expressionless.

"Hi Frank, it's Randy. We met the first day at the Chiki Tiki."

"Oh, hey," he says. "Didn't recognize you without your massage girl."

"Yeah, sorry about that. Sometimes we don't know when to stop."

"I just figured she was high or something. The Missus and I party, but we know better than to bring anything onboard."

Mango Mike, his entourage, and the beagle pass by in the hallway again.

"What's going on?" I ask Frank.

"They busted some couple this morning," he says. "The Bermuda cops bring sniffer dogs on when we dock. If the dog smells something, they search your room. If they find something, anything, even a joint, it's a big fine and a huge hassle."

"Noted," I say, thinking about the joint tucked in the

cigarette pack in Jackie's purse, which I was carrying for her not an hour ago. "Can I buy you a beer?" I ask Frank.

I order a cask-conditioned ale for each of us, and return to my desk wondering if they have sniffer dogs in the malls, before I nod off again.

I awake to gentle pressure on my shoulder.

"Excuse me, Miss. Would you have anything by that famous American novelist Randall Burns?"

It's Geoffrey.

"Didn't mean to interrupt you," he says, holding up my empty beer glass. "Looks like you were pretty busy."

"Resting the synapses. I'm rewriting a scene from my show and it's been slow going."

He pulls up a chair and orders two beers from a circulating waitress.

"If you need motivation, just think of that TV show *Fleabag*."

"Never seen it."

"She got her big break at a fringe festival. Alan Rickman, Rowan Atkinson, Russell Brand, Robin Williams all did fringe festivals. And now, you've inspired me. I may try performing next year at the Moosefin fringe. I'm getting to that age where it's now or never."

"Tell me about it."

Our beers arrive. We stand and toast. "To now or never," I say.

Geoffrey and I wander the stacks, running our fingers along the book spines. Above us hang strings of soft white lights. I detect Geoffrey's earthy aftershave. He stops every time he finds a Canadian author: Robertson Davies, Alice Munro, Michael Ondaatje, William Gibson.

"Have you read *The Shipping News*?" he asks.

"Yeah, but Annie Proulx isn't Canadian, is she?"

"She earned her master's degree in Montreal and did time in Newfoundland."

"Didn't know that."

I consider stopping for all the New England writers but don't want to upstage Geoffrey.

He leads me through a pair of French doors to a small, dimly lit room. Michael Bublé comes on the sound system. There's a gas fireplace in one corner and the ship's DVD collection in the other. Turns out Geoffrey and I have similar taste, particularly in obscure foreign films.

"You are the only person I've ever met NOT from Norway who's seen *Elling*," Geoffrey says.

"You are the only person I've ever met NOT from Israel who's seen *Late Marriage*," I say.

He points to a DVD for the Mauritanian movie *Timbuktu*.

"It's on my list, but Jackie's not big on subtitles."

I spot the movie *Brokeback Mountain* but for some reason don't say anything.

We finish our beers and I order another round.

"Jackie seems like a real character," Geoffrey says.

"She has a wicked sense of humor, but she's kind of an introvert. She reads a lot."

"How long have you two been together?" Geoffrey asks.

"About six months. This is our first vacation."

Our beers arrive. We toast again. "To first vacations," Geoffrey says.

"Has the writer-performer of the *Chronic Single's Handbook* ever been married?"

Normally, I deflect this question but this time I answer it. "Not yet. After two years in a relationship, I usually need a break. But finding the next girlfriend has gotten harder. Seems once single people hit fifty, most just give up. The guys settle for massage parlors and, instead of settling, the women just quit dating. How long have you and Theo been together?"

"Thirty years."

"What's the secret sauce?"

"Luck and we try to mix it up."

"If you don't mind me asking, like, how?"

"In the early nineties, we tried simple living. Sold the house and moved to a small apartment in town. Got rid of our cars, TV, and didn't buy anything but food and underwear for an entire year."

I tap his beer glass with mine. "I commute by bicycle, live beneath my means, no TV."

"We also tried veganism, ayahuasca, polyamory. Now, we're trying something called 'apartners.' We live in separate apartments, get together for sleepovers a few nights a week, and take vacations together. We've only been doing it for a year, so the verdict is still out."

"Jackie suggested this cruise. She's very athletic. We laugh a lot. She speaks and reads Chinese. A great cook. Likes to smoke pot. She's really the performer in our relationship."

I wonder if I'm sounding defensive.

"Speaking of performers," Geoffrey says. "What do you think: Is Trump going to be your next president?"

"The election isn't for another six months and I'm already sick of it. Sick of the ranting about climate change, immigration, billionaires, race, gender. I just want to sit in a bar with my girlfriend and watch sports."

Geoffrey checks his watch.

"Speaking of which, I'm meeting Theo for dinner. Hope we can do this again."

"Definitely."

As I'm packing up my computer, *Infinite Jest*, a novel by none other than David Foster Wallace, catches my eye. It's a thousand pages, a subwoofer of a book. As I'm thinking that I should be avoiding Foster Wallace and his post-modern negativity, I drop it in my bag.

For dinner, Jackie and I are seated in what she says is her favorite restaurant in the world, The Mayfair Arms Tearoom in St. George, a major tourist town at the opposite end of Bermuda.

The restaurant décor could generously be described as rustic: graffiti on the walls, dollar bills hanging from the ceiling, and wood flooring, tables, and chairs that have all seen better days. The restaurant is not as nice as the ship's library. It's not as nice as the ship's Chiki Tiki bar, but Jackie is excited and I'm smiling and agreeing as much as I can, hoping to get through this without hurting her feelings.

So far, tonight's incidentals, which I may have mentioned are on me, have included the ferry ride over here (ten dollars each) and a round of Rum Sweazels (fifteen dollars apiece), which taste worse than they sound.

Jackie orders the goat-fromage torta (twenty-six dollars) and I order the mesquite-broiled hogfish (thirty-eight dollars), a recommendation from our waiter.

"So, did you get a lot of work done in the library?" she asks.

"Some."

"Did you meet anyone interesting?"

"That guy Frank from Quincy was there. Did you know they bring drug-sniffing dogs onto the boat?"

"I knew. Did you run into anyone else?"

"Mostly, just worked on my script."

"Is there a bar in there?"

While Jackie waits for an answer, I play with my curly straw.

"Oh, and Geoffrey popped in and bought me a couple of beers," I say.

"What did you talk about?"

"You know, this and that, my show."

Later, back in the room, I'm *in*-digesting the hogfish special and the hundred-dollar cab back to the ship because the ferry had stopped running.

I shower, chew a Pepto-Bismol tablet and join Jackie in bed.

She's reading *Cosmo*. The cover story is "Why Men Are Clueless."

I reread the first page of *Infinite Jest* for the fourth time. The critics were right: It's impenetrable.

"That's a big, fat book you got there," Jackie says, looking over. "You must be wicked smart."

"Frickin' smart. Since when do you read *Cosmo*?"

"When I feel like it."

"How's that cover story?"

"Pretty good. I just filled out a survey for you. You scored a hundred percent."

I clear a bit of Pepto-Bismol from a molar with my tongue.

"I know you hated the Mayfair Arms," she finally says.

"Sorry, yeah, the hogfish didn't live up to its billing. Also, I think I'm a little grumpy from not sleeping."

She throws the magazine against wall.

"Oh, is that my fault too? You're just a fucking snob, like your girlfriend Geoffrey."

And then she's off.

"As in Mr. Moosefuck, Ph.D. All you guys think the same: no degree, no brain. My mother sent me to Oak Hill Junior College, a finishing school for girls, but it sucked and I dropped out. I guess being with me is slumming." She pauses. "I had husbands who made more money than you'll ever make."

OK, so she didn't go to Harvard. Neither did I. I went to a state school, so I can't look down my nose at anyone.

"I know how you are," she says. "You think anyone who watches TV is a moron and anyone who wears headphones in public is a retard and the postman is a lazy cretin, and the library is run by dykes and anyone on Facebook should be killed. You are the biggest hypocrite. You use Facebook to spam about your fucking book and show. You know what you are? A hater. You hate everyone."

I think to myself, the word is "misanthrope."

She says, "Yeah, and a stuck-up phony."

Then we're back to the Canadians, and of course, no fight is complete without a mention of Lenny.

"Your friends are clueless, too — especially that fucking Lenny, who thinks he's got it over everyone because he's got money," she says. "And you think you're so special because you got a book deal."

She pauses for a breath. "Like you're some kind of *artiste*."

I stare through her, recalling Abe's advice on arguing with a woman: Let her run till she exhausts herself.

"No-o-o. Mr. Simple Living doesn't like shopping or malls or cruises. You keep that crappy old car even though you can afford a new one. You'd rather ride around on a *bicycle*. What are you trying to prove? Do you think I want to live like a college student? When we get married, you're going to crack open those mutual funds, and that twenty-year-old bed, thirty-year-old fridge and hundred-year-old couch are history."

Simple Living? That's a new one.

"And you still have a flip phone. This is the fucking twentieth century."

Twenty-first.

"You go skiing at expensive resorts, have brand-new skis, took a trip around the world just so you could whine about it. You say you're more into experiences than stuff. That's such New Age, Cambridge bullshit. You like nice restaurants as long as you don't have to pay, as long as Lenny pays or I do. You don't care about the environment or the poor. You're just a cheap fuck!"

Why is she so upset? And what did she mean, "when we get married?"

But she probably has a point.

Sometimes I am clueless.

And a cheap snob.

I consider throwing *Infinite Jest* against the wall for effect but worry about straining my wrist and abandon the idea.

"Husband number two was cheap like you and he got breast cancer. Bet you didn't know guys' boobies can get cancer. You're not even listening!"

She yanks a handful of my chest hair, leaps out of bed, and storms off to the balcony to smoke a cigarette. I lie there, pretending to read.

Ten minutes later, Jackie opens the sliding door. "Get out here. Now," she says. I offload the book and head out. She hands me a lighted cigarette.

"I have a confession," she says. "I spied on you and Geoffrey in the library."

First, I am flattered, and then I am furious but bite my tongue because all I want is to get through this cruise with our relationship still intact. I say nothing.

"Hello? Hello? Anyone home? Say something!" Jackie says.

Before I can respond, she turns away from me, leans on the railing, and looks out at the ocean.

I say nothing.

After a long moment, Jackie says, "I'm sorry. I'm sorry for being such a moody twat." She turns back to me. "You know, I love your quirks. I fell for you the first time we met, when you said you were done apologizing for your show. That's how I've been feeling because most guys say they can't deal with me. They say I'm too much. I fuck them a few times and they disappear. But you seem to really get me."

I pull her close. "I think you're fascinating. A pain in the ass but I'm never bored. I'm sorry for hurting your feelings. I didn't love the restaurant but I love you."

We hug for a long time, listening to the water licking the side of the ship.

"Look at us. We can fight and make up just like grown-ups," she says into my shoulder. She lifts her head, big eyes, big smile. "I told you going on this trip would be great for us."

That night, I dream that my show is a success and I've become famous, so famous that a big publisher has given me a seven-figure advance to write a memoir. The book has just come out and I'm doing a book signing — at Madison Square Garden. Ricki, Harriet, my mother, and Edgy and Artsy from *Match.com* are there; my biological father has come to apologize for never sending me a birthday card; even Lorraine Zlotnik, the girl who wouldn't let me hold her hand in second grade, is there.

After signing a bunch of books, I pause to shake out a hand cramp. A woman in line clears her throat to get my attention. Scarlett Johansson.

"I didn't know you were Jewish," she says.

"Yup."

"So am I!"

While I'm signing her book, she retrieves a white yarmulke from her purse and starts to write her phone number on it, then pauses to ask, "So, what ever happened with Jackie?"

I wake up sweating.

"Good dream?" Jackie asks, already awake and sitting up reading Zig Ziglar.

She makes us some in-room coffee. Then we have sex. Then we drink more coffee and smoke a couple of cigarettes. Then she wants more sex. Then she says, "I know, let's get some lunch at Fantasia's and we can do a little shopping at the other mall and then go snorkeling at the Dockyard lagoon.

And then. And then. And then.

I'm feeling what Moody would call "over-stimulated." In layman's terms, I'm done doing.

"How about we take a couple of hours apart and snorkel later this afternoon?" I ask Jackie.

Her face shrivels. She grabs her phone and pulls up of our pre-trip agreement and reads out loud:

"Section Three, Paragraph One states, 'In the mornings on

Bermuda, Randall shall do whatever Jackie wants for at least three hours.'"

We follow the crowd down the gangway to the snorkeling beach, which is packed with spit-roasting bodies covered with the aforementioned skin conditions. In the lagoon, another crowd bobs motionless, faces down, like corpses after a maritime disaster. I rent snorkeling gear for us (fifty dollars for three hours). The gear smells like toilet bowl cleaner.

The snorkeling is tolerable, then enjoyable, because I don't have to talk to, listen to, or entertain anyone. I bob, scream into my snorkel, and practice my breathing exercises: Full, deep inhalation. Hold. Slow, cleansing exhalation. My mind and mood resets. A green and blue parrotfish stops to check me out. A blue tang swims by. I hang out for an hour beyond our agreement and kiss Jackie goodbye under the moongate.

I return to the ship's library, again populated mostly by men but no sign of Geoffrey or Frank. I take a seat at the same desk with the same note about the librarian being back tomorrow and use the desktop computer to email Abe, Lenny, and Joey.

All's well, haven't killed each other — yet. Three more days to go. Hope I don't run out of oxygen.

I work steadily for three hours, periodically looking around to see if Jackie is spying on me. Then I pack up and stop by the jewelry store on the way back to the room.

After dinner at Listeria, Jackie wants to go dancing at a club in Hamilton, a tourist spot we've yet to visit.

She's wearing a T-shirt she bought today. The front says "Caravaggio" above a hand holding a severed head by the hair. The back says, "49% maniac motherfucker, 51% kinky genius."

"Nice," I say. "I didn't know you liked Caravaggio."

"Oh, didn't I tell you?" she says. "I majored in art history at finishing school."

That night, we take the ferry to Hamilton (ten dollars for two). The club, which is mostly devoid of patrons, has a cover charge (twenty dollars each). I buy two Rum Sweazels (thirty-five dollars with tip).

Soon after we find a table, the hip hop music starts. And then the rap or gangsta or crunk or new jack skiffle or whatever the fuck they call it. By the time the salsa starts, I've had it and bolt for the bathroom. On the way, I see a sign that says "Hamilton Sports Bar, upstairs." When I return, an island guy is chatting up Jackie. I march over. He leaves.

"We've been here an hour and haven't danced once," she says. "People are noticing."

"Let's compromise and go to the sports bar upstairs. The Sox are on."

"You're so Caucasian."

"Don't play the race card with me, princess."

"You jerk, it's my time and I want to dance."

After two more Sweazels, a song finally comes on that I recognize, "Bust a Move." I grab Jackie's hand and we join a handful of over-fifty couples on the dance floor.

The Sweazels kick in and I do the Twist, followed by the Pony, the Swim, the Hora, and finally the Y.M.C.A. I feel Jackie's hand on my ear.

In the cab back to the boat (fifty-four dollars), there is a long stretch of silence, which Jackie interrupts to inform me that we're not going back to the room because we're not done dancing. No, the fun will continue at a Seventies and Eighties Midnight Dance Party on Deck 9. I consider asking Jackie if she's familiar with the paintings of Edvard Munch, but instead decide, once again, that the best tack is just to go along for the ride.

The Dance Party is in a ballroom with patterned carpets and upholstered chairs at tables with tablecloths. A few older couples are seated, waiting for the music to start.

"Whose Bar Mitzvah?" I ask.

Jackie heads to the bar and orders a single malt scotch (forty-five dollars). I get a water.

We find a table and sip. The DJ mounts the stage and starts with the song "Ain't Gonna Bump No More."

I stand and extend a hand to Jackie. "We doing this?"

She's happy again.

On the dance floor, we go all out. At one point, I bump Jackie's hip, which starts her hopping around on one leg, fake-moaning, "Oy, oy, oy, my lumbago is acting up again." Then she hip checks me in the ass and I limp around, yelping, "Is there a specialist in the house?" At the end of the song, a few onlookers clap as Jackie jumps on my back for a piggyback ride to the table.

We sip our drinks and kiss, finally in sync. Then I hear Jackie say, "Oh, crap, your Canadian rump-wrangler is waving at us. Can't we just ignore him?"

I turn. Geoffrey and Theo are sitting at the far end of the bar. They smile and wave again.

"Let's just go over and say hi," I say. "We'll make it quick. Promise."

Geoffrey and Theo are dressed in polo shirts, linen shorts, and no socks. They're both wearing white boating sneakers.

We exchange drunken, sloppy hellos and handshakes.

Geoffrey gestures to Jackie's T-shirt. "I love Caravaggio. Love, love, love that painting, 'David with the Head of Goliath.' Did you know that's Caravaggio's face not Goliath's?"

"Yeah, I knew," Jackie says.

She gestures toward Geoffrey's boating sneakers.

"Did you know that in school we called those skippies?"

There is a short awkward silence. Then the song, "Turning Japanese" comes on.

"Good to see you, both!" I grab Jackie's hand. "Let's go, Honey; it's our song."

The next morning, I awake at nine o'clock, feeling oddly sharp and rested. Jackie is half awake and stroking my chest.

"I had a really fun time last night," she says. "Didn't know you could dance."

"M-m-m," I mumble, still coming to. Did I just sleep through the whole night? For the first time in weeks?

"So glad we did this." She gives me a long kiss, and then says, "OK, time for a shower."

I'm contemplating making coffee when she calls out from the bathroom, "Could you see if my hair dryer is in the closet?"

When I open the closet door, her clothes are everywhere: on the ground, dangling from hangers, and overflowing from open drawers. I can't see one thing of mine.

She comes out of the shower wrapped in a towel looking gorgeous. "Sorry about the mess," she says.

"No biggie," I say.

"I'll clean it up while you're in the library. Let's get something to eat. I'm starving."

After a late breakfast, we go our separate ways.

In the library, I return *Infinite Jest* to the stacks, return to the librarian's desk, and continue rewriting my script.

I work non-stop for an hour until I'm interrupted by gentle pressure on my shoulder and a familiar whisper. "I got you something."

Jackie pulls out a Caravaggio T-shirt in my size.

I'm flattered. Then annoyed.

"Thanks," I whisper. "Do you want to leave it in the room? I'll be down in two hours."

Jackie swirls her tongue in my ear and then whispers. "I'm bored and I miss you and it looks like it's going to rain. I know this is your time to yourself but can I hang out? You won't even know I'm here."

I'm smitten. Then crowded.

"Sure. I guess. OK."

As she wanders around the stacks, guys check her out, for a change.

I return to my script but when I look up, Jackie is waving a copy of *Infinite Jest*, which falls to the floor with a thud. Every head in the room turns. A guy nearby picks it up and offers her his seat. She gestures, thanks but no thanks.

I'm proud. Then irritated.

She is holding the book again, open now, with two hands, pivoting it from right side up to upside down, and then up again, slowly rotating it around and around like a steering wheel.

I want to laugh. I want her to leave.

She sashays over. "I wish there was a big strong man to explain this book to me." She sits on my lap and whispers in my ear. "Can I suck your cock?"

"I thought we had a deal," I say, knowing it's no use mentioning our contract.

The rest of the day is not worth going into, except that the ship finally leaves Bermuda for the trip back to Boston.

That night I don't sleep and neither does Jackie.

I awake the next morning sweaty and out of breath. Jackie is still asleep. On the way to the bathroom, I stumble over her clothes, which are strewn across the floor like her Brookline bedroom, on a good day.

I pick up her bathing suit, a white-bowed flipflop, and a high-top sneaker.

"Just toss those in the closet." Jackie is rubbing her eyes, watching.

I slide open the closet. More of the same. I start matching shoes and stuffing her dirty clothes into an empty pillow case. "Will you please leave my things alone?" she asks. "I told you I'd clean it up."

"That was yesterday and now it's today."

"Come on. I'll get to it. Promise. Let's not fight."

"Fine," I say, as calmly as possible.

We head to the gym where we order breakfast smoothies. For me, the Megaton Shockwave. For Jackie, the Lady Howitzer. Both drinks include Black Seal rum and Red Bull. After finishing our beverages, we have to lie down in the stretching area until the rum subsides and the Red Bull kicks in. We work out at top speed and race back to the room to see who gets to shower first.

When Jackie emerges, she says, "I know. Let's get stoned and go in the hot tub."

"What about the sniffer dogs?"

"We're not in Bermuda anymore. All cool."

Out on the balcony, we smoke the joint, but I insist we exhale into a wet washcloth. When we're done, we flick the roach into the rolling ocean and share a cigarette before heading to the hot tub on deck 12, the sundeck we visited earlier in the week.

Jackie wears her scarlet one-piece and I wear my board shorts and long-sleeve rash guard shirt. We snag an empty hot tub and order drinks from a waiter.

Bubbling water. Steel drum bands. Sun above, girl by my side, drink in hand, and only forty-eight more hours until I can sleep alone in my own bed. My body is purring from the workout and humming from the weed.

A few minutes later, a body rush, an updraft, a downdraft, an air pocket, to the edge then back. When was the last time I was this wasted? Jackie rests her head on my shoulder.

My face feels cold and then hot, a thermal head rush. When it passes, I realize Jackie is slumped forward, eyes closed, her face inches from the foamy water.

"You OK?" I ask.

"Let me be," she says.

Her tawny skin is pale.

I pull her upright, then slide one arm under her legs, another under her shoulders, lift and lay her down on the hot tub deck.

"Let me *bllleee*." She's slurring.

I get out of the whirlpool to lift her head up until she's sitting. Her eyes are closed. Her head flops to the side. I hold her face with both hands. "Jackie! Jackie!"

The lifeguard rushes over and holds two fingers to her wrist.

"Her pulse is weak," he says.

She opens confused eyes. "Let *meee bllleee*. White guys won't let me *bllleee*."

She shuts her eyes and her head flops again. Another lifeguard runs over, walkie-talkie engaged.

He lets her head hang between her knees; she seems to come around. She lifts her head and sips from a cup of water. She puts her head in her hands. "I'm OK," she says, still slurring a little.

Dr. Rosen appears at the side of the whirlpool with two guys and a wheeled stretcher. They load Jackie and we all descend the elevator in silence.

What if Jackie dies?

What if she lives and Rosen finds weed in her blood?

They wheel her into the same exam room we were in the other day and slide her off the stretcher onto the exam table. They take her pulse. They take a vial of blood. They hook her to an IV.

I tell Rosen what happened, mostly. "We had one of those rum protein drinks, worked out, and got in the whirlpool with some pina coladas." I avoid looking at the clock. It's eleven A.M.

Jackie is still pale, fluid drips from her IV bag. I feel like crying.

Rosen asks a few more questions and takes notes. He and the others leave. Jackie sleeps. I nod off in a chair by her bed.

Five or ten or fifteen minutes later, Rosen reappears with a tablet computer, two nurses, and one of the lifeguards.

"She didn't have a heart attack or a stroke," Rosen says. "Her vital signs are almost normal, but she's still a little dehydrated. This was likely a vasovagal episode, a sudden drop in blood pressure and decreased blood flow to the brain, which leads to fainting."

Rosen addresses me: "Working out, drinking, and jumping into a hot tub is not recommended for people your age. I believe there are signs on our whirlpools advising against consuming alcohol or other medications."

He seems to emphasize "other medications." He suggests Jackie remain here for a couple more hours. Afterwards, we will be free to enjoy the rest of our cruise. He says either "Be well" or "Behave" and leaves.

Jackie naps. I nap or something like it.

"Burns! Burns!" Jackie's voice sounds as if it's inside my head. "Snap out of it. You've been staring into that trashcan for the last ten minutes. I need something to eat."

"Rosen said not to eat for an hour," I mumble.

"I don't care what he said. I'm hungry. Get me something."

"Like what?"

"Figure it out. Get me chicken tenders. And a sweater."

I start to open my mouth.

"Also, get me a copy of the latest *Cosmo*. And some dark chocolate. Get a move on. I'm suffering here!"

She sits up. "My back hurts," she says. "I don't know what they did to me on that stretcher. Get Koop back in here."

I summon Dr. Rosen.

Jackie starts in. "My back is sore. I think it's from the stretcher ride."

"I'll send a nurse in to check you out."

"Also, I want to see the bill. I don't want any mischarges."

"We haven't written it up yet."

"I'm sure you have some idea."

"Well, there's the emergency treatment and stretcher charge. We'll charge you for the IV. Then there will be lab charges and my fees. And an hourly fee for this room."

Jackie rants about the bill and the bumpy stretcher ride. I'm embarrassed and follow Rosen out.

In the hallway outside the room, I apologize to him. "She's very upset."

When I return, she's even more upset. "I heard you out there, Benedict Burns backstabber."

"Jackie, look, I didn't mean to upset you, but you're being a little difficult. Rosen's not a bad guy."

"He's a condescending, kraut jackass is what he is."

"Let's just get you better. I can help out with the bill."

"Damn fucking straight you'll help out with the bill. It's an incidental." She starts to cry. I go to hug her.

"Get away from me. You make me sick. Just get my stuff and the chicken tenders and get me a chocolate donut, too."

When I return a half hour later, she's asleep. Room service delivered her chicken tenders, which are all gone. I put a bag of miniature chocolate donuts, her *Cosmo*, and a rose on a table by her bed.

I sit in a nearby chair and tap a tongue depressor against my knee, thinking: This is not going to work.

The lack of boundaries was cute for the first couple of months. But now, she stalks me in the library, reads my mind, and she's a slob. And she's a terrible listener. She reminds me of my deceased mother, whose stock line was: You'll be fine.

"Your girlfriend Ricki got a boob job and dumped you because she thought she could do better? You'll be fine.

"Caught encephalitis on your trip to Asia? You'll be fine.

"Haven't slept in two years? Guess what . . ."

I watch Jackie sleep, still pale, IV still in her arm.

I am such a douche. I need to cut her some slack. I take out a little blue-velvet box and lay it next to the rose.

That night in the room, we skip the sex and actually sleep.

In the morning, Jackie is out on our deck sipping a cup of herbal tea. I make a cup of coffee and join her. She hands me an envelope. Inside are two tickets for the eight P.M. show of *Betsy Carmichael's Bingo Palace* and a card: "I love the earrings. Thanks for putting up with me (again). Love, Jackie."

I smile and hand her an envelope with two tickets to appear on the four P.M. *Best Couple* game show.

"I'm going to rest a little more and then apologize to Rosen," she says. "How about you do your own thing, and we meet later for lunch, and then hit the show?" She draws my face to hers and kisses me. "I'm a lucky girl."

At 3:45, Jackie and I are sitting side-by-side on the stage for *The Best Couple* game show along with three other couples decked out with frozen drinks and hoodies. I'm wearing a tie and Jackie is wearing a leopard print top and her leather pants. I am determined to make sure Jackie has a good time.

Our host is mincing Mango Mike. "Welcome to our wild and crazy, cruise version of *The Newlywed Game*, called *The Best Couple*," he says. "Tonight, we have four couples competing for the grand prize of ... yes ... another cruise! Here's the format: First, the ladies go offstage and the men will guess how their ladies will answer some intimate questions. Then we bring the women back to see how well their men know them. Next, it's the men's turn on the hot seat. Prepare to be titillated!"

He sweeps his hand toward the exit. "Ladies, complimentary drinks await you at the bar next door."

Jackie parades across the stage behind the other three women. Even Mango Mike can't help watching her.

Ten minutes later, they return, drinks in hand.

"OK, folks. Time for some reckoning." Mango Mike gives the audience a thumbs up and turns to address Jackie first.

"What does your man love most about you?"

Jackie thinks a minute and then says, "My pervy sense of humor?"

"Hee hee," says Mincing Mike. "Let's see what Randall said."

He pauses while I turn over the card with my answer.

" 'Her pervy sense of humor!' One point for Jackie and Randall!"

The audience claps and hoots. Jackie points to her bicep and flexes it.

Mango Mike moves on to the next three couples who all bite the dust. No points.

"The next question is: Who smells worse in the morning — you or him?"

Jackie doesn't miss a beat. "He probably said I do."

I turn over my card. Mango Mike shouts, "Right again. He said 'she does!' "

A handful of people clap.

Jackie and I high-five.

The other three women answer that their other half smells worse in the morning, which is what their partners predicted. Two points for us and one point for each of them.

Time for the men go offstage. I head to the open bar with the other guys and order a shot of Jack Daniel's. After ten minutes, we return.

"OK," says Mango Mike. "I'll start with you, Randall. Who would Jackie say you would rather make love to: Melania Trump or Michelle Obama?"

I ponder a moment. "Melania has eyes like Jackie so definitely Melania."

The audience murmurs and mutters.

Mango Mike pauses and waits for Jackie to turn her card. "Correct, she said he'd pick Melania. Three points now for Randall and Jackie."

Jackie and I share an open-mouthed kiss that elicits a few hoots from the audience.

The second guy answers, "Both Melania and Michelle," and his wife gives him a not-so friendly punch in the arm. No points. The next one says, "Neither." And gets it right. One point. The third answers, "I plead the fifth," and gets no points.

Mango Mike says, "OK, couples, final question, starting with you, Randall. What is the one word you use that Jackie wishes you wouldn't?"

Without pausing, I say, "Shay-Shay?"

Mango Mike looks crestfallen. "Sorry, Randall, I think she said ... " he pauses to let Jackie turn her card, but she just sits there. Mango Mike gingerly takes the card from Jackie's hand and reads it. "She wrote, 'Lenny.'"

The audience is quiet.

"You two were on such a roll," Mango Mike says, with a downturned mouth. Then he smiles with a theatrical wink, "But you're still in the lead." He pauses. "If you don't mind my asking, what's a 'Shay-Shay'?"

Tears form in Jackie's eyes. She storms off the stage.

After making excuses to Mango Mike, I race back to the room and find her clothes, rumpled and child-sized, on the floor. On the bed, a note: "Have an excellent time jerking off."

Nothing about where she is or when she'll be back.

I check the buffets, the gym, and the sundeck. Still no Jackie.

Two and half hours later it's 7:30, only thirty minutes to *Betsy Carmichael* and still no Jackie. I text her.

She texts right back:
On my way.

After nixing the idea of going to the show on my own, I smoke a third cigarette on the balcony and watch the butt drift back toward Bermuda.

At eight, I hear the door open.

"Hi," she says. Her eyes look swollen. In fact, her entire face looks swollen.

"You lose a fight?"

She doesn't answer. From her bag, she takes out two cold packs, and lies down holding them to her face with both hands, eyes closed. She mumbles something about a friend she made and mentions that "he" invited her for a drink, which turned into two, then three, which is why she's late.

"Did he coldcock you?" I ask.

"You wish. I got a liquid facelift at the spa." She quickly adds, "Don't worry, I'll pay for it. Dr. Elke said the swelling will go down in a couple of days."

"Are you drunk?" I ask.

"Little bit." She smirks as best she can with a swollen face and then grimaces.

"I need a cigarette," I say.

Outside on the deck, I pace, take out my little notebook, and put it back in my pocket. I take a couple of puffs off a cigarette, throw it overboard, and light another one.

I need to manage this.

I flip the butt over the side and open the sliding door. "Get out here now," I say.

"Fat chance." She's sitting on the edge of the bed.

I come inside. "OK, what's going on?" I ask. "We were having fun at *The Best Couple* game and then *pow*."

"*Pow*? Is that all you have to say? You embarrassed the shit out of me. You think 'Shay-Shay' is funny? You don't know when to stop. This whole trip you've made fun of everything at my expense. One: It's a Rum *Swizzle* not a Sweazel. And two: It's the *Dorian Whisper* not the *Durian Whisper*. Is Durian for my benefit because I'm Asian and you think I smell?"

I reach for my pen and little notebook.

"And three, you're such a racist!" she says. "Like grabbing me for 'Turning Japanese' in front of those fucking Canadians.

I'm afraid to have you meet my mother. Who knows what crap will fly out of your mouth?"

I jot down a few counterpoints.

"And you're a misogynist. You get a boner watching David Ortiz but hate women's basketball because you say they suck. Well guess what? *You* suck!"

I switch to shorthand.

"I try to plan a fun, crazy day and end up in the ER. I do all the work in this relationship. What do you do?"

Before I can open my mouth, we're back to misogyny.

"And the way you talk about women's bodies. What if we got married and I put on weight?"

She has a point.

"You could stand to lose a few pounds, pal. And I know how you feel about my moles. Why do I waste my time with assholes like you?"

Then she bangs a U-ey.

"And why is it always about *your* feelings? What about *my* feelings? How do you think I feel when you use the word 'snatch' all the time?"

What?

"I hate that word. It's in your show. Your whole show is offensive to women. Why do I always end up with schmucks like you?"

She shifts to her ex-husbands and details I didn't — and don't — care to know. As I'm attempting to make sense of my notes, a hand snatches — I mean grabs — my little notebook and launches it across the room.

There's a long silence.

I'm sorry," I say.

"You're always sorry. How about not fucking up in the first place?"

I think: Wait, haven't *you* been apologizing for crap you did? Like multiple times?

Her voice becomes vague, distant. I feel myself shrinking, fading, drifting away like a lost balloon or a broken kite.

She fades back into view. I look at her swollen face and realize she's preparing for life as a single woman.

"... and you're such a drama queen," she says. "I'm sick of all your lists and little notebooks and nonsense. You never got married because you're damaged. You and your space and your fucked up friends. What's our future, Mr. Ambivalent, hot and cold, clueless chickenshit?"

"Define future?"

"*Uchhh!* I can't stand this!"

"What?"

"You and your waffling bullshit!"

"I love you but I agree we have some stuff to work on."

"*I* don't have stuff to work on, *you* do. Answer my question."

We sit there in silence. She puts her head in her hands. I decide to go off script.

"Have you ever heard of 'apartners'?" I ask.

"Is this more David Foster Wallace mental shit stains?"

"No. I read about it in the library. It's our fix. We'll get married and live-in separate places, like Jack Nicholson and Anjelica Huston and Robert Parker and whoever he married."

"I don't want to live in separate houses! That's insane. And Jack Nicholson never married Anjelica."

"Just listen. That way I get my space and you get your marriage and we hang out every weekend and one or two nights during the week. We'll have fun like we always do. No fighting over my sleep or your messiness or money. Tim Burton and Helena Bonham-Carter do it, did it."

"Yeah, and he never married her, either!"

I ignore this and go on. "And twice a year, we get a week to do other stuff, like Joey and Monique. You can have all the anal you want. Just don't tell me about it."

An ice pack slams into the wall.

"I told you from day one, I wanted a normal marriage: shared checking accounts, a house, and not some weird Lenny-hooker thing."

She starts crying into her hands. "I thought you might change, get better if I was patient. We have so much fun together. What's wrong with my head? And don't repeat that line from your show that 'marriage is no barometer of mental health.' Never married at fifty-seven and performing *The Chronic Single's Handbook* is not mental health."

I start to feel woozy. A vasovagal episode?

Jackie doesn't seem to notice. She digs out the old gripes, like my being a back-stabbing, stuck-up kvetcher, as well as a trove of new ones: my twenty-year-old jeans, thirty-year-old Ralph Lauren Polo shirts, leather bomber jacket that's too small, ridiculous Morton Salt sailor's hat, and torn, stained bathmat.

She alternates between bullying and crying, berating me and berating herself. Retreat or fight? Blast her or hug her? At fifty-seven, I should know how to fix this but I don't.

"I hate you," she says. "You and your fucking fringe festival. Say something!"

My mind goes blank.

"Get out, asshole!" A *Cosmo* thwacks against the door.

I'm on the top deck, one layer above the Chiki Tiki, at a railing next to a fenced-in basketball court.

An amber sun fades under ashen clouds. It's cool and misty. I kick an empty cup into the water and watch it bob and disappear. More plastic in a dying ocean.

You'll be fine.

The first two weeks after a break-up are great. No one to report to, no fighting, and I usually sleep through the night.

I take out my phone and scroll through our selfies, the happy couple, The Best Couple.

Maybe Jackie was my last chance, my insurance against a life of battling the Dark Place every Christmas, New Year's, and Saturday night I don't have a date.

I retrieve a photo of our pre-cruise agreement. I should have known this wasn't going to work. I've never had luck with women, starting with Harriet.

When I was seven and Harriet was fourteen, she invited me to watch her favorite new show, *Dark Shadows*, with her after school. I didn't really get what the show was about, but I remember that whenever this guy Barnabas appeared, Harriet would squeal and hug my head to her chest or press my hand to her lap and squirm. I started running home every day after school to be with her. One day, Harriet pricked her finger, then mine, and touched the tips together, declaring us vampire lovers. She kissed me on the mouth. Soon after, she introduced me to a game called, "Tell me if this hurts." One day, we were all set to play when my mother came home early and noticed the cuts on my arm. The next day Harriet was sent away to "boarding school." Whenever I asked what happened to Harriet, her father, my stepfather, would say, "Go ask your mother." Instead of saying, "You'll be fine," my mother would say, "Don't you have anything better to do?"

I look down at the swirling ocean. Spotlights illuminate black water. I look closer expecting to see baitfish drawn to the light. Not a one. I Google "Does drowning hurt?" Apparently, once you stop thrashing, and water enters your lungs, you fall unconscious, asleep, pain free.

If I died, and one day God said, "You've been a good boy, I'm going to let you relive your five best days on earth," half of those days would be with her. Jackie that is, not Harriet.

I put away my phone.

Maybe all is not lost. Maybe I'll be a hit at the fringe festival: five-star reviews and theater babes in black body stockings. A book signing at Madison Square Garden.

And maybe Neil Simon will buy me a house in Tahiti and Natalie Portman will wash my feet every night.

Success didn't save Foster Wallace — he hanged himself at forty-six.

Maybe I should marry Jackie.

Hats on trees, clothes on floors, pumpkin faces that stay that way, ex-husbands and KY Jelly, moles and subscriptions to *Cosmo*.

Marriage didn't save Foster Wallace, either.

I close my eyes and grip the railing, the ship droning under my sandals. A few minutes pass.

From behind me, I hear a ball being bounced on the basketball court.

There's a guy in what looks like a dress shirt with rolled up sleeves, a cigarette in his mouth, shooting baskets.

I move closer: grey beard, blue blazer on a chair. Dr. Rosen, un-Kooped.

"Oh, it's you," he says, noticing me staring.

He stuffs his cigarette into a can of Coke, and then bricks a ten-footer.

I step onto the court and grab a ball. We shoot in silence. A few go in. Then we take a break.

"Got another cigarette?" I ask.

He extends a pack of Marlboro red. "I'd appreciate it if you don't mention this to anyone," he says.

We puff and look through the chain-link fence out at the water.

"Your better half came by this morning and apologized." he says. "How is she doing?"

"OK, more or less. I guess we've been real pains in the sphincter."

"This is a cruise ship, Mr. Burns. You don't know half of it."

Rosen tells me that he just got divorced, which is why he's working on the cruise. He wanted to get away.

We talk about traveling, and I tell him about my world trip. Then I admit that my "better" half just kicked me out of the room.

"What now?" he asks.

"I'm not sure," I say. "Is it her? Is it me? I'm not sure it's salvageable."

"Hmmm," he says, picking up the ball. "If you need a place to sleep, there are empty beds down in the infirmary."

He takes another shot and misses. He's about to take another, when he turns to me and says: "The way I see it, relationships go well until you realize the other half isn't going to save you."

III

THE FRINGE

Two weeks later, on May 22nd, my flight lands in Calgary, Alberta, Canada's Wild West, home to badlands, oil sands, black gold, blue collars, rednecks, rodeos, and theater festivals. Which one doesn't belong?

In the terminal, I claim my one piece of luggage, the green backpack I took on my world trip that I now use as a prop.

A cab ride later, I find myself at the Greyhound station. I wipe crumbs off a plastic chair on its last legs and sit. Across from me, a guy about my age is wearing granny glasses, the cracked lenses held on his head with a smeary underwear band. Fruit of the Loom.

There are no women in the station. Not in plastic chairs, not behind counters, not in the coffee shop.

Two dark-skinned guys take seats across from me. I'm guessing they're Canadian Indians or, more correctly, First Nations Canadians. Their knuckles, throats, and arms are riddled with rough-cut, grey-green tattoos, featuring: spades, clubs, dots, and a clock with no hands. One guy is straddling his one piece of luggage, a clear plastic bag with a brown paper bag inside.

The guy beside him asks, "How long you in for?"

Felons, in Canada?

I listen to them talk about the oil crash and construction gigs. The guy with the bags bends over and opens the plastic bag, and then the paper one.

Is "zip gun" one word or two?

He digs out a beaded necklace. Then another and another. "Made them myself," he says.

A uniformed man orders the four of us, the only passengers, to line up. He dons blue latex gloves and searches our carry-ons as we board. He examines the necklaces. "Nice," he says.

I locate a crumb-free row and settle in as Great Plains, treeless steppe, and golden prairie fan out and roll by.

I saw above me that endless skyway
And saw below me her tawny valley
The dust clouds clinging and the wheat fields whining
A voice was nagging and her gaskets blowing
And I was paying the incidentals and never sleeping.

I haven't spoken to Jackie in two weeks, half a billing cycle, not since I slept on a cot in sick bay. Jackie's disembarking words were, "Don't bother apologizing. Ever again." Last week, she appeared in my Tinder feed. Her profile featured one of our Christmas selfies with me blacked out. She specified, "No left-wing pin heads, right-wing fetus lovers or insomniacs or artist wannabees." I considered faving her. I considered reporting her. Instead, I called Abe who said I'd probably hear from her now that I'm out of town. Then I called Joey who said to focus on my show, which is about all I can handle right now.

Two hours later, I arrive in the town of Moosefin. A cab drops me off at a low stucco house, where I'll be bunking for the next two weeks. There's a white Camry in the driveway. Hanging from the hood is an electric plug, probably for an engine-block warmer, which I'm hoping won't be needed now that it's almost summer.

To make travel affordable for performers, the festival offers "billeting," which means locals provide free lodging. Joey said accommodations can range from a queen bed with down pillows and ensuite bath to a sleeping bag in an unfinished basement decorated with mousetraps.

A week ago, I received an email:

Due to the unprecedented demand for housing, we may not be able to find you a billet. Please consult the attached list of hostels and inexpensive hotels. Or check Airbnb.

I consulted the list. One hostel didn't answer the phone. Another had a lower bunk in a twenty-person dorm. *Airbnb* had rooms an hour away in towns named Mucklik and Cheapshot. A town named Drumheller had rooms with hourly rates. Any of these options would require commuting back and forth by Greyhound. Sharing a sleeping bag with a nest of mice started to sound good.

Joey said not to panic.

Two days later, there was another email from the festival about a friendly couple with a spare bedroom and a shared bath.

"Gay OK?" the note asked.

I called my inner circle with the good news.

Abe: "Here's all you need to know about gay guys. Big fat, bearded, hairy ones who wear lots of flannel are known as bears. The little fat ones are cubs. Skinny hairy ones are called otters. If you get hairy ones, be sure to clean the little wigs out of the drain before you shower."

"Abe..."

"Let me finish. Twinks are young and skinny without body hair and kind of swishy. No drain wigs."

"So, let me get this straight, otters and bears aren't swishy?"

"Hold on. Then there are gay jocks and gym rats. You'll probably get along with them. They're also some known as wolves. Let's not go there."

"Abe, what's your source for this info?"

"*Pornhose.*"

Lenny: "They won't bother you. They'll be too busy cornholing each other. But you should sleep on your back. If one of them says, 'Bend over, I'll drive,' run like hell. And whatever you do, don't crap in their bathroom. The smell of shit turns them on. They like to fling it around like chimpanzees.

"Also, see if they have any poppers in the medicine cabinet. Snorting them is a rush and it relaxes your sphincter. On second thought, skip the poppers. Oh, and I almost forgot the most important thing. You remember the hanky code from the movie *Cruising*?"

"Lenny, will you quit fucking around. This is important."

"A green hanky in the left back pocket means booger-play. Yellow in the right front, means: piss on my face and I'll blow a wet fart in yours. And be sure to check out the local strip clubs, what we used to call the 'Canadian Ballet.'"

Joey: "You're from Massachusetts, the most progressive place in the world. These guys are even loaning you a bicycle. Focus on your job."

As the cab speeds off, I'm focused on the front lawn, on the largest rabbit I've ever seen. It has periscoping ears like a Doberman and muscular haunches like an SUV. I stare. It flexes. I hit the doorbell.

A tall greybeard answers. He's wearing a cowboy hat with a little feather and a tight white T-shirt. Good pecs for a guy my age. His shorts are not too long and not too short. No hankies. On his feet, high-top Converses without socks. Probably a gym rat.

"You must be Randall Burns from the States. Welcome, I'm Barclay."

I extend a hand for a shake as he extends arms for a hug. We meet somewhere in between, then break.

"How was your trip?" Barclay gestures for me to come inside.

"Decent," I say. "Stayed in Ottawa last night. WestJet to Calgary today, then Greyhound to Moosefin."

"The Hound? Oh, please, tell me you're kidding."

"Yeah, it was a little sketchy."

"A little? Didn't you hear about the psycho who cut the head off another passenger a few years back? Now, when you ride the Hound, you're supposed to ask the driver, 'Where you be heading?' Cute, eh? But to be honest, we've got plenty of sketch around here, too. Moosefin is known for its quads, dink hats, junkies, and peeler bars."

I'm guessing a "quad" is a four-wheel drive and a "peeler bar" is probably a strip club, the Canadian Ballet. A "dink hat" might be a condom, but I decide not to ask.

Barclay adds: "But no handguns. We don't pack like you do in the States. Most Canadians are pretty mellow until they see a puck or an unlocked bicycle."

"Speaking of which, I brought a Kryptonite lock for your bike. Thanks again for letting me use it."

"Better use my lock, too. Or better yet, stash the bike inside the theater and then use both locks."

The first thing I notice about someone's house are the smells: pickling litter boxes, vinegary beer empties, smoky coffee grounds. Then the sounds: the churn of an old fridge, the crunch of grit on a foyer floor. Barclay's place is odor-free and crunch-free, like my place. There are a few pastel color schemes but nothing too swishy.

He's cleared a shelf in the fridge for me. There are no crumbs on the counter or lettuce shreds or body hair in the kitchen sink.

"We don't have a garburetor," he says. "Organic matter goes in the compost bin."

"Garburetor" must be Canadian for disposal.

From the living room, I hear the voice of Bea Arthur, a *Maude* rerun on TV. Why am I not surprised?

"We'll all be sharing the washroom," Barclay says, indicating a door to my left.

I peek in. The "washroom" mirror is free of toothpaste spatter, the shower drain is free of wigs.

"We only have one house rule: Please put the lid down when you flush."

Maybe Lenny knows the meaning behind this.

"Not a problem," I say, spotting a problem. The toilet paper roll is facing the wrong way. The next leaf should be draped on top of the roll, not tucked underneath. I'll fix it for them later.

My room has a desk with a gift basket of fresh fruit and a futon on a raised wood frame. At the foot of the bed, there's a matching bath towel, hand towel, and face towel all neatly folded. On the wall, a few photos of a cuddling couple, Barclay in his cowboy hat with a younger guy with eye shadow. Jackie put eye shadow on me. My body starts to feel unseasonably warm.

Barclay seems to notice. "When it's sunny, the place gets hot. We have an air conditioner in the living room. Just leave your door open at night and you should be cool enough."

He hands me a black leather keychain with several keys and a manila envelope bearing the Moosefin International Fringe Theatre Festival logo. "I'll leave you to get organized," he says.

I empty the envelope onto the desk. IDs and lanyards, schedules and pamphlets, agendum and addendum, statements of purpose and statements without purpose, unwritten rules and undocumented documents, dos and don'ts and I hope-you-already-dids. There's also a phone app for checking ticket sales and a copy of my signed and dated, "Tolerance, Trigger Warning, and Diversity Awareness Agreement."

I download the app: one ticket sold.

I consider the pamphlets.

I consider calling Joey.

I lie on the futon.

Ten minutes later, I check my phone: Still only one sale.

I fire up my computer and open *Pornhose* for today's recommendations. In Alberta, "Morning Moose for Moosefin Mama" has garnered five stars. A friend in Boston — in other words Abe — has liked "MILF Cock and Ball Torture" and "Mummified Wife with Nipple Clamps." He and Amy must be fighting again.

An ad appears for *HatTrick*, the Canadian version of *Tinder*. I install it, create a profile noting that I am an actor at the fringe festival, and swipe several fifty-something women near Moosefin.

But am I not an exotic American in a Canadian backwater?

I swipe five more women in their forties, ten in their thirties, and fifteen in their twenties.

My swiping is interrupted by a text from the festival about changes to the ticketing procedures. I still haven't read the original ticketing procedures or, for that matter, any procedures.

When I was a magazine editor, I always prioritized tasks into three piles: low, high, and too hard. The too-hard pile was for items so thorny that they were best ignored and left to sort themselves out.

After prioritizing my piles of Moosefin *moosellanea*, I have an ant hill of low-priority tasks, a mole hill of high-priority tasks, and a Whistler Blackcomb of too-hard tasks.

I decide to attack two tasks not in any pile: groceries and a temporary gym membership. *Google Maps* recommends a Safeway and a GoodLife Fitness three kilometers away. I multiply three times .62 — less than two miles and near the fringe festival grounds.

I grab my backpack and, heading to the garage, notice the Camry is gone. I unlock a side door and find Barclay's bike in the middle of a newly painted garage floor. I unlock it, adjust the seat, and hit the streets of Moosefin.

The neighborhood: low stucco houses, two-car driveways, and a giant evergreen tree on every front lawn — all pleasant, genteel, gentile, Canadian flyover, middlest of middle North America.

I pass a lingerie store called The Panty Bar and a gas station called The Petrol Bar. Gas for only $1.22? Oh, right, it's per liter not per gallon.

Google Maps directs me down Snail Run to Salmon Child Road, which mushrooms to four lanes and features a sign: "Speed limit 80 kph." As I'm converting to mph, a quad passes me. Then an eighteen-wheeler. Then a Camaro offering a bird-in-hand and encouraging words to this first-time visitor. "Get off the highway, asshole!"

Douche bags, in Canada?

I pull over at a place called The Bar-Bar. The décor is "Contemporary Detritus." Dangling from the ceiling is a crowbar, a shock absorber, and hip waders. Mounted on the walls are wood skis, a stuffed crow, Alberta license plates, and TVs tuned to American baseball. The bartender is sporting a Husqvarna beard, a woolen beanie, and forearm tats that are colorful and non-jagged. A Canadian hipster, a lumbersexual.

I grab a stool at the empty bar. Today's special is a Bloody Caesar and a burger for twenty dollars.

"What's in the Caesar?" I ask the bartender.

"New in town, eh? Vodka and Clamato juice. It's Canadian for Bloody Mary."

"Maybe not. Can I get a burger, medium-rare?"

"In Canada, all burgers are well-done."

I sample a can of Kokanee, Canada's Budweiser, and a bag of what must be a local specialty, ketchup-flavored potato chips.

"Is there a Safeway or GoodLife around here?" I ask.

"They both moved five years ago."

I finish my beer and order two Slim Jims and two bags of ketchup chips to go.

The bill is thirty-five dollars Canadian. Multiplied by the exchange rate of .75 and it's still a rip-off. I pay with a credit card and tip a few Loonies, Canadian one-dollar coins, which each weigh as much as a curling puck or stone or whatever they call it.

I give up on groceries or a gym for now and check my ticket sales: Still only one sold, but there's a hit on *HatTrick*. Then it disappears.

Flakes, in Canada?

At Barclay's, the Camry is back in the driveway but no sign of the rabbit. I lock the bike to a snow blower in the garage using two Kryptonites, and slip in a back door and go to my room.

There's a knock on my barely open bedroom door. Barclay peeks in and scans my haul from The Bar-Bar.

"You won't last a week eating that junk. Why don't you join us for dinner?"

"Sounds great. What can I bring?"

"I'm making fish and chicken so some Sauvignon Blanc would be great. There's a place about three kilometers away on Crow Flies Road called The Booze Store. Dinner at six thirty."

I head out again to pick up the Sauvignon Blanc and make it back without any honking or birds-in-hand. Parked beside the Camry is a black Trans Am, which reminds me of Jackie's car, until I notice the rusting quarter panels. I ditch the bike in the garage and lock it to a chainsaw.

Barclay is in the kitchen wearing a denim apron that says, "Will act for food." He's monitoring a sauté pan and a bamboo steamer.

"You're back in one piece," he says, turning to me. "Congrats."

"Performer, bike, and wine all intact." With a flourish, I remove the wine from my backpack.

"Two bottles? You got us pegged as lushes. Good call. Park them on the counter, wash up, and join us at the table. Dinner's in about ten."

In the washroom, I take a moment to flip the toilet paper roll, use a piece of toilet paper to close the door, and then rub down the light switch, door knob, and toilet handle with a Lysol wipe from the canister I brought.

I try not to think about poppers, hankies, or bathhouses.

Lenny is such an idiot.

I continue wiping down the sink taps, the shower handles, and finally wash my hands. Three times. I don't open the medicine cabinet.

The dining area is in the living room behind a taupe sectional with bold accent pillows. There's familiar catchy, twangy, folky music playing on the stereo.

"Is this the Be Good Tanyas?" I ask.

"Yes, they're Canadian but their music is Americana," Barclay says. "Go figure."

He's sitting at the table with the guy from the cuddly photos who is wearing a flannel shirt with the sleeves cut off. Slim with hairy forearms. No eye shadow. An otter. He's also wearing a baseball hat with a Canadian maple leaf logo. On my trip around the world, most Canadians I met sported at least one item with a maple leaf; the message being: I ... am ... not ... American.

"Randall, this is Allistair," Barclay says.

Allistair stands. As I'm bracing for a hug, he extends a hand for a shake and squeezes mine a little too hard. We take seats across from each other. Barclay is at the head of the table, as if he plans to be the adult in the room.

The table is chrome and glass, and set with water and wine goblets, dinner forks, dessert spoons, and a small centerpiece of yellow flowers.

From my seat, I glance out the window. The rabbit is back and appears to be staring in at me. "What's with the rabbit?"

"Oh, that's just Carmine," Barclay says. "He guards the house. We saw him chase a dog off the lawn one time."

"We saw him chase a Bruins' fan off the lawn one time," Allistair says, holding a bottle of Sauvignon Blanc.

"Good thing I don't follow hockey." I watch as Allistair fills my twelve-ounce water glass with wine and my eight-ounce wine goblet with water. Barclay cracks open a beer and hands it over, too.

"Cheers," I say, raising my beer. "And thanks for the hospitality. I was getting worried I'd end up in a dorm or a cardboard box."

We toast. They each chase their beer with wine and wine with beer. I pace myself and sip my beer.

The cuisine is straight. Baked salmon with lemon slices, broiled chicken breast with mustard sauce, lots of vegetables and few carbs, the way I usually eat. Barclay serves me and then Allistair.

Barclay asks, "So, have you done a lot of fringe festivals?"

I knew the sizing up would come at some point and prepped for it. Back in Boston, I checked out their websites. Allistair and Barclay are both equity actors with agents, have MFAs, teach theater at U of Alberta, and specialize in singing and dancing, as well as clowning and stage combat. Their show, a musical comedy called, "My Best Friend's Gerbil," won Best of the Fest last year.

"I've done a few small ones in the States," I say. "But this is my first Canadian fringe. I'm a little late to the game. I did the corporate thing for twenty years. Saved some money. Traveled around the world. Wrote a book and thinking about writing another. I thought, why not try performing to sell some books?"

"Sure, performing isn't that hard," Allistair says. "Why not just try it to sell some books?"

Before I can process Allistair's remark, Barclay says. "A novel, eh? Self-published?"

"No, I got lucky. It was picked up by a small literary press out of New York."

"Kudos. That doesn't happen much these days," Barclay says.

Allistair cracks open another beer and says abruptly, "If that asshole Trump becomes president don't even think about moving up here. We're building a wall."

"In Boston, we don't care much about politics," I say.

"Interesting." Allistair picks up his phone and starts scrolling.

"This fish is excellent," I say.

Barclay opens another beer and refills his water glass with more wine. He sits back in his chair as if waiting to be entertained.

Allistair looks up from his phone. "What do people from Boston know about Alberta?" he asks.

I take a sip from my beer. "Well, we've all heard of the Land of the Living Skies and ..."

"I believe that's the slogan for a province called Saskatchewan," Allistair says.

"Polar bears?" I ask.

"Northern Manitoba," he says.

"Revelstoke ski area?"

"Interior BC."

"Alberta Clipper snow storm?"

"Bingo."

Barclay pours me some more water.

Allistair peers over the rim of his glass, one of Jackie's favorite gestures. "We got our start performing at a World Heritage site in Alberta called Brains-Splattered-on-Ground Buffalo Jump."

"I think I might've heard of it," I say.

Barclay represses a smile and says, "That would be 'Head-Smashed-In Buffalo Jump.' It's a hundred-meter cliff in southern Alberta that native people used for driving buffalo to their messy demise. We gave tours dressed as pioneers."

Allistair says, "Then I graduated to working attractions in Ass Hat and Yellow Neige."

Barclay says, "He means Medicine Hat and Yellow Knife."

These two have stolen my routine. They refill each other's water glasses with more wine.

I root around for something clever to say, but all I can summon is an excerpt from my show: "I know how to say 'Speak English?' 'Got Pepto-Bismol?' and 'Send the evacuation helicopter' in three languages."

There's a short silence.

Barclay offers me some roasted vegetables. Allistair takes off his hat and puts it on backwards.

I feel like I'm being tag-teamed and not in a good way. First the geography quiz, then the Abbott and Costello routine. And, yeah, I probably insulted them with my remark about performing just to sell books. Barclay seems OK, but Allistair seems like a typical twenty-something dick hole. I decide to play the non-threatening newbie, the *man-génue*.

"Any advice for this festival?" I ask. "I've only sold one ticket so far."

Barclay smiles. "Not to worry. Most people buy at the last minute. I read your listing in the program. Your show description and photo are pretty good. And your venue at The Rod and Gun Club is decent. Eighty-nine seats, central location."

"Where should I hand out postcards?"

Barclay says, "We usually flyer people queued up for other shows."

Allistair cuts in. "Your *venue*," he emphasizes with air quotes, "is in the Gun Club basement, something out of your *Texas Chainsaw Massacres* — axes and dismembering tools on the wall. The good thing is that it stays cool even in summer because the freezers are filled with murdered animals. Except that time when the electricity went out and the freezers leaked a tasty, pink ooze all over the floor."

I spoon more chicken onto my plate and offer some to Barclay, which he declines, and then to Allistair, who also declines.

"What's your venue?" I ask.

"We're in the big theater upstairs from yours," Barclay says. "It's always good to check out the competition. Want some recommendations?"

"Sure," I say, taking out my little notebook.

Barclay: "See 'God is a Scottish Drag Queen.'"

Allistair chimes in: "Definitely 'Two Guys and a Guy.'"

Barclay and Allistair: "She was a Great Dad."

Allistair refills everyone's water glasses with wine.

Barclay. "What about 'Gender Enders?'"

Allistair: "No, skip that one. It's going to be a piece of crap."

"Well then," Barclay says, pushing back his chair. "Dessert anyone?"

"Thanks," I say, pushing back my chair. "That was a great meal and I'm stuffed so no dessert for this boy. Can I help with the dishes?"

Allistair says, "Not a chance. Barclay here is *very* particular."

I look at Barclay. He smiles. "Don't worry about it."

I clear my dishes and retreat to my room.

Later, Allistair knocks on my door and pokes his head in. He's still wearing his maple leaf hat on backwards. "We're watching some TV. Want to join us?"

Not particularly, I think.

"Sure," I say.

In the living room, five guys are sitting on the sectional but no Barclay. A few are wearing preppy polo shirts. No one looks over thirty. The coffee table is littered with half-empty beers as well as bags of what I'm assuming is Canadian brand junk food: All-Dressed Ruffles, Dill Pickle potato chips, Hawkins Cheezies that look like Cheetos, and Hickory Sticks that look like potato sticks. There's also a package of giant Tootsie Rolls.

I decline Allistair's offer of a beer or snacks.

"Everyone, this is Randall," Allistair says. "He's from the U Ass of A. Boston, home of the big bad Bruins."

I walk the length of the couch and shake hands with Courtney, Cameron, Drew, and someone named Steff or Stiff, and someone else named Chris or Bris. I grab an open seat at the end of the couch nearest my room and immediately forget everyone's names.

Someone asks, "What's the deal with Trump?"

I say, "Your guess is as good as mine."

Someone else mentions a crush on New England Patriots' wide receiver Julian Edelman.

Someone else says, "Jews are so exotic."

I wade in, "Edelman is only half Jewish."

Someone asks which half.

Laughter.

I say, "The wrong half."

Silence.

Someone calls out someone for being an anti-Semite. Someone says something about Hongcouver, slang for Vancouver because of all the Asians living there. Jackie has relatives in Vancouver. Someone says something about Edmonchuk, slang for Edmonton because of all the Ukrainians there.

Racists, in Canada?

RuPaul's Drag Race comes on the tube.

The MC, who I'm guessing is RuPaul, is tall and Black and wearing a large blond wig with a voice more feminine than Maude's.

On the screen, drag queens sashay and swish, flounce and mince, glide and waft. My couch mates applaud. I reach for a beer.

Allistair gestures at one of the contestants and covers his mouth, smothering a gasp. The contestant has a red wig that matches their red beard. Allistair says they met on a cruise, slept together, and the contestant left something unsavory on the sheets.

"You mean as in Winnie?" asks one of the guys on the couch.

"As in lawn carp?" asks another.

I fake a yawn. Maybe I'm not as progressive as I like to think. Maybe I'm just a middle-aged, homophobic, vanilla prude. Maybe I need to find another place to stay for the next two weeks.

"Bigger than this?" asks another guy, holding up a giant Tootsie Roll.

I can feel them watching me pretending to watch TV.

I was in a fraternity once. I was a pledge once, too. These guys are busting on me, the hetero American in the room. Boys will be boys, regardless of orientation.

That night, I hardly sleep. Even with the door open, it's too hot. I open *Eat, Pray, Love* featuring Elizabeth Gilbert in Rome stuffing her *punim* with pasta but that doesn't help.

In the morning, my head is buzzing and my throat is sore. Probably something I caught from the Hound. I check my phone. Still no changes in ticket sales or hits on *HatTrick*. Carmine the rabbit is outside the window watching me.

In the kitchen, Barclay is hoisting a canvas messenger bag across his shoulders.

"Gotta run," he says. "Help yourself to anything. There's fruit in the fridge."

No sign of Allistair. I grab an orange to get some vitamins in my system and return to my piles and pamphlets. After an hour, I pull the shade down on Carmine and catch some sleep.

At six P.M., I bike to the fringe festival's preview event being held at The Rod and Gun Club, which is in an area of town Allistair referred to as the "Hershey Highway."

Adjacent to the Gun Club is a storefront offering bail services, a minimart offering cash loans, and a street mission offering Jesus. There's also a pawn shop, another pawn shop, and the Rusty Pole Tap and Grill. A broken second-floor window above it is covered with a sheet.

A juvie-looking guy in surgical scrubs and a juvie-looking girl in pajamas are sharing a cigarette outside the mission. He pulls something out of his pocket, blows on it, bites off a corner and offers it to the girl. These two are what Barclay referred to as a "heat score," a magnet for police.

In front of the Gun Club, a relaxed-fit crowd starts to line up. Stripes and checks, little and black, coifs and makeup, trekking poles and golden retrievers. Slumming suburbanites.

I approach a stocky woman with a bristle-top hairdo in the shape of a maple leaf. She has a lanyard with a stop watch around her neck and a clipboard in her hands.

"Hi, I'm one of the performers," I say. "Randall Burns? *The Chronic Single's Handbook*?"'

She skims her clipboard and flips the page.

"You preview after *Trump the Musical*. How long is your piece?"

"A minute forty-five."

"FYI, if you go over two minutes, the clowns will get you. And ... B ... T ... W ... I got your request to use two theater chairs as props for your show. Sorry. Fire hazard. And ... N ... O ... There's nowhere in the theater to store your props; you'll have to take them home after each show. You can go downstairs to the green room and wait until your name is called."

She looks to someone behind me. "Next!"

I don't move. "Sorry to be a pain, but would it be OK for me to bring my bike inside?"

"No. Lock it up over there."

I follow her index finger to the sidewalk and what is either an abandoned wheelchair or a bike rack bent in half.

"Next!"

After locking my bike to the half-rack using two locks, I go inside. The Gun Club has been jury-rigged into three theaters: a two-hundred seat "Beast" on the main floor, my eighty-nine seat "Belly of the Beast" downstairs, and a twenty-five seat "Outback" in an art studio behind the Gun Club.

The lobby walls are adorned with animal parts, including heads and pelts, skins and bones, skulls and spines. The room is set up with buffet tables with chafing dishes and card tables with unfolded folding chairs. A blackboard menu lists moose lasagna, venison meat balls, and bear stew.

To the side, is a display with a sign for "The Scat Museum," and a table piled with actual shit: the Milk Duds of a jackrabbit, a poutine pile of bear crap, a tubular coyote turd with hair in it, and of course, the green lawn carp of a Canada goose. I look around to see if anyone is watching, then bend and sniff. Nothing. I grab a plastic fork off a card table and poke the lawn carp; it has a hard, clear coating. I return the fork to the table.

I follow the signs to the Beast theater, the venue for tonight's preview. An open door leads to a raised professional-size stage with professional-grade lighting, dozens of high-beam howitzers affixed to the ceiling and along the floor. Suspended from above, wings of black cloth. I imagine cameras snapping, ovations standing, and women moistening.

I locate the downstairs green room, which *is* a commercial kitchen, just as Allistair described. It's packed with the competition: men with wigs, women with beards, cute chicks, fat chicks, and one smooth blonde with impressively high breasts. The crowd is speaking in Canadian: "Double-double," "All janked up," "I have to joush up my hair."

The walls are outfitted for mayhem with saws, axes, giant scissors, and machete-sized filleting knives just as Alistair described. It reminds me of *that* Christmas at Ricki's and her mother's arsenal. The thought of Ricki gives me heartburn. Or maybe it was my lunch of Slim Jims with a side of ketchup chips. I need some real food.

On the other side of the room, a group of performers is grazing a long table featuring Tootsie Rolls, Baby Ruth bars, a vat of popcorn, and a chafing dish of bear stew. I fill a paper plate with gloppy grizzly bits.

Barclay and Allistair, dressed like rodents with their hands in fake bandages, are in a corner with a bunch of people, some in capes, some in feather hats, all in bare feet. Considering that I'm wearing khakis, a black T-shirt, and lace up shoes, I look like I'm slumming.

Allistair waves me over. He bites into a giant Tootsie Roll and winks. "Hungry sweetie?"

"I'm good," I say through a mouthful of bitter grizzly.

"Don't break your teeth on the buckshot," he says.

Barclay introduces me to people standing in his group, including Amanda, the blonde with the impressive breasts.

I think "high" but say "Hi," and then add my old go-to line, "Having fun?"

She looks me up and down, says, "Excuse me" and leaves.

Everyone else begins to disperse.

I toss my plate of bear into the trash.

On a nearby table is a Moosefin festival program packed with ads, show descriptions, and actor bios. The program is an inch thick, probably thicker than the Moosefin phone book. I start reading: "The Moosefin International Fringe, one of the largest fringe festivals in North America, is modeled after the Edinburgh fringe festival in Scotland, which is the largest in the world."

I skim the performers' bios: *The Moth*, *This American Life*, Canadian Comedy Award winner, CBC, BBC, NBC.

A bunch of farmers? Really, Joey?

Performers pace around the green room, rehearsing their previews, timing themselves with their phones. I time myself with my watch. My first effort is two minutes and five seconds. I cut a sentence and try again.

After, several run-throughs, I sit on the corner of a chest freezer and check my ticket sales: no change. And nothing on *HatTrick*.

Blonde Amanda is sitting on the far end of the freezer. Except now she's holding a baby — a real, live baby. Amanda uses a real baby in her show? Clever.

She adjusts herself under her blouse and the sounds of suckling and slurping ensue.

I look away as best I can, and then notice a sign on the other side of the room, "Belly of the Beast. Keep Out."

"Excuse me," I say, without turning to look at her, and head for what will be my venue for the next ten days. The half-dozen light cannons on the ceiling are lit. Black curtains hang from a jungle gym of metal tubing to create a little black box theater, a crude version of the big theater upstairs. Instead of a raised stage, flat black rubber tiles have been arranged in a rectangle on the floor. I count off my steps along the rectangle: about eight-feet deep by sixteen-feet wide, a little bigger than my living room rug, plenty of room for my show. The seats are set on risers like you'd find in a high school gym. I count eighty-five, four fewer than advertised.

"Hey!"

I'm jolted from my calculations.

"All those universities in Boston, you'd figure people from there could read a sign." The woman with the maple-leaf bristle-top is in the doorway, a bullhorn in her hand. She raises it to her mouth and yells, "Got it?" and leaves.

Back in the green room, most of the performers are crowded around a flat screen to watch the preview event going on upstairs. I stand next to a guy with circa 1980s pleated pants, black and white saddle shoes, and straying reddish hair. He looks like he was dressed by Woody Allen's mother. I'm guessing this isn't a costume. I'm guessing he's on the spectrum. He introduces himself as Harvey Feldman.

Feldman is four inches shorter than I am. I have an urge to pat him on the head.

"You're Randall Burns, right?" he says to me. "Read about your show, a modern *Portnoy's Complaint*." He leans in. "You realize we're probably the only Jews at the festival."

"Call me Burns," I say. We shake. He has big hands for a small guy.

"*Shhh*!" Someone points to the flat screen.

The MC for the preview event is wearing a blond wig, a fur bikini, and has thick, athletic arms. He is well over six-feet tall. It occurs to me that this is only the second Black person I've seen in Alberta, and they've both been on TV.

"Greetings. I'm Leto," the MC says to a packed audience. "Your hostess for the opening night of the forty-fifth annual Moosefin International Fringe Theatre Festival."

Applause.

"This year's festival is bigger, badder, and busting out all over." The MC adjusts his full, furry bikini top. "We have two-hundred theater companies, fourteen-hundred performances at forty venues stuffed into ten days of madness. There's singing, dancing, comedy, acrobatics, and, of course, clowns. It's unjuried, uncensored, and anything goes. Consider yourselves warned."

Two clowns run out on stage dragging a giant hockey bag.

Leto continues: "For tonight's preview, we've selected forty acts that will entice you with a two-minute preview of their shows. But if a performer goes over the two-minute limit ... "

From the hockey bag, one clown extracts a volleyball net and throws it over Leto. The other throws a bed sheet over Leto. They take out giant foam hammers and foam baseball bats and whack away at Leto who squeals, "My hair, my chest hair!"

Someone hands me a brown paper bag with a bottle and a strong odor of hootch. I pass the bag on without sipping from it.

On the screen, Allistair and Barclay run onstage in their gerbil costumes and chase a shrieking guy in a business suit. Leto giggles and applauds. He's changed into chest-high fishing waders with no shirt.

I head to the bathroom where I lock, piss, shake, and wash. My hand is on the door handle when I realize I have to piss again.

When I return, Leto is in a low-cut evening gown. Someone from the audience offers him a brown, paper bag shaped like a bottle. He swigs and hands it back to the crowd.

"Love that Screech." Leto says.

I return to the bathroom for another piss and hang out to do some voice exercises in front of the mirror. My intestines start squirming. I park myself on the toilet, head in hands, bowels recalcitrant. I practice bathroom Zen and imagine my colon doing cat-cow, fire-log pose, warrior I, warrior making a II, cobra, cobra-head peeking out, cobra-swallowing eggplant, child pose, child-squatting-behind-couch pose, bacon strips on Persian rug pose, up dog, down dog, dog crapping in my deeded parking spot, but nothing helps. Even my shit is scared. Someone pounds on the bathroom door. "Hey, Randall Burns you're on deck."

Upstairs, another short-haired woman with a clipboard points me toward a short queue along a black, fabric wing leading to the stage.

Leto announces the next performer. "And now we have a fringe fav, Harvey Feldman, all the way from New *Yawk* City doing a bit from his new show, *Kvetching Cage Match: Philip Roth vs. Woody Allen*, twenty memorable characters in one unforgettable hour. Lay it on thick for Harvey."

Feldman stumbles onto the stage. People laugh. He drops the microphone. People laugh. He impersonates Alvie Singer and Annie Hall, Alexander Portnoy and his mother, Hannah and all her sisters, a woman called The Monkey, Broadway

Danny Rose and Zelig. Feldman slips from character to character, male to female, not a seam showing. He races around the stage and jumps in the air. He pauses to let punch lines land. People laugh. A lot. I time him. He finishes in a minute and a half. He yells to the audience: "Who wants a free ticket?"

The audience screams. "I do, I do." He runs around the crowd handing out tickets and exits through the back of the room.

The guy presents as a *schlemiel*, disheveled and inept, but on stage he kills. I make a mental note to check his bio.

I watch a couple more acts. *The Proctologists*: Two guys with giant flashlights on their heads. The Onion Dip guys do a bit from their new show *Jiggy Pop Live on the Hershey Highway*. The one who plays Jiggy rolls around the stage on chocolate kisses, while his associate throws candies into the audience. The clowns come out after them. A woman in the audience yells, "Jiggy, I want to be your dog!" The crowd laughs and claps.

A guy in a wingy, blond toupee, Trump in *Trump the Musical* goes on.

I'm next.

I feel myself fading out, fading in, and can't make out what Trump is saying because of all the ponging and echoing, whirring and clicking in my head.

Trump finishes. Leto takes a yellow hanky from his red-spangly tank top and dabs his forehead.

"Leto shouldn't have drunk so much Screech. Leto is fucked up."

Big applause.

"You sure know how to make a girl feel special." He throws his sweaty hanky into audience and they dive on it.

"OK. Next, we have Randall Burns from Boston, *Massa-two-shits*. His show is *The Chronic Single's Handbook*, adult situations, adult language, and more adult situations. He's going to do a piece called, *The Day I Was Almost Gay*. Ooh-wee, Leto remembers the day he was almost gay."

I avoid looking at the blanched skeletons and snarling, stuffed heads on the wall.

Clapping drowns any remaining pongs, pings, whirs, or clicks.

Show time.

I stride onstage, grab the mic, and launch into my piece.

"When I was in my twenties, I hitchhiked from Boston to California, went to the beach and three hours later, got a second-degree sunburn. Then I met a guy, a very pretty guy with a face like Sharon Stone ... "

The rest of the story unspools, kink-free, smooth as a golden prairie. I let the last line land. Pause. Laughter. Clapping.

I head back down to the green room tingly, queasy, woozy, and feel a pat on my back. My fellow Jew, Feldman. "Nice job," he says.

Maybe Joey was right; maybe I can pull this off.

At the preview after-party, people are crowded around the Scat Museum table, which is now serving as a bar. Everyone has a can of Kokanee and is playing catch with the plasticized crap.

I buy a beer and lean against the table, watching. Allistair and Barclay are by the stage yukking it up with Lady Rottweiler of the maple leaf haircut, who I've learned is Morag Fitzgibbon, director of the Moosefin fringe.

Amanda is seated a few feet away from me wearing some kind of printed poncho. Her arms are hidden and holding something the size of a football. I feel grossed out, then turned on, then lonely.

A guy hovering her is talking to another guy about udder covers, baby backpacks, and baby front-loaders.

Jackie hated kids. I imagine her whipping plastic coyote turds at these two.

Someone taps my shoulder and says, "Nice piece." It's Morag Fitzgibbon.

"Thanks,'" I say.

She turns to Trump and says, "Nice piece."

She turns to Feldman and says, "Nice piece."

I return to standing alone.

Feldman wanders over, examining one of the coyote turds. "Nice piece," I say to him. He laughs.

"No, I really mean it," I say. "You're a pro. How long you been doing this?"

"A while," he says.

As we talk, performers come by and pay their respects to Feldman — Jiggy Pop, covered in what I'm assuming is chocolate, the MC now in a mini skirt, the guy from a show called *Pretending Things Are a Cock*.

I say to Feldman, "Seems to be a theme at this festival."

"Yeah, drag queens, cocks, all things anal. It's an open secret that Moosefin is the most gay-friendly fringe festival."

"You don't say."

Fucking Joey.

Feldman continues. "But it's not all gay. You've got the whiney one-man shows that are more therapy than theater. Or, please, the women way past their prime who insist on doing burlesque. Then you have the ringers. See that older guy by the stage? He's a former Hollywood actor, performing an off-Broadway play called *Underneath the Lintel*. The younger guy over there? Former Broadway cast member in *Jersey Boys*. Don't see their shows unless you want feel worthless and suicidal."

Hollywood? Broadway? I feel worthless and suicidal.

Feldman checks his phone. "Opening night tomorrow and I'm only half sold-out. It's bullshit. Audiences used to be bigger with half as many performers and no putrid show times like Sunday at ten P.M. or Thursday at noon. I used to sell out every night." Feldman reaches up to put an arm around my shoulder and gives it a squeeze. "It's a tough time to be starting out."

I experience a moment of panic, and then some warm and fuzzy.

"Tell you what," he says. "I'll add you to the private performers' Facebook group. I'll be flyering in here tomorrow. Join me after your tech rehearsal. I have an idea for you."

A small group of performers is walking by with a brown paper bag and a stuffed animal. Feldman waves them over. "We got a Moosefin Virgin here. Time to pop his cherry."

Feldman gives me a wink. "Gotta bolt. Enjoy."

The guy holding the bag waves it in my face and says, "Spread 'em." He pours a shot of thick liquid into my mouth and tells me to hold it. It tastes like rum, very strong rum. Another guy holding the animal, which turns out to be a stuffed moose, steps in and holds it up to my mouth, ass first. Everyone then recites something about the shores of Newfoundland and the prairies of Moosefin and a moose's ass and Trump's ass and a beaver's beaver. In unison, they say, "Do you?"

I say, "I do," as best I can through a mouthful of booze.

They say, "Then down your Screech and kiss some bungus."

I down my shot with the moose butt hovering my face. I consider how many faces this ass has sat on. I close my eyes, pucker up and give it a peck. It's sticky.

From across the room, Feldman gives me a thumbs up. A hot-looking woman is sitting on his lap.

A few Kokanees later, I teeter out to the sidewalk. Someone in clown-face is scrutinizing a bike. "Fucking *skids* stole my bike lights."

My bike lights are also missing. *Skids?*

I ride home in the dark.

The next morning, I awake to the jab of futon slats through

cotton batting. I grab my phone. No hits. No tix. I check email. There's a note from Geoffrey.

Hi Old Man:

Theo and I wanted to wish you luck at the fringe. Sorry again, we'll miss you but we recommended you to some Moosefin friends. Break legs!

— Geoffrey

There's also a note from Jackie. Abe was right. She misses me. I open it.

To: R. Burns

Subject: Misc

Message: Your half of cruise bill incidentals and my ER visit. I know you'll review every charge with a scientific calculator, so I attached all receipts.

Payment sooner rather than later appreciated.

Jacqueline Chin-Rosenthal, Realtor

As I'm considering whether to block her, I check the time: Nine A.M. Did I just sleep through the night without drugs? A week after breaking up with Jackie and my insomnia has cleared up? Why am I surprised?

Sleeping with her was literally a nightmare. After our bedtime routine of tongue cuddling, booger and ear-wax checks, back-zit popping, breath and armpit sniffing, we would retreat to neutral corners of the bed and doze off.

Minutes later, Jackie would begin the Wild World of Sports and not in a good way.

Offside, encroachment, reaching in, holding, pushing, charging, roughing, over-the-back foul, loose-ball foul.

"Ouch!" I'd say.

"Sorry," she'd say. "I'll go back to my corner."

Again, we'd doze off, and then restless-leg syndrome, frog

and scissors, axel and lutz, somersault in pike position, single-leg takedown, flying kidney kick, tombstone pile-driver.

"Will you knock it off!"

"Sorry, Burns, bad dream."

Next: restless elbow syndrome, restless elbow to head syndrome, hooking and slashing, right jab and rabbit punch, clothesline and horse collar, half nelson, Peruvian neck tie, and tap out.

The next morning, she'd complain about my snoring.

No matter, I don't need any bad karma or distractions here in Moosefin. It's time to move on. Instead of checking her math, I *PayPal* her the full $1,225 and sign it simply, "Be well."

Later, when I go to leave, the house is quiet with no sign of Allistair or Barclay or their vehicles. Carmine is at his post on the lawn.

I arrive at the Rod and Gun Club at four P.M. for my technical rehearsal. In the lobby, the folding tables and chairs have been removed, the chafing dishes cleared, and the Scat Museum and animal parts relocated. In their place, are two bars and rows of booths for tickets and food.

A door along one wall reads, "Beast," the two-hundred-seat main theater used for the preview. I head to a door in the far corner for the Belly of the Beast, my eighty-something-seat basement theater.

The downstairs kitchen has been taken over by an oversized porta potty emblazed with a pair of smiling half circles and the words "Privacy pod and lactation lounge for pumping and breastfeeding." I look for Amanda, but there's no sign of her.

The door to The Belly is ajar with a new sign: "Quiet! Show in Progress." I knock twice and wait for a response.

"Enter the dragon."

A smurf about five-five and probably twenty-five with a knit hat and shrubby face stands up from a plywood desk to greet me.

I extend a hand. "Randy Burns reporting for rehearsal."

"I'm Sea Bass, short for Sebastian, but don't call me that unless you want to perform in total darkness."

On his desk, there's a roll of black tape, a console with sliders and buttons, an empty six-pack of Mountain Dew, and a stack of paperbacks with the spines facing away. Sea Bass will be running my lights and sound. We have three hours to rehearse my one-hour show.

"Let's do it," I say.

Sea Bass leads me to a storage area behind the stage. Against one wall is a stack of folding chairs. Along another, a row of trunks and some capes and tights on hangers. Items are labeled with show names, including *Kvetching Cage Match*, Feldman's show. In front of a lighted mirror, there's a desk and two metal chairs.

I decide against asking Sea Bass if I can borrow chairs for my show or add my backpack to the props section. I don't want to appear high maintenance on our first encounter.

"This is your green room," Sea Bass says. He looks down the hall. "That's our new, improved, all-pronoun, all-gender, genderless washroom. But once the house opens, customers can use it, too. You could be taking a leak, and in the next stall, a beautiful chick could be taking a nasty dump. Genius."

He starts to say something about the "titty shed in the kitchen" but is drowned out by the rumbling and squealing of big iron.

The noise subsides, but it reminds me of the disposal and kitchen sounds at the Harvard Square Storytelling Hour, only much louder.

"Was that a train?" I ask. "Could that happen during my show?"

"Yup. That would be the Canadian Pacific Railway. We're next to the switching yard. This is a *fringe* festival, remember? It's all good, bro."

"I read that all props had to be flame retardant," I say. "Do I have to spray them with something?"

"Dude, ignore the manual," Sea Bass says. "Ignore Morag, AKA 'The Rag.' Help yourself to whatever you need, chairs, props, storage. Fill your boots. She's a boomer bitch. Everything is a midlife crisis with her. She totally hates my music. Enjoy your Top Forty, you cunt!" He jabs a middle finger at the ceiling.

A guy who reads books and hates on bitchy, middle-aged women. My new *bufu* or *bff* or whatever they call it these days.

We review the schedule. I'm performing seven shows. According to Sea Bass, my first show times are good: Wednesday at seven P.M., Thursday at nine, Friday at ten, Saturday at seven. And then bad: Monday at ten, Wednesday at four, Friday at noon.

"Every year, the festival crams in more performers," Sea Bass says. "They collect more entry fees and give performers shittier and shittier show times. And the audiences aren't getting any bigger. It sucks for you."

"Yeah, everyone keeps telling me that," I say, thinking, no filter and a bad attitude. I like that in a coworker.

I hand him a copy of my script. "This is my first big fringe festival, so I only have a few lighting cues: 'on' at the start and 'off' at the end and a few spotlights in between. Since you're the expert, any suggestions appreciated."

"Get changed. We'll see how she goes there, eh?"

In the green room, I get into my get-up of a purple aloha shirt, olive Bermuda shorts, and black flipflops.

I notice a new varicose vein and consider rethinking the shorts. Fuck it.

Out on the black floor tiles, my stage, I set up my props: in the right-front corner, my backpack; in the left, a book hand-scrawled with the title *The Loneliest Planet: A Handbook for the Chronically Single*. I add two folding chairs and place them side by side. One chair is for me as the narrator, the other for the imaginary women I battle during the show: ex-girlfriends, new girlfriends, bar girls. I'm planning to add Jackie to a future show. Under my chair, I place a pair of oversized black reading glasses for channeling an imaginary shrink based on Dr. Moody.

Sea Bass is back at his table behind the seats. A jazz-blue light reflects off his glasses, but the rest of him is in the dark. I hear a series of clicks. The stage lights dim, then brighten, turn blue, then red.

The Barenaked Ladies blasts over the sound system.

"Did you know these guys are Canucks?" Sea Bass shouts from the dark.

"Didn't know that," I shout back.

Later, when a song called "Be My Yoko Ono" comes on, I don't think of Jackie. Not even twice.

"OK, ready," I say after five minutes of positioning, and then repositioning my props.

"For your opening, do you want a wash?" Keys click, the whole stage lights up.

"Or this?" *Click-click*. My corner of the stage gradually lightens.

"The second one," I say.

"OK, run your show."

I dive in. Words, phrases, and gestures materialize when they're supposed to. I clip along, developing a rhythm.

Sea Bass stops me and tries some lighting configurations: one is bluer, one is redder.

"Which does the artist prefer?" he asks.

"The artist defers to your good judgment."

He futzes. I wait.

"Continue," he says.

I restart for two minutes. Then he stops me. This pattern continues. He has me repeat the same line over and over until he has the effects he wants. Red light for romantic scenes. A halo glow for a lonely scene. A spotlight for scenes in which the Dr. Moody character offers theories on why the narrator is still single: the fish theory, the valency theory, and other medical excuses.

An hour later, we've completed only fifteen minutes of my show.

"There's a note in your script that calls for an overhead spotlight to show you're being interrogated by a South African police officer," Sea Bass says.

"Yeah, the narrator meets a twenty-one-year-old girl in a bar. She's invited herself back to his hotel. He's not sure whether she's a prostitute or just a girl looking to be wined and dined by a rich Westerner."

"Same diff." Sea Bass says. "We know she's a hooker. You know she's a hooker. She's twenty-one, and you're what? Forty-five?"

Something like that.

"Anyway," I say, "the next scene is in a club in Cambodia. A bar girl sits next to the narrator and starts rubbing his knee and within minutes says, 'Me go hotel you.'"

"Do you mind me asking, how much of this play is true?"

"I'd say about twelve percent."

"Is that a firm estimate?"

"You ask a lot of questions. Aren't we running out of rehearsal time?"

"There's no one scheduled after you. We got all night."

"I thought it was the South African police interrogating me not Sebastian Doo-Right of the Moosefin Mounties."

I get a blast of spotlight. Through closed eyes, I see lightning and thunderbolts that resemble blood vessels.

"Too much, wise guy," I say.

Click-click.

We've now been at it for two hours and we're only halfway through my show. I'm cranky. I'm hungry. I start to forget lines, lose my place, my rhythm. The assembly line in my mind gets all janked up. I have to call out to Sea Bass, "Next line?"

He's starting to remind me of Joey, another nitpicker. Who cares if the light is pink or red? Is this more about Sea Bass than my show? What's with these theater people?

We finally wrap up after three-and-a-half hours. Sea Bass turns up the house lights. I stow my props and meet him at his desk, where I can now see the titles of his books: *Bangkok 8; No Money, No Honey;* and *Off the Rails in Phnom Penh: Into the Dark Heart of Guns, Girls, and Ganja.*

"A learned man," I say. "Hoping to meet a nice girl to bring home to mom?"

"Me and the boys are going on holiday to Southeast Asia. When I heard about your show, I asked to be the tech."

"Want to go for a beer?" I ask.

"Nah, but thanks, anyway. I'm meeting a friend."

We walk out of my theater together and are standing outside the lactation suite when the door opens. Amanda emerges with her blouse mussed and the baby asleep on her shoulder.

"Hey," says Sea Bass, grinning.

She gives us the once-over and goes upstairs to the lobby.

"See you tomorrow night," I say to Sea Bass and follow her.

Upstairs, the lobby is crammed with people lined up to buy tickets, drinks, moose meatball subs, and deep-fried nonsense.

The walls, bare three hours ago, are now covered with four-color, movie-caliber posters promoting various shows.

I have no posters because I didn't want to spend two dollars apiece for them.

I consider calling Joey. I consider finding a graphic designer in Moosefin. I consider creating something simple in Microsoft Word, which would still cost two dollars apiece to print. I transfer the problem to the too-hard pile and get in line for Canadian Tex-Mex.

Jiggy Pop approaches the line with a tray of chocolate stuff. He ramps up the volume:

"Introducing *Jiggy Pop on the Hershey Highway*, folks. Five-Stars at the Edmonton Fringe festival, opening tomorrow night in Moosefin. That's right. The same guys who brought you *Onion Dip*.

"Brown-eyed brownies anyone? Rabbit Milk Duds? M-m-m. Just like Bugs Bunny used to make."

He hands out chocolates on little plates printed with his show schedule, website address, and reviews of *Onion Dip* and other fringe shows he's done: Four stars, Edinburgh. Five Stars, Winnipeg. Five Stars, Washington D.C.

I take one.

At the food window, I order a taco in a bag. The bag features an ad for Jiggy Pop and another for Harvey Feldman.

In my pocket, I finger a stack of show postcards, the DIY specials I created with Word, card stock, and my inkjet printer. The cards feature my photo and a show description on one side, and my show times and venue on the other.

Four guys with musical instruments swoop in singing a song from their show, *You've Got Male*. They hand out postcards shaped like penises topped with steel wool for pubic hair.

Fifteen feet above, a guy is sitting on a bicycle, balanced on top of a pole, juggling squirrel-shaped puppets. He flings the puppets into the crowd and then balances upside down with one hand on the bicycle seat. A few feet away, Amanda is holding the baby in one arm and handing out cards with the other. The baby's onesie advertises her show, *Dairy Queen: A Mammary Musical*.

I take one of her cards. On the flip side, is the juggler's show, *High-Wire Homo*. His credentials: Cirque de Soleil, Ringling Brothers, Hollywood stuntman."

Did I mention I'm fucked?

I spot a guy standing alone and slap a postcard in his hand.

"Thanks," he says and hands me one of his.

I hand another to a couple in line for wild game poutine. They say, "*Merci*" and "No *anglais*."

I start dispensing cards willy-nilly to people on the food line, the drink line, the ticket line. I give out forty cards in five minutes. At twenty cents a card, that's eight bucks' worth.

I hear someone calling my name. "Burns!"

I turn. Feldman.

"I've been watching you, man. Handing out postcards like that is useless. You gotta talk to people. You gotta have some kind of shtick. Observe."

He drags me over to a group of people eating, drinking, and talking. He cuts in. "Hey there. I'm Woody as in Allen." He pauses and points to my shaved head. "And this is Bruce Willis. Welcome to Moosefin."

Laughter.

Feldman grabs several of my postcards and starts passing them out. "This is a must-see show. It's to *Die Hard* for. First show tomorrow night, downstairs. Only a few tickets left."

He approaches another group. Same routine. A woman asks for a photo of me with her little boy. I lean down and put my face next to the kid's, smiling like someone who isn't repulsed by children.

"The chronic single with child," Feldman says.

Laughter.

"Email us the photo so we can post it," Feldman says, giving her one of my postcards. "First show tomorrow night. A few tickets left."

Feldman shoves the remaining cards in my hand. "Your turn, grasshopper."

Fifteen minutes later, I rejoin Feldman, who is checking his ticket sales.

"Almost sold out," he says. "Now we're talking."

I check mine: Ten sold. I'll take it.

"You really know your shit," I say.

"I should. I've been doing the circuit for years. Like anything else, do it enough and you learn the angles."

"So how did everyone get their posters up here and all over town?" I ask. "There was nothing yesterday."

"Most people bring their own staff or hire locals."

"But what if I'm a cheap-wad Jew and all I've got are these?" I fan out my remaining four-by-five-inch postcards.

"Not a problem. Give them up."

He walks over to a wall with some open space, counts out three cards, and arranges them in a row.

"Lend a hand."

As I hold the cards to the wall, he pulls out some clear tape from his pocket and tapes the cards in place, then arranges three more below. We repeat this one more time until the cards are three wide by three deep. He steps back. "Voilà. A mini poster. You're in business."

"Feldman, I owe you big."

"All in due time, boychick," he says. "Now listen to Papa Feldman. Tomorrow night, hit the lines at the best-selling shows. Flyer my line. Put on something goofy. Get in character. Tell people something, anything. Say you're taking a trip around the world looking for the woman of your dreams, but you're not having any luck. Ask them for advice."

Jiggy Pop walks by. Feldman grabs him. "Hey, Jig. This is Burns, a fellow U of Asser. Good guy."

Jiggy offers a flaccid left hand and moves on.

Feldman gives my cheek a little tweak. "OK, my man, gotta split."

I recheck my ticket sales: fifteen.

A couple eating cheese curds from a Styrofoam plate stops next to me.

I clear my throat. "Greetings folks, I'm Bruce Willis and I'd like to recommend *The Chronic Single's Handbook*. Tomorrow evening in the Belly theater of the Beast at seven P.M. Don't be late, now."

They laugh, take a card, and move on, dropping one of Feldman's postcards in the process. I pick it up: Degrees in theater and English literature; wrote a book on Jewish comedy; taught high school theater; wrote a one-man show called *Old Shul* about Sid Caesar, Jack Benny, and George Burns; then *Old Shul II* about Don Rickles, Jerry Lewis, and Mel Brooks, and *Old Shul III*. Five years ago, he retired from teaching, put all his belongings in storage, and now he lives on the road lecturing and performing. He's done a hundred fringe festivals in North America, the UK, and Australia, and has been written up in *The New York Times*, *The Washington Post*, and the *Chicago Tribune*.

My mind goes blank. I put his card in my pocket and bike home.

The next morning, I have two texts.
One from Feldman:
Break a few tonight. Meet later at onion cake truck, chazzerai for dinner. Me and some performers seeing Eddie Izzard, a stand-up from the UK. Got you a ticket.

I text back:
Thanks. I'm in.

And one from Jackie:
An audio clip of her singing "Turning Japanese," with her own lyrics featuring the phrases: "never-married headcase," "waffling, clueless liar," and "the loner who dies alone."

I delete it.

That night at the Rod and Gun Club, I park my bike at the bent bike-rack under the pinhole gaze of the two juvies. They may be down-and-out but they dress *au courant*: high-water pants, low-ankle socks, Achilles tattoos, and large-screen iPhones.

"Donation for the cause?" the guy says, sliding a pair of Dr. Dre's off his ears. I shrug to indicate I'm all out, but several Micronesian-sized Loonies clang in my pocket. Busted.

"How's the festival going?" he asks.

"My first show is tonight," I say.

"I'll rub the genie for luck." He caresses his girlfriend's bubbly hindquarters.

I fork over a Loonie.

The Rod and Gun lobby is sprinkled with people buying tickets. A group of old ladies in floral dresses and straw fedoras are sipping Kokanees by the Beast theater door. *Jiggy Pop*, is the next show. I pretend to study the Jiggy poster on the wall and eavesdrop.

"Herb and I love their earlier work," says one lady.

"I thought 'Onion Dip' was very daring," says another.

"Their writing has matured," says a third. "It's sharper, more astringent. And did you try their onion dip? It had quite a kick."

A few people are lined up outside my theater for my seven P.M. show. I knock on the door. Two men with salt and pepper crew cuts and paisley cardigans whisper, "He must be the performer. He really *does* look like Bruce Willis."

The door opens. I turn back and say, "See you soon."

Inside, a woman about the size and shape of Morag is seated by the door, a spool of tickets, a tablet computer, and a cashbox on the table in front of her. "How are my sales?" I ask her.

"Is your app not working?" she asks.

"Thought I'd double-check with you."

"We've got what the app's got."

She also has Morag's cheery demeanor.

Sea Bass is seated at his plywood table, and for a change, the Barenaked Ladies is on the sound system.

"How's it?" he asks.

"So far, so good" I say. "Twenty-two presales."

Sea Bass and I go about our business. I pop the first of three Ricola drops, arrange the props on my little stage, and hit the head for a piss. Then, for a change, I hit it for another piss.

In the mirror, I notice a small swelling under my eye. A stye? Did I catch something from the moose puppet?

Sea Bass sticks his head in as I'm washing up. "Five minutes to house," he says. "Did you give the front-of-house gash your show programs?"

"The short, nasty one?"

"Yeah, that's The Rag's cousin, AKA, Do-Rag."

"Will do. Thanks, dude," I say.

From my backpack, I take a stack of my self-published programs and pause before Do-Rag. Eventually, she removes her earphones.

"Could you pass these out to people when they come in?" I ask.

She puts on her earphones. "I'll see what I can do."

In the green room, I do some voice exercises.

Meeee. Maaay. Myyyyy. Moooo.

Meet my mom at the movies.

My mouse and monkey wear mini-mittens

Meeee. Maaay ...

Sea Bass comes back stage: "OK to open the house?"

"Yeah, sure. How's the audience look?"

"Not bad for a first show. About twenty-five outside and a few more presales that haven't shown up yet. Also, you got a reviewer. A chiquita from *Moosefin LGBTQ* online. They like edgy stuff."

After he leaves, I hear the shuffling noises of the audience taking their seats. Joey says if you can hear discrete conversations, it's going to be a small crowd. If it's a drone of white noise, then you've got more than twenty. I pick out some words and phrases about politics and food.

Is Joey wrong for a change?

The lights go down. A spotlight appears on the stage illuminating Do-Rag.

"Welcome to the Twenty-First annual Moosefin International Fringe Theatre Festival," she says. "We'd like to acknowledge that we are that we are on Treaty Six land and thank the First Nations peoples who were here long before us. With this treaty, we extend our hands and hearts in peace and friendship."

From the back of the room, someone who sounds like Sea Bass, groans.

Do-Rag indicates the emergency exits and asks people to shut off their phones. She mentions a tip jar to support the fringe. She mentions everything but my show.

My skin starts to tingle, my throat feels like there's a Loonie stuck in it, and now I have to take a shit. I hate performing. Why do I do this?

Because I am an artist and need to express myself, to share my deepest feelings, to connect, give back, enter that place where I vanish into the moment. On that stage, I am in service to the universe, to the audience. I help people to remember and to forget. I embody the human condition.

What horseshit.

I want to be worshipped, feared, the biggest shlong in the room. I want to be God, Jesus, Colonel Kurtz, and Ron Jeremy.

I want to be recognized, idolized, and begged, "Can my wife please lick your balls?" I will never again have to fabricate on an *OKCupid* profile.

These people paid to see me. They are my fans, my lemmings, my fish, my punks. This is my space: Come in, sit down, and shut the fuck up. I'm Kanye West, Sid Vicious, Dirty Harry.

People will line up to buy my books, to buy me drinks, to be my subjects.

Do-Rag exits stage right. The spotlight goes out.

When I went bungee jumping in South Africa, I stood there, frozen. I had to be pushed off the jump platform. I feel an imaginary shove onto the stage. The lights come up. Sea Bass is out there somewhere. He has my back.

I hold an empty beer can for a prop in one hand and, with the other, reach for something in space, and begin.

"It's a spring morning in Boston and I'm standing in front of my medicine cabinet."

I pretend to examine some pill vials and then the beer can.

"Vicodin, Ambien, or ... Heineken?"

A few titters from the audience.

"What do newly unemployed people have for breakfast?"

Full laughter.

And too soon, it's over.

"Thank you all for coming," I say to the audience. "Hope you enjoyed it. The show is based on a novel that was published last year. If you're interested, only twenty dollars Canadian."

Thirty or so people shuffle out of the theater. One remains.

High Doc Martens, high calf muscles, a sleeveless down sweater.

"Samantha from *MoosefinLGBTQ* online," she says. "Mind if I ask you a few questions?"

"Sure."

Firm handshake for a small girl. Jiggy Pop could learn from her.

"I liked your show," she says.

"Thank you." We exchange smiles.

"So, it's based on a novel that was inspired by actual events?"

"A typical novel is eight hours of material. I hired a theater director who boiled it down to a one-hour, one-man show."

"Cool. How much of the show was inspired by actual events?"

"About twelve percent."

"Which twelve?"

"I got laid off from my job, took a trip around the world, and had a rotten time."

"Any other actual events?"

"Um, eh, yeah, no."

"What do you think of Donald Trump?"

"Um, eh, yeah, no. I follow sports not politics."

"Help me out here, bro."

"He and I are both from New York, so I can't really be objective."

"New York? The program says you're from Boston?"

"I grew up in New York and live in Boston now."

"Boston is supposed to be a racist town. What's your experience?"

"I'm Jewish. I haven't had any problems."

She looks at my shoes, pants, and then my bald head. Her mouth presses tight as she scribbles into her reporter's notebook. She flips to a new page. My armpits feel damp.

"I recently got dumped by an Asian woman," I say. "Does that count for anything?"

"*Quelle* bummer. So, in real life, you took a trip around the world and had a rotten time. Apparently, you had a good time in Cambodia. Did you really pay for a hand job?"

While I look at her Doc Martens for an answer, Samantha launches a follow-up question. "Only one?"

Next thing I know, I'm seated next to Feldman upstairs in the Beast theater for Eddie Izzard's show, two-hundred seats, all full. Feldman bought me a deep-fried dough-thingy, one of Moosefin's famous green onion cakes. A wax paper slick seeps and spreads. We wipe our hands on the seats.

Jiggy Pop takes the saved seat next to me. He and I exchange slippery left-handed handshakes. When Eddie Izzard comes on stage, Jiggy moves to the other end of the row. Midway through the show, Feldman says that he's taking off. I watch him move down two rows to sit with a woman I don't recognize. Eddie Izzard is brilliant.

The next morning there are no emails from Feldman or Abe or Lenny or even Jackie. I check the ticket sales for today. Only two.

I inventory my clothes: One T-shirt, one sock, and one pair of underwear pass the sniff test. Jackie claimed she could wear one pair of thong underwear for six days. She'd rotate a different triangle corner to go between her legs each day, flip it over, and repeat. Gross pig. What did I ever see in her?

The house is quiet as in dead. No *Maude* reruns, no Be Good Tanyas, no Barclay or Allistair. Carmine isn't even outside.

My phone vibrates with a text from Feldman.
Congrats on the review.

> *Review?*

Here's the link. Also, drinks tonight at 10:30, beer garden.

It isn't a question.

> *I'll be there. Thanks for invite.*

Then I read the review of my show.
Had the audience laughing at all the right times.
Great for the chronically single and very married alike.
Highly recommended
Four stars out of five

I read the reviews of other shows.
Jiggy Pop: *Five Stars*
Feldman: *Five Stars*
Allistair and Barclay's show: *Two stars*

The front door slams. Allistair's yells, "Fucking cunts." The fridge door opens. The *kssst* of a bottle being opened. The front door slams again. Outside, I watch the Trans Am peels out. Should *schadenfreude* be italicized?

I post my review online. When I look again, Abe, Joey, Lenny, and a few others have liked it.

I head to the kitchen where the groceries I bought yesterday are clumped in a corner on the counter: three cans of sardines and a box of bran cereal. I also have a bag of salad and a quart of low-fat yogurt in the fridge to counteract all the crap I've been eating.

After breakfast, I still have only two tickets sold and Carmine isn't where he's supposed to be.

My phone vibrates.

Someone I don't care to name has texted me a link to a chirpy news story about Connie Chung and Maury Povich.

Delete.

Outside the Rod and Gun Club that night, the juvies are at their post. At least someone is where they're supposed to be today.

The girl is wearing a wool cap with a little pair of knit moose antlers protruding and a jean jacket opened to a pure collar bone. Not a bra strap in sight. Her boyfriend is standing behind her, hands on her shoulders.

I hand him a Loonie. "Keep up the good work," I say.

"I'll rub the genie for you." His hands slide down her jean jacket into her breast pockets. She inhales. I inhale.

Inside, I get to work handing out postcards.

"Hi, I'm Bruce, as in Willis. Come see adult situations, adult language, and more adult situations, including a visit to a body spa named The Curious Finger."

People seem entertained. I start to enjoy myself.

A decent line forms outside my theater, including a few of the old ladies who saw Jiggy Pop yesterday and a guy wearing a cowboy hat with dozens of fringe show tickets sticking out of his hat band like feathers. He has owly glasses, a T-shirt that says "Got My Fringe On," and a belly the size of a beer keg. I give everyone a little salute as I enter the theater.

The Barenaked Ladies is blasting for a change. Do-Rag and two other women are at the ticket table looking put upon. I extract a stack of programs from my shoulder bag and hand them over, smiling. "How you doing tonight?"

Do-Rag ignores me and yells into the darkened theater. "Will you turn that crap down?"

The music gets louder.

"I'll take care of it." I excuse myself and return to the lobby.

I reenter with a paper bag under my arm, nod to Do-Rag, and go inside.

Sea Bass is fiddling with his console. "Fuck her," he says.

"Look, I know they're a-holes but the music is a little loud, even for me. And dude, I cannot afford to be a diva this early in my run."

I hand him a six-pack of Mountain Dew.

He cracks one open and turns the music down a little.

"So, I read the review. You crushed it," he says. "It's a start. Tonight, you got reviewers from *The Moosefin Star Herald* and *TheatreMoosefin*. Should be a good house. My crystal ball says thirty to thirty-five."

I think: Then why does my app say only two? but say nothing. I change, set up the stage, take a piss, and then take two more for luck.

Sea Bass's head appears in the green room doorway. "OK to open the house?"

"Sure."

I hear the drone of a good-sized audience entering the theater. Then silence as Do-Rag gives her speech with no mention of my show.

Lights down, then up, me on stage, beer can prop in one hand, imaginary medicine vials in the other. As I'm saying my opening lines, I think about pure collar bones and bubbly hindquarters.

The audience laughs at something I say and then laughs again. I sit, stand, move across the stage, upstage, downstage. Lights change to red, blue, green, and back to white. I check the clock in the back of the theater. Forty minutes have elapsed.

The line about fishy female genitalia is coming up. I imagine the old ladies cringing. But Joey said to sell it, swing for Lansdowne Street.

And so I do. "Your twat stinks so bad, seagulls follow you home."

An old lady in the second row wearing a straw fedora *does* cringe. The audience goes quiet. I go quiet. We're all waiting for something.

Croaking laughter emanates from the rear of the theater. It ripples through the audience. Even the old lady laughs.

Ten minutes later, it's over. There's some applause and, after delivering the pitch for my book, one of the old ladies comes up to me.

I prepare for the worst.

"You've got some balls," she says. "How much for your books?"

She buys two.

A woman with toned arms steps forward, hand-in-hand with a guy with a full head of hair.

"We loved your show," she says. "Incorrect. Funny. Courageous."

They introduce themselves as Marnie and Oscar.

Marnie has a black bra strap racing down her back.

They buy two books, exchange a look, and then say, "Want to meet us in the beer garden for a drink?"

"Sure. Be there in a few."

The theater empties, but no reviewer materializes.

On my way out, I stop by the console, "Hey, Sea Bass.

Thanks for getting the laughing going when all seemed lost. I owe you."

"No worries. Always happy to help a bro."

I do a lap around the beer garden, passing the food carts, the drink ticket lines, a cop eating pierogies, and tables of old ladies sipping draft beer out of plastic cups. No sign of Oscar and Marnie.

Feldman is at a table with other performers. His hair is tucked under a black top hat. Tight white T-shirt, leather vest. A young woman I don't recognize is on his lap, feeding him puffs off a cigarette.

He waves me over. "Here's my boy. How about a beer?" The girl on his lap gives me an unreadable look, stands, and leaves.

I pull up a chair and squeeze in. Jiggy is sitting across the table wearing a shirt printed with fake abs — Iggy Pop forty years ago. Trump from the musical still has his flying-wing hairpiece on, a blue suit jacket, and a pink tie flopped down to the ground between sequined flipflops and toenails painted red, white, and blue.

Feldman slings an arm across the back of my chair. "Hear, hear, fellow weirdos, this is Randall Burns of *The Chronic Single's Handbook* — MoosefinLGBTQ is a big fan."

A round of polite applause. A waitress hands me a sixteen-ounce can of Alexander Keith's IPA, Canada's good stuff. Feldman pays and leans over to say he has something to do and that he'll be back in ten minutes. He gives my thigh a friendly squeeze and leaves me sitting next to a younger guy who looks vaguely familiar.

"Bris," the guy says. "We met at Allistair's *Drag Races* party the other night." We exchange a normal handshake. "You were a good sport. How are your shows going?"

"Two shows down; audiences pretty good," I say. "How about you?"

"Not bad. Eighty yesterday. Sold out for tomorrow. Good

reviews from *The Herald* and *TheatreMoosefin*. I think I'm all set."

"They were supposedly at my show tonight," I say. "But no one came up to interview me."

"Sometimes reviewers have to rush off to other shows. I wouldn't worry about it."

Bris introduces me to someone to his left, then stands, and takes off. This sequence repeats several times over the next half hour: Someone asks how my show is going, I ask the same, they start looking over my shoulder, introduce me to someone else, and leave. Am I getting the old hand off? Is it me? Or is this just theater?

Marnie and Oscar finally appear. I stand to greet them and go to shake Oscar's hand as Marnie is extending hers to me. We eventually get the handshakes sorted out.

"Let me get you another Keith's," Oscar says, leaving for the bar. Marnie and I remain standing.

"We loved your show," she says to me. "Really impressed with your writing."

"Thanks for the kind words," I say. "Are you local?"

"No, we're from Edmonton."

Oscar returns with three Alexander Keiths.

We toast the Moosefin fringe festival.

I notice a manila envelope protruding from Marnie's handbag.

"Are you a writer?" I ask.

Marnie glances at her feet, her lambswool flipflops, and then produces the envelope. "We were wondering if you might have time to look at our script."

I feel flattered, then put upon.

"What's it about?" I ask.

She gives me a pitch about a sumo wrestler with a peanut allergy, secret yogic texts, undead steam punks, a Roman Catholic homunculus, a man-eating tree, and a jubokko or a jikininki or something that begins with the letter "j."

"Sounds like middle-grade fantasy," I say.

"Yes!" Marnie's says. A black bra strap emerges from her blouse.

"Here's the issue," I say. "Fantasy is not really my thing. Why don't you give me your card and, if I can recommend someone, I'll drop you a note?"

"That would be great," Marnie says. She places the envelope back in her purse.

There's a moment of silence for the manuscript.

"Well, we should be going," she says eventually. "Hope you enjoy your stay in Moosefin."

"Let's keep in touch," Oscar adds.

As we're shaking hands, Marnie looks over my shoulder and says, "Look, Oscar, there's Auntie Morag. Let's go say hi."

Feldman returns as the beer garden is closing, and then it's only me, him, Trump, Jiggy, and Bris, who is carrying a bag of cold onion cakes.

As we exit, a guy from a food truck offers us a leftover pizza.

We spill out onto the darkened street.

"Leftovers are for closers," says Jiggy.

Bris cuts in: "*My Left Foot*, Daniel Day Lewis. *Left to Die*, Barbara Hershey."

Trump adds, with a phlegmy German accent: "*Left Luggage*, Jeroen Krabbe, Isabella Rossellini."

I can't think of anything clever, so I eat a slice of pizza I don't really want. We pause in front of a church where spotlights cast shadows on the stone façade.

Jiggy wiggles his ass, and then starts making hand puppets. First a bear, followed by a moose. He starts marching zombie-like with his fingers outstretched. "*Nosferatu*," Bris yells.

Feldman and I stand watching, shoulder-to-shoulder. Bris and Trump start jousting with their arms, their shadow lances stabbing through each other's bodies as Jiggy's shadow-Nosferatu approaches from the side.

Abruptly, I feel Feldman's hand on the back of my head, pulling me toward him. Then his lips on mine and an oversized tongue enters my mouth.

I taste onion.

I taste beer.

I pull away.

Is this some kind of improv scene gone off the rails?

Did I just get punked, poop-shanked, or some other prison slang I don't know the meaning of?

I feel myself fading in and out, and have to remember to breathe.

"What the fuck was that?" I say.

Feldman is watching the others again. He smiles without turning. "It just seemed right."

I stare at his profile.

Silence.

Finally, I say, "I … Anyway, I gotta get going. Early day tomorrow." It sounds lame even to my ears.

Feldman turns to me. "Sure. Sleep tight."

Jiggy is riding Bris piggyback, his rhinestone sneakers bouncing in the air. I hear Feldman yell, "*Top Gun,* bitches!"

Back at the wheelchair rack, my bike and locks are still intact, but the lights are gone again. A half hour later, I find myself back at Barclay's with no idea how I got there.

I wake the next morning with a headache and a sour taste in mouth. No apology text from Feldman. Ticket sales for tonight's ten P.M. show: zero.

I check *HatTrick*. A fifty-year-old woman named Pam appears in my feed. She is long and blonde in what looks like size four jeans.

Her profile:

If we go out and you don't look like your photo, you're buying me drinks until you do.

I immediately invite her for drinks.

She immediately answers:

A show about massage parlors and curious fingers? I'm in! Late tonight at beer garden?

I respond:

Deal!

I text Barclay about using the washing machine. He texts back:

Help yourself. Sorry I haven't been around much. And sorry about the review, know the feeling.

Review?

I read it, and then dial Joey, "Call me!"

I hang up and immediately call two more times, leaving the same message. This is our three-call code for an emergency. I pace my room watching clips from the movie *Betty Blue*, which fails to cheer me up. My phone buzzes on the tenth lap.

"OK. What happened?" he asks.

I can't bring myself to tell him about Feldman.

"I just got a two-star review."

"What did you get on your first review?"

"Four, but that was from a puny publication, *MoosefinLGBTQ*."

"So what? It's your first bad review, a flesh wound."

"My roommate got two-stars and I haven't seen him since."

"Look, Burns. Ignore them when they love you, ignore them when they hate you. On your world trip, you wanted to come home after two weeks. Suck it up. You've got a job to do."

"Look Joey, this is no time for platitudes. I have five more shows here."

"OK. Read me the worst stuff."

And so I do:

"Misogynistic bullshit"

"Diary of a sex tourist"

"Nothing is off limits: navel secretions, eye cheese, toe cheese, cum shots"

"Audience was clearly uncomfortable"

"Wouldn't leave him alone with my six-year-old daughter"

"Bruce Willis? Ha!"

"An hour of my life I'll never get back."

"Perfect!" Joey says. "Post that your show is controversial and include a few of the bad quotes with a bunch of good ones from the first review. By perseverance, the snail reaches the ark. Go get 'em, Burns." He hangs up.

After posting as Joey suggested, I throw a load into the washer without sorting whites and colors. Then, I wipe down every surface in the bathroom with Lysol and take a long shower using my roommates' loofah to scrub off Feldman. When I brush my teeth, I take an extra minute to brush my tongue.

After my clothes are washed and dried, I dress in my goofiest outfit: a wide-brim sun hat, a travel wallet around my neck, cargo shorts, black knee socks, and black dress shoes. Yeah, this was Feldman's idea. Yeah, I'm a fucking patsy.

I call Joey again and he answers on the first ring.

"What now?"

"Remember I told you about that guy, Feldman? The New York Jew who knows everyone and is like the mayor of the Moosefin fringe?"

"Yeah?"

I take a deep breath. "The little shit-weasel kissed me on the mouth last night. I mean tongue and all."

Joey exhales loudly into a mutual silence.

"Wow," he says. "OK, look. I deal with this crap all the time. It's theater, Burns. I'm not telling you to suck it up but you got to figure this out. You can't sabotage your run over some little pecker's smooch. You've got a show tonight."

"Oh, and Jackie started texting."

"Enough Burns. Go hand out some fucking postcards!"

Over a breakfast of bran flakes and Tootsie Rolls, I notice that Carmine has returned to his post.

When I get to the Rod and Gun Club, the juvies are at their post.

"Do you two have names?" I ask.

The boy looks up momentarily surprised. "I'm Spooner. And she's Chloe."

I hand over two Loonies. "Thanks for watching my bike."

Spooner grins. Chloe just looks sullen.

The lobby is packed with prey buying tickets. Performers who got good reviews have taped their star ratings to their posters on the wall. No sign of Feldman, Jiggy, or anyone else from last night.

I hit a group of middle-aged women.

"Greetings, ladies, your fringe won't be complete until you see *The Chronic Single's Handbook*, the personal journey of *Eat, Pray, Love* with the sexual frustration of *Portnoy's Complaint*. Twice your daily requirement for adult situations."

They take two cards. I move on.

I work the room for half an hour and manage to part with twenty cards and even get some valuable advice from two older women who've had their share of Kokanees before three in the afternoon.

The smaller woman nudges the travel wallet around my neck. "Got much cash in there, young fella?"

Next, she considers my black lace-up shoes, black socks, and sunhat the size of a snow saucer and says, "I think you need a woman to dress you, honey."

"How about you two?"

They take a card.

Every time I unload one, I feel lighter.

While leaning on the wall next to my makeshift poster, a trio of twenty-somethings pass by. I point to the poster. "I heard this is an excellent show."

They look at the poster, then at me, laugh, and take three postcards.

Later, I feel compelled to see Feldman's show and sit in the back row. He naturally gets a standing ovation from a full house. After the applause dies down, he says, "If you enjoyed the show, please tell your friends. If you hated it, tell your enemies. I'll be up here shamelessly flogging my CDs and chapbooks. Buying from me is the most direct way to support the arts because you know the taxman won't see a penny of it. Have a great evening."

The little putz is a pro.

As I'm heading back to the lobby, my phone buzzes. Joey has sent an article about Julie Andrews, Rodney Dangerfield, and everyone else who had a rocky start but stuck it out. He includes a quote from Robert Strauss, whoever he is. "Success is a little like wrestling a gorilla. You don't give up when you're tired. You give up when the gorilla is tired."

Delete.

My phone buzzes again with a text from Feldman:

Saw you in the audience. Thanks for coming. Can't return the favor tonight, but am sending Jiggy and Amanda. Beer tent later?

The gorilla calls. I respond:
Sure.

I attempt to see *Walking While Gay in Saudi Arabia*, a comedy, and Barclay and Allistair's show, but they're both sold out. I squeeze into *Pretending Things Are a Cock* and *Sperm Wars*. Both are great. It's now nine thirty. I'm on in half an hour.

Inside my venue, Do-Rag is all smiles and asks for my programs. Something isn't right.

Sea Bass calls out, "You've got some funny fans, dude."

"What?"

"You haven't seen the comments on your post?"

"I've been in shows the last couple of hours. You know silence your phones and all that."

When I turn on my phone, I'm assaulted by three voicemails from Morag.

"A board member was offended by a comment on your post, please remove it."

Then:

"Take down that post, now!"

Then:

"If I have to drag you off the stage, I will!"

I go online to locate the post I made earlier and spot the offending comment.

That reviewer doesn't know her cunt from a skunk's asshole.

The comment is from someone named Action Jackson. The face is grayed-out, but I recognize the economical prose style, the evocative use of metaphor, the B-cups, and the Aaron Hernandez hoodie. Her comment garners fifty responses starting with passive-aggressive remarks from folks claiming to represent the ASPCA, the League of Women Voters, *OBGYN Today*, and the makers of Preparation H, followed by flames from a who's who of goodie-goodies, busy-bodies, low-lifes, crackpots, and shysters: PETA, NOW, LeBron, Bono, Jane Fonda, Greta Thunberg, Al Sharpton, Alan Dershowitz, and of course, Justin Trudeau.

Sea Bass pokes his head into the green room. "Five minutes to house."

While I'm changing into my show outfit, my phone buzzes with a note from *HatTrick* Pam, which gets bumped by another note from Morag:

You are done if that doesn't come down!

I text Morag:
Sorry, been in shows all day. Post is down.

I open Pam's note:
Not going to make it tonight. Still in Corner Brook getting sorted. The Ex cleaned out bank account. Could you wire $300 for plane fare? God Bless.

My phone buzzes again and again:
If you want to see Pam alive, send $5,000
Melt Flab with Keto.
Poly Alberta Speed Dating. Make friends tonight!
Cure ED with black quinoa extract.
HatTrick has terminated this user's account. We apologize for any inconvenience

I toss Feldman, Pam, Bono, LeBron, and Morag into an overflowing too-hard pile, silence my phone, and start my voice exercises.

Sea Bass pops in. "Two minutes to house and looking grim, my friend. No presales, three walk-ups, and two performer comps. This is one of those nights that separates the men from the skunks' assholes."

The show goes all right except that Jiggy and Amanda leave midway through.

On my way out of the theater, I encounter Sea Bass by the Lactation Lounge.

"That was a tough one," he says. "That crap review probably didn't help." He pats my back. "I'm headed to The Bar-Bar later. Buy you a beer?"

"Sure."

I head to the beer garden. Feldman is standing by a table with the performer crowd. He waves me over.

"What's shaking?" he says, keeping his hands to himself.

"Not much."

"Saw the write-up. Ouch." He looks over my shoulder and waves to someone or something. "No worries. We've all been nailed."

I can't tell if he's empathizing or patronizing.

"You know how it is," he continues. "Just gotta shake it off."

I can find nothing to say.

Feldman doesn't seem to notice and says, "What the hell?" He pats my back as he heads off. "You're going to be OK."

I take a seat next to Jiggy. "Thanks for coming to my show," I say. "You doubled the audience."

"That was a little rough," he says. "At what point do you think you lost the audience?"

"Probably the moment I came on stage."

He doesn't laugh and turns to talk to someone else.

At the other end of the table, I notice that Feldman is back and has his arm around the waist of a younger guy I don't recognize. I go to the bar for a beer.

When I return, Feldman, Jiggy, and the younger guy are laughing uncontrollably.

"What was the worst show you ever saw?" Feldman asks, loud enough for everyone in earshot, including me, to hear.

"A show so out-and-out bad it must have been on purpose? To mess with the audience, like an Andy Kaufman show?" Jiggy asks.

"No, just plain bad," Feldman says. "An hour of your life you'll never get back."

The "hour-of-your-life" comment sounds familiar.

They mention some shows I've never heard of. None of this strikes me as funny.

"Yeah, that guy got a measly one-star review." Jiggy says. "I was the only one in the audience, so I couldn't leave!"

Jiggy had no problem leaving my show.

I leave. In the lobby, I buy a moose-meat poutine and some caribou pierogies but pass on the onion cakes.

The Bar-Bar is empty except for two guys watching TV. One has long, grey hair with a matching moustache and goatee, a grey hoodie, black skinny jeans, and black leather sneakers. He's either a gym teacher or an artist. The other guy is wearing a Bengal-striped dress shirt like one I own, cuffed pants, and Reagan-era tasseled loafers. He's either a banker or a banker. I sit two seats from them at the bar. A toilet plunger and tailpipe dangle ominously from the ceiling. The Bar-Bar has been redecorated.

Martin, the lumbersexual bartender from my first day in Moosefin, comes over. "Good evening, Mr. Burns. Ketchup chips with a Kokanee chaser?"

"Trying to watch my figure," I say. "Just the beer, thanks."

A Canadian sports show is on TV. The announcer is an attractive middle-aged Asian woman who looks familiar. I lean over and ask the guy in the tasseled loafers, "Is that Hazel Mae, the Red Sox sportscaster?"

"Certainly is."

"I'm from Boston. We were wondering what happened to her."

"She's Canadian," he says. "You stole her and we stole her back. You here to kidnap her?"

We both laugh.

"No," I say. "Here for the fringe festival."

"Attending or doing?"

"Doing," I say

"I'm Rod from Moosefin," he leans toward me, hand extended.

"Burns from Boston," I say.

"What's your show?" he asks

"It's a comedy about loneliness. *The Chronic Single's Handbook*." I resist adding, "It sucks."

"You've got to be kidding. Did you meet a guy named Geoffrey on a Bermuda cruise a few weeks ago?"

"Yeah," I say. "He was with his wife, Theo. Good guy."

"Geoffrey's in our Gray Guys Facebook group and he posted about your show," Rod says. "Small world, eh?"

He turns to his friend. "Hey, Erik. You're not going to believe it. Look who we got here."

I exchange handshakes with Erik. Turns out Rod *is* a retired banker and Erik *is* an illustrator. Both are divorced with grown kids.

I hand Rod one of my postcards and leave a bunch on the bar.

He reads it. "So, your show is about middle-aged guys, Ambien abuse, and hookers? What do you think, Erik? I'm buying this man a beer."

Rod leans in and lowers his voice. "All right, level with me. What do you think of Trump?"

Before I can answer, he says, "You might as well know I'm a conservative, a big fan of Reagan, Bush, and the old trickle down. I think Trump is the only person who might stand up to the Chinese and their trade policies. The only reason he's sucking up to the Russians is to scare the Chinese. He's smarter than people think."

A Trump supporter, in Canada?

Erik cuts in: "They say that maturity is the ability to hold conflicting opinions in your head at the same time. For example, Rod talks like an idiot, and he's been my best friend for thirty years."

"Right, and Erik is a pussy-grabber from way back," Rod says. "Doing his part to make North America great again."

Erik says, "Fuck off, Rod," and turns back to the TV. I buy the next round. We toast Hazel Mae.

Sea Bass enters with a few friends and stops by to give me a high five. "Glad you made it," he says. He glances at Erik and Rod. "You should check out his show for a good laugh. He's great." Then to me, "See you tomorrow night, Burns." Sea Bass gestures to the bartender to put a beer for me on his tab and sits at a table.

Erik raises a questioning eyebrow.

"That's Sea Bass. My lighting guy. He's all right for a millennial."

More people trickle in. Erik takes my pile of postcards and hands them out. Even the bartender takes one.

Jiggy comes in with Amanda, who is wearing a tight sweater. I wave. They don't. As they pass by, Erik says, "A drink for the lady?"

Without turning, Amanda says, "Fuck off, old man. Go home to your grandkids."

Rod, Erik, and I exchange glances, eyebrows raised to where our hairlines used to be.

That night, I barely sleep and my stomach feels like shit in the morning. On the way to the bathroom, I find a rabbit blivit on the floor. Then I notice that my big toe feels sore and, upon closer inspection, has a purple tinge. The rest of the morning is a blur of cramps, runs, and Pepto-Bismol. I call 800 Ask-The-Nurse. The woman who answers says it's unlikely I caught black plague from a rabbit, a moose puppet, wild game poutine, a shower faucet, or a light switch, but I should visit an ER if things get worse.

I wash my hands, sheets, clothes, bedroom floor, the doorknobs, assorted surfaces in the bathroom, and then my hands again. On the bright side: I've sold thirty tickets and don't think about Jackie or Feldman.

I arrive at the theater a half hour before my seven P.M. show. Do-Rag and Sea Bass are bickering. This is starting to feel like any other middle-management job. I send Sea Bass inside and hand Do-Rag my programs. She dons her headphones and ignores me.

As I'm pacing around backstage, a message from Jackie

comes in. No text, just the one happy photo from our cruise, a selfie of us in surgeons' masks kissing in our room.

I know what she's doing: She's peeing on me, marking her territory, stringing me along. I'm not interested in being her check-down receiver, part of her bullpen, or her plan B.

Delete.

More cramps ensue. I retire to a stall in the any-sex, all-gender, bias-free washroom. The toilet paper roll is facing the wrong way. I set it right.

The washroom door opens. From between the stall panels, I see hands fluffing a blonde head of hair. Someone who identifies as a woman. She leans in to the mirror, pulls something from her bag, and dabs her throat.

I catch her scent. I catch mine. A courtesy flush for the lady? I retract my feet and stifle a sneeze.

"Wow," the fluffer says. "Who sliced the *fromage*?"

Nowhere to run.

"A little of the old Montezuma's poutine, hey?" she asks.

Nowhere to hide.

"Whoever you are, no worries, we've all been there."

I hear the door close.

Back in the green room, Sea Bass pops in. "Five minutes to house. Looks like forty people, your best night yet. Oh, and one suggestion: When you're pitching your book, spread a few across the stage and hold one up in your hand." He pauses and sniffs. "Dude, what did you have for dinner?"

The show goes smoothly. No cramps, hiccups, or goofs except for a train squealing during the domination scene. When it happens, I pause and shrug for the audience, while holding the imaginary head of a woman to my crotch. I get a few laughs and spot Erik with Rod, who is wearing a red MAGA hat. Even Spooner and Chloe are there, seated in the last row.

And then it's over.

"Thank you all for coming." I say. "And do me a favor —

spread the word. I'm from the U Ass of A and I need all the help I can get."

I hold my novel up. "I also have these puppies waiting for new homes. Only twenty dollars Canadian. Limit ten to a customer."

A dozen or so people come up to congratulate me: Mostly strangers plus Rod, Erik, and two women I don't recognize. One of them is Erik's cousin, Alice. I notice a stripe of cheekbone, the hollow of an eye socket, collar bones like handles. She's wearing a drapey, blousy top that looks like something from the Stevie Nicks collection. The other woman is apparently Erik's girlfriend. I immediately forget her name.

Rod says, "Meet us at the beer garden. We'll get a table."

A soft, round, balding guy trudges up. "My wife died two years ago," he says. "Not sure why but your show made me feel better." He shakes my hand and leaves. He doesn't ask me to read his script. He doesn't ask me for anything.

Next is Chloe who hands me a bouquet of dandelions and doesn't say a word. Spooner waves from the back, and they leave.

I sell five books.

In the beer garden, Erik waves from a table that includes Alice, Erik's girlfriend, and Rod without his MAGA hat. Feldman and company are at a nearby table. I resist looking at them.

Our table is crowded with all the Canadian food groups: gyro thingies locals call donair, pierogies, tacos in a bag, spinach dip, and beer. As I sit, Alice grabs a handful of thick blonde hair, flips it one way, then the other, then back again as if she's casting for something.

After a few toasts and questions about my book, talk turns to Hillary Clinton, Hollywood, Wall Street, and their favorite Canadian show, a sitcom called *Corner Gas*.

After an hour, most of the food and the second round of beer are gone.

"I'm beat," says Rod, standing up. "Don't want to turn into a pumpkin, eh?"

Erik and his girlfriend, whose name I still can't remember, stand and say they're ready to go, too.

"Alice?" Erik asks.

"I think I'll stay a bit," she says, and then turns to me. "Keep me company?"

Rod sticks out a hand. "Keep in touch. I'm counting on Trump to make North America great again."

"We'll do our best," I say.

When they leave, Alice moves into the seat across from me. "I really liked your show," she says.

"Thanks. If you don't mind, let's talk about something else," I say. "Can I get you another double bloody Caesar?"

"*Mais, oui*," she says.

When I return Alice is wearing a green and yellow knit hat with the words, "Edmonton Eskimos" on it. I briefly think of Jackie and her forest of hat trees.

"You follow Canadian football?" I ask.

"No. I'm just a lame Canadian, always cold. I need to find a rich American to buy me a condo in Miami."

I smile. Her blouse is hanging off her shoulder like a hint. A ski hat paired with sheer clothes. Kooky and contradictory.

"By the way, how's the Montezuma's poutine?" she asks.

The washroom fluffer? I smirk and say, "You might want to ask Aunt Fern who's waiting upstairs."

"What?" she says.

"You've got something green between your top front teeth."

"How unflattering." She leans in, lips parted. "Get it for me?"

I flex my biceps, crack my knuckles, flutter my fingers. "There's a price for this procedure," I say.

"Never mind. Canadian insurance doesn't cover overpriced American specialists."

Alice leans back and flicks the piece from her mouth with the tip of a painted fingernail.

"Can I have a look at one of your books?" she asks.

I take one out of my backpack and hand it over. She looks at the front. She looks at the back.

"How much?" she asks.

"For you, only twenty dollars, Canadian."

"That's not much of a deal."

"I'll sign yours with a personal message."

And I do.

"To my Dear Alice:

"My regards to Aunt Fern and the gang."

I draw a little heart and sign my name.

She writes her phone number on a twenty-dollar bill and signs it:

"Alice's Poutine Clean-Up Service"

Back at home, I fall into bed at one and wake at three to the odd sound of groaning and grunting. I roll over and cover my head with a pillow. More grunts.

I finally get up and tiptoe to the living room.

From the hallway, I see the back of a human head that I recognize as Allistair and, in his lap, the Y-shape of a pair of ears. Carmine's ears.

On the TV, two horses are fucking.

Still half asleep, I sit by Allistair and Carmine on the couch. The coffee table is strewn with Tootsie Roll wrappers, empty beer bottles, and a box of Kleenex.

The TV show shifts to hippos fucking, then lions and tigers and bears. There are close-ups of moose cocks, a spiny anteater with a four-headed shlong, a corkscrew pig dong, and lots of reluctant, biting females.

We watch animal porn in silence.

"Can you hold Carmine a minute?" Allistair gets up and goes to the washroom.

Carmine is warm and muscular. I check his coat for fleas. He moves around on my lap, a *lapin* lap dance. I get an erection and think of Alice but not Jackie.

Allistair returns and says, "OK, I'll take him now." I hand Carmine over, wait for my erection to subside, and then say, "Have a good night," and go back to bed.

In the morning, I text Alice and suggest The Bar-Bar for drinks. She responds right away:

I'll pick you up at seven.

That evening I sit on the lawn enjoying the breeze and the freedom of not having to do a show that night. Carmine keeps me company. Alice finally pulls up in a black hatchback. She's only fifteen minutes late. I had expected at least half an hour. Carmine flexes. "Easy boy," I say.

She's wearing peach-colored lipstick. In an exposed ear, a silver, five-pointed star. There's a blue-feather woven into her blonde hair.

"What's with the rabbit?" she asks.

"Long story," I say and leave it at that.

At the Bar-Bar, Alice heads straight to the washroom. I grab two seats at the bar.

"Back again, eh?" asks the bartender. "Hot date with some local talent?"

"One can only hope."

"Impress her with an authentic Canadian drinking experience, the Snakebite: Yukon Jack and lime juice."

Alice returns. I smell vanilla moisturizer, the stuff Jackie uses.

She moves her stool into my personal space. "Hey, Martin," she says to the bartender.

"Oh, hey, Alice."

I feel my forehead wrinkle.

"I went to high school with his mother," Alice says.

Martin turns away to clean some glassware.

"So, how about a Snakebite?" I ask.

"Yukon Jack? You sure know how to treat a girl."

"Stick with me sister, and you'll be farting through silk."

"Do we really want to go there, Mr. Poutine?" She laughs. "Besides, I believe I've heard that line before."

"Robert Mitchum stole it from me."

The shots come and go.

Alice opens her coat revealing a low-cut, white T-shirt and a collarbone crossed by a black band. She hooks the band with two fingers and repeats a line from my show: "She had an exposed bra strap that looked like a ribbon, a gift for the right guy."

More shots come and go.

"So, you take trips around the world, perform at fringe festivals, and then claim you're a starving artist?"

"Yeah, look at me." I point to my waist. "I'm wasting away to nothing here."

She reaches for my stomach and pinches some skin. "You could stand to lose a few pounds."

No boundaries. My kind of woman.

"Been thinking about your show," she says. "A little kinky, hey?"

"I thought it was 'eh'?"

"Some of us in Western Canada prefer 'hey.'"

A couple more shots come and go.

"Now that I've seen your show," she says slurring a little. "And bought your book." She puts a hand on my arm. "I feel like I know you, like I can tell you anything."

Uh, oh.

Sure enough, Alice talks about DUIs, hospitalizations,

shoplifting, assault with a ski pole, bail, armed husbands, more bail, junkie boyfriends, lithium, anxiety disorders, and insomnia.

Moody always said that where most people see red flags, I see a red cape. He also said I have a thing for injured sparrows that eventually bite me in the neck.

Alice stops mid-sentence. "You're not gay, are you?"

I try not to think of Feldman's tongue in my mouth.

"Never mind," Alice says blurrily, shaking her head. "You're not."

She unhitches my watchband.

"So, Mr. Burns. Ever been married?"

"Nope. No kids, no ex-wives, no pets. I don't have the herding gene."

She asks Martin for a double bloody Caesar. I order a beer.

"I made a video," she says, swaying a little, while hauling out her phone. "I want your professional opinion."

We lean into each other to watch on the small screen. First, complete darkness, and then a spotlight revealing a moist, red circle. The camera pulls back, and I can see it's the hole of a jelly donut. The head of a peeled banana enters the frame and prods, pokes, and finally penetrates the red circle. The pale head moves in and out, at first slowly, then persistently, desperately. The red circle expands until, eventually, the donut is splayed open. The banana head collapses beside it covered in red jelly.

The video makes me hard. Then it makes me sad.

Alice grabs my hand. "Let's go, you Yankee pig-dog," she says blurrily, stuffing my watch into my shirt pocket.

She turns to Martin and says, "Put it on my tab, little man."

"Can you drive?" she asks me, weaving. "I'm a bit pissed."

At her place, I go around and open the car door for her.

"I'm impressed that you like rabbits," she says, holding onto my arm for balance. "That's my spirit animal."

Inside, we remove our shoes at the door.

"Make yourself *comftable, comfortbluh.* You know what I mean," she slurs. "Be right back."

I sit on the couch and consider Alice's three full bookcases. I like a woman who reads.

She returns in a few minutes with pin-holed pupils, as I'm examining the spines of her books.

"You could say I'm a spiritual dabbler." She twirls, wobbly. "New Age. Buddhism. Wicca. The whole lot. Keeps me off the streets."

I think of Harriet and *Dark Shadows*.

I think of Jackie for no reason.

Alice reaches for my hand. "Let's go."

Her bedroom smells of burned sweet grass, used in smudging rituals for healing and possibly human sacrifices. We sit facing each other on her bed. She regards me with her pinholes.

"Here's the deal, Randy Burns. I like you but this is only for one night, OK? There is no future here. Let's just have some fun."

I suppress a cough. My sore toe throbs for the first time all day. I get hard.

She puts her hand on my forearm. "You seem nervous. When was the last time you had sex?"

I'm unable to speak.

"Poor thing. Let's get you off." She has a serious, focused look as she straddles me and starts peeling off her clothes and then mine.

Black bra, skin pure and white as Saskatchewan in January. Not a mole in sight, the only blemish is a yin and yang tattoo on her shoulder.

Alice reaches for something on her nightstand. Vanilla moisturizer. My favorite. She rubs her hands together, warming the lotion.

"Poor, sad, sweet baby."

She brings me to the edge. Slows. Back to the edge. Alice could teach Shay-Shay and Jackie a few things.

She gathers my balls as if she's testing them. I feel her lips next to my ear. "Nice and full, hey?"

Then they're not, and for a moment I forget where I am or why I'm here.

When I open my eyes, Alice is staring blankly at me; the engine is revving but no one's at the wheel.

I think, time to run for it. But instead, out of guilt or habit or gender equality, I whisper. "Anything I can do for you?"

She snaps out of it. "Sweet baby," she says.

She reaches across me and opens the drawer to her nightstand. I lift my head and see purple butt plugs and, still in its wrapper, a "Pegging the Sissy Kit" with a picture of a guy on all fours and a woman in a waist harness with a purple dildo protruding.

Alice grabs a black rabbit-shaped device from the drawer and flips over, holding the vibrator aloft like a hara-kiri knife.

"Tell me a story," she commands.

"What kind of story?" I ask, feeling drained, literally and figuratively.

"Like something from your book."

"OK, I meet you in a bar."

"A Cambodian bar," she says.

"OK, a Cambodian bar. And..."

"You're with a friend and I'm lost."

"OK, I'm with a friend and..."

"And you take me to your hotel room. You and your friend want to tag team but I say, I don't do that. You throw me onto the bed and start choking me, and then both of you are fucking me, a double-pen. You cum on my face. Your friend cums on my face and then..."

She flips on the rabbit and works herself.

I stroke her pulsating arm, whisper in her ear, and sing what

I can remember of an old, classic Little Feat song:
>Well, I was out late one night
>I seen my sweet Alice in every street light.
>Alice, my sad, sweet Alice
>And if you feed her weed, whites, and Yukon Jack
>She be willin' ...

Alice moans and flails, and eventually conks out.

I watch her for a minute and then, as I'm reaching for my shirt, she stirs and raises herself up onto her elbows, wide awake. "Want to break in my pegging harness?"

"Sounds like fun, but I have a hair appointment in three hours," I say, as if it would make any difference to her at this point.

At seven A.M. a cab drops me at home, feeling soiled for the second time this week. I skip the Lysol wipes, take a hot shower, and get into bed.

Four hours later, my phone buzzes. A text from Jackie:
I really miss the kosher gerkin.

OK, she's extrasensory. I contemplate letting her know that she misspelled *gherkin* but don't. I contemplate hitting Delete but don't.

I check ticket sales for tonight: Zilch. Then again, today is Monday and I'm not on until ten. Sea Bass warned that tonight's show and all my remaining shows were on shit days at shit times. No worries. I go back to sleep.

My alarm wakes me at five P.M. Four tickets sold and a dozen comps reserved. In my email, there's a note from Morag marked "Urgent."

To Randall Burns:

This is a formal warning regarding your show due to repeated violations of your "Tolerance, Trigger Warning, and Diversity Awareness" agreement.

In particular, you have been cited for the following:
1) 27 May 2016: Failure to promptly remove a misogynistic Facebook comment.
2) 28 May 2016: Someone who said he was a friend of yours wore a MAGA hat at your show.
3) In addition, you were identified on several occasions lurking outside the Lactation Lounge, creating an uncomfortable environment for nursing women and their children.
Any more violations and we will be forced to cancel your run.
Sincerely,
Morag Fitzgibbon, Director, Moosefin International Fringe Theatre Festival
Falguni Chichimecacihuatzin-O'Malley, President, Moosefin International Fringe Theatre Festival.
PS: Mx. O'Malley, myself, and my staff will be attending your show tonight to assure that everything runs smoothly.

I immediately leave three voicemails for Joey.

When I enter the theater at nine thirty, Do-Rag is all smiles. I don't ask her for my ticket sales nor do I offer her my show programs. Sea Bass points a middle finger toward the ceiling, as I pass him on my way to the Green Room. After some handwashing and piss breaks, Joey finally returns my call but I don't answer. Instead, I think about his advice about gorillas and snails and arks. I take out my little notebook and write until I hear Do-Rag giving her spiel.

When I come out on stage, Morag and her crew are seated in the first two rows. A half-dozen or so other people are scattered around the theater.

The show goes reasonably well, and I direct my seagull joke to Morag, who cringes, and then looks away. At the end, instead of my usual book pitch, I whip out my little notebook and read my prepared statement.

"Dear Moosefin Community:

"Recently, I have been called out for being a racist, a misogynist, and a homophobe. I know I have disappointed many people and I accept full responsibility for the contents of my play. But it is essential that the people I have hurt know that I see them and hear them. No one is more disappointed in me than myself.

"For me, theater has always been a way to combine artistry and activism, an education of the soul. In this show, I had hoped to examine the trauma that comes from inequality and the continuous cycle of pain in our marginalized communities.

"True, I am a privileged white male, but I am also Jewish. I have been there. And to that end, I will share a personal story.

"Every year on Passover, my family tells the parable of 'The Running of the Jew.' Historically, Jews have been blamed for plagues, famines, and rounding errors. Of course, we are not blameless: Many Jews have done bad things. You've probably all heard of Bernie Madoff, his cousin Bernie Sanders, and all those Jewish welfare babies?

"Anyway, 'The Running of the Jew' is the story of a Jewish boy who lived in a Polish peasant village. One day, he was walking his pet ferret in the woods when some proud boys chased him, beat him, and set the ferret on fire.

"Through tears, the boy asked: 'Why did you burn my little Hymie?'

"The proud boys said: 'Because you are a devil worshipper. Your high priest has a goat's head and naked girls kiss his behind. You eat witches' cakes made of menstrual blood, virgin's urine, Christian semen, and onion dip.'

"Through tears, the Jewish boy said, 'Are you talking about gefilte fish?'

"The upshot of this story is that the little ferret is me. It is you. It is all of us who are fighting to be heard during these trying times.

"To help compensate for the pain I have caused, and so that I can move forward with my recovery, I have decided to cancel the remainder of my run here in Moosefin. This will be my last show and your last opportunity to purchase a signed copy of my book for only twenty dollars, Canadian.

"*Ganbei, Namaste, l'chaim*"

The audience is silent. Then there is some light clapping from the back of the room. Morag's crowd files out quietly. A few people I don't recognize buy books.

After packing up, I lug my bag and props and meet Sea Bass at his plywood desk.

He's stands up. "You nailed the speech, dude. Going to miss you."

I open my arms for a hug. "Don't forget to write after you get the clap from all those bar girls," I say.

"For sure."

I walk around the upstairs lobby one last time, removing my posters from the walls and humming the tune to "Ain't Gonna Bump No More." I dump my remaining postcards, twenty-five dollars' worth, into the trash.

At midnight, back at the house, I find a bottle of champagne, a joint, and a note on the counter that says, "Condolences. May drugs and alcohol comfort you in this difficult time." There's also a stack of clippings of bad reviews from Allistair and Barclay's performances over the last ten years.

In my room, I change my flight to Boston to tomorrow and start packing.

My phone buzzes, another text from Jackie:
Have I mentioned my pussy misses you?

Then a text from Feldman:
Heard about your resignation. Beer garden tomorrow night, just us.

I text Feldman:
Raincheck? Heading out of town. Thanks for everything.

Coming from the living room, I hear the familiar sounds of snorting, grunting, and groaning. Allistair and Carmine are watching animal porn again. I take a seat on the couch and open the champagne. We pass the bottle back and forth.

"I don't know how you guys deal with all the rejection and nonsense," I say.

"There's only one option: If you have a bad run, you have to get your dick, I mean stick, back on the ice."

I light the joint and we pass in back and forth.

"Where's Barclay?" I ask, between hits.

Allistair cracks open a beer. "Once a year, we open up our relationship for two weeks. Barclay has this thing for old ladies with huge tits." Allistair doesn't mention what his thing is.

"My cousin Joey has an arrangement like that with his wife. Twice a year she goes back to France to sleep with a woman and he gets to hit the local massage parlors. Seems to be working." I pause. "Can I hold the rabbit?"

Allistair pulls Carmine away. "Sorry, bro. I'm done sharing."

At five A.M., I wake up with a hangover, strip the bed, and sweep the floor. On the dining room table, I leave a signed copy of my book and a gift certificate to the Bar-Bar.

Then I text Jackie:

Hey, Action Jackson. Quitting the festival a little early. Apparently, some people don't like Jews. More soon.

IV

THE KINK

My first day back in Boston, the weather is overcast, pallid, and listless. The second day, ditto. Friends leave messages that I don't answer — especially the ones from Joey. I spend the third day on a bench in the Boston Public Garden scrolling my cell phone and observing the fauna: guys wearing wool hats and no socks; a Lane-Bryant-sized woman sporting headphones and a suit who spits on the sidewalk as she walks by; a child foraging in his nose and retracting his finger to consider his find.

The general public never fails to horrify me.

I think of Jackie calling me a rotten, miserable hater, which reminds me of a session with Moody ten years ago, soon after Ricki and I had broken up for the third time.

"Let's review." Moody's tone was on the smug side of sincere. "You feel for the poor but don't want them in your neighborhood. You envy the rich but complain about their greed. And you're repulsed by what's in between, the middle, the bourgeois, the bland, and the boring, which is most of humanity."

"So?" I said.

"So, you've chosen to disconnect from the world and wonder why you feel sad, angry, and frustrated that you're alone and can't land a relationship."

"Sounds like you're calling me a misanthrope with no game," I said.

He raised his voice.

"Randall, I'm saying that you've limited your options to skinny, edgy women your age — like Ricki — who are equally disgusted with the human race but can function well enough to hold down a job. Occasionally, you find an 'outlier,' as you call them, usually after a long drought, and the connection turns into an all-consuming, overwhelming, Technicolor love story, but neither of you can maintain the intensity. No one can. Then you take a break. Then get back together and repeat. You both get hooked on the drama until one or both of you hits the wall."

My cell phone buzzes. I check the message.

Maybe Moody had a point back then, but the point now is that Moody the expert is getting divorced and Jackie the outlier just texted, asking to meet tomorrow at One If by Land, what used to be our favorite coffee shop near her apartment in Brookline.

I decide to arrive at the coffee shop thirty minutes early to reacquaint myself with the terrain, to secure a perimeter, and dig in.

It's only been a month since the cruise that sucked a thousand leagues, and I'm still not sure who dumped who. Or who has the negotiating advantage today. Or what I want from her. Or she from me. And who has she been fucking the last four weeks?

I lock my bike to a no-parking sign and pick my way through what was once a sidewalk into what was once One If by Land, but is now Crank, part of an indie coffee chain.

Like everything else these days, the décor is ambiguous, half-and-half. The seating area suggests a boho bookstore: post and beam, exposed brick, leashed dogs, and unleashed children. Behind the counter, the caffeine-sequencing lab: glass and stainless, beakers and tubing, presses and grinders. Are you supposed to drink this stuff or snort it?

The front section is filled with people sitting alone, some still in their pajamas, backpacks on the opposing seats, drinking Crank beverages, and munching food from Tupperware containers brought from home. Their tables are littered with iPads, USB hubs, external hard drives, wireless mice, and cables strung to too-few power outlets.

In the back room, it's more of the same — twenty-somethings at their mobile, global headquarters. I spot a guy packing up and idle nearby. A bearded dude in a knee-length nightshirt and fluffy slippers comes from the other direction and idles, too. He has hairy ankles and several inches on me. I summon my performing skills and attempt to stare him down.

Another table opens nearby. "No worries, *sir*," the dude says, "I'll take this one."

I say nothing and claim my seat.

A few minutes later, he comes over.

"Excuse me, *sir*," he gestures to the outlet under my table. "Mind if I plug in?"

"No worries, bro," I say, without looking up.

A woman with a stained hoodie, two kids, and a baby in a stroller sets up at a long table nearby. She heaves the baby out of the stroller and starts to breastfeed. I try not to think about Amanda, lactation lounges, or tolerance warnings, but feel triggered anyway. The two older kids, boys of about three, stand on their chairs and start banging the table. The mother raises her voice, "Rinaldo, Beckham, sit down. Now!"

Jackie always joked that hipsters liked to name their kids after foreign soccer players. She also joked that there was a simple solution for overpopulation and global warming: "Eat more kids."

Someone blonde, slender, and unusually punctual enters my field of vision. She's wearing a black leather blazer over a charcoal jersey dress, black nylons, black ankle boots and crimson lipstick. A thoroughbred in a petting zoo.

Jackie's breasts seem higher and she's not wearing a hat. When our eyes meet, her expression is flat.

Little Rinaldo is in the aisle playing with something in his diaper, blocking Jackie's path. The mother still nursing apologizes and shouts at the boy, "Sit down, Rinaldo. Don't make me come over there!"

I smile and say to Jackie, "Stir-fried brat with oyster sauce?"

She drops her bag on the table and doesn't smile.

I move forward, wrap my arms around her, and receive a quick pat on the back. We separate. I pull out her chair.

She sits back in her seat and crosses her arms as if she's expecting something. We stare past each other.

"Large black?" I ask, when I can no longer take the silence.

"Chamomile," she says in a low voice. "I'm on the wagon."

OK, who has she been fucking?

When I return with our beverages, the dude in the nightshirt is plugging a second device into the wall socket next to Jackie's knees.

He ignores me and goes back to check the rig on his table, then comes over again and says to me, "I'm sure it's not intentional, but the plug keeps coming out."

"Look, bucko," I say, standing up. "You've got two cords strung under my table. I'm trying to enjoy coffee with my wife."

I'm surprised by my gusto. Maybe it's the caffeine. Or maybe it's because one of Jackie's favorite activities was messing with millennials.

The guy continues to stand there and says nothing.

I say, "You know, in some states fighting an elderly person is a hate crime."

He looks confused and glances at Jackie for a verdict. I'm waiting for her to say, "Me Cambodia." Instead, she offers to switch tables with him.

"Traitor," I say to her, as we stand to move.

No laugh. No smile. Nothing.

After we sit down, she takes out some Purell. I extend my hands. She hesitates, squirts me first, and then herself. I think, well, at least that's something.

Rinaldo and his family have been joined by more children, and another mother who immediately distributes crayons and paper to the little horde. The mothers blather on about tiny houses, heirloom avocados, ethically-sourced hammocks, Trump and Ponzi, Trump and Caligula, Trump and Mel Gibson.

I whisper to Jackie, "Do you hear that nonsense?"

"I haven't been following the news lately," she says, her voice trailing off. I want to reach for her hand but don't.

"Turning Japanese" comes over the sound system. I flex my eyebrows and start lip-syncing the words, my hand resting flat on the table, hoping she'll reach for it. I flutter my fingers as a hint. She leaves me hanging.

I take off the sippy top from my coffee and swirl the backwash. Jackie does the same with her tea. The mothers next to us momentarily quiet down.

"So, how have you been?" Jackie asks.

My body becomes hot and fluey. Do I say I missed her? That I want to get back together? Do I want to get back together? Do I tell her about Alice?

"In hipster *schpeak*," I say, "You could say the Fringe offered some 'teachable moments.' Like getting good reviews one day and shitty ones the next."

Or like getting kissed by a guy.

"On the other hand, I learned I can hang with the big dogs but may need to pasteurize my material for wider appeal."

Jackie is looking at her hands, not me. "Well, you gave it your all."

Pause.

She looks up. "When are you going to look for a real job?"

There's the cheap shot. Isn't she the one who bought me brass balls for Christmas for trying something she said most people our age wouldn't think of trying?

"I'm not sure what's next," is all I can summon. "What about you?"

I sip from my empty cup as the crowd buzz starts up again.

"After you left," Jackie says, looking over my shoulder, "My mother suggested I volunteer somewhere to get out of the apartment. Do something useful, meaningful. So, I'm helping out now at *Homeless Not Helpless*, that newspaper street people sell in Brookline."

She takes a flyer from her purse and hands it to me. "They have literary events and readings."

I hold the flyer close. I hold it far. Jackie sighs and finally hands me her reading glasses.

"You should go some time," she says.

You?

A middle-aged couple wearing skinny, high-water jeans and hoodie wife-beaters that say, "I CAN'T ADULT TODAY" passes by. They both have loud tattoos on their shoulders.

Jackie watches them and shakes her head. "If we end up like that, I propose a murder-suicide."

We?

After another fifteen minutes of meaningless conversation, she stands. I stand, too.

"Well, it was nice seeing you," she says. Her tone is toneless.

I say, "Yeah, me too."

She picks up her bag and makes no move to hug me. "Thanks for the tea," she says. "

As I watch her leave, I feel like crying.

Back at home, I begin a novel about a Jewish guy and an Asian woman. Then I change it to a Zoroastrian guy and a Croatian woman. I write two sentences and get lost thinking about Jackie. She seemed angry: the crossed arms, the sighing, ignoring my jokes, defending the dude, the crack about getting a real job. Didn't she text me first? Was it something I said? Did she find out about Alice? And what's this about being on the wagon?

She's probably been fucking that shit-bag Adam, Lenny's

real estate buddy she met New Year's Eve. He always brags about his volunteering, psyllium cleanses, and vacation properties.

Or maybe it's her ex. I bet she's still working for him.

Or she's cleaning up on *Tinder*, *Shiksamingle*, or *Match* with all those neutered suburban guys who can't wait to remarry.

I log onto *Pornhose* and find myself on the Canadian channel. Today's recommendations: "Inuit Nookie," "Celina Dion Croon and Poon," "Pegging in Winnipeg."

I flip to *Shiksamingle*, then *Tinder*. No Jackie, but I've got a bunch of Likes. On Facebook, I have a friend request from, of all people, Ricki. I check out her profile. She's put on a few pounds.

I spend the next two hours vacuuming and re-vacuuming my apartment. I make three doctors' appointments for GI, purple toe, and zoonotic diseases, and check my phone, my email, then phone again. Nothing from Jackie or anyone else. If I had a TV, I would have turned it on and off a dozen times, which is why I don't have a TV.

I call Abe:

"My advice to you, young man, is to avoid pepperoni pizza; it puts zits on your dick."

Translation: Get a regular job and marry Jackie.

Then Lenny:

"Don't know what to tell you, Burns. I got kinda burned out on the eight balls and mother-daughter tag-teams, so I spent a couple of weekends with Deborah."

"What? You're spending your weekends with Deborah?"

"Did I mention she's got a friend in her forties who wants to meet you? Got to dash. Go easy on the pepperoni pizza."

What is this? I go away for two weeks and everything changes?

I get dressed and head to Squats, my gym, the low-budget

alternative to the Minuteman, my first visit since leaving for the Fringe.

Everything here seems familiar, unaltered, soothing.

- The men's steam room is still closed due to "inappropriate behavior." Lenny says it's probably an infestation of Australian jumping crabs.

- The self-flushing urinals still spray anyone within ten feet.

- The guy who vapes and conducts FaceTime meetings while taking a dump, is still at it.

On my way to the weight room, I notice the new all-gender bathroom. Fuck.

Later, I'm back home resting on the couch, listening to Enya, and not answering Joey's calls, when I get a text from Jackie:

Seventies Mayhem at Brookline Theater next week. Airplane *or* Deathwish?

She caved?

I stand up, sit down, and then vacuum some more, wondering how long I should wait before responding. A day? A week?

I set the timer on my phone for three hours.

Fifteen minutes later, I message her:

Definitely Deathwish

We nail down plans via text as if we're both trying to avoid a phone conversation.

Her last text:

Remember I'm on the wagon.

Joey texts. This time I respond and agree to meet him tonight at seven-thirty, face-to-face, at the "Office," where we used to meet when my mother was dying.

While walking there that night, I think about what I want from Joey after all his nitpicking and the fact that I blew a thousand dollars on the Moosefin Fringe Festival just to be humiliated. An apology? The kind he usually gives, complete with tortuous monologs and chin-up slugger banalities?

What if he doesn't apologize at all?

Or what if he gives me something like half an apology?

For that matter, why do I keep listening to him? Or any of my idiotic friends? Even on my trip around the globe, I followed the advice of a guidebook that was often wrong. Not a little wrong but a lot wrong. The guy who wrote it tried to cover his ass by claiming that in life, experts are right about seventy percent of the time; the rest is experience and destiny. What crap.

I descend the stairs to the center platform of the Park Street T-stop, our "Office," twenty minutes early. The walls, ceiling, and floor of the platform are covered by tiles. It resembles a public bathroom. On the tracks below, mice dart around a third rail. I've never seen one get electrocuted, but there's always a first time. Homeless people and off-duty fast-food workers, still in uniform, mill around.

Things could be worse.

I take out my pocket notebook, skim some notes, put it away, and then lean against a pillar and review the subway map on the wall.

A guy in a wheelchair rolls out of a nearby elevator. He has thick white hair and is wearing a Harvard T-shirt and a crimson scarf. He parks himself in a corner and pours something from a bottle into a Starbucks cup. He smiles and takes a sip, savoring whatever it is. It reminds me of Warren Zevon's take-away from his bout with cancer: "Enjoy every sandwich."

Joey arrives at 7:21, nine minutes early, looking like Monique dressed him: skinny black shorts, and hanging from his narrow, bony shoulders, a black wife-beater that could pass for a halter top. He seems to have aged in the last few weeks.

We great each other with sanitary elbow bumps.

He kicks a Subway sandwich wrapper off the platform onto the tracks.

"Look, I screwed up," he says. "I'm sorry. I should have done more research before sending you off like that. At least you gave it a good shot. Remember the story of Rick Ankiel, the Cardinals' pitcher who ... "

I throw a hand up. "Don't give me the old Dale Carnegie bullshit."

"That's all I got."

"Forget the stories. What exactly *are* you sorry for?"

He takes out *his* little pocket notebook and recites from a list: the gay-themed festival, the ringers, the gay ringers, the platitudes, the listening but not hearing.

My internal organs start to unwind.

"Things change," he says. "I guess the festival changed."

I say nothing.

"Burns, we're almost sixty," Joey says. "We have what, fifteen good years left?"

He glances at the guy in the wheelchair, savoring the contents of his Starbucks cup. We point to each other and say in unison, "Enjoy every sandwich."

"I got a story for you," Joey says.

I scratch my nose with my middle finger.

"Look, I already apologized and this one took some digging."

He tells the story of Paul McGowan, a football player voted the best college linebacker in 1987. McGowan lacked size and speed but was a hard worker. He got up at six A.M. to lift. He studied film of the competition. He was drafted by the Minnesota Vikings, but was cut before he played a single down. At his exit interview, a coach said, "I know it doesn't seem fair, but we never said we were going to be fair when we drafted you." McGowan settled for playing Canadian and Arena football.

"He never made it back to the NFL," Joey says. "He moved on. Became a firefighter. Got married."

A week later, I meet Jackie in the theater lobby. She is blonde and hatless, sporting the earrings I bought her on the cruise and wearing her night-burglar outfit: fitted black military pants, black paratrooper boots, black pea coat opened to expose her collar bones. She's already bought our tickets.

I'm wearing the same outfit I wore on our first date: navy chinos and a button-down dress shirt — tucked in — a little equestrian above my left pec, a spray of brown and grey chest hair at my open neck. I'm also wearing the Polo hoodie she bought me for Christmas.

She looks me up and down. "Let's go for a walk," she says.

In the parking lot behind the theater, she pulls out a joint. "Looks like I picked the wrong month to quit weed."

I say nothing.

Jackie pauses mid-light and considers me over the joint. She says nothing and lights it. We take a couple of hits, and then she heads to a nearby mini-mart. I follow.

She asks the clerk for a pack of Newports and when he hands it to her, she says to him, "Looks like I picked the wrong month to quit ciggies."

Her fingers graze mine as we share a cigarette outside the theater. I get a double shot of oxytocin.

Inside the theater, we score aisle seats. I put my arm on the armrest between us and flutter my fingers, but she leans away.

When the lights go down and the previews roll, she retrieves a flask from her thigh pocket. "Looks like I picked the wrong month to quit booze," she says, taking a swig. She hands it over without looking. I take a sip. It isn't smoky bourbon. It's herbier, grassier, and nasty. "What is this?" I ask.

"Green Chartreuse. French for '110 proof.'"

I swallow hard and return the flask. She takes it and crosses her legs.

On screen, Charles Bronson and Hope Lange are sitting on a Hawaiian beach.

"Isn't that cute," Jackie says, looking at the screen. "He called her fat, but he's the one with the little gut."

I say nothing.

As we watch, we pass the flask back and forth. I take sips I don't want, but it's something to do.

Onscreen, Jeff Goldblum's character is stalking Hope Lange and her daughter inside a supermarket. He's pretending to check out some melons. I drop my hand onto Jackie's knee. She removes it and passes me the flask.

I take a long swig as Goldblum and fellow thugs follow Hope and her daughter home.

"Time for the old in-out," I say.

Someone behind us says, "*Shhh!*"

Jackie says nothing.

At the hospital, Hope is dead and her daughter has seen better days.

"Hey, Bronson," I say, slurring. "Spare some change?"

"Will you please be quiet?" says another voice from behind us.

As I'm passing the flask to Jackie, the cap falls to the floor. I bend over to retrieve it.

In the dim light, I can make out her leg, a band of golden skin exposed above the top of her boot. The next thing I know, her calf is in my mouth and I'm growling.

"Quit it, you fuck!" Jackie squeals, swatting me on the back of the head.

I haul myself up, cap in hand, and then she's on me with a 110-proof kiss, tongue barreling deep. I hear her moan. Or maybe it's me.

A voice erupts behind us: "Why don't you two get a frickin' room."

As the credits roll, I rest my head on her shoulder. "I'm blasted," I say.

"Me, too," she says, happily. "Let's go get a drink."

We walk unsteadily to a nearby bar, arm and arm.

My phone buzzes in my pocket.

"Do you need to get that?" Jackie asks.

"What? Who cares?" I say.

At the bar, she orders more Chartreuse. I order a beer.

We sit in bleary silence for a while.

My phone buzzes again.

"Must be important," Jackie says.

I rest my head on her shoulder.

"What would you do if someone raped me?" Jackie asks.

"Go for your guns."

She sits up and looks me in the eye for the first time in a month. "I never had any guns."

Then she reaches for my hand. "I have a confession."

Here it comes, the sock full of coins.

My phone buzzes again.

"I really missed you," she says.

I say nothing because I know I'm about to puke. I bolt for the bathroom and vomit a stream of green, some of which lands in the bowl. I rinse my mouth out in the sink and notice the flowery décor, the sitting room, and the lack of urinals. I pop three Ricolas, exit quickly, and forget to check my phone.

When I return, Jackie says, "My poor little pale face looks extra pale." She strokes my cheek and recites from one of our favorite childhood cartoons: "Drizzle, Drazzle, Drozzle, Drome; time for this one to go home."

We walk arm and arm to my bike, and she tells me to stay alive until next Saturday, when we'll meet at a bar to watch the NBA finals.

Later I check my phone. There's a text from Deborah with a photo of her friend, who looks like Taylor Swift, only with a few lines around her mouth.

I arrive early at Rapinoe's, a new sports bar Jackie wanted to check out. The wall-to-wall TVs are tuned to the NBA finals. I circle for seats. The crowd is young and debating the usual crap: "Trump vs. Idi Amin," "sriracha vs. aioli," "maker spaces vs. coworking studios."

I snag two bar seats just as Jackie makes her entrance. I turn to watch as the crowd parts. She's wearing a green Celtics warm-up jacket, matching Celtics shorts, and sparkly green Converse high tops. Amber legs. Blonde hair. Cherry red lipstick. No hat. And, once again, the earrings I gave her from the cruise. Who cares if the Celtics aren't playing? I'm happy to see her, and she looks happy to see me. We kiss.

"Sweet threads," I say to Jackie.

A bartender appears. I order beers for us.

After a few sips, we put coasters on top of our beer mugs and go outside to smoke part of a joint, then return to our seats to watch the game. She rests her hand on my thigh. I stroke her blond hair.

The bar erupts in hoots and applause to a LeBron James power dunk.

"He's such a jerk," Jackie says in her stadium voice.

"Who? LeBron? How would you know?"

"Look at that beard — only a jerk wears a beard like that."

"What are you talking about? The guy is a wonder of nature, built like Gronk, moves like Nureyev."

I put down my drink. "Oh, I know," I say, winking at her. "You don't like him because he's gay."

Two gender-trenders sitting nearby look over and scowl.

"Not true," Jackie says. "I don't like him because he's Polish."

We low-five.

A guy wearing cropped pants that expose his hairy calves takes a seat at the bar.

Jackie shakes her head. "Say it ain't so, Joe."

"Nice clam diggers," I say to Jackie.

"Yes! That's what I want. Seafood," Jackie says, sitting up and looking around. "I want seafood."

A bartender with a pink beard tosses down two menus and steps back with his arms folded.

"Do you have bearded clams?" Jackie asks, sweetly.

"Do you see it on the menu, lady?" the bartender says.

"How about rocky mountain oysters?"

The bartender's expression, even with the pink beard, would have shut down most people, but not my Jackie. She absently runs her finger down the menu and points to a blank space. "I'll go with the fresh, seafood *twat-alingus*."

The bartender snatches the menus and stomps away. The couple a few seats over is now glaring at us.

"You crushed it, dude," I say to Jackie.

We low-five again.

There is an amiable silence.

"I really missed you," I hear myself say to Jackie.

"Say that again," she says, hopping onto my lap. I wrap my arms around her and bury my face in her hair, which smells herbal and comforting. I feel the vibration of her feet tapping a beat against the chair.

"I really missed you," I say.

"Oh, Daddy." She sits up. "Let's toast."

I wave down the other bartender, the clean-shaven one, and order two Green Chartreuses on the rocks.

Jackie wriggles in my lap like Carmine the rabbit.

The drinks arrive. "Time to get my rocks off," Jackie says in my ear. She takes an ice cube from her glass and drops it down my shirt. I yelp. She laughs.

"Oh, come here, my furry, little Jew," she says, hugging me tight.

Out of the corner of my eye, I see the bouncer goose-stepping in our direction.

We walk hand-in-hand down Cambridge Street across Charles Street toward the Ritz-Carlton bar, where there'll be no one under forty. As we're cutting through the Common, a guy in a full-length down coat, a little much for June, totters toward us. One of his sleeves is missing. Aqualung.

I tug Jackie's arm to move her away from him but she pulls free.

"Spare a dollar for some Chink food?" he says, holding out a grimy hand. His eyes are flickering and unfocused.

The next thing I know, Jackie is pressing a hand to the side of his grey-stubbled face and reaching into her jacket to pull out a ten-dollar bill, as if she'd been storing it there for something like this. She folds it into his palm.

"You're going to be OK," she says.

His eyes settle.

I watch her, thinking, Who *are* you? And what have you done with Jackie?

At the Ritz, we sit side-by-side on a couch. Jackie orders two soda waters.

"After last week, we need to look after your liver." She caresses my abdomen and smiles. "I never had anyone attack my calf like a Doberman. It was kind of hot."

We look at each other, her hand resting on my belly. She licks her lips. I reach for my soda.

"This is nice, isn't it?" she says after a minute.

"It is. It's very nice," I say, meaning it.

She lays her head on my shoulder. I close my eyes and breathe in vanilla moisturizer, piney shampoo, and her sweet floral breath.

"Burns?" She nuzzles closer. "We're so good together."

She looks up at me, her face inches away. "I'm willing to take another chance on you."

My arm around her goes numb. It takes everything in me not to move to the other side of the couch, the room, the country.

She interrupts my silence. "I know how you are, and I'm sure your friends have said their usual crap about me. Abe probably told you to suck it up and suffer like him. And I bet Lenny told you to just dump me."

I don't disagree with her.

"But I love you. And I missed you. Like I said, we're good together. We laugh. We cry. We party hard. You listen to me. You take care of me when I'm sick. I like your body and you like mine."

I listen to her, trying to process, parse, compare costs and benefits, calculate net present values and future returns.

She puts her hand on my face. "We're going to be OK, my little scaredy boy. Trust me."

I decide this isn't the best time to mention my trust issues.

"And just so you know," she says, narrowing her eyes, "I didn't fuck anybody while we were apart."

There's a silence.

I kiss the top of her head and finally say, "I love you, too, and I want us to be together. I'll quit waffling. Maybe we should try couple's therapy."

She shakes her head. "I've tried that before with three different husbands and you see how well that worked. My mother says Western therapy is bad for Asian women. Also, I'm working on my shit. I'm taking yoga, meditating, and seeing an acupuncturist. Besides — and I mean this in the nicest possible way — you're the one who's never been married."

I decide not to mention that Moody said I might never be marriage material.

"Fair enough," I say. "*I'll* go to therapy. It's always worked for me. Give me three months."

"Take six. I'll even sleep on the couch sometimes till you get fixed. You know, because of your sleep issues. And by the way, about your purple toe? My mother says it's not plague, it's gout. There are pills you can take. It's all going to be fine."

My internal balance sheet appears and recalculates. Did *I* just cave? What does "sleeping on the couch sometimes" mean? Two days a week? Once in a while? One or two times — period? And what does she mean until I get "fixed." Did she mean just my sleep issues? What about all my other issues? I've been trying to get fixed my entire life. What am I a fucking dog? Was there something more to her Doberman remark?"

Then again, no one has ever wanted to pin their life and happiness on me. And this could be my last chance.

I start to feel relieved. The right person, the right next move, is right in front of me.

I wrap my arm around her and pull her close, settling in, absorbing her.

After a minute of calm, she bolts her head up and turns to face me.

"Why don't we join a gym together? Not the Minuteman. A new one. I'll teach there and get us membership discounts."

I feel my jaw tighten. I miss the Minuteman. I miss seeing Lenny. I miss seeing Abe, at least when he's allowed to go.

I say nothing.

She slumps back. "Never mind. It was just a thought."

Pause.

"Are you going to pull down your dating profiles?" she asks.

"Yes, definitely, of course."

She whispers into my ear. "Want to come over and fuck me?"

The sex is just like I remembered, except for her kissing technique, which has improved, probably because she was fucking somebody. In spite of everything, I sleep through the night.

Monday morning, I call Moody and leave a message.

He returns my call with a text:

Randall, as I said earlier, I have moved on and done all I can do for you. I urge you to find another therapist. I will be happy to forward them your records.

Sure. Fine. No worries.

I find a handful of shrinks online who will take my cheap-ass Obamacare insurance and contact several who specialize in "men's issues." One even has a similar last name, Byrnes. Also, he is the only one who returns my call. When I call back, he actually answers and says he has an opening this week. Not a good sign that he's so available, but I take the appointment, anyway.

His ground-floor office is next to an artisanal pickle shop in Somerville, a hipster town neighboring Cambridge. The building is webbed in scaffolding.

The waiting room is empty, and the office door is ajar. I peek in. He is poking at an iPad and waves me in. Dr. Byrnes is big and round, grey and balding, shirted and tied. He's wearing pressed khaki pants and penny loafers with lavender argyle socks and a wedding ring. Another middle-aged guy dressed by his wife.

He has my records and has already spoken to Moody. On the stick or too eager?

I take a seat on a buff-colored cloth couch opposite his buff cloth chair. The desk and bookcases are chipped and scratched, off-white melamine. Beige and boring?

We start with my backstory. Mother and stepfather deceased. Biological father, don't know and don't care. One sibling, a stepsister Harriet, lives in San Francisco, is sixty-four, probably still has a great ass, and is getting married for the fourth time; we haven't spoken in a dozen years. I also have a group of long-time friends scattered everywhere, and a cousin, Joey, here in Boston.

Relationship with mother was hit-and-run. When I was seven, she left the family for six months to carry on an affair with a younger guy. After dinner, my stepfather would retreat to his room, often overheard him crying. In mother's absence, stepsister Harriet took care of me, got bored with me, and got pregnant — not by me. Soon after mother returned, Harriet was sent to boarding school.

I mention that Moody said I see relationships with women as power struggles between humiliator and *humiliatee*. Thank you, Mom and especially you, Harriet.

Byrnes listens and takes notes on his iPad.

I lay out the current problem. "I'm in love with this woman Jackie. She's Chinese. Chinese American. And my type — skinny. And she's my age. But my track record with relationships isn't great." I pause. "Can you turn me into someone who can marry her?"

Byrnes looks up and smiles. "You might be in luck. I just got in a new shipment of fairy dust."

Another bad sign: This guy isn't funny.

"You said you're planning to see Jackie, what, two to three times a week? That's good for now. In a few weeks, we'll bump it to four and later to five. Expect some roiling anxiety and sleepless nights. At times, this might feel very unpleasant. But try not to think of it as your last chance."

His eyes are grey and tired. Is he up for the task? Am I?

"You seem really competent," I say. "But I'm concerned that you are the only shrink with immediate availability."

"I appreciate your honesty. I'm semi-retired and only take clients I like. Your insurance only reimburses me for forty minutes, so I'm clearly not taking you on for the money. You're a writer. My spouse is a singer. I like artist types. I expect our time together will be challenging and possibly entertaining."

Ninety minutes later, I leave with a plan, a reading list, and some hope.

Jackie likes the plan. She cleans up her apartment, replaces the milk crates with an armoire, moves her shoes to a closet. We rediscover all our favorite activities: Weekends on her Bermuda Triangle couch, partying to romantic comedies, and binge-watching seventies and eighties mayhem.

So far, I'm sleeping OK. I have four nights to myself, which gives me enough space to miss her. The sex is fine. Or close enough.

I meet with Byrnes twice a week. Each session, we run over forty minutes. Sometimes, we run over sixty minutes. At the end of the sixth visit, he announces, "I think it's time to bump Jackie-time up to four nights a week."

I choke. He pats my back and rubs my neck. "Inhale, then exhale, and text if it gets ugly," he says. "You're doing great."

Jackie is pleased with the news. She immediately moves stuff into my place: a blow drier, some shampoo, some lube. We stay at my place two of the four nights the first week. She moves in some more stuff: moisturizer, a loofah sponge, more shampoo, a phone charger. She starts to text more frequently to say "hi" and "thinking of your cock." If I don't feel like responding at the moment, I don't. Our agreement is that I have six hours to get back to her for a non-emergency.

One night the following week, I have trouble sleeping at her place. My head is a swirl of moles and thinning hair, which is suddenly prominent as her roots have darkened. I imagine hands around my throat, a life-preserver out of reach. I get up to piss every twenty minutes. After Jackie leaves in the morning, I text Byrnes.

He says anxiety is to be expected, a little insomnia never kills anybody, and how about that reading list?

I head to the library and borrow *The Squid and the Spaceman: What's Your Attachment Style?* I read the first fifty pages.

My Synopsis:

- Attachment style explains how you connect with other people, particularly in romantic relationships.

- The Spaceman wants to be close — close to the door. To create space in their relationships, they focus on other people's imperfections.

- Famous examples: J.D. Salinger, Leona Helmsley, Felix Unger.

The next night, Jackie stays over. I ask her to sleep on the couch. "Mr. Spaceman needs some space?" she asks. "Already?"

I haven't even discussed the book with her. Women are freaky.

The next day, my day off, she hangs around into the afternoon. At four P.M., I start pacing around the living room, then around my little outdoor deck. I go to the gym. When I come home for a shower, she's still there. I go back to the gym. I come home at nine, and she's finally packing up. "See you in a couple of days," she says, giving me a deep kiss that feels more like a violation than affection.

The next night, I read about "The Squid."

My Synopsis:

- Squids are needy and desperate for a relationship, looking for a life-preserver, someone to keep them from going under.

- Famous examples: Cyrano de Bergerac, Vincent van Gogh, Jennifer Aniston.

- One cure for attachment disorders is to have a child.

I slam the book shut. This is bullshit.

Later, Jackie texts about Wednesday and Thursday, which are supposed to be my nights off.

I respond:

Sorry. Got plans. Wednesday, drinks with Abe. Thursday, helping Lenny plan his August party. We're invited.

When can you fit me in, Mr. Sardine Can?

Next Friday, per our agreement

She doesn't write back.

I check out another Byrnes' recommendation, *The Farmer and the Clown,* a children's picture book. Byrnes says children's books can tap into subconscious issues.

My Synopsis:

There's a sad, old bachelor farmer with a pitchfork and a bad back. A train carrying the circus goes by his farm and a little clown falls off the train, which keeps going. The farmer takes in the little clown, happy to have some company. But the clown is sad without his little clown family. Soon, the farmer feels crowded having the whiney clown in his space. Eventually, he is bored to tears with the little clown, who just mopes around the house. Instead of stabbing the little clown with the pitchfork, the farmer consults a local wise man, who tells him to try thinking of others besides himself. The farmer goes home and attempts to cheer up the clown. After a few attempts, he succeeds and, in the process, cheers himself up as well. One day, the circus train comes back and the little clown rejoins his clown family. The farmer is alone again but is no longer sad. Even his back is better. He is probably just relieved not having the boring, needy, whiney little clown in his space all the time.

For some reason, after reading the book, I call Jackie. She is glad to hear from me. I am glad she's glad. She talks about her day, her mother, her gym routine, the missing side mirror on her car, her dripping toilet, and again about her gym routine. I am completely bored but can't get her off the phone. After twenty minutes, she gets another call. "Got to run," she says.

The next time I see Byrnes, he is wearing a priest-collared shirt and a sweater vest, items I recently saw previewed on the cover of GQ. A tuft of grey chest hair protrudes from his collar.

I go on and on about needy little clowns, boredom, and how Jackie can talk about nothing for hours. "I know this sounds fucked up, but in an ideal world, I'd skip all the 'how was your day' calls, the shopping, and other meaningless crap and just be with her for the good times. I want a little thermostat, so I can dial her up when I miss her and dial her down when I don't."

Byrnes sits there and listens. He looks a little bored.

"How do you and your wife do it?" I ask.

"Maybe you should examine what boring means for you. It could be low-level anxiety around something you want."

"What I want is to get away from her. I'm rarely bored by myself. I'm bored when I'm with her and she can't stop yakking."

"What would you rather talk about? Could you try changing the subject?"

"Sometimes I don't want to talk, and I don't want to listen. I just want to be alone or go to the gym. Now that you mention it, I don't want to walk down the street and hold her hand, either. That's so girlie. No one wants a real man anymore. Masculinity is a bad word these days."

"Boredom and anxiety are things you can learn to sit with. Things that pass."

At dusk on Saturday August 6th, Jackie and I arrive at

Lenny's annual "Summer's Eve, Douche-Free, Blowout BBQ" at his place across from the Boston Common. Jackie hasn't been here since the New Year's party. I was ready two hours ago, but she kept stalling because she wanted to be fashionably late.

We take the elevator direct to Lenny's foyer with its twenty-foot ceilings and walk by the Hogged-Back Growler photo without looking. I slide an arm around Jackie and steer her through the living room onto the deck.

There are at least a hundred people roaming the rose-stone flooring, sitting on upholstered benches, lounging on chaise lounges the size of queen beds, facing a wall of TVs tuned to the Red Sox game taking place a half-mile away.

Most of the women are wearing beachwear for middle-agers: one-piece bathing suits and cover-ups that cover as much as possible. Lenny's girlfriend, Deborah, is in jean shorts and one of Lenny's old dress shirts over her one-piece. Jackie and I are wearing Bermuda shorts and black T-shirts.

We pass a fire-pit filled with flaming glass beads and a hot tub filled with young women in bikinis. Asian women in short kimonos circulate with drinks and appetizers. Shay-Shay sees us and waves. Jackie frowns and jabs my cecum.

Rachel saunters over, reintroduces herself to Jackie, and then says, "What a bummer. You two just missed seeing Gronk and Peter Wolf. They left about fifteen minutes ago."

"Which one made a move on you?" I ask Rachel, winking.

"Gronk's a little young," Rachel says.

Jackie cuts in: "I'd fuck Peter Wolf any time."

There is a short silence.

"Anyway," Rachel finally says, "Lenny was looking for you guys. He's over there trying to blow his hand off."

Jackie grabs my hand to move on. In mid-stride, I turn back toward Rachel, and mouth, "Sorry. Talk to you later." She gestures with the buckle-up gesture, followed by the fingers crossed, followed by the pistol to the head.

"I saw that," Jackie says.

"What?"

"All of it."

Lenny is holding court at the tequila bar, where he's lighting a roman candle. Jackie and I join Abe and Amy, Joey and Monique, Deborah, and a few people I don't recognize.

"Check out my Jason Pierre-Paul imitation," Lenny shouts, holding up a giant flaming straw that shoots red, green, and blue fireballs into the fading light. He throws the straw over the railing, and holds up one hand with all fingers folded except the middle one.

"I see he's in his usual not-so-rare form," Jackie says in a low voice.

"You're just jealous because he's almost as funny as you are," I say, trying to lighten the mood.

Lenny comes over, shakes my hand with his middle finger still extended, and then gives me a hug.

He hugs Jackie, too. "Glad you guys could make it. Plenty of grub and drink. We even special-ordered seafood twat-alingus."

I sense Jackie stiffening beside me.

"And before I forget ..." Lenny reaches around the bartender and grabs an unopened bottle of Green Chartreuse. "All yours," he says, handing it to Jackie. "Every time I drink this stuff, I end up breaking the bottle over somebody's head." He returns to his fans.

I seat Jackie at a table and bring her cherry stones, a lobster tail, and a glass with rocks for the Chartreuse. I hold her hand while we eat. I do everything I think I'm supposed to do, following the operating instructions I learned the hard way. She watches other people milling around and eats in silence as if I don't exist, as if I wasn't sitting right beside her.

"Is there anyone who's going to be here that I need to know about?" Jackie asks, delicately biting into the lobster tail.

Just then I realize I never got back to Deborah about meeting her friend.

"What?" I finally respond.

Before Jackie can say anything, Joey and Monique join us. He's carrying a huge plate of ribs, fried oysters, and crabmeat poutine, Monique's favorite, and sets it down for all of us. Monique compliments Jackie's shorts. Jackie compliments Monique's leather miniskirt. Monique and Jackie joke about Lenny's tacky décor and how Abe and Amy are arguing for a change. I turn my attention to Joey.

I gesture to the plate he brought over. "Greasy and slimy, our two favorite food groups," I say to Joey.

We dig in.

"What's shaking?" Joey asks me through a mouthful of French fries.

I dip a fried oyster in poutine gravy. "I just started a second novel."

"Excellent," he says. "We should turn it into a show."

I don't respond.

"Oh, come on," Joey says. "Did Michael Jordon give up when he got cut from his high school basketball team? Did Dr. Seuss give up after twenty-seven rejections? Did J.K. Rowling..."

Under the table, I feel Jackie squeeze my hand a little too hard. After a third helping of fried oysters, I feel my colon squeezing a little too hard.

Monique asks Jackie, "Want to dance?" Before she gets up, I whisper in her ear, "Got to hit the head. Be right back. You OK?"

She shrugs and heads off with Monique.

Fifteen minutes later, I emerge from the bathroom and find Jackie standing outside the door with her arms folded across her chest. "What took you so long?"

"Sorry, my stomach was a little upset."

"Oh, really? Your stomach's upset? How about me? I can't *believe* you told Lenny about the seafood twat-alingus. And the Chartreuse. What else have you told your friends? Where's my privacy? *Our* privacy?"

Abe's newest relationship epiphany: When a woman starts ranting, it's usually the third atrocity that's the real problem. So far, I only counted two: abandonment and a privacy violation, so I wait to see what else Jackie's got.

"Why do you always spend so much time in the bathroom?" she says. "What were you doing in there? And don't tell me you were busting out a sidewinder."

This is about my bathroom habits?

Jackie tries to push past me.

"You can't go in there," I say, blocking her. "It's now a Superfund site."

"I bet Shay-Shay was in there jerking you off. Move!"

"C'mon Jackie. Give a guy a little privacy."

"Why? You don't care about my privacy."

I put my fists against my chest, wing out my elbows, and set up in a pass-blocking stance in front of the bathroom door.

Jackie fakes an outside rush and spins to the inside.

She jabs my stomach, shoves my shoulders, and yanks my ear. She tries a bull rush, and then gives me the old rip-and-swim move. I poke her crotch.

"Pig!" she howls.

She swings for my crotch. I swat her hand away, and then make a run for it down the hall to the guestroom. She takes the bait and follows. When she charges in, I kick the door shut, throw her onto the king-size bed face down and jump on top of her, wrapping my legs around hers. The old Bangkok corkscrew maneuver. I grab a fistful of her hair but then hesitate. *Is this getting out of hand?*

Jackie says in a muffled voice: "I know you hate me, you bastard. Go ahead, hit me, choke me."

She tries to flutter kick her legs but can't.

I reach around into her shorts.

"You're hurting me!" Is she smiling?

" 'No' means ... you got *no* balls, girlie boy," she says.

Does that mean stop or go?

She's no longer struggling. We're spread like two starfish with me on top.

"Finish the job, you fucking pin dick." She *is* smiling.

I pull down her shorts and finish the job from behind. We climax together.

The next morning, she has black and blue marks on her thighs and serves me breakfast in bed.

That week, Byrnes is about as useful as Abe, Lenny, or St. Jude.

"Maybe Jackie is overly jealous or maybe you acted like a jerk," Byrnes says. "All I know about Jackie is what you tell me."

"You're not being helpful and I'm paying you a lot of money."

"Dr. Moody said that was your favorite line. I'm very sorry, but I can't referee your fights or give you the formula for discerning her motives. But the silver lining is that you two muddled through a trust issue and ended it with some sex you enjoyed. Life is about muddling through."

"That makes me feel *so* much better," I say. "Does this strategy work with your wife?"

Byrnes face registers nothing. "That really isn't relevant to our work here," he says, quietly. "But since you brought it up again, let me clarify: I don't have a wife. I have a husband."

Over the next month, Jackie and I settle into a new routine and muddle through the bump to four nights a week. I stop watching the clock and waiting for her to leave when she's at my place. But at her place, I leave when I feel like it, which is usually early. I'm back to sleeping OK, and we have sex two to three times a week, mostly when we're stoned.

On my days off, I see my friends, work out at the Minuteman, which I rejoined, and work on my novel.

At my next meeting with Byrnes, he says: "From what you've been saying, things have been going well. Let's up Jackie time to five nights a week."

"What if I'm bored?"

"We already went over this. Ask for what you want or sit with it."

"What if I'm crowded?"

"Remember that's also anxiety. You say you want a relationship and never have any luck. A month ago, you missed Jackie and worried that she might not want you back. As soon as she was back, you got panicky. You oscillate from squid to spaceman. We need to slow the oscillating."

Byrnes assigns me another book: *The Giving Tree*, a children's picture book by Shel Silverstein.

I announce the news to Jackie. "Byrnes says we're making progress, so we're going to five nights a week."

She is pleased. She calls her mother. They talk in Chinese using their coliseum voices.

Our new schedule: my place three nights, Friday, Saturday and Sunday; hers on Tuesday and Wednesday. I'm on my own Mondays and Thursdays.

Jackie moves in more stuff. She cleans my place and throws out some of my stuff, coincidently, the same kind of stuff Ricki used to throw out: shirts with holes, shoes with Shoe Goo, a bag of used but reusable plastic bags, a box of empty but reusable plastic water bottles.

She quits cigarettes and starts chewing gum, the pink fruity smelling stuff that snaps and crackles like frying crickets. She greets me with the same suburban-mom question every night we're together: "How was your day?" Before I can answer, she shows me her latest purchases: shoes, bags, clothes, and other stuff. A few days pass and I notice a couple of milk crates are back in her bedroom to accommodate the new stash.

On Monday, my day off, she hangs around till five P.M.

At her place on Tuesday, we're awoken at seven A.M. by hammering, sawing, and rap music. "They're renovating the unit upstairs," Jackie says. "Can I stay at your place till it's done?"

More stuff accumulates in my bathroom cabinet where there is suddenly no more room. And whenever she replaces a toilet paper roll, it's facing the wrong way. A milk crate appears in my bedroom. Then another.

On Thursday, my other day off, I ask her to please abide by her part of the bargain and leave at the agreed time. "I have work to do," I say.

She salutes and says, "Whatever you want, Colonel Cosmonaut."

By Saturday morning, Jackie has officially annexed the bathroom: hair irons and hair dryers, removers and thinners, shea butters and tea gels, coconut mousses and pear drenches; crap fills the cabinet and covers every flat surface. The mirror is spattered with toothpaste spots. The shower drain has a wig. I move my toothbrush, dental floss, and Irish Spring soap bar to a saucer under the kitchen sink.

The rest of Saturday, she works from home, as in my home, in her pajamas, hair in rollers. She looks like a bad Carol Burnett imitation. She farts indiscriminately in front of me. No "excuse me" or decorum of any kind.

I try retreating to the spare bedroom, which is my office. But I swear I can feel her pinging me through the walls. Instead of fighting with her, I go to the bathroom and weigh myself. Almost 163, three pounds overweight. This relationship is making me fat. I go to the kitchen and chop enough salad for a week. I broil enough boneless, skinless chicken breasts for a week. I weigh myself again. Still 163 pounds. And Jackie is still on the couch.

"Will you quit buzzing around the apartment?" Jackie asks.

I go the gym. I come home and she's still on the couch. I take cover in the bathroom, fan on, texting the shrink, my friends, Joey.

Lenny is the only one I can get hold of.

Me: *I can't take any more.*

Burns, you got to block the mind reading.

Me: *You're not going to recommend an aluminum foil hat, are you?*

Those don't work. I tried. When any chick stays over, I wear noise-canceling headphones, so they can't talk to me and keep a white-noise machine by the bed so they can't read my dreams.

"What are you doing in there?" Jackie calls through the door. "Are you watching porn?"

That night, no sex. She thrashes. I thrash. I don't sleep more than two hours. In the morning, I feel hung over, but she doesn't seem to notice.

Monday morning, my day off, I tell her I need a full twenty-four hours to myself. Monday night, instead of staying at her place with the construction, she checks into a motel around the corner from my condo. She sends me photos of the moldy shower curtain, a bathtub ring, and a desk clerk with Elvis mutton chops. She texts:

I need my Daddy to protect me from the creepo!

Instead of answering her, I put on my new, noise-canceling headphones and read *The Giving Tree*.

My Synopsis:

There's a tree and a glommy little boy. The boy takes the tree's apples to sell for cash, then the limbs to build a house, and then the trunk for a boat. In the end, all that's left of the tree is a stump. Upshot: The little boy is a taker.

At our next session, Byrnes offers a different synopsis. "Sometimes relationships are not about keeping score with internal spreadsheets."

He is wearing yellow argyle socks. What does he know?

"My condo is three rooms," I say. "No space. And I feel like I have to entertain her all the time."

He recommends a non-date, date-night, a children's game called parallel play. Jackie and I will do our own thing, but in the same apartment.

I attempt an adult discussion on parallel play with Jackie.

She salutes. "Aye, aye, Mr. Challenger Space Shuttle."

That night, she sits on the couch with her tablet and her phone and plays intermittently with both. She smokes some weed. She smokes some cigarettes on the balcony. I say nothing. She drinks some Chartreuse. She chews some gum. I agree to watch a video with her in a few hours when we go to bed. She smokes more weed.

I go into my office, close the door, put on headphones, and begin writing my own children's book called *Lucy the Lamprey*.

Jackie starts pinging through the wall. I throw the headphones in the trash, come out, and tape a sign to my office door: "He-Man Woman Hater's Club: No Girls Allowed." She laughs and calls me a little rascal. I close the door behind me.

The pinging continues. I know she's checking up, watching for a mistake, any hint that I'm deviating from the program, that I'm not going to marry her. Her mother has probably been telling her she's wasting her time with me. I turn on my new white-noise machine.

My office door opens. "Can I help you with something?" Jackie asks. "I can hear you thinking."

"I'm fine," I say.

"I'm bored. Let me sit on your lap while you work. I'll be quiet. You won't even know I'm here."

I say no.

She sits on my lap. I get hard. She starts unzipping my pants.

I'm angry. I'm hard. She goes down on me, but I can't cum and now I'm really angry.

"I have to get some work done," I say.

"Oh, all right. Godspeed, John Glenn."

She returns to the living room but doesn't close my office door. I note the micro-aggression.

In bed that night, I renege on watching a movie with her. A micro-retaliation. She reaches into my pajama bottoms. I push her hand away. A macro-rejection.

She leaves promptly the next morning on my day off.

The following Wednesday is our ten-month anniversary. I take Jackie for drinks at the Ritz, and then for dinner at her favorite Thai restaurant on Boylston Street. While we're eating our satay, I get a call from Lenny. I ignore it. Another call. I ignore it again.

Then a text:

Spiraling, my man. In the Dark Place. Anniversary of my mother croaking. Deborah wants us to buy a place together. Did too much blow. Starting to freak. Need to get out of my head and away from the railing.

"Is that one of your friends interrupting our anniversary?" Jackie asks.

"It's Lenny, a three-call, Dark Place emergency. I told him he could join us."

"You fuckers." Jackie throws down her napkin and goes to the bathroom.

I ask the waitress for another chair. I order Lenny's favorite dish: double steak, double pork, and double lobster in extra hot and spicy green curry, with a side of brown rice.

Lenny is there in minutes. I greet him with a long hug. Jackie emerges from the bathroom, sees Lenny, and bangs a U-ey to the bar. She returns with a shot of green booze in each hand. Chartreuse. Lenny reaches for one, as if Jackie brought it for him, as if she's also his good friend.

We listen to Lenny ramble. We watch him ignore his food. I rub his back.

"Do you want advice or an ear?" I ask Lenny.

"Just an ear," he says.

"You should visit your mother's grave," Jackie says. "And you should let Deborah move in for a little while."

She pauses. "And maybe you should see his Dr. Byrnes," she says nodding toward me, "Randall could go with you."

Who? Do what?

Lenny and I look at each other. Micro-headshakes.

Lenny stands up. "You are *da* best," he says to us, but mostly to me. He kisses Jackie's cheek. Then he kisses mine and leaves.

A bottle of Taittinger appears. A happy anniversary cake appears. A dinner check never appears.

Jackie and I walk home in silence. She reaches for my hand. Warm, smooth, soft.

We undress and get into bed. I'm wiped out and angry but not sure why. I roll over to my side and don't sleep. I feel Jackie's hand reach into my pajama bottoms. I stop her, hold and caress her hand, and then move it to her side. Then it's back again. "It's our anniversary, aren't you going to fuck me?"

"I'm kind of tired. How about tomorrow morning?"

"It's your day off and you'll throw me out like some cheap slut."

"I promise not to."

There's a long silence. I try to ping her thoughts but can't.

"Your dickhead friend ruined our night," she finally says.

"He said he was suicidal."

"Bullshit. He's just another rich guy who thinks people should be at his beck and call."

No wonder she has no friends.

I want to tell her that she has jealousy issues. I want to tell her that she has compassion for homeless people but not for people I care about. I want to tell her that she's a bad listener. I want to tell her to go sleep in her own apartment. I want to tell her that her mother is right about me. Instead, I tell myself, *Lucy the Lamprey* is going to be a bestseller.

I go into the bathroom and turn on the fan. I text Byrnes, Joey, Lenny, and Abe:

I'm done.

My phone dies. I flush the toilet. Jackie is waiting outside the door.

"I bet you can't wait to ditch me."

I get hard. I fuck her as slowly, as carefully, as under control as I can. I don't want to bite her or choke her and leave marks a police officer could see.

"You didn't cum," she says.

She gives me a hand job. I still don't cum. She grabs her phone and goes into the bathroom. I hear Chinese, then the fan.

Thirty minutes later, she flushes, and comes out.

"Are you gay?" she asks. "It's OK, you can tell me."

I lie awake all night. Thoughts orbit like space trash.

Then it's eight A.M. I must have dozed off for an hour or so. Did Jackie leave? Did she say goodbye? I'm hungry. I'm on a diet. I have a hard on. My balls hurt. Blue balls. *Blue Boy* magazine. Am I gay? I check one testicle, smooth sparrow egg.

I check the other one. I feel the stringy mess of vessels around it. Then a nugget. No wonder I can't cum. I have cancer.

I Google "nugget on my nuts" and find an article called, "The Lump on My Junk." The author is gay. Maybe I *am* gay.

I pull the covers over my head and review my gay history:

Age Five: I let Harriet stick household objects in my ass, such as Mom's toothbrush, Dad's Cross pen, and raw carrots.

Age Six: Joey and I rubbed weenies in a weenie war.

Age Seven: Vice-principal, Mr. Trowbridge, called me into his office and asked me to sit on his lap. He reached down the back of my pants and cupped my balls. It felt good. He did the same to Joey. To this day, on Joey's birthday, I always send a card, "Mr. Trowbridge misses your little nuts." To this day, I like having my balls rubbed.

Age Nineteen: Went to gay bar with a gay friend. Guys bought me drinks. I thought: So this is what it must be like to be a hot chick.

Last Fall: Jackie dressed me up like a girl and I went along with it. I kind of liked it.

Two Weeks Ago: Feldman full-on kissed me. I didn't like it. Did I?

Now, I find out my shrink is gay.

Maybe I need to have sex with a guy once and for all. A safe, supervised environment in case I want to kill myself afterwards. Dr. Byrnes? I could ask him for a blow job and not look.

Isn't he always telling me to ask for what I want?

Or maybe it would be more polite if I offer to blow him. He'll probably want me to teabag him, too. I try to imagine his fat, hairy orangutan balls. I imagine a mouth full of his pubic hair and gag.

It's eight thirty and my appointment with Byrnes is in an hour.

Another gag reflex. I need to eat something. But I'm on a

diet. Maybe something small. A carrot. *No, definitely not a carrot.*

I should drink some coffee or I'll get a headache. But caffeine makes me anxious. Headache or anxiety? Straight or gay? To teabag or not to teabag?

What's wrong with me? I'm paying Byrnes. He should blow me.

I take the sheets off my head, touch the lump on my junk, pick up my phone, and call Lenny's urologist, who says he'll squeeze me in this afternoon.

Today, Byrnes is wearing a lavender dress shirt, lavender tie, penny loafers and his yellow argyle dress socks. I'm wearing shorts and Keen sandals with no socks, a short-sleeved shirt, and a baseball jacket. I cross my legs, uncross them, and cross them again. I look out the window at the men on the scaffolding next door. Nice biceps.

"Randall," Byrnes finally says. "You've been sitting there for almost five minutes and haven't said a word."

My head feels warm. There's something churning in my stomach, climbing into the back of my throat. I cover my mouth but can't stop it from coming out.

"I think I want to have sex with you."

He doesn't flinch or move. He must have known I was gay and just waiting for me to ask for his shlong.

"Do you really?" he asks.

"No. But this thought has been revolving around my head for the last twelve hours. I'm supposed to be sharing all my thoughts with you right?"

His loafers seem to have moved closer. I retract my sandals. He says nothing.

"No offense," I blurt. "But I don't want to be gay. I have enough problems. I love Jackie but don't like having sex with her. And now she thinks I'm gay. Her mother thinks I'm gay. Her mother never misses a diagnosis. There's a lump on my junk that could be cancer. I don't want to die."

Byrnes sits up in his chair and retracts his feet. "Have you ever wanted to kiss a man?" he asks.

"No."

"Had sexual dreams about men?"

"No."

"Watch gay porn?"

"No."

I feel like my sandals are being drawn across the floor toward the penny loafers.

"I want to be a performer, an artist," I say. "I'm supposed to make myself do things that scare and repulse me. I went bungee jumping because I'm afraid of heights. I get on stage because I'm afraid of public speaking."

"But you're not attracted to men."

"Sometimes I see a good-looking guy and imagine Jackie fucking him. I might be able to get it up for a guy wearing makeup. With long hair. And breasts. And a vagina. I saw some lady boys in Cambodia who were sexy. If one of them wanted to give me a blowjob, it might have worked. But anal sex grosses me out. No offense."

"Well, how do you feel about Jackie at the moment?"

"I hate her! I love her!" I yell. "I don't know how I feel!"

My feet settle back under me.

"I'm wondering if this is all just mental detritus floating around in your head," Byrnes says. "Have you ever hit a woman?"

"No, but I told you how I yanked Jackie's hair and bit her and left marks. She seemed to like it, but I'm a little freaked out about it."

"When was the last time you got in a physical fight?"

"When Joey threw my baseball down the sewer."

"When was that?"

"I was seven. That was a tough year."

"Been in any fights since then?"

"I'm Jewish. We're configured more for running and hiding."

I glance down. My legs are extended. My Keens are millimeters away from Byrnes' penny loafers.

"Shouldn't I just try gay sex to make sure I'm not gay?"

"Can't answer that. Do it if you want to. But I don't think you're gay. Everyone has crazy thoughts. You don't need to engage them."

Byrnes' shoes are back under his chair. Mine are back under the couch.

"Sorry if I offended you with any of my gay comments."

"No worries," he says. "I have another book for you."

We exchange hugs after the session. I don't get a hard on.

Later, I bike over to Lenny's urologist. He feels my balls. I don't get a hard on. Maybe Byrnes is right. His petite, blonde radiologist ultrasounds my balls. I don't get a hard on. Maybe Byrnes is wrong.

The diagnoses:

- The lump is not cancer; it's a varicocele, a varicose vein. First my legs and now my ball bag? "Live with it," the urologist says.

- My problem cumming is probably stress. For back up, he gives me a sample of Cialis. "As you get older, you lose sensitivity in your penis. Get a younger girlfriend or a more understanding one."

I see why Lenny likes this guy.

I text Jackie the good news:

Dr. Homo says I'm not gay. And the urologist says I have a varicose vein in my nut sack.

Then I lie.

He says no sex for seven days.

Jackie and I have a decent week. I barely sleep, but we go out for drinks and dinner and movies. We hug and kiss and she sits on my lap and calls me Daddy. We don't have sex. The ache in my balls goes away, but I don't tell her.

The night before my next session with Dr. Byrnes, I read his latest literary recommendation, a children's picture book about OCD called *Around and Around Planet Worry*.

My Synopsis:

There's this little douche bag named Dana who worries about everything. But I don't blame him: He has a girl's name, a cartoon mother with no breasts, and a cartoon sister with no breasts. Are they all hermaphrodites? The sister teases him but never gives him a hand job like Harriet did when I was seven. In school, kids tease him for being a little homo. To deal with this, the poor bastard constantly checks and rechecks, counts and recounts, makes lists and spends too much time in the bathroom. Who doesn't? Still, his parents take him to a shrink who has a dyke-y haircut and nerdy glasses à la Elizabeth Warren. The anti-white-male tone of the book annoys me. But I get the message: I need to cut Jackie some slack. The poor thing suffers from OCD.

That night no sleep.

Two days later in Byrnes' office, I don't care what either of us wearing. I need answers.

"Is Jackie the right one? Why do I feel so crowded? How can I love her and not want to have sex with her? Would this get better if I married her?"

Byrnes casually takes notes as I ramble on.

I talk about feeling connected but asphyxiated, about domination and humiliation. I circle back to connected, back to asphyxiation, on to living with someone, my need to stop drinking coffee, about Shay-Shays and hand jobs and Jackie's thinning hair.

"We have so much fun when we party. She's my favorite person in the whole world, ever. But she's gone back to giving gobbly kisses and gulping blow jobs. And I've tried to get past the moles, but they seem to be multiplying."

I pause and locate Byrnes' shoes, near his chair where they should be.

"Any suggestions?" I ask.

"Your thoughts sure are loud."

"What does that mean, 'loud'? Will I ever be able to live with someone? Even if I were gay, I still wouldn't want to live with someone. And she's the one who likes anal sex. Maybe she's the gay one. No offense."

"I can see your thoughts circling around and around." He adjusts his feet but doesn't extend them.

"You're not helping. Maybe I have the wrong shrink. How did I end up with a gay shrink? No offense."

Byrnes sighs. "Regarding Jackie, you are exploring the possibility of a long-term relationship. She can talk about marriage all she wants. You are exploring."

"I don't have to marry her in six months?"

"You don't have to marry her ever."

"What if she leaves me?"

"We're orbiting planet worry. I don't want to talk about Jackie any more. Another thought for you, and then you need to leave: The world is not a kind place for sensitive men. Ease up on yourself."

"Does that mean I'm going to die alone? How much can you change for someone you love?"

"Keep reading. I'll see you next week."

We stand.

"Would you like a hug?" he asks.

"Only if you mean business."

We both laugh and then hug. No erections are exchanged.

On Friday, I jump on Jackie. It's been a week. I cum. She cums. We repeat Saturday morning. Saturday night, we don't have sex. Or the night after. I'm fine with it. She says nothing. But later she says, "You know, plenty of guys would love to fuck me."

The following night, she calls me a porn addict, asks if I've been sneaking out with Shay-Shay, and suggests I try Viagra. I don't mention the Cialis, which scares me. As I've mentioned, I don't want to end up in the emergency room with a three-day boner.

I consult the sex experts:

Abe: Smoke some weed.

Lenny: Smoke some weed.

Joey: Smoke some weed.

Tuesday and Wednesday Nights: Jackie and I smoke some weed. We have sex and both cum.

Thursday (my day off): I have a weed hangover and am too fried to write, so I go to the gym.

Friday: I don't want to smoke weed and don't want to have sex. Jackie seems OK with that.

Saturday: Jackie tries to sit on my lap while I say, "no means no." We have sex anyway but I don't cum.

Sunday: I say no and mean it. We have sex anyway. I don't cum and neither of us sleeps.

Monday (my day off): Relief.

The next week in Byrnes' office, I look at his bookshelf, at his tie, at his face but not his feet.

"Is Jackie fucked up or is it me?"

"I don't think either of you is 'fucked up,'" he says. "But at your age, sex two to three times a week without Cialis is pretty good. If she wants any more than that, she will need to find herself a much younger guy. Then again, this may be how she connects with men. You have to try negotiating with one another."

"How do I present this without upsetting her?"

"You have pretty good people skills. Do your best. How is your writing going?"

"I'm not done talking about Jackie."

"I am."

"*You* are? Now, *I'm* offended."

"We're just repeating ourselves. With OCD, the more you react to the obsessive thoughts, the more you strengthen the cycle. In your case, you keep asking questions when you know the answer."

"Which is what?" I can't help myself and glance down. His socks are lime green with yellow polka dots.

"You have no control over her behavior and you don't sit well with uncertainty. Ha! You just hooked me into this circular discussion again. You're good!"

We both laugh. He extends his legs and I extend mine. Our feet briefly touch in the middle. I leave mine there. He retracts his.

I start talking about how inconsiderate Jackie has been and how hopeless middle-aged sex is.

Byrnes says OCD is like a hiccup or a record with a skip. He says the brain has trouble sorting what's important and what's junk. It's like your mental inbox is overrun with Fox News, Al Sharpton screeds, and toe-fungus cures.

This all sounds fine and good, until I notice a tenderness in my groin. I mentally trace the tenderness down to my scrotum. Is this the varicocele? Did I spell it correctly? The urologist said to live with it. But it hurts like blue balls. I follow Byrnes' advice and try not to engage any of these thoughts.

Instead, I look out the window. Dust spews from a sidewalk grinder. My right arm starts to itch. Is dust entering through the leaky old windows? My left calf starts to itch. Somewhere a cell phone is ringing. How am I supposed to get better in this kind of environment? Maybe I should I say something to Byrnes. What can he do? He's not going to move his office for me.

Finally, Byrnes says, "I can see there are a lot of distractions today."

Patronizing prick.

Byrnes discusses another component of OCD, the compulsions. We discuss my need to create lists and to monitor my moods and aches throughout the day, something both he and Moody suggested I do. He talks as if I — not Jackie — is the little dickhead Dana from the OCD book.

What does Byrnes know? His grey chest hair is sticking up over his collar and tie knot. How did his husband let him leave the house like that? It's sloppy and not right for a man his age. I'm about mention it when he cuts me off.

He says today I should notice repetitive thoughts and consider not reacting to them. I take a deep breath. He's right for a change. Who cares where his feet are? I know I'm not gay. If he wants to play footsie, I'll ignore his flirting and inappropriate behavior.

Then I notice an ache in my left foot arch, like a thumb tack. Is my plantar fasciitis coming back? Maybe it's only a pebble. I think about taking off my sandal and checking. But I don't want to do it in front of Byrnes; he might think I'm flirting.

I catch myself thinking about how I will now have to see my fleece-artist podiatrist who pushes two-hundred-dollar orthotics that never work. And what if the toe injury from Moosefin isn't gout as Jackie's mother said? Maybe I should see a rheumatologist.

I give in, remove my sandal, and look at my foot.

"Everything OK?" Byrnes asks.

"All good. Probably stepped on a rusty Bowie knife or a Gila monster. Does my toe look swollen?"

"No, it looks OK."

The foot pain and scrotum pain subside. The noise outside subsides.

"Anyway, as I was saying, I like women my age and their life experience — I just don't love their bodies or having sex with them."

Byrnes says: "Middle-aged sex may be one of those irresolvable issues, a gray area, an imperfection of life. How is the writing going?"

The construction continues at Jackie's place and she asks to stay with me again. "You won't even know I'm there."

Monday: Round One

Micro-aggression: I find a piece of chewing gum stuck to the underside of my dinner table.

Micro-passive aggression: She burps and farts during dinner and then complains about my cooking.

Macro-invalidation: She asks when I'll look for a regular job.

Tuesday: Truce

As we walk to Rapinoe's sports bar in silence, she reaches for my hand. I feel the warmth but can only think of the chewing gum.

Wednesday: Atrocities

Jackie harps on my shortcomings: The duct tape on my raincoat, the Bondo on my car, the Bondo on my raincoat, the duct tape on my car, Windows XP on my computers, heel taps on my flipflops, my velour tracksuit, and tube sock collection.

Jackie: "It's not eighties vintage if you actually owned it in the eighties!"

Me: "It was all fine until you moved in!"

Thursday: Escalation

She bitches about my mismatched pots and pans, my thirty-year-old refrigerator, the toaster oven with a broken handle. "I'm sick of using pliers to make a piece of toast!"

Then there is my diet: "Eat something besides salad. Those sardines smell like ass. Are you trying to tell me I'm fat?"

And then my twenty-year-old mattress: "It has a crater in middle because you've been sleeping alone your whole life. Wake up. I'm your girlfriend. Act like it. Get a new mattress."

Friday: Council of War
Abe: "This is who you are. If she wants a big spender, she should date Lenny."
Lenny: "Ditto."
Joey: "Replace the bed. Stay the course."
Byrnes: "Sitting with it is one thing, but you also need to assert yourself sometimes."

Saturday Night at Home: Dresden
Elephants in the room, eggshells and hot potatoes, thin ice and thin lines and lines in the sand; yelling, crying, stomping, and refrigerator kicking; raincoat in garbage, raincoat out of garbage, toaster in the garbage, cosmetics over balcony, sardines over balcony, a call from the neighbors; biting, pinching, fucking, and fleeting post-coital clarity.

Me: "You have expectations I can't meet."
Jackie: "Are you just going to let me walk?"

Monday Morning: A Text
I miss my furry little Jew

Delete.

Monday Afternoon: A Text
Sorry for being a bitch. I love you the way you are.

Delete.

Monday Night: A Long Email

I've been under some stress and didn't want to add to yours. Sorry. I know how hard you've been trying with Dr. Pillow Biter. Sorry. I know how concerned you were when I fainted on the cruise, how concerned you are about your varicocele. Sorry. I was going to wait till I got results before whining, but I'm a little scared. Will you come with me to my doctor's appointment on Wednesday?

More fainting? Her va-jay-jay? Her colon from all the anal she used to get? I read on.

It's too embarrassing to tell you in person. There's blood in my poop and I've been burping and farting a lot.

No shit, Sherlock.

Wednesday morning at Mass General, I carry Jackie's purse. She's quiet. I reach for her hand. Sweaty, shaking. I wrap an arm around her and kiss her head.
I check her in with the turbaned check-in person.
"Relation to the patient?" he asks.
"Fiancé," I say.
"Congrats," he says.
An hour later, I meet Jackie in the recovery room. I slip on a surgeon's mask, reach under her top sheet, and prod her breasts with a tongue depressor. "Dr. Cosby will see you now," I say.
She smiles and pushes away the tongue depressor. "Anyone ever tell you that you have an inch worm for a penis?"
A male doctor pulls aside the curtain. I retract my hand from under Jackie's sheet.
"She has an ulcer," he says. "She'll live. She just has to act her age. And you probably won't need that tongue depressor or mask."
Jackie reaches for my hand.
The doctor continues: "I have prescribed antibiotics and

acid suppressing medicine. We'll need her take it easy until we know how she reacts to the treatment. That means no driving, no all-night raves, no smoking, or Green Chartreuse. Is there someone responsible at home to take care of her?"

He glances at my hand holding the surgeon's mask and tongue depressor. Then looks at me, eye to eye, man to man.

He turns back to Jackie and softens: "OK. We're good."

I drive Jackie home in her Camaro. She dozes, mouth open, eye sockets deeper than I remember; her face lined and fragile, handle with care. I'll follow Byrne's advice and do my best to make her happy and comfortable. No internal spreadsheets. I took good care of her when she had the flu and when she fainted on the cruise. Maybe I'm not that broken.

We pull into my driveway. Jackie opens one eye and reaches for my hand. "My mother is flying in tomorrow to help out."

That night, I put Jackie to bed, in my bed. I count her pills, water her, read her a bedtime story, *The Giving Tree*. Her synopsis: "The tree really loves his baby." She goes to sleep. I go to sleep and really sleep.

In the morning, I take Jackie's Camaro to Logan to pick up her mother who is flying in from Boca Raton.

Jackie told me to look for a seventy-something who thinks she's the first lady: feathery short hair, big Sophia Loren sunglasses, a cream-colored pantsuit. "Call her by her first name, Grace. She agreed not to bring any of her stinky herbs. And remember: She can smell fear."

Grace has a carry-on wheelie, which she insists on wheeling herself. Older men check her out.

"Where's the thirty-year-old Civic I've heard so much about?" She has a slight Chinese accent.

"We figured you'd be more comfortable in this."

She insists on opening her door herself.

"How's our girl doing?"

"OK. But everyone feels better when their mom is there."

There's a moment of silence. I assume Grace knows that my mother passed five years ago.

At my place, we look in on Jackie and decide to let her sleep.

"Nice apartment," Grace says. "Where's the old refrigerator I've heard so much about?"

She inspects the egg tray, vegetable drawer, and freezer. "These old Kenmores last forever. Where's the old raincoat I've heard so much about?"

A ballbuster like her daughter. Like my mother. I suddenly miss my mother.

I take the raincoat off a hanger and model it. She runs her finger along the duct tape repair while I'm still wearing it.

"I do my own tailoring," I say.

I show her the flipflops with heel taps.

"I also do my own shoe repairs."

I point to her cream-colored ballet flats. "My rates are very reasonable."

I detect something that could be a smile.

I show her the pullout couch. "I'll be staying at my friend Lenny's place so you and Jackie can have time together."

"You sleep with Jackie. We're all adults and you're getting married soon, anyway."

She seems to be waiting for a reaction or confirmation. I say nothing.

"So, where are the sardines I've heard so much about?"

The first week Grace stays with us goes surprisingly well. Jackie goes in to work a few hours a day. I sleep well with Jackie in my bed. No pressure, no sex, no asphyxiation. Two nights in, Grace tells me to go out with friends because I deserve some time to myself.

That night I stay at Lenny's to give Grace and Jackie some alone time. Lenny is up in his room with Shay-Shay. I'm on his balcony, overlooking the Common on a warm September night, and have a moment of clarity. I've been with Jackie almost a year. Maybe I can do this: the domestic scene, the relationship scene, the mother-in-law scene. Maybe I won't die alone. Maybe seeing Byrnes has paid off. Even if he is gay.

The next night, Grace makes dinner for Jackie and me. There's a bottle of wine. Jackie isn't supposed to drink, so Grace and I polish it off. Grace becomes animated. She talks about being single in her seventies. "I need to stop dressing like Nancy Reagan." She models skinny jeans she bought from a vintage store in Cambridge.

"Does this make me look easy?" she asks with her hands on her hips, standing a foot away from me.

"I used to have a cute little figure like Jackie." Grace touches my arm coyly. I tingle inappropriately.

"I wish Jackie was as frugal as you are," she says, leaning forward to whisper in my ear. Another tingle.

Jackie says something in Chinese. Her mother says something in Chinese. I don't want to get caught in the crossfire and duck into the bathroom.

Later in bed with Jackie, she's rolled over facing the wall. I reach for her.

Jackie removes my hand. "Don't," she says.

I'm not sure what "don't" refers to, so I try something safer. "You need anything?"

"Don't," she says.

I roll away from her and face the other wall.

An hour later, we're still in the same position. I sense that she's still awake.

"You and my mother are getting to be real good buddies."

"Mothers usually don't like me," I say.

"I have some things to tell you that you're not going to like."

"Don't," I say.

"First, I'm twenty-thousand dollars in debt."

I think, OK, separate bank accounts.

"After my second husband — the older guy — died, I was stuck with bills I couldn't pay."

Does "prenuptial" have one "n" or two?

"I got a job in a real estate office."

Industrious.

"One of our clients was a middle-aged white guy. He had a townhouse in Beacon Hill. He offered me five hundred dollars for sex. I took it. A bunch of times."

Maybe too industrious.

I roll onto my back, stare at the ceiling, and process in silence. A couple is two. Several is three or four. A bunch is usually less than a dozen, maybe five or six. Six times five hundred dollars is three grand.

My girlfriend was a hooker.

My girlfriend was a hooker?

"I never told anyone before," she says.

My girlfriend was a hooker!

"Burns, say something."

Blue screen.

"That was sixteen years ago. How many times have you paid for sex?"

Too hard pile, too hard pile

Do loop, do loop.

Jane, stop this crazy thing!

"Your thoughts sure are loud," she says, starting to cry.

I reach for her hand.

I kiss her cheek.

We have sex for the first time in almost two weeks.

In the morning, Jackie and I don't mention last night's revelations. Instead, we cut deals:

- I won't do any more fringe festivals and will talk to Abe about working part-time for him at Gillette in Boston.

- Jackie will volunteer more at *Homeless Not Helpless*, make some female friends, so I won't be her only social outlet.

- I'll buy a new bed and a new raincoat.

- She'll stop calling me cheap.

- Our sex life needs work, so I'll buy two tickets to a local fetish conference for inspiration.

I have indigestion for the rest of the day.

On the fourteenth day after Jackie's diagnosis, she goes to the doctor. She is better. Time to get on with her life but go easy on the smoking and drinking. I still have indigestion and wonder if ulcers are contagious.

The next day, I drive Grace to the airport. She removes lint from my collar and gives me a parting speech. "Once I go, Jackie will have no one. She needs to get married while she is still cute. You're a good guy, and I would like to have you as a son-law. But if this isn't your thing, you should move on."

I hug Grace goodbye, feel inappropriate stirrings followed by indigestion.

For what I figured to be a loose, laid-back event, the fetish conference is pretty uptight. At check-in, we're handed a square of paper with four red, thumb-size peel-and-stickies. These go over the camera lenses on our phones. Privacy. A handout of don'ts includes: public nudity, sex in the bathrooms, touching without permission, and misuse of personal pronouns. I skim sections on service animals, bodily fluids, and something called "chux."

"They're absorbent, disposable pads. They keep your goo off people and things," Jackie says.

The conference is in Rhode Island, the Nevada of New England, a state where prostitution was legal from 1980 to

2009. Inside the conference center, the event resembles any of the computer expos I attended as a writer for *Personal Computer Computing Week* and features booths and products, seminars and lectures, cliques and loners, and of course cosplayers: Witches, wenches, warlocks, guys in leather kilts, women wearing chain-link neck ties.

Jackie is wearing a spandex catsuit with a long tail, an outfit I've never seen before. "From a previous life," she says. I leave it at that.

She's dressed me in a dark suit, white button-down, tie, and tasseled loafers. "You're my owner," she purrs.

We stop at a booth for a surgeon specializing in body modification: cropping ears like an attack dog, splitting tongues like a snake, restoring foreskins, removing nipples, tattooing eyeballs. Maybe he could take care of Jackie's moles. Jackie picks up a brochure for anal stretching. "Might make you less uptight, Mr. Vanilla *Haole* Boy," she says.

I let the comment pass.

We skip a table for the Sex Workers Union of New England and stop at a paraphernalia booth. I scrutinize a piercing play kit with twenty-gauge needles and a photo of what could be a spiny anteater or a scrotum stuck with three-hundred pins. Jackie fondles a "Pegging the Sissy Kit." I briefly think of skin as pure and white as Saskatchewan in January.

Jackie fingers a device called a Violet Wand, the first thing she wasn't familiar with.

"It's for electricity play," says a booth guy about my age. He's wearing a hat with a propeller on it. "Delivers a sexy shock," he says.

He talks about coils and output ranges, glass electrodes and branding electrodes, mylar floggers and ball-chain whips, remote controls and the Internet of Things.

Jackie and I look at each other and share eye rolls.

"Newbies, huh?" He turns to a couple with sharpened teeth.

Jackie and I grab a conference program off his table and review the afternoon lectures, which I read out loud to her:

Non-Monogamy: Moresomes and gangbangs, elephant walks and double penetration, polyamory triangles, polyamory quads, polyamory pods. "Swingers have sex, polys have conversations."

"*Oy vey*," I say.

Fluid Play: Sphincters and scat, fisting and lactating, mucous and urine, bukkake and blumpkins. There's no mention of Purell or hazmat suits.

Breath Play: Choking and throttling, strangling and self-hanging, smothering with a pillow, smothering with a bag, making friends with your dry cleaner, smothering your dry cleaner, your friend the carotid artery. Jackie takes my hands and wraps them around her throat and makes faux gagging noises.

In the seminar wing, we enter a long, dark hall of candelabras and closed doors. Feather dusters, bullwhips, and leather masks hang from the walls like medieval art. There's a water fountain and a bathroom, but I decide not to chance either one.

We find a door for a seminar called "Tantric Kundalini: Awaken the Sexual Energy Coiled in Your Spine."

"Might loosen you up, Mr. White Bread," Jackie says. Her cracks are starting to annoy me, but I say nothing and focus on the lecture.

After thirty minutes of postures and posturing, cleansing and energizing, nostril breathing and breaths of fire, rules and more rules, I feel something in my spine like sciatica.

The next lecture is "Domination for Dummies," the name of a scene from my show. A must-see. The lecture description: "For tops, bottoms, switcheroos, and the undecided."

The lecturers, a couple in normal jeans and collared shirts, lists their credentials: He's a pagan, warlock bottom. She's a wiccan, Buddhist switch.

The room darkens. A hushed quiet. I reach for Jackie's hand. A blinding light on a wall. A near-death experience? Worse, a PowerPoint presentation: flogging and caning, biting and kicking, cock and ball tortures. I choke Jackie's hand. "*Ow*, you fuck!" she yells. The audience laughs.

There's a slide of a wooden X against a stone wall with a woman manacled by her wrists and ankles. "St. Andrew's Cross," Jackie whispers. Then a slide of what looks like a padded saw horse with ankle straps. "The spanking bench," Jackie whispers. My future wife knows a lot more about sex than I do. She's top and I'm bottom. Humiliator and humiliatee. Not cool.

The bondage slides: ace bandage mummification, spread eagles, hog-ties, frog-ties, shrimp ties, reverse shrimp ties. I'm getting hungry.

Jackie and I slip out a side door as the lecturers discuss safety, contracts, postmortems, and how yes means yes and anything else means no.

"*Oy vey iz mir*," Jackie says. "These people and all their rules."

Saturday night we decide to try some things we learned at the conference, minus all the rules, regs, and uptight nonsense.

Jackie arrives at my place at seven P.M. wearing a pinstripe skirt-suit, hair up in a power bun, as I had instructed.

She sits on the couch.

I stand over her. "Who said you could sit?"

She stands up.

"*Now*, sit down, close your eyes, and open your mouth."

She sits, smirks, and opens wide.

I toss in a pill and hand her a beer. "Drink," I say.

She swallows. "What was that?"

"A Quaalude."

"They don't make Quaaludes anymore."

"Can't fool you. It was Ecstasy."

"Where would you get Ecstasy?"

"Lenny."

"I have an ulcer, remember?"

"Geez, I'm so sorry!" I say. "It was really just a vitamin. Want some Pepto-Bismol?"

She stands up, jabs my chest, and then stomps around the room. "You can't just give in like that. I'm your whore. You can't be a honky, pussy boy. Get into it or this isn't going to be any fun."

She marches into the bathroom.

I call out: "I'll do better. I mean, I'll do better, you gook slut."

I hear the toilet seat go down and reflect: We're trying to save our sex life, our relationship, lay the groundwork for a marriage. I need to get this right, to boss her around, own her, rule her. She liked it when I made her black and blue. I can do this. I'm a performer. I just need the right mindset.

I perform some tantric kundalini, breaths of fire to ignite the sexual serpent at the base of my spine. Then I fire up my internal spreadsheet of debits and credits, tits and tats, slights and grudges. I just took care of her for two weeks and put up with her horny mother. What does she do for me? Criticizes my clothes, my apartment, my Bondo jobs, and she's the one in debt. She actually *was* a hooker. How do I know she's not still hooking? Did I mention her twenty-thousand-dollar debt?

When she comes out of the bathroom, I'm fired up.

I study her immaculate suit. "On your knees. Give me ten."

"This is a twelve-hundred-dollar outfit."

"Shut up, slope. And address me as 'sir.'"

She smirks, gets on the floor, grunts and groans through three pushups, and collapses. I feel myself getting hard.

She stands and dusts herself off, dirt from the floor smudging her chin. Instead of giving her a napkin to wipe it off, I hand her a condom containing a key and four twenties rolled up inside.

"Stick this in your cunt. Tonight, you're my wallet."

She smirks again.

An hour later, a cab drops us at the Kennedy Hotel in downtown Boston. I scan the lobby: men in suits, women in suits, a bow-tied piano player. There's a window partly obscured by floor-to-ceiling curtains. I grab Jackie's hand. "Let's check out the view."

At the window, I draw the curtains behind us. We have two feet of private space, front row for an exclusive show.

We look out at the skyline. The piano is playing the theme from "The Way We Were."

"I hate this song," Jackie says.

I press a finger to her mouth for quiet, and then point to the bottom of the curtain. We see passing wingtips, cap toes, and dress pumps. We hear people chatting, arguing, and laughing as they walk past us, unseen. I smell leathery aftershave and floral perfume.

"Give me your panties," I whisper.

Jackie reaches under her skirt and hands me a slingshot of lace. I rub it around my crotch, over my nose, and around my head. Jackie smiles. I smile and then throw it out the window.

"You asshole, those cost fifty bucks."

I press my finger to her lips again for quiet. She still has dirt on her chin. Disgusting pig.

I notice a burning in my spine. Is the kundalini kicking in?

"Suck me off," I say.

I drop my pants. She smirks, kneels, and then licks gently in the crease of my thighs, working her way into my boxers. I feel myself poking inside her cheek.

She pauses for a breath. I look down at the top of her head, at her blonde power bun and think of my stepsister Harriet's favorite hairdo for special occasions: her prom night, her first wedding, her fourth.

I grab the back of Jackie's head and force myself deep into her mouth. I pump and buck. She starts to gag. I don't let up, can't let up.

My girlfriend, my future wife, is the class slut. How many ball bags has she licked? My spine shudders.

I pull out, yank her power bun free, and give her the load. A dribble travels down her cheek, mixes with the dust on her chin.

Jackie's eyes are wet and blinking fast. Is that fear or excitement? With her, is there any difference?

"Find me a cigarette and meet me out front," I say, zipping up and leaving her still kneeling.

Outside at the taxi stand, I smoke the cigarette she gives me, and then instruct her to walk two feet behind me as we head home.

When we get there, I order her to take off my shoes and get me a beer.

She carefully removes my shoes, massages my feet, and then goes to the kitchen. I hear the *kssst* of a Budweiser being opened. She comes back and hands it to me, eyes cast down.

"Now go into the bathroom, take off your clothes, and lie in the tub," I say.

I stand in the doorway, holding my beer and watch her undress. When she's in the tub, I put the beer on the sink, drop trou, and point my unit at her.

"You don't have the balls," she says, looking up at me.

I spray her size-five, baby-girl feet. She just lies there motionless.

I work my stream up her body, pause at her moles, pretending to dissolve them.

She's quiet. We're both watching me work.

On her stomach, I focus on a cluster of three squashed currants, a hair in one of them. That's an attractive new development. I zap them. Her abs tighten.

A mole on her breasts, one under her armpit, one at a fold on her neck. I pause, chug the rest of my beer, and then restart the flow around her collarbones. Her eyes are closed now. She exhales and exhales again. Is she getting off on this?

I see a tear dribble from the corner of each eye and run down her cheek. I stop at her throat.

"Fuck you," she says in a quiet voice.

I ask her, "Are we still playing?"

"Fuck you," she says again. "What do *you* think?"

Then I detect a smirk and consider spraying it off her face but stop myself. My work here is done.

"I didn't think you had it in you," she says.

We stare at each other for a moment.

I'm not sure how I feel about this game. Guilt? Shame? The magic legal term, remorse?

After she showers, she climbs in bed next to me. Neither of us speaks. I turn out the light and we turn our backs to each other.

As soon as Jackie's asleep, I take my phone into the bathroom and Google: "I pissed on my girlfriend: sick or hot?"

I find a research article "Sex and Sadism" authored by, no surprise, a Canadian.

My Synopsis:

Many people, men and women, enjoy the pain, suffering, and humiliation of others. In fact, it is so common, scientists believe human beings are wired for sadistic pleasure.

Variations:

Sadomasochism: Fantasy play between consenting adults. More than ninety percent of men entertain at least one deviant fantasy in their lifetime.

Sexual sadism: Often includes demeaning victims in public and non-consensual encounters. Perpetrators often believe their victims enjoy it. Implicated in sex crimes and murder. Other characteristics of perpetrators: impulsiveness, antisocial behavior, sensation seeking, fascination with violent sports, art, and film.

Conclusion:
Enacting sadistic fantasies is a primary motivation behind sexual maiming and murder. Sadomasochism and sexual sadism differ only in degree.

I lie awake all night, and in the morning, I ask Jackie, "Are you OK? Should we do a postmortem?"

"We're good," she says, adding that she's just a little tired, a woman's excuse for anything they don't want to do.

"I think I'm going to see if they're done renovating my building," she says.

The moment the door closes behind her, I feel instant relief.

A few days later, I get a text:
Forgot to tell you. Tonight is the annual Homeless Not Helpless *poetry reading. I got us two tickets. At six. Dress like a mensch. Don't be late.*

At six, I meet Jackie at the venue, a Jewish temple in Boston's West End. We exchange perfunctory kisses and take seats toward the back of the function room. I go to the bar and buy the only alcoholic option, a glass of white wine for me and a sparkling water for her — on the way in, she informed me that she was back on the wagon.

The room is filled with people dressed in either business casual with blazers and blouses, like Jackie and me, or boomer hipster with black turtlenecks, black pressed jeans, and white Converse All-Stars.

On the stage, a white millennial walks over to the microphone. He's wearing skinny jeans and a *Homeless Not Helpless* T-shirt. His tightly curled hair seems to hover on his head.

"Nice Jewfro," I whisper to Jackie.

She presses her finger to her lips for quiet.

"Welcome everyone and thank you for coming. I am Josh Goldstein, the director of *Homeless Not Helpless*, and tonight is our annual reading of original work from the At-Risk, Youth of Color, Poetry Ambassadors."

Behind Goldstein stands a chorus line of teens of varying hues. He motions to two of them to come forward.

"And tonight is a special cause for celebration," Goldstein says, pointing to the taller of the two teens. "Jermaine just got accepted into BU."

The audience applauds.

"And," Goldstein points to the other teen. "Enrique here is going to be a father!"

Pause.

The audience seems unsure how to react. They look around before settling on a light applause.

I turn to Jackie and mouth the words, *"Mazel tov."*

"*Shhh,*" she hisses.

What's up with her?

The lights dim. The teens on stage start swaying and clapping out a rappy beat. Jermaine steps to center stage and chants:

"Eat me, you:
Heineken sippin'
wine sniffin'
sushi nibblin'
Uber hailin'
Bianchi ridin'
garage parkin'
Newton livin'
tax evadin'

Wall Street snortin'
charity deductin'
lawyer hirin'
Aspen-skiin'
SPF wearin'
Obama suckin..."

I stop listening and nurse my glass of wine. When the piece is done, there is polite applause, which gradually gets louder. I whisper to Jackie, who is smiling and clapping, "Were we just insulted?"

Her smile disappears. She grabs my hand and drags me past the bar to the lobby.

"Why is everything a big joke to you? I am so sick of your racist comments. All you white people think that just because we had a Black president, everything is fine for us people of color."

You white people, *us* people of color?

Now she's rolling, blowing through red lights, onto the autobahn, Mach I.

"I've been patient with you for almost a year," she continues. "You and your weird phobias, your duct tape, and your refrigerator and all your wishy-washy waffling bullshit. You need to take a dump or let someone else have the bowl."

Does she mean shit or cut bait?

"I'm sure you hooked up with some theater slut up in Moosefin. And what about all your comments about fat girls? You're a fucking misogynist. You're fucked up like George Clooney. No wonder you've never been married."

I seem to recall that George Clooney got married, but am pretty sure this not the time to correct her.

"You should leave now. I hope you and Dr. Flamer have a good laugh talking about me tomorrow."

She stomps back into the event.

I head outside and bum a cigarette from an at-risk poetry ambassador smoking by the entrance. I take out a dollar and offer it to him. He leaves me hanging.

The next day Byrnes is wearing a tie with skinny jeans and Doc Martens. He seems to have lost weight. Whatever. I get right to it.
Me: "Am I a racist?"
Byrnes: "You're white and live in Boston. You're a racist."
Me: "Am I an inflexible misogynist?"
Byrnes: "You're drawn to intense, unconventional women, and you're always disappointed and angry when they act out. Biting and peeing on your girlfriend turns you on a little, but mostly it makes you feel bad. You're ambivalent about being in a relationship and don't deal well with uncertainty. Life is about making difficult decisions when faced with uncertainty. You're willing to compromise for Jackie about sex, marriage, your career. But there seems to be one thing you're unable to compromise on: your personal space. You may have discovered your line in the sand."
Did he answer my question?
Me: "So, am I douche bag? If I don't marry Jackie, am I going to die alone?"
Byrnes: "Those thoughts sure are loud. Before you make any decisions, take a week and read these."
He hands me two more picture books by Shel Silverstein: *The Missing Piece* and *The Missing Piece Meets the Big O*.

Ten months later, I'm in Edinburgh, Scotland, at the largest fringe festival in the world.
Following a killer performance by Feldman, I come on stage for my two-minute preview, grab the mic, and begin:

"With apologies to Shel Silverstein, this piece is called, 'Missing Something.'

"A man was missing something, so he went looking for a woman. He went wine tasting and book grouping. He went to First Fridays and Third Thursdays. He went to Killington and Cancun. But mostly he went to the Dark Place.

"One day, he met a woman. They ate. They drank. Mostly, they laughed.

"Eventually, it was time to have sex. Because they were both middle-aged, it was not pretty but they didn't mind. They liked being each other's missing something.

"Then it came to pass that the man wanted space, for he had been single most of his life and liked having time to himself. Also, spending time alone made him appreciate her more.

"This bothered her greatly. She was not happy being alone, especially in a relationship.

"She became angry. And the angrier she became, the more space he wanted.

"One day, she said, 'If your space is so important, take all you want, and have a nice life.'

"This made him sad but he said, 'Maybe we are not each other's missing something.'

"This made her angrier. 'You will surely die alone,' she said.

"This made him even sadder.

"One day, he met a wise man who said: 'Everyone is afraid of dying alone. But do you want to be with someone who doesn't like you for who you are?'

"The man thought and thought some more. Finally, he said, 'Let me get back to you.'"

ACKNOWLEDGMENTS

Special thanks to many folks for making this book possible, including: Epsilon Books; my indispensable editor Carey Adams; and my beta readers and prose pros: novelist Erica Ferencik; fiction writer K.M. Halpern; author and artist Meia Geddes; telemarker and fellow-UVMer Tony Adams; and cousin, writer, and safari guide Mathew Dry. I'm also indebted to the New England Indie Authors Collective (NEIAC): Judah Leblang, Jason M. Rubin, Stephanie Schorow, and Susan Phillips; my mother Judith Ross for her great sense of humor; and author Marlene Shyer, my model of persistence and fearlessness.

OTHER WORKS

GOD BLESS CAMBODIA
(NOVEL, The Permanent Press, 2017)

A chronically single guy takes a trip around the world hoping to change his luck with love. A gritty, bittersweet romantic comedy that combines the personal journey of *Eat, Pray, Love* with romantic frustration of *Portnoy's Complaint*. Adult situations, adult language, and more adult situations.

"A very entertaining story about a guy who sets out to change his life..." — *Booklist*

"...this story of a flawed character's midlife crisis becomes an easy one to relate to." — *Kirkus*

Available at *Godblesscambodia.com*.

TALES OF A RELUCTANT WORLD TRAVELER
(ONE-MAN SHOW)

Sixteen weeks, four continents, three bungee jumps, and Randy Ross couldn't come home soon enough. This is the story of how a Boston homebody turned a solo trip around the globe into a comedy novel and a one-man play. Part travelogue, part theater, and part off-kilter author talk. A must-see for book lovers, writers, travelers, whiners, kvetches, and misanthropes.

"Absolutely hilarious" "animated story-telling" "a theatrical experience" — *Utah Theatre Bloggers Association* (2020 Great Salt Lake Fringe Festival)

"Entertaining" "sardonic kvetching" — *Fringe Festival KC* (2021 Kansas City Fringe Festival)

Website: *RandyRossmedia.com*, Facebook: *RandyRossWriter*.

ABOUT THE AUTHOR

Randy Ross is a Boston-area writer, performer, and former executive editor for *PC World* magazine. His fiction, humor, and erotica have appeared in *The Drum*, *Black Heart Magazine*, *Side B Magazine*, and *Calliope*, among others. His first novel, *God Bless Cambodia*, was published by The Permanent Press in 2017. His one-man shows, *The Chronic Singles Handbook* and *Tales of a Reluctant World Traveler*, have been featured at indie theater festivals around the U.S., Canada, and the U.K. *Randyrossmedia.com*

Printed in the USA
CPSIA information can be obtained
at www.ICGtesting.com
LVHW041505040924
790015LV00008B/61